One – the Collection

Anna Ellis

Three Birds Press

One – The Collection

One Night

One Week

One Night

One Summer

CHAPTER ONE

Jasmine

H E ALWAYS STARTS WITH the boobs.

My husband is a breast man, always has been, always will be. And thankfully I still have a great pair, even after three kids. Or so he keeps telling me. I don't need his admiration, even though it's still nice to hear it. I can look in the mirror and check for myself.

But Basil certainly shows me enough, unable to keep his hands to himself whenever the kids are occupied or asleep. After nearly twelve years of marriage, it's nice to be still wanted. I hear so many of my friends complain that their husbands barely touch them anymore.

I don't have that problem. Basil and I have always had a healthy sex life. He'd like it to be healthier, but I think he does okay.

Calling your sex life *okay* shouldn't be what a married couple strives for though, is it?

I think a lot about different positions, how we can make things better than okay. Basil cringes when he sees my bills from Victoria's

Secret, but then he's all smiles when I stand before him wearing the sexy red bra with the cute little bow at the front, and the lace panties to match.

I think about sex more than Basil realizes because I've never been able to tell him things like that. I've never been anything but eager and available, but I have a problem initiating, or even telling Bas what I want, how I want it.

I'm shy that way.

But some of the things I think about—I wonder sometimes why don't we try something different—in the shower, on the couch after the kids go to sleep? Why don't we ever try and watch ourselves in the mirror when we have sex? What would it look like, his great, giant cock sliding in and out, like a big dump truck driving into a construction site and then backing out? But faster.

How am I supposed to tell my husband that? That I equate him to a dump truck?

His cock inside me. In and out. In and out.

In...

A sigh escapes when Basil pushes inside me, bypassing the area between my legs entirely. It's like it's a foreign land to him now and you know how men are about asking for directions. He used to give me everything I could ever want down there, spending hours—maybe not hours, but definitely long minutes—bringing me to orgasm. There was oral, an embarrassing amount of oral sex before the kids came along. There were fingers everywhere, all the time—here and there and everywhere.

I think about how it used to be sometimes.

I'm not sure what happened.

I love Basil, and our marriage is strong. We make a good team, especially now since we're outnumbered by the kids. I still think he's great looking—still a head full of dark curls with no sign of hair loss and his body is amazing from all the running he does. I love him, and more importantly, I still like him, which is something not all of my friends can say about their husbands.

I'm lucky to have him, so I shouldn't complain if our sex life is less than mind-blowing.

It's actually kind of...dull.

As Basil enjoys himself on top of me, I look up at the ceiling to see if the cobweb I noticed last week is still there. If I stand on the bed I could get it with the Swifter.

Basil curls his hands under my bum, shifting my hips to give him a better angle.

I should stop letting a cobweb on the ceiling distract me because this is good. Basil is good. He has moves, even though they're more than a little predictable.

I prepare for the flip; for him to switch positions so he can have more boob play. I prefer to be on top because I can always come that way.

Isn't that a line in a song – She only comes when she's on top.

I think it is.

I should stop thinking about a song and enjoy my husband.

Basil

JASMINE IS ALWAYS SO quiet. Sometimes I'd like her to open up and really let me have it, but then I remember that we have three kids that are asleep down the hall.

She does make little whimpering noises, almost like a meow. When I hear them, it's like a crack to the balls, but in a good way.

Her breasts jiggle as she rides me. My wife has amazing breasts. Full and still firm with perfect-sized nipples that I can't keep from biting.

I think she likes it when I bite. Not enough to hurt, just a nipple—nibble. A nipple nibble.

I like to nibble on her nipple.

I reach up and catch one tantalizing pink nipple in my mouth as my thumb finds her clit. There's that little meow, and she steps up the pace, her tiny hands braced on my chest as she rocks her hips up and down.

Up and down. Again...and again.

Up and...I need to think of something other than how my cock feels when she grips me like that or I'm going to come too quick for her to get any enjoyment.

Does Jasmine still like having sex with me?

I watch her face. Her eyes are closed, head leaning back. Another mew but she bites her lip to stifle the sound. I suddenly arch my hips, driving up and her eyes fly open with a gasp.

"You like that?"

"Yeah," she says in a breathy voice.

I do it again, aiming for the infamous G-spot that I still have never been able to find. But I must be doing something right because Jas grips my wrist with a firm grip, and I take that as an instruction to thumb her clit faster.

That works, because about ten seconds and one final thrust later, Jas comes with a wordless cry.

It's my signal to let go, and I do, with both hands cupping those breasts.

Jas rolls off me and flops back on her side of the bed. Her dark hair falls as perfectly as ever, not even mussed from our lovemaking. In fact, other than the deep breaths as she fights to slow her heart rate, and those rosy pink nipples still erect and moist from my mouth, Jas looks like she just woke up.

I'd like it if she'd let herself get mussed up once in a while.

Her eyes fly open while I'm still staring at her. "What?" she asks with a furrow between her eyes.

I shake my head, wanting to tell her she's beautiful, but Jasmine never appreciates compliments. "Was that okay?" I ask instead.

"It's always okay." She leans over and kisses me briefly, not like the make-out sessions that we used to have. Her kisses had been so deep and intense that it felt like she was ripping out my soul.

I miss those kisses.

After the perfunctory kiss, Jas throws her bare legs over the side of the bed. "The kids'll be up soon. Are you all packed and ready to go?"

Today we leave for Aurora Resort to spend a week at the lake. A week with our three kids, and our best friends, and their kids. It's a great time, and we look forward to it all year. The kids can go a little crazy, Jasmine can have some much-needed downtime, and I get to watch the bikinis on the beach.

But it also means that this will probably be the last time I get to have sex with my wife for the week. Staying in a tiny, two-bedroom cabin means absolutely no privacy.

I sigh as I pull myself out of bed. I should have remembered that earlier. Maybe I could have gotten a blow job out of it.

CHAPTER TWO

Jasmine

AURORA RESORT IS LOCATED on the shores of Lockport Lake, in the wilds of Eastern Ontario. I have no idea where exactly it is because I am directionally challenged, plus Basil always drives while I play Wizard, a Euchre-like card game, on my phone.

I'm quite the card shark in the family, or I would be if anyone played with me.

My brother Mahak and his wife Melissa first told us about the resort years ago. They only went twice, preferring to vacation with their neighbours rather than us. My brother has an interesting relationship with his neighbours; Melissa is always talking about Wendy-this and Tia-that, and lately, she's been going on and on about this Jacey woman. They seem to be more like a best friend group than simple neighbours.

I don't really understand neighbours like that because I barely know Mrs. Pearson on the corner and Rick and Randy two doors down, but Mahak always has his own thing going on.

Our best friends are Claire and Billy, who we met six years ago during our first year at Aurora. We had come up with our other best friends Matt and Shawna, and the six of us developed a great friendship during the week together, so much that we planned the next year's vacation before we left. We've been coming back ever since and now have a series of framed photos on the wall showing how much the kids have grown since our first time here.

Matt has been my best friend since grade two and this is the first year he and Shawna won't be joining us.

He told me about the divorce a month ago and I'm still trying to process.

The rain that chased us here from the city is starting to ease up, now light enough to stop the ripples on the lake. We'd arrived with the kids ready and eager to swim and scream and race around the resort, but instead, it had rained the whole way up, and they were told they needed to help Daddy bring in the bags, and then wait until Mommy finished with the unpacking before heading to the Big House.

I thought there'd be a mutiny until Basil broke out the secret stash of toys, the ones we never tell them we're bringing. The kids—Lily who is eight, and the twins, Sebastian and Dominic who just turned six, figured out last year that there's usually a new toy for each of them in the stash.

I glance in the bedroom, where Basil is still sprawled on the bedroom floor playing superheroes with the kids.

"Wonder Woman can save him." Basil waves the Wonder Woman doll at the twins as an army of stormtroopers close ranks around Iron Man.

"Not without Superman," Sebastian argues, gesturing to a prone man of steel. "And he's hurt."

"Superman is strong and fast, but Wonder Woman can hold her own against him," Basil explains. Three little faces stare in rapt awe as super-geek Basil tells of some comic books lore that has Wonder Woman and Superman fighting each other. With a shake of my head, I turn away to finish unpacking the cooler.

Not long after, Basil calls time out for him and Wonder Woman and joins me in the tiny kitchen area with a bemused expression on his face.

"Did Wonder Woman save the day?" I ask, pre-packing three Tupperware containers, each with twenty-seven carefully counted Goldfish into the bag for beach day tomorrow.

"She always does," Basil says, grabbing a bottle of water from the cooler.

"And you always play with her. Is there something I should know about?"

"Just that I had the biggest crush on Wonder Woman when I was a kid. This new one is good, but nobody's going to beat Lynda Carter in my mind. The way she filled out that suit." Basil closes his eyes with a sigh. "She'll always have a soft spot in my heart."

"Because she gave you a hard-on?"

Basil laughs with delight at my unlikely comment. I know he wants me to be more playful and flirty when we're alone, and I try, but it's not me.

"I guess I was a breast man, even back then." With a quick glance over his shoulder at the kids still in the bedroom, he leans close and grabs my breast. "Nothing has changed, has it?"

I smile at the feel of his fingers. "Not really."

And that's why it still works with Basil. He may annoy me at times, and I know things are less than exciting in the bedroom, but we still love each other, and he's a great father to the kids.

The rain eventually stops completely in time for us to take a quick walk along the beach before heading to the Big House for an early dinner. By the time we climb the steps to the wrap-around porch, I'm as excited as the kids to see Billy and Claire.

We had bonded quickly when we first met, since the six of us had been the only ones at the resort with children.

Or child—I had been pregnant with the twins at the time. We found out later that Claire conceived at Aurora, with her daughter Rachel arriving a few months after the twins. It's great that the kids are the same age so there's never any worry about making friends.

Guests mill about inside the Big House and excited chatter spills out onto the wide, wrap-around deck overlooking the lake. The bar is busy and the couches set before the fireplace are crowded with people getting reacquainted. There are quite a few guests that are like us, coming back for the same week in July every year and I smile and wave as the ones I recognize catch my eye.

Claire quickly finds me and once the kids are settled in the playroom, we disappear onto the far corner of the deck, the same place Shawna used to drag us when she wanted a contraband cigarette.

Claire hands me a glass of wine and sinks into the Muskoka chair beside me with a happy sigh.

The gray rain clouds are slow to leave, like the last guest at a party, but blue sky peeked out from between them. "It's going to be a nice sunset," Claire says.

"And because I had a nap in the car, I'll be awake to see it," I joke. For me, Aurora is all about relaxation, something I solely need.

Having three kids is nothing compared to the thirty I deal with during the day. Basil and I are both teachers; Basil tackling the teen hormones as a high school math teacher while I try to keep up with the energetic nine-year-olds and their issues with multiplication tables.

"I like these rubbery cups," Claire says, touching her glass with mine "I don't know how many glasses I've broken when I'm drinking outside."

"But not when Shawna is around," I remind her, catching the pettiness in my voice.

"I'm going to be drinking a whole lot more this year now that she won't be around. I still can't believe they broke up. I never thought Matt would have the balls."

"She left him," I say sadly.

"Have you talked to Matt?" Claire doesn't take long to ask the question of the summer. Since Matt broke the news, every time we texted or DM'd each other, Claire always wanted to know if I'd spoken to Matt.

"Yesterday," I admit. "The kids are bummed that they're not coming here this year, but Shawna took them to Florida for the week, so they won't even remember Aurora after Mickey gets through with them."

"Did the *boyfriend* go with them?" Claire asks cattily.

Matt told me that Shawna had an affair with some guy she'd met at the gym, some big muscle-bound idiot, as he put it. I haven't heard Shawna's side of things yet, nor do I want to. My loyalty is to Matt, and always will be, and I can't understand what this gym jock could have that would pull Shawna away from Matt. Matt has everything going for him—he's cute and funny, and a great father, and even though I'm a married woman, I'll admit Matt has the best butt in any man I've ever seen.

"I hope she took him because wouldn't have a clue how to deal with those kids without help. Oh, that wasn't very nice of me, was it?" I blink quickly, feigning innocents and Claire laughs.

Shawna is the classic Type A control freak, and sometimes a little too intense to vacation with. She has a need to plan everything, from playdates for the kids, daily activities scheduled to the minute, as well as date nights for her and Matt planned three months ahead. She spends so much time organizing their life that sometimes I think she forgets to live it. Matt is much more spontaneous and hands-on. He tells me about stealing the coloured markers that Shawna used for the family calendar to actually colour with the kids.

I gaze at the couples venturing onto the deck. Aurora is still more of a couples resort, but more families come every year now, thanks to Shawna's insistence about a kids' club, lifeguard and playroom in the main building. Now we can enjoy our wine in the evenings while the kids wreak havoc with the ping pong table and Wii video games.

I give a silent thanks for Shawna's perseverance. It's the only thanks she'll get from me tonight.

I miss Matt.

There's an empty spot beside Claire where Shawna used to be, but I feel the loss of Matt more as Claire and I sit and drink our wine on the deck,

As we enjoy our drinks, Claire tells me about their plans for the rest of the summer, even though she's told me twice already. I try to keep my mind from wandering to Matt, worrying about my oldest friend, or asking myself if Basil's lacklustre performance that morning was partly my fault when a splash draws my attention to the water.

The lakefront is broken into two parts; the family area, the long strip of golden sand stretching far out into the water, and the adults' only section, which has a long pier dotted with chairs and ends with a drop-ff of ten feet of cool water and a short swim to the floating dock.

Scanning the water, I see a man climbing the ladder onto the floating dock. With a soft sigh, I lean forward, resting my arm on the railing, not even pretending not to watch him. It's too far a distance for me to see his face, but what I do see of his body grabs my attention and doesn't let go.

Thick, muscular shoulders that could carry the weight of the world or at least a hundred and fifty-pound woman like myself tapers to narrow hips and legs the size of tree trunks. He looks like he spends hours in the weight room on a regular basis; unlike Basil, who focuses on cardio and personal bests for his runs.

Water boy—Water Man, more like it, with capital letters—is not my type, but there's something about him that's definitely appealing.

The weak sun peeks from behind a cloud and lands in a puddle around him, showcasing the bald head glistening from his swim and the salt-and-pepper beard, making the fuchsia swim trunks glow like they're on fire.

"Not many men can pull off a pink bathing suit, but it sure works for him," Claire muses, following my gaze.

"He could pull off just about anything," I say in a low voice.

"Including your clothes?" Claire laughs and I join her. Is it sad that it's funny thinking of anyone pulling off my clothes?

I sip my wine, watching Water Man with the pink shorts, wondering what it would be like if someone pulled off my clothes.

Basil

THE NEXT AFTERNOON, I stop at Billy's cabin before we take the kids to the Big House for camp. Four counsellors look after eight kids, taking them swimming and canoeing and for long walks in the woods. It's free babysitting, and I love it, plus the kids are always exhausted at the end of the day and fall asleep as soon as their heads hit the pillow, sleeping much deeper than they do at home. Jasmine says it's the fresh air. I don't really care what makes them sleep so well, only that it allows Jas and I to hang out with Claire and Billy, keeping a close watch on the kids via the cordless baby monitor.

"It's weird without Matt here," Billy says as we troop across the lawn after the pack of excited children. "I can't believe it's over between them. It must be worse for you because you see them all the time."

Matt and Jasmine grew up five houses from each other and ended up living five blocks away. Despite that, we never saw much of Matt and Shawna on a purely social level; the kids play hockey and baseball together, but Jasmine keeps our schedule busy with kids' activities, family time and other friends.

For a while, I've wondered if Jas kept things that way because she didn't want to get together with Matt and Shawna too often. She might love Matt like a brother, but Shawna has never been anyone's favourite person.

However much we did socialize with Matt and Shawna, we saw them more than Billy and Claire, who live an hour and a half away.

"I saw him at hockey the week before she left," I tell Billy. The hot July sun had already dried the lawn, soaked by yesterday's rain. I hate being at Aurora in the rain, especially when we first get here. It's such a waste when you can't go out, and although the kids don't mind getting a little wet, I prefer not to. "He didn't say anything about it."

"Maybe he didn't know."

"How could you not know?" I ask. "Wouldn't it be obvious—your wife sneaking around at all hours?"

"How *could* you know?" Billy laughs. "I've no idea what Claire does during the day. She could have a whole Army platoon stashed in the bedroom when I'm at work and I'd never know. I just try to keep her happy, stay out of her way when she's not, and hope for the best."

"Why Army guys?" I ask.

"All the books she reads have covers with Army guys on them with their shirts half off. I guess that's her type." He gestures to himself. "As you can tell."

I have to laugh because Billy looks more like a beach bum than a military man with his floppy blond hair and constant stubble. "I have no idea what type Jas likes. All of her books are on the e-reader and I can't see the covers."

"Sometimes Claire reads the good parts to me," Billy confides. "Hot. You better hope Jas reads the ones like that."

Is it wrong that I have no idea what types of books Jasmine reads? I know she likes sappy, romantic movies so it makes sense for her to read books like that but I can't see her getting caught up in the heaving bosoms or throbbing manhood type of reads.

But who knows?

Since we found out about Matt and Shawna, I've worried more about my marriage than I ever have, even when the Jason Statham lookalike started working at her school. I had no idea Jasmine even knew who the actor was until she pointed him out while I was watching Fast and Furious.

"He looks like the new teacher at the school," Jasmine had said, sounding a little too excited to make the connection.

Was I jealous? Maybe a little. But I trust my wife and I know she's not going to throw our twelve-year marriage away over nice arms and firm abs. I have good abs and she's always commenting on the muscles in my legs, so there's nothing to worry about.

I never understood the bald head when I still have a head full of my own hair.

Is still Jasmine happy with me? If Matt's marriage—which had always seemed rock solid—broke up, it can happen to anyone.

"Do you ever worry that you aren't making Claire happy?" I ask Billy.

"I made her very happy this morning," he jokes. "And plan to do it again tonight. The kids always sleep like little logs when we're here."

"It's the fresh air." We reach the steps up the deck and the kids have the brains to stop at the bottom and wait for a woman to pick her way down, sparkly flip-flops slapping each step.

I can't help but notice that she's a very sexy woman with sun-kissed and boat-blown blonde hair, wearing what might possibly be the world's smallest black bikini for breasts that size. My head swivels in time with Billy's as she walks by us with a smile, lowering her dark glasses in an 80s movie move as she passes.

"Hello, boys," she says in a husky voice.

"Hey, there." Billy smiles at her, the same smile I see him use on Claire after a few beers have gotten him in the mood. It's pretty obvious when Billy's horny, plus he has no qualms about telling everyone. "Welcome to Aurora," he adds.

"Oh, I'm no virgin to this place," she purrs, sweeping past us to the kids with a gaze so blue, it puts the sky to shame. "Cute kids. Are they always around?"

"No, never," Billy says quickly.

"Hardly ever see them," I agree.

She smiles. "Nice. I'll be at the beach."

"We'll be right there." Billy almost trips up the steps in his haste. "Just getting rid of the kids."

"Daddy!" Rachel pouts. "Why did you say that? We're never leaving your side!"

Billy grimaces and hustles the kids up the steps to afternoon kids' camp.

CHAPTER THREE

Jasmine

AT AURORA, HAPPY HOUR officially begins at four o'clock, which gives the few parents with kids there a half-hour to drink as much as possible before picking up the kids at camp. I have twenty minutes left, sitting quietly with my book and a glass of lukewarm Pinot Grigio when Claire sinks into the chair beside me and gives my arm a nudge.

"Check this out."

'This' is tall and gorgeous with an Angelina Jolie-type body—willowy, non-existent hips and breasts that rival mine. She's older but still model gorgeous with cheekbones I could use to cut the kids' chicken fingers and masses of blonde hair piled up in a messy bun. Claire always points out women to me. I used to think it was because Claire is jealous, but now I realize it's more admiring than envious.

I watch as the woman pulls a lounge chair along the sand, obviously looking for the optimal beach spot. There's no cover-up hiding the black bikini and it's small enough to leave nothing to the imagination.

Even I have to admit the view is impressive.

She holds a wine bottle in one hand, one of the resort's rubbery glasses caught between her fingers. I wonder why no one is helping her and can't help but marvel at how good she looks even struggling to carry it all. I can't even carry a grocery bag into the house at the end of the day without looking like something the cat dragged in.

The woman notices our attention and smiles like she's used to it. I raise my half-empty wine glass and then watch, frozen with trepidation, as she veers towards us like she's about to join us.

"I think she's coming over," Claire hisses.

And she does, dragging her chair around an umbrella stuck in the sand to settle beside me. "Well, if that wasn't an invitation, I don't know what is," she says in a breathy voice. "Y'all look so friendly sitting here smiling at me."

"I thought I'd say hi," I say, trying to hide my awkwardness. Was I smiling? I glance sideways to Claire, who always says she lost the art of small talk when she decided to stay at home with the kids.

I'm never the one to make friends; it was always been Shawna who could muscle her way into any conversation and leave with new Instagram followers. Every year when we say goodbye to Aurora, she has a handful of new names added to her Christmas list.

Claire and I were the followers. I don't want to admit that I'm at a loss without her, because there are so many things I like about Shawna *not* being here.

"And hello to you, too. I'm Carson." She clinks her bottle against my glass before refilling her glass and offering it to us. When

Claire and I shake our heads, she sets the bottle in the shade of her chair. It's too hot to carry a bottle around; already, my half-drank glass is uncomfortably warm.

"I'm Jasmine," I say. "And this is Claire." Claire leans forward with a wave.

Carson waves back before turning her attention to me. "Jasmine. I don't know if it's the green bathing suit, but you look so much like the Jasmine in Aladdin. But I'm sure everyone tells you that, don't they?"

"All the time." Disney's Aladdin first came out when I was five and I've hated the movie ever since. I should be the only dark-haired, dark-eyed Jasmine in the world; who wants to look like a copycat to a cartoon character? "Is this your first time at Aurora?"

"Oh, no." She shakes her head a little too vehemently. "We come every year. Usually, one week in August but my husband thought a change would be good and wanted to do July. That's him over there in the hot pink shorts."

My gaze flew to the man I spied on the dock yesterday. I clamped my jaw shut, not wanting to look like a gasping fish. "That's your husband?"

"That's my Wyatt. Aren't those shorts a hoot?"

"A hoot," I echo. "You won't lose him when he's got them on."

"Oh, he always comes back to me." Carson takes off her sunglasses to reveal eyes so pure and blue that it isn't fair to the other blonde-blue-eyed women in the world.

Luckily, that's not me and Claire.

"I don't think Wyatt needs the shorts to get the attention," Carson says with a smirk. "Being how he looks like he does."

"He's...impressive." I stammer over the word. I could say he's super hot as well, and sexy enough for me to keep him in my mental file for when I'm alone with the Rabbit. How he's built so nicely that it makes me want to climb him like a tree and wrap my body around him and refuse to let go.

I give a start, praying I didn't say any of that aloud.

"What about you? Are you virg—newbies?" Carson pops her sunglasses back on and leans back in her chair, hot husband forgotten.

I sneak another peek at Wyatt who is talking to a couple of men by the water, making the others appear scrawny and washed out beside him. He won't be forgotten by me any time soon.

"We've been coming here for years," Claire says.

"Years! And we've never met you before," Carson marvels, clapping her glass with her hand. "I'm so glad we're all here this week. Now, are you two together?"

"We're here with our husbands," I say quickly. "That's them out there, paddle boarding." I point to where Billy lays across a paddleboard, his lanky frame tipping over the side as Basil makes a herculean effort to stand up, his legs shaking with the effort to keep his balance.

"They're cute," Carson says admiringly.

A little too admiring, maybe. But I'm still proud of the boys. They might not be in Wyatt's class, but they're no embarrassment to us.

Claire must agree. "They are," she says firmly.

"We should all have a drink when they come in," Carson says brightly.

"We have to pick up our kids soon," Claire says apologetically.

"The kids' camp is great here," I add. "Lots of activities during the day, which tires them out at night. It's a very early bedtime."

"For the kids," Claire cuts in. "Once they're asleep, we're free to do what we want."

"That sounds like fun. Let's meet up tonight at the fire and get to know each other a little better."

"Sounds great," Claire says quickly. I'm glad she's able to answer because my gaze is caught by a hot pink bathing suit approaching.

"Oh, there's Wyatt now." Carson waves. I lose all moisture in my mouth and gulp the rest of my wine as I watch him saunter across the beach to us.

"Wow," I hear Claire say under her breath.

"Hey, beautiful." Wyatt's voice sounds like gravel crunching under a tire, which is suddenly the sexiest sound ever. Especially when he looks right at me when he says it, even though I know he's talking to Carson. He kisses her cheek before sitting on the edge of her lounge chair, facing us.

"Wyatt, honey, this is Jasmine and Claire. New friends for us! They've been coming here for years, so isn't it a shame that we haven't met them sooner?"

"Definitely. "Wyatt leans over to me, extending a hand. I let it engulf my fingers. Even his handshake is strong and sexy.

Up close, Wyatt is even better looking than I imagined, and I'm not embarrassed to admit I did my share of imagining last night. I've seen enough of the Marvel movies to recognize Thor and Wyatt looks like a more mature version of him, but better, with a beard and bald head. And the tattoos—one shoulder is covered by a sun and a dragon covers the opposite collarbone.

I think I might have a thing for bald guys, since the new sixth-grade teacher, Stephen Lyle, started at the school with his shaved head and deep dimple.

I'm embarrassed to admit there's been some fantasizing about Mr. Lyle but he's about to be thrown over by Wyatt.

The bald head, the nicely groomed beard—too long to be a missed shave, too short to be one of those hipster beards—not to mention the muscles make up for a very nice package. Even the pink bathing suit works.

I mean, it *really* works.

Basil

MY FAVOURITE TIME AT Aurora is at night after we put the kids to sleep.

Mainly, because putting the kids to bed is so easy here. We forgo the night bath time because the kids are already water-logged from swimming, and I race through one book without the usual issues of Lily wanting me to read a chapter from one of the Fairy books and the boys wanting Geronimo Stilton.

Sleepy eyes are half-closed by the time I finish a chapter of Harry Potter and Jasmine and I wait for a never-ending fifteen minutes until they're asleep. Then with the baby monitor tucked into the pocket of my shorts, we set off with a bottle of wine to the fire pit at the edge of the beach.

The camp locks the gates at night so no one can get in after eight pm. Plus, they have security guards by the road, so it really is a safe place. The kids are old enough and have been here long enough to know Mommy and Daddy hang out with Claire and Billy at night, and to yell into the monitor if they need anything and Daddy will come running.

Jasmine always tells them she'll come running, but two years ago we proved that I can get there quicker.

Jasmine may feel guilty about leaving the kids alone, but I always tell her it's no different than if the kids are asleep and we're watching a movie in the basement rec room.

"So who is this woman again?" I ask as Jasmine quickens her steps to keep up with me. All through dinner, Jasmine went on and on about this woman she and Claire had met, with Claire tripping over Jasmine's words to get in her own observations.

They didn't say much about the husband, which worried me a bit. I've never been a jealous person, but Jasmine never has any problem giving her opinions on the attractiveness of men, so when she doesn't, I have to wonder why not.

"Her name is Carson, and she's blonde and gorgeous and she wants to meet up for a drink tonight," Jasmine explains again.

"Yes, but why *us*?"

"Why not us?" Jasmine demands.

"Well, even though you're the real catch in this relationship, you've pretty much described this woman as a goddess. I have to wonder what she wants with us mere mortals. Are we to be some sacrificial part of a midnight ritual?"

She rolls her eyes in the moonlight. "I think you're reading too many of those dragon books. The ones where they sacrifice the maiden to appease the monster?"

I chuckle. "I don't know which of my books you've read, but they're nothing like that."

"And I'm sure Carson and Wyatt don't mean to sacrifice us," she says impatiently.

"You don't know that. They might."

The bonfire is blazing when we arrive, glowing orange-red and reaching high into the dark sky. Small groups of chairs are pulled around it. A few older kids, granted the reprieve of an early bedtime, dance around toasting marshmallows, but most of those gathered sit quietly chatting with others.

I catch sight of Billy and pull Jasmine towards them. The first thing I notice is Billy grinning from ear to ear, and I see then the blonde we saw on the stairs.

Is that the woman Jasmine is talking about? *Thank you*, I pray to the god of wandering eyes.

And then I see the husband, and my face freezes in sort of a grimace.

He looks like Thor, twenty years in the future, but without the hair, and with the addition of some lines on his tanned face. I expect to see Mjolnir resting in the sand by his chair.

The woman catches sight of Jasmine and stands with a wave. "Jasmine. You made it."

Jas holds up the bottle. "And with wine."

Thor stands up, towering over even Billy, who has a couple of inches on me. "Hey," he says, offering a meaty hand. Am I imagining the hint of an Australian accent? "Wyatt Peak."

Even though I can't compare with those arms, I'm confident I have the better last night. "Basil Cope-Patton," I say, enunciating my fading accent. "Good to meet you."

"I don't think I've ever met a Basil before." The blonde covers our still clasped hands. "I'm excited. You sound very British."

"Not much anymore," I admit. Wyatt releases my hand, but Carson twins her fingers with mine.

"I liked the paddleboarding demonstration earlier," Carson says with a smile. "Jasmine pointed you out."

"And did she point out when I fell off head first?" I ask ruefully.

"Oh, we saw that too," Jasmine says as she steps through the cluster of Muskoka chairs to sit beside Claire, which happens to be right beside Thor.

"Great."

"I can never stand up on those things," Thor—Wyatt—growls, doing a great job intimidating me until he smiles.

It's a sweet smile for a man who looks like him, helping him lose about ten years. I bet there is a dimple underneath the beard.

"It's easier to just lie flat," Billy says lazily.

"No one should ever just lie flat," Carson says, sounding surprisingly sexy for a conversation about water sports.

Then I twig that maybe she's not talking about paddleboarding.

Carson and Wyatt's movie star good looks are intimidating, but despite that, they're nice and down-to-earth and we have a good time with them, spending a couple of hours of good conversation around the fire with several bottles of wine.

They're not Matt and Shawna but it's nice to have the extra faces.

We skirt over the basic background facts before diving into our histories at Aurora. Of course someone—Billy, I think—brings up

Matt and Shawna and we talk about the breakup of their marriage. It's like detailing the progression of a traffic accident.

"It's always sad when a marriage ends," Carson says with a rueful smile at Wyatt. "Both of us are divorced and it's not a fun time."

"Matt's handling okay, but he's worried about the kids," Jasmine says.

I've always wondered about Jas and Matt. Yes, they've known each other since they were kids, but in my opinion, it's not easy to be friends with a woman. When Matt and Jas sit and reminisce about the past, is Matt looking at Jasmine and wishing he could take her to bed? My wife is a beautiful woman—

My quick glance at her catches Jasmine smiling at Wyatt with pink in her cheeks and a shine in her eye.

And he's smiling right back at her, with a knowing *yeah, you want me* look in his eye.

Does she want him?

Even though Matt is my friend and I miss having him around, part of me was glad when he cancelled so I wouldn't have to watch him and Jasmine in their own little friendship bubble. I love my wife, and I trust her completely, but it's not fun watching her with a man she clearly enjoys the company of. Because then I have to wonder if she likes his company better than mine.

"Do you have kids?" Claire asks directing her question to Carson.

Carson is also a beautiful woman, in the complete opposite of Jasmine so I can't even compare the two.

But I'm ashamed that I do.

"No kids for me." Carson's lack of regret tells me she's not the mothering type. "Wyatt has a sixteen-year-old son."

"He lives with his mother in Edmonton." Wyatt's tone is regretful. "I get him over Christmas, two weeks over the summer and March break."

"You must miss him," Jasmine says sympathetically. Score another for Wyatt. Hunky and sensitive.

"He's a great kid." I can tell from Carson's few words that he's anything but. "And while I have regrets about not being a mother, Wyatt and I feel that bringing children into our lifestyle would be difficult."

"What lifestyle is that?" Claire asks.

Carson and Wyatt look at each other, and Wyatt gives a tiny shrug and shifts his gaze. "How long have you been coming to Aurora?" Carson asks us.

"Seven years," Claire supplies.

"It's a beautiful place, isn't it? But in those seven years have you never noticed why it hasn't really taken off as a family resort?"

"We come as a family," I tell her.

"From what I understand, your friend insisted on making this a family-friendly place." Carson picks her words like she's stepping on slippery rocks to cross a river. "And a lot of people appreciate that. But in the weeks that we've been here, there haven't been a lot of kids. Just adults. Lots and lots of consenting adults."

"So?" Billy asks, clearly as mystified as I am at the word consenting.

Carson gives a delicate laugh and runs a finger along Billy's hand that's resting on the arm of his chair. "There's no easy way to tell you this."

"Tell us what?" Jasmine frowns.

Carson glances at Wyatt again. "Aurora is a resort for swingers," she says lightly.

CHAPTER FOUR

Jasmine

"SWINGERS?" CLAIRE ECHOES.

All I can think of is the playground for the kids, the tough, colourful slide and climbing apparatus. There aren't any swings for the kids.

"Swingers, like couples who share?" Billy asks. He looks wide awake for once, his eyes huge and staring.

"Sharing, wife-swapping. There are many names for it. We call ourselves swingers but I prefer to say we practice polyamory," Carson explains.

"We?" My head pops up and I stare at Carson in amazement. "You do this? You two?"

I can't look at Wyatt.

Carson nods with an easy smile on her face. "We do. And have for years. You're telling me that as long as you've been coming here, no one has ever approached you to play?"

The years at Aurora blur as they race through my mind. How I could have missed this? I've spent most of our time at the resort with Matt and Shawna, Claire and Billy, and none of them have ever mentioned anything untoward or suggested playing, other than in the park with the kids. "No," I say shortly.

"Actually..." Billy clears his throat. "About three years ago, there was a woman." He shrugs sheepishly and gives Claire a sideways glance. "I thought she was just coming on to me, but maybe that's what she had in mind."

"I've had people ask me if we're coming to the opening night bonfire," Claire offers. "We've never gone because of the kids."

"That's when set-ups happen," Wyatt says in his growly voice. "Hook-ups."

"Hook-ups happen at the bonfire?" Basil demands. "At Aurora? You're telling me that couples swap, or wife-share, or whatever it's called right here on the beach?" He shakes his head, more angry than offended. "Why didn't we know any of this?"

"We've always been in our cabins when this is going on." The laugh bubbles out of me, inappropriate to be sure, but I don't know how else to deal with this.

Swingers. At Aurora. Where I've been bringing my kids for years. "Did you know about this?" I demand of Claire and Billy.

Billy shakes his head, and then with a look at his wife, shrugs. "I didn't know anything, but I remember comments."

"Looking back, there were comments that I never picked up on," Claire admits. "I had no idea at the time, but they kind of make sense now."

"So both of you..." I trail off with a glance at Basil. "Why not us? Why didn't anyone ask us?"

It's pathetic that I'm more upset at being left out than not knowing.

"I'm sure the others thought you were already in a relationship," Carson says quickly. "From what I've picked up, you're very close to your other friends. I'm sure it was accepted that the six of you had something going on."

"But we didn't!"

"And that's okay," Carson soothes. "There's nothing wrong with that. We thought you should be filled in about what goes on around here, in the off-chance you didn't already know."

"And we thought we'd ask if you wanted to try it with us," Wyatt adds.

I glance at Wyatt; at the sharp blue eyes and the smile hiding behind the beard. "You want us to try swinging with you?" I repeat slowly.

"Yeah," Wyatt says.

We head back to the cabins soon after that, the four of us trailing single file across the lawn.

"Did that just really happen?" Claire kept repeating, each time becoming more and more excited.

"I can't believe this place is some swingers' club!" Billy seems happy with the idea, but then again, nothing really fazes him. When he came home from work a few years ago to find Claire lying at the bottom of the stairs with her ankle bent at an impossible angle underneath her, apparently all he said was, "Hey, that looks broken."

Then he scooped the crying kids up and bundled them into the car, dropping them at his parents before taking Claire to the hospital.

Basil, on the other hand, is clearly upset. His mouth tightens into the same expression he gets during dinner with his parents when his father admonishes him for becoming a teacher instead of following in his footsteps to join his dentistry practice.

Not that Basil could ever become a dentist. His dental hygiene is impeccable, but he has a thing for bad breath. So much he refuses to kiss me in the morning until I brush my teeth. When I'm mad at him, I'll go a whole day before touching a toothbrush.

I have no idea why he's upset about this, though. But his stiff back and measured steps tell me he's really annoyed.

"They should have told us," he complains as we stop under the trees by Claire and Billy's cabin. They left a light on inside, the same as we do, in case the kids wake up.

"Who?" I ask because it's the first thing Basil has said since we left the bonfire and I'm not sure who he's referring to.

"Aurora," he snaps. "This place. How could they let us bring children here when this is going on?"

"What exactly is going on?" Billy asks. "It's not like people are doing it in the woods or in front of the kids. We've been coming here for years, and we had no idea what was going on, so I wouldn't worry much about the kids."

"Obviously, they're discreet," Claire adds.

"How do you know? Maybe the orgy happens after we go to bed."

"I don't think there's an orgy," I say quietly.

"How do you know?"

I raise my hands to fend off his anger being directed at me. "I know just as much as you do, which is nothing, but that's not a reason to get so upset. What are you so angry about anyway?"

He fumes for a moment before taking a deep breath. "I thought it was very presumptuous of them to ask," he says, sounding more like a formal Englishman than I've ever heard him.

"Well, how would they know if we would go for it if they didn't ask?" Claire demands and Basil turns to her with wide eyes.

"Are you going to go along with it?"

Giving Billy a sideways glance, Claire sets a hand on Basil's arm. "Bas, we just heard about this and I get that you're upset."

"I'm not upset!" He scrubs his face with his hands. "I'm not sure what I am."

"Why don't you and Jas talk about this first, and Billy and I will do the same. Tomorrow at breakfast, we'll hash it out between the four of us. It's been a long day, and I, for one, have had a lot to drink, so I'm not sure I'm thinking straight." She smiles at Basil, raises her eyebrows when she glances at me. "Sound good?"

"Sounds like a great idea," I say firmly, taking Basil's hand. "See you at breakfast."

I lead Basil back to our cabin, wondering what I'm supposed to say to him.

Basil

I FIND JASMINE AT the door to the kids' room, staring into the room lit by the flower nightlight we brought from home and listening to their even breathing.

"Do you think they woke up?" I whisper, my lips close to her ear.

Jasmine shivers, or maybe I scared her. "No." She gives her head a shake and turns away. "Too tired."

"Let's go to bed," I suggest. Sometimes we'll sit up reading, or have one last drink together by our own fireplace, but not tonight.

"Do you want to talk about this?" she asks, slipping out of her shorts and folding them neatly on the chair. I watch as she pulls off her sweatshirt, noticing the blue lace of her bra and how it dips between her breasts. "Bas?" This pulls my attention away from her breasts and back up to her face.

"I don't know what to say."

"Neither do I, but I think—"

I kiss her before she can finish her thought.

I meant it to be a quick kiss, a quick peck to say goodnight, but Jasmine grabs the front of my shirt and pulls me closer, her mouth open and eager. Her arms wind around my shoulders, one hand stroking my back.

It's been a long time since we've kissed like this, like we did when we first met, sitting close together in the movie theatres, in the front seat of my car, on Jasmine's parents' front porch.

I'm suddenly breathless.

I don't know if it was the conversation by the fire or the wine, or maybe it was the heated glances Wyatt kept giving her, but Jasmine seems different tonight. Usually, she's soft, pliant, gentle with her touches.

That night she's none of those things.

She kisses me, long and deep, her hands reaching around my back to dip into the waistband of my jeans, fingernails scratching against my ass.

"I want you," she says against my mouth.

To my ears, she sounds surprised at the admission but maybe it's because I'm surprised that she would say such a thing. Jasmine has always been generous with her *I love yous* but never has she given instructions to me in the bedroom.

And that sounded a lot like she wanted me to do something.

I reach for her breasts, but Jasmine tugs me by the hips toward the bed. I lay down beside her when I hear the cry through the walls, rather than the baby monitor still in my pocket.

Jasmine makes a clicking sound of disappointment and draws away. "I'll go," I say softly. "Get ready for bed."

I don't know why I say that. I don't want her ready for bed, I want her ready for me—warm and open and naked.

I pull myself out of her arms and head for the kids' room.

It's Dominic. Bad dream. By the time I soothe him with a back rub and a hug, fetch him a drink and then help him to the bathroom, twenty minutes have passed.

Will Jasmine still be awake?

At the door, I stop. Jasmine left the lamp beside my bed turned on and in the dim light, I see her curled up underneath the blankets, fast asleep.

I back away with disappointment, heading for the bathroom on the other side of the cabin to brush my teeth and to get rid of the pressure that started when my wife kissed me.

To be honest, I was turned on long before we got back to the cabin. I got hard at the first mention of swapping or sharing, or whatever Carson called it, glad I had changed into my jeans rather than still wearing my loose bathing suit. All I could think of was being with another woman. Carson's sharp lines and edges rather than Jasmine's gentle curves. Or even Claire's athletic lankiness, her long reddish hair swinging around her shoulders.

Another woman, who isn't my wife. Feeling her touch, the weight of her body against mine. Different breasts...

I think a lot about different breasts as I fight to fall asleep.

CHAPTER FIVE

Jasmine

I WAKE UP WHEN Basil crawls into bed.

For a resort targeting swingers, they really don't have suitable beds. The mattresses are the type found in a family cottage, still there years after their prime. The bed frames squeak, the headboards creak—these are not beds that anyone can be quiet in.

It's always so very dark at Aurora; no streetlights or headlights marring the pitch blackness. I like it. It helps me sleep—usually.

I roll over as a signal to Basil that I'm awake.

"Jas?" Basil's voice is tentative, like when he's checking out if I'm asleep when he wants to have sex. Soft enough voice not to wake me if I'm in a deep sleep, but loud enough to jar me out of a fitful sleep.

"I'm awake." After such a heated kiss, a crying child makes it impossible to catch up and I've lost the mood. But I don't want to tell him that and prepare for his moves to start.

"Do you really want to do this?" he asks instead.

I yawn. "Do what?" I ask, thinking he's talking about having sex. Since when has he asked if I wanted it? He just makes a move and it's a yay or nay from me.

Usually yay, sometimes a more enthusiastic yay than other times.

I hear him roll onto his side and blink into the darkness as I try to make out his profile. I see a flash of white from his teeth but that's it. "What they suggested. I don't know what to call it."

"Do you?"

"I asked you first."

"I'm asking you second but I really need you to answer first," I say honestly.

A deep sigh and a pause. Basil likes to think before he speaks, which is usually a good thing, except for when we're arguing and he makes me wait minutes before a comeback. That drives me crazy.

"I don't know if I can," he says finally. "Thinking of you with Wyatt or Billy—Billy might be okay because I trust him, but you want Wyatt, don't you?"

I don't answer.

"Tell me what you think," he begs.

"I think I want to." It's a small voice that doesn't sound like me, but the words are mine.

"Why?"

There's hurt and disappointment in Basil's voice, as well as confusion and a bit of anger. But I focus on the hint of eagerness I can make out between his other emotions, and cling to that like a lifeline.

"It's not that I don't like being with you," I begin. "I think that was pretty clear before I fell asleep."

"But it's not always like that." He sounds resigned, disappointed maybe. I hate the thought that I disappoint him.

"No. It's not," I agree. The mattress creaks as I shift under the blankets. "But it's not why I want to either. I think there could be a little more excitement between us. Almost twelve years of marriage, three kids—things can get a little stale for anyone."

"Do you think they're stale?"

"Don't you?"

Another deep breath and I'm glad for once that I can't see his expression. "Maybe a little."

I prop myself onto my elbow. "I think Carson's right about marriages breaking up because they lose the passion. That's what leads to cheating, like Shawna and Matt. I'm not saying either of us will ever be unfaithful, but if we do this, it might take away some of the curiousity that could lead to an affair."

"Or it could lead right to an affair. You might get a taste of a new man and want to keep tasting."

I smile and reach out until my hand touches his chest. "Is that what you're worried about?"

"Of course it is," he burst out. "Look at him! He looks like Thor, without the flowing blond locks."

"He does sort of," I admit, resting my hand over his heart. "But I love you, Bas, and no matter how well Wyatt swings his hammer, I'm still going to want you."

Basil is silent for a moment. "Did you actually just make a comment about his hammer?" he says finally.

"I thought it was funny," I say defensively.

Basil gives a huff of frustration. "I'm never going to be able to look at Thor the same way again."

I chuckle and inch closer to him on the bed. "I want you," I say. "Always. That's not going to change. But I've only ever been with one other man, so yes, I'm curious about what it would be like with someone new. And I'd like to be able to find that out while I'm still in love with you."

"What if it does something to us?" Basil asks in a gruff voice.

"We won't let it."

"What if it does something to our friendship with Claire and Billy?"

I pause as an image of Basil and Claire flashes through my mind. They wouldn't be my first choice, but it's not the worst option. Can I live with knowing my husband and best friend had sex? I think so. Will it bother me? Yes, but I can push it down, deal with it later when I have the time and the mental energy.

"We can't let it," I say finally. "It'll be a thing that happens one time and we won't talk about it. It doesn't have to change anything."

"But it will."

"But maybe it won't be a bad thing."

"And maybe it will." Basil huffs. "You know me. I always look at the negative. If you want this, then...okay."

He gave in quicker than I expected, which reinforces my belief that this is something Basil wants too. "It has to be what you want too, or you'll start resenting me for making you do this."

"But if we don't do it, and you really want to, then you'll start to resent me," he counters.

"We don't have to decide tonight," I say. "Sleep on it and we'll talk to Claire and Billy tomorrow. This has to be something we both want, or at least what we can live with." I lean over and give him a clumsy kiss, still not able to see in the dark. "I love you."

"I love you, too," he says and rolls over.

It's a long time before I can fall asleep that night.

Basil

J ASMINE AND I DON'T get a chance to talk about it with Billy and Claire until lunch, and even then we wait until the kids are ushered away by the counsellor to camp. Alone, the four of us huddle close together, not sure what to say.

"Did that really happen?" Claire whispers. "Last night. They really asked us to have sex with them?"

"Think so." Billy has a wide grin on his face, and I understand how he feels. Part of me is doing a singing and dancing routine worthy of Broadway at the thought of having sex with a woman—*with permission from Jasmine.*

The other part of me is sitting at the farther corner of the theatre with a scowl, not enjoying any part of the show because even though I get to have sex, so does Jasmine, with a man who is not me.

This isn't going to be easy.

"They want us to *swing* with them." I can tell Jasmine is nervous about the thought, but there's a tinge of excitement in her voice as well.

That's what is making it difficult. This is something *she* wants to do, not me. If it was up to me, I'd be curling up beside my wife tonight.

Maybe. There's the whole being torn about this again.

"I don't think that's what you call it," Claire says with an un-characteristic giggle. "Share?"

"Swap," Billy says like he knows what he's talking about, even though I know he's only slept with three women in his life, and not one of them was someone else's wife.

"Do we need to prepare for this?" Claire asks. "Should we read something?"

"Like Fifty Shades?" Jasmine laughs. "I don't think that's going to help us. I've never read anything about swingers."

"Me neither. Maybe I should Google it." Claire pulls out her phone.

"It's a one-time thing," I say derisively. "I think we have all we need to know."

"You're going to Google swingers?" Jasmine asks like I hadn't spoken.

"You'll only get pictures of swingsets." Billy covers Claire's phone with his hand. "I already checked."

"It's called polyamory," I say, leaning back from the table. There are still a few clusters of guests eating, but the early lunch seating is over. "That's what Carson said."

Polyamory. Jasmine mouths the word like she's testing it out.

"I think that's what your brother is into," I add, a little too maliciously to be purely informative.

"Pardon?" Jasmine's eyes pop.

"Mahak?" Claire asks, a slow smile crossing her face and I remember at the last minute of her comments over the years about how attractive she finds Jasmine's brother. "*Really*?"

"Well, you just gave her the go-ahead, so thanks, bro." Billy gives me a thumbs-up.

"What does it matter if Mahak and Melissa are swingers?" I regret saying anything, wishing I'd shared the info with just Jasmine.

"How do you know that they are?" Jasmine demands.

"Mahak's always talking about other women, dropping names."

"They have friends! Neighbours."

"Yeah—that. They do a lot with those neighbours. You telling me you've never wondered?"

"No, I haven't wondered if my brother and his wife are swingers because he has friends," Jasmine says in an icy voice.

"And Melissa—she seems the type, you know." I don't know what makes me keep going since I can tell from Billy's expression that I'm digging myself deeper.

"And what type is that?" Jasmine hisses angrily. She jerks her head to a nearby table where a sixtysomething couple sits. "Do they look the type? Do I?"

"No. I don't know." I shrug. "I don't know anything."

"No, you don't," she says. "Especially not about my brother."

"What does it matter what Mahak does?" Claire wants to know.

"It really doesn't." Jasmine sighs. "It's just that I was always the good daughter, while Mahak was more of a troublemaker. And this makes me feel like I've crossed over to the dark side. It's kind of...dirty." But she doesn't seem upset when she says it.

"It does, doesn't it?" Claire sounds excited, as does Billy. I guess I'm the only hold-out.

But I've already agreed, so I guess I'm not the hold-out. Now we have to find out who goes with who. As I listen to Claire and Jasmine's conversation about bathing suits, my gaze drifts over Claire's face.

I've always thought she was pretty; like her body, her face is long and lean, her wide mouth the central focus, as well as the hazel eyes. I've never noticed the sprinkling of freckles on her arms or the definition of her biceps.

There's a lot I've never noticed about her. I have a feeling that tonight I'm going to learn a lot more.

Chapter Six

Jasmine

I FEEL LIKE A teenager when, after lunch, I ask Claire what bathing suit she thinks I should wear.

There's a nervous excitement surrounding us as we sit at the table in the Big House and I wonder if the other guests can sense it. Most of them—if this is a swinger's resort—have been in this situation before, so they should be able to relate. Anticipation practically sizzles through me, like I'm getting away with a crime.

Claire studies me, running her gaze over my chest and for a moment, I wonder if she's picturing me naked. "Your bikini," she decides. "Definitely the bikini."

"Are you sure?" I ask in a low voice, not wanting Billy or Basil to overhear. "I feel kind of bloated today."

Claire raises her eyebrow. She's really good at getting only one to rise, like Jack Nicholson, only not as sinister. She flicks a finger toward my chest. "Bikini," she says firmly. "It doesn't matter if you look as bloated as a nine-month along pregnant woman, no one is going to notice a thing when the girls are out to play."

"Why, Claire." I clutch my chest. "I didn't know you cared."

"I'm jealous," she says frankly. "Are we good to go to the beach now?"

"Hang on." I glance at Claire's face, excitement dancing in her eyes. "If we're doing this, shouldn't we decide on...you know...who?" I hope they know what I mean because I can't form the words that will ask if my husband is going to have sex with my best friend or a beautiful stranger.

Honestly, I have no idea which is the worst option.

"We'll let them decide," Billy says easily, leaning back and hooking his arm around the back of my chair.

"I think they already have." Claire scoffs at my blank expression. "C'mon, Jas, you'd have to be blind not to notice how Wyatt was checking you out yesterday, and last night."

"It was kind of obvious," Billy agrees.

I glance at Basil, who looks as stunned as I must.

"I'm fine with that," Claire announces. "You go ahead with the big guy. I'm good with..." She visibly swallows and for the first time, I can sense her nervousness. "Basil."

There's an awkward silence when she says his name, not just from me, who feels like Claire's just kicked me in the stomach, but Billy and Basil too.

"If that's okay," Claire adds in a rush. "Jas and Wyatt, Billy and..." There's a perceptible pause. "...and Carson. Me and Bas."

"I'm good with that," Basil says quickly. I'm not sure if he feels like he's rescuing Claire or is really good with the thought of having sex with her.

Why wouldn't he be? Claire is a beautiful woman.

"Well, okay, then," Billy drawls, pushing his chair back from the table. "I need a beer real fast, and then let's go meet our new friends."

We walk across the lawn to the cabins in silence. Basil's hand brushes mine and I grab his thumb and hold tight. Right now, I honestly don't know if this is the right decision. The four of us can have fun this week without anyone else.

And then I think about Wyatt's pink swim trunks. When will I ever get another chance to check out Thor's hammer?

The giggle slips out as we stop at the fork in the path that leads to the cabins—left for Basil and I, right for Claire and Billy. The cabins are a good twelve feet apart, close enough for a shout to be heard across the path.

Would anything else be heard?

"Hang on," Claire says as Basil leads me to the left. "Jas?"

As I look into her hazel gaze, I know exactly what she's going to say. "It's fine," I tell her.

"Are you sure?" she implores. "I don't want anything to come between us. Not even because of a great snog."

"Shag," Basil corrects. "I think that's what you mean. And thanks—that you think it's going to be great."

"How can it not be? When it's this?" Claire does a little shimmy and another giggle burst out of me. Even Billy laughs. "But Jas…" Her expression is now serious.

I step forward and hug her. "We won't let anything come between us," I promise. "It's going to be fine. A one-time thing."

No one corrects me.

Basil

As soon as we step inside the cabin, Jasmine heads for the bedroom. I follow, thinking maybe we're going to finish what she started last night, but Jas has her phone in her hand.

She looks up at me as she puts the phone to her ear. "I'm calling my brother."

"Put him on speaker," I suggest, flopping onto the bed. "He'll be at work though."

"He'll have to find a quiet place to talk." She sits cross-legged on the bed and puts the phone between us.

"Mahak Bennet."

Jasmine and her brothers, Mahak and Rajesh, are the only Indian family I know with such a Caucasian-sounding name. Their father was a minister working in India when he met their mother, fell in love with her and eventually brought her back to Canada when Jasmine was three. Jasmine has only the faintest hint of an accent, but her brothers, especially Mahak, still have the lyrical intonation to their words.

"Mahak, it's Jasmine. Basil and I are here at Aurora this week," Jasmine says firmly. Her interactions with her family are interesting to watch. It's like she's demanding respect with every conversation, which sometimes makes her sound like a bitch.

I'd never tell her that, of course.

"Hey, Mahak." I give a little wave.

"Basil," Mahak says shortly. "Why are you calling me if you're on vacation?"

"We're at the Aurora Resort on Lake Lockport." Jasmine enunciates each word. "Shouldn't you be telling us something about it? Something you should have told us years ago?"

Mahak suddenly laughs. "Look, Jas, as much as I'd love to have this conversation with my little sister, I'm leaving for a meeting right now. Call Melissa. This is her thing anyway."

"So she's a swinger, but not you?"

Another chuckle. "No, Jasmine, we're both part of that lifestyle, but I think we'd both enjoy it better if you let her explain."

"Will she?" I ask.

"Have you ever known Melissa not to talk about something? Have a good time, and we'll catch up when you get back."

A click and I glance at Jasmine. "Are you going to call—"

"Damn right I am!" In only a moment, Jasmine has Melissa on the phone. My sister-in-law has barely enough time to say hello when Jasmine accosts her. "You sent us to a swinger resort!"

"Oh, that's right, you're at Aurora this week. How is it?"

"The same, but now that I know that it's filled with couples who like to swap, it feels a whole lot different."

"Are you seriously just finding out?" Melissa asks incredulously. "I thought you've known for years and were fine with it."

"I don't know if we're fine with it. The kids, Melissa! What were you thinking?"

"They haven't got a clue. You've got a couple more years before you have to start being really careful."

"Really careful? So you and Mahak..?" Jasmine glances up at me as she trails off.

"Well, yeah. We have been for years."

My wife closes her eyes. "What does this mean?" she whispers.

"It doesn't mean anything," Melissa says in her usual abrupt voice. She is the bossiest woman I know. "Our marriage is great—better than great, and I think it's because of this. You have a good marriage, or so it seems, so if this is something you want to try, it won't come between you. Unless you let it."

"But how?" I can relate to the desperate quality of Jasmine's voice.

"Do you really want details?" Melissa laughs. "Because, trust me, this swinger stuff will curl your toes."

"No details necessary," I say since Jasmine seems to be at a loss for words.

"If you meet a couple that you like, go for it. You're in the right place. Everyone but you two know what's going on."

"Billy and Claire didn't know anything either," Jasmine says defensively.

"Well, from the sounds of it, Billy never seems to know much," Melissa scoffs. "I can't believe people pay him to take care of their money."

"You've only met him once!"

"I'm a very good judge of character. See, I knew you'd come around to Aurora. I just didn't think it would take you this long."

CHAPTER SEVEN

Jasmine

AFTER MY TOUCHING HEART-TO-HEART with my sister-in-law, I stare at Basil. "You were right," I accuse.

"I didn't know I was right!"

I exhale with a huff as I pull myself off the bed. "So this place is legit."

"Is that what you were concerned with? Not the whole bending our marriage vows?"

"Is that what you think we're doing?" I stop before I reach the dresser where I've unpacked my clothes. "Bending, not breaking?"

"It sounds better," Basil admits. "Although, I'm sure your father wouldn't agree."

"Please don't mention my father." I buried my face in my hands. "Maybe we shouldn't do this."

"Hey." I let Basil pry my hands away from my face. "This is what you want. You're just scared. What did Shawna always say? Put on your big girl panties and get on with it."

"Shawna," I moan. "We'd never be doing this if they were here. She would have hated Carson on sight."

"That she would have," Basil agrees with a chuckle.

Instead of my big girl panties, I change into my bikini, nervously posing in front of the mirror.

"You're only going to the beach," Basil says when he catches me preening. "Nothing will happen this afternoon."

"I feel like we're doing something wrong just planning this," I confess. "Like if something is going to happen, it should happen naturally and we shouldn't force it."

"Then don't. All we're doing is hanging out with a couple that we just met. Pretend they're new friends—that's it. Maybe we won't like them at all and this swapping thing will never happen."

I study Basil's face, unsure if he's hopeful or disappointed at the thought. I never imagined the conflict going on inside me at the thought of having sex with another man.

Probably because I could never have imagined being in this situation.

I nod. "I might not even like Wyatt," I say.

But I know that's not going to be the case.

By the time we get to the beach, it's dotted with chairs and umbrellas, but Claire and Billy got there in time to grab a good spot, with chairs for all of us. My stomach tightens when I see Carson, wearing another itty bitty bikini, this time in bright blue, and Wyatt chatting easily with them.

Am I the only one nervous about this?

But by the grip on my hand, I can tell Basil is as uncertain as I am about the whole thing.

"Beautiful day," Wyatt says with a welcoming smile.

For a moment, I don't think Basil is going to let go of my hand, that he's going to sit down still attached. But at the last second, just as I open my mouth to stop whatever is going to happen, he squeezes it tightly and drops it.

"It is a beautiful day," I say instead.

We sit. We make awkward small talk. We arrange our things; towels, sunscreen, water bottles. I pull out my book, but it sits unread on my lap as I stare out at the lake.

How am I supposed to do this?

I don't even know this man. Is a base attraction enough to allow me to be intimate with him? When I was younger and single, I was never one for casual hookups and Basil is only the second man I've had sex with. Both were the result of long-term relationships. I met Wyatt only yesterday, and now I'm supposed to have sex with him?

I sneak a surreptitious glance at him. Today he's wearing dark green trunks and he looks as good in them as he did in hot pink. His body is nothing short of amazing—muscles and flat abs with a smattering of hair across his chest. Another peek and I'm convinced it's grayish, like his beard.

How old is Wyatt?

What's his last name?

"Would you like to go for a swim?" Wyatt asks. I turn to him with a start when I realize he's asking me.

"Sure," I stammer. Anything is better than sitting there like a bump on a log, trying to convince myself that it would be a good thing to let something happen tonight.

Wyatt stands and offers me a hand. With an apologetic glance at Basil, I take it and let Wyatt help me to my feet.

"Back soon," he throws over his shoulder as he leads me away from the others.

I take a last look at Basil. He nods, and I exhale, not realizing I was holding my breath.

"Carson can sit in the sun all day, but I need water," Wyatt confides as we step around the other beach lovers. He's still holding my hand, his grasp warm and oddly reassuring.

I push away the thought that I had been holding hands with my husband only a short time ago.

"The same with me," I say, pretending that I'm having a simple conversation with anyone. If I push the idea of sex aside, I might be able to get through this without embarrassing myself. "But I don't like to swim with Claire, because she, like really swims, and the same with Basil. I go in with the kids but—" I'm not sure why I stop myself, or why it sounds like a car coming to a screeching halt in my mind.

"But what?" Wyatt prompts.

"I don't really want to talk about my kids."

"Ah." We reach the water and Wyatt gingerly takes a step in. "What do you want to talk about?"

"I'm not sure."

"Do you want to talk about why I'm here with you and not with my wife?"

"Maybe," I say shyly.

Wyatt nods. "Let's go out to the floating dock."

Instead of wading into the waves, we head for the pier instead. The wood is hot under my feet and I step quickly, dodging those that have pulled chairs onto the pier, others that sit with legs dangling in the cool water. When we're almost to the end, Wyatt stops and drops my hand.

"Race you?" he asks with a mischievous grin that has my stomach flipping over at the sight.

"Where?" I ask stupidly.

"To the floating dock. I'll even give you a head start."

He had me at *race you*.

I glance to the dock and back to Wyatt, appraising his body like I haven't already studied every inch of it. "I don't need a head start." But I take one anyway—five leaping steps and I flatten into a racing dive. Wyatt laughs as my body knifes into the water.

Despite my unfair head start, Wyatt quickly catches up. I can tell he's holding back by the way he matches me stride for stride. A few feet away from the dock, I stop swimming with a laugh.

"I give up," I gasp.

"I'm not letting you." Wyatt grabs me by the waist and drags me through the water, both of us laughing.

The feel of his hands helps with my second-guessing, as does the way he manhandles me to the ladder. I scramble up to the dock as quickly as I can.

"You said you didn't need a head start," he accuses as he sits on the edge facing out onto the lake, his toes dipping into the water.

"Didn't mean I wasn't going to take it." I tuck my hands under my thighs, a puddle growing around me as everything drips.

"A little competitive, are you?" Wyatt arches an eyebrow with an amused grin.

"Just a little."

We sit quietly, the dock still rocking and waves slapping against the sides. "So you're the talking sort?" he asks finally.

"What's that supposed to mean?"

"I mean, some people jump into this without a thought. It's like they're being given a free pass and they grab it, without a thought about the consequences. And then there are others who think and think about it and need to discuss every aspect. They need a certain comfort level before anything happens."

"What are you?" I ask, trying not to feel offended.

"The talking sort," Wyatt admits. He brushes my shoulder. "It's all good."

The rigidness in my body softens at his touch. "What do you talk about?"

"Anything you want. Anything that gives you that comfort level. It's not worth it if you're having second thoughts." He splashes his feet in the water. "If this isn't for you—"

"I've never done this before," I interrupt.

"I know. And that's okay with me."

"And you're okay with me?" I blurt, gasping after the words are out in the world. "I mean...if..."

Wyatt bows his head and watches his feet slice through the water. "That's a silly question."

I honestly don't know what to say, so I stay quiet for long minutes. The sound of wood on water, the distant sounds of laughter from the shore makes it very peaceful on the dock.

Or maybe it's sitting beside Wyatt. Because as *impressive* as he looks, as much as he might resemble a bad boy with the baldness and the beard and the muscles, I can tell he's a nice guy.

I like nice guys.

Of course, I've never known anything different, so I wouldn't know a thing about a bad boy either.

"What do you do?" I ask to finally break the silence.

Wyatt meets my gaze with a hint of a smile. There goes that stomach flip again. "Firefighter," he says like it's nothing. Like firefighters aren't some kind of superheroes.

"Of course you are."

"What's that mean?"

"I should have known. You even look like you could be in one of those calendars, maybe the ones with the firemen and the cats."

Another arch of his eyebrow. "You like looking at pictures of firemen?" he asks with a knowing smile.

"I like cats."

Wyatt laughs and my stomach warms. Maybe this will work. Because even if I'm nervous about how this will affect my marriage and my friendship with Claire and Billy, there's a part of me that is never going to forgive the rest of me if I turn down this chance.

"I think you're beautiful," Wyatt says casually.

I snort. "I don't think so. Have you seen your wife?"

"I think you're beautiful," he repeats.

I stare at him. He actually looks like he means it. "Thank you," I say.

That settles it. Done deal.

Basil

I CAN'T STOP STARING at Jasmine out on the floating dock with Wyatt. She keeps laughing. He makes her laugh.

I don't remember the last time I made her laugh like that, with her face lighting up with every word as if she would rather be with him than with anyone else.

"Bas?"

I look up when Claire says my name. I get the impression that it's not the first time.

"Sorry—what?"

"I asked if you want to take one of the canoes out." She looks pointedly at the dock. "Might be a good distraction."

I smile wryly. "Sounds perfect."

Billy is asleep on his lounge chair beside me, with Carson on her stomach, head buried in her arms and earbuds in. I don't know if she's asleep or not, so with a last glance at them, I follow Claire down the beach to what we call the marina, where there are a half dozen canoes to use, as well as a selection of kayaks and paddleboards.

It doesn't take long before Claire and I are paddling in the opposite direction of Jasmine and Wyatt.

It's not unheard of for me and Claire to do something together. In past years, while the kids were in camp, Jasmine would be absorbed in her book, while Billy slept beside her. The rest of us would play in the water, or volleyball on the beach. One year Claire announced she was joining me on my morning runs. That lasted a day, since she cajoled me into going for an early morning canoe ride the day after, rather than running.

Lockport is a closed lake and during our first year here, Claire, Billy, Matt and I canoed around the whole thing, leaving Jasmine with Shawna and the kids.

I ask Claire if she remembers that day.

"I don't think Jas ever forgave us for leaving her behind," Claire throws over her shoulder.

"I did get quite the cold shoulder from that," I admit. "But I think Shawna was more upset on Jas' behalf. She was pregnant—what was I supposed to do?"

"Drag her along in a dingy behind us?"

My attention is fixated on watching Claire paddle. She's wearing a black Speedo—practical, no-nonsense, but giving me an excellent view of her back and the way it tapers into her waist before flaring out into her hips.

She's wearing shorts or I'd be staring at her ass the whole ride. Even now I can't get enough of her back, her muscles flexing with each reach of the paddle.

"Claire?" Watching her paddle, with the realization that tonight I'll most likely be seeing her out of her bathing suit is making me uncomfortably hard. "Are you okay with all this?"

I'm asking if she's okay with me, but I can't bring myself to use those exact words.

She doesn't respond and I'm about to ask again when she turns slightly. "I've always thought you were cute, you know."

"Really?"

Carefully, Claire swivels so that she's facing me, causing me to clutch the sides as the canoe rocks. "You know that."

We had set off along the shore of the lake, and when I glance back, Jasmine, Wyatt and the beach had disappeared. I forget about them and focus on Claire.

"Actually...no. I don't."

"You're a smart man, Basil. Don't you remember that time when I kept holding your hand?"

"You'd had a bit of wine that night, so I didn't think anything of it."

"When you kept joking about necking with other women—you kept asking me to run off into the woods with you?"

"And you said no, if I recall correctly."

"I wanted to. But I knew you weren't serious. It was all a joke to you."

"And you really wanted to run off into the woods with me?"

"I did."

I don't know what to say. The thought of being wanted puffs up my chest, but it's coupled with a sharp pang of regret. Not that I would ever cheat on Jasmine, but we are at a swinger resort. What if someone had approached us years ago? Would we have taken them up on it?

Could I have been having sex with Claire all this time?

"Your face!" Claire laughs. "I've never seen you speechless before."

"I'm not speechless, I just don't know what to say."

"It's the same thing, Basil."

"I've spent this whole time wanting to apologize for you being—not stuck, but you know, stuck with me, and here I find out you've had secret fantasies about me."

"Aren't all fantasies secret?" she asks, rather than admit or deny.

"So you've fantasized about me?" Taking the bull by the horns here. I shift on the uncomfortable seat, glad that standing is frowned upon in a canoe.

"So what if I had?"

"Like what? Can you tell me?"

Claire leans forward, causing another rock of the boat. "You do understand the *secret* part of fantasies, don't you?"

"Seems only right that you tell me, now that we're about to take our relationship to the next level."

"I'm not sure you should call it that."

"Relationship, or next level?"

"Next level. That suggests we're moving here," Claire stacks her hands one on top of the other. "Rather than *here*." Hands side by side.

"You're saying this is going to elongate our relationship."

"It might elongate something," she drawls.

"Why, Claire." I enunciate my accent even more because I know she likes it. "I never knew you cared."

"If things are elongated? Maybe a little," she teases.

I grin, suddenly giddy at the thought of being with Claire. It's surreal to think that tonight—

I want it to happen tonight.

"How do we do this?" I ask once the six of us are back at the beach. Wyatt has pulled his chair closer to Jasmine's, while Claire is sitting on the end of my lounger.

Clear selections have been made.

Jasmine looks surprised that I asked the question.

"Does this mean you'd like to try it?" Carson raises an eyebrow.

"Yes." I glance at Claire, then Jasmine. Billy has an excited grin on his face. "We do. The kids will be at a sleep-over at the Big House tonight."

"Perfect timing. We'll meet at the bonfire tonight, and see what comes up."

"At the fire?" Jasmine asks nervously.

Carson laughs. "I think it would be nice to have a few drinks together before we go our separate ways. I usually have a time limit," she says. "Because we're in each other's room. Let's say two hours—"

"That long?" Billy asks, and we all laugh.

"Oh, yes." Carson gives him the sort of sexy smile perfected by on-screen sirens like Scarlett Johanson. For a moment, I think twice about my choice of Claire.

But then I glance at Jas and see how she's staring, entranced by whatever Wyatt is saying to her. For me to change my mind would rearrange everyone and I can't do that to her.

Even though I'm a little nervous about Wyatt and Jas. Maybe I should say something to him, warn him how Jas takes a little bit to get warmed up, how he should be gentle with her—

I stop myself. Jas is a big girl, and she's the one who wanted this.

"Ninety minutes," Carson continues with the rules. "If you need more time, hang something on the doorknob outside, but I'll tell you now that if there is anything hanging outside my door, I'm going to cozy up who will have me for the night." She gives Wyatt a stare I can't read, but obviously, he understands because he nods with a secret smile.

I'm really nervous about Jas.

CHAPTER EIGHT

Jasmine

IT FEELS LIKE A first date.

But worse, because I know exactly what is going to happen. There's no wondering about a first kiss—I think we'll be doing a little more than kissing.

To say I'm nervous is an understatement.

I have all the signs—butterflies in the stomach, knees threatening to knock together under my very short skirt, accelerated heart rate. When Wyatt releases my hand to unlock the cabin door, I notice my fingers are trembling.

And it's not just because I think Wyatt is hot, because oh my god, I do! He's beautiful, and manly and *Sexy*, using capital letters and italics.

I can't stand not knowing what he's going to do to me.

I don't even go to the thought of what I'm going to do to him. When I start to wonder about that, things start to go hazy because how am *I* going to please this hunk of manly manhood?

He ushers me into the cabin and my attention zooms to the bed. Wyatt and Carson have one of the smaller cabins—one room, with a king-sized bed taking centre stage, a tiny sofa and uncomfortable wing chair grouped around the obligatory fireplace, and a wall full of windows overlooking the lake.

Immediately, I head to the curtains to pull them closed, leaving my personal time with Wyatt private.

But he stops me. "Leave them open," he says in the husky voice that sounds like he's got a bad sore throat.

"But someone might see us."

Wyatt moves behind me and I hold my breath as he slides a hand around my waist and down my thigh. "Is that a bad thing? I think you'll look glorious being fucked. And when you come?" His fingers reach the hem of my dress and curl around it, pulling it up inch by inch. "I can't wait to see that."

"But do you think—?" His lips press against my neck and halt my protest and I sag against him. How does Wyatt know my neck is so sensitive? Basil barely even remembers that.

"Do you want to talk or do you want to fuck?" Wyatt says. I can feel the smile on his lips as he presses another kiss behind my ear. My insides tingle from his words as much as his touch.

"Well, I...I'd rather not talk," I stammer.

Wyatt stiffens behind me and pulls my shoulder back so he can see my face. My quickly reddening face. "Really?"

"I don't want to talk." I try again in a low voice, my gaze dropping under his stare.

"Do you want me to fuck you?" he asks roughly. Mutely, I nod. "Tell me."

"Yes," I whisper.

"Say you want me to fuck you." He kisses my neck again and a gasp escapes me at the touch of his touch. And then he steps away, leaving me chilled. "It's the only way this is going to happen."

I squirm under his stare. "I can't."

"You can, and you will. Because I plan on making this a night to remember for both of us." He pulls me against him and I feel his hardness.

I did that to him. The realization sends a rush of dizzying desire through me.

"I want you, Jasmine. Tell me you want me too."

I love the way Wyatt says my name. *Jazzzz*min. Drawling and slightly mocking, like the smile on his face. "I want you," I whisper, my excitement giving me courage.

He moves around to face me, tilting my chin with a strong finger so our eyes meet. "What do you want me to do to you?"

Just about anything right now. "Fuck me." The words are barely a breath, but Wyatt hears me.

"How do you want me to fuck you?" Wyatt's voice is low, intense, like the weight of the world rests on the question. And it feels like it does.

"Anyway?" I can't handle more questions. I'm so turned on that I might have difficulty giving my full name right now.

"That'll do." With a swiftness that takes my breath away, Wyatt lifts me up, his fingers biting into my ass as my legs automatically wrap around him. "I like to fuck hard," he says, those blue eyes studying me. "And rough. You okay with that?"

It's all I can do to nod. Still holding me, Wyatt lifts his chin and I kiss him, a tentative brush of my lips. But when he moves his lips against mine, he opens them slightly and suddenly we're kissing, *really* kissing. His tongue sweeps inside my mouth and I wind my arms around his shoulders.

I think the low moan comes from me.

Through the haze of desire, I can tell he's moving, still carrying me but I don't know where, nor do I care. I haven't been kissed like this since Mark O'Neil felt me up in the front seat of his dad's car when I was seventeen.

Mark O'Neil gave me my first orgasm that night, and it feels like I'm about to explode right now, especially the way Wyatt flexes his fingers on my bum like he's moving ever closer to what is undoubtedly the centre of my world at this moment.

I think I might be grinding against him.

Wyatt stops and I have an instant to lift my head before he throws me onto the bed. I land with a *humpft* and then giggle.

"That's so hot," Wyatt says, pulling off his T-shirt.

I can only stare at the pecs and biceps and the overall picture. He's standing close enough to the bed so that I only need to reach out and touch. "What is?" I ask with difficulty.

"Your laugh." He lands on the bed beside me, lying on his side and cupping my chin with a gentle hand.

"You think my laugh is sexy?"

"The way you giggle is." His smile is bemused and slightly embarrassed as he strokes my chin with his thumb. "I wanted you before I even saw what you looked like. I heard you laugh at the fire the first night and told Carson it needed to be you."

"Really?" I whisper.

"Really." He leans over to kiss me and I feel his weight as he rolls on top of me. But only for an instant because he keeps rolling and I end up on top of him.

Tucking my legs on either side of his hips, I sit up. With a swift movement, Wyatt pulls my dress over my head, leaving me in only my bra and underwear. I take a deep breath and fight to urge to cover myself, clutching his shoulders instead. His hands cup my breasts.

"And then I saw these the next day and that was it," Wyatt says with a grin.

Something explodes inside of me; not the orgasm I want, but instead, a feeling of self-worth and pride. I've never felt so wanted in all my life.

"I want you to tell me what you want," he says, his hands slowly moving down my back.

"I can't," I admit.

"You can try." His hands massage me, rough and powerful, at odds with the gentleness of his earlier kiss.

"Okay." And then I lean down and kiss him, wanting more of his mouth.

I lose track of how long we kiss. It's all about lips and tongues, Wyatt's hands roving along my back, my breasts. Eventually, the flick of his fingers against my bra fastenings rouses me enough to realize my bra is hanging off my shoulders and I break the kiss long enough to sit up and shrug it off.

Right away, Wyatt curls up and finds my nipple with his mouth. Eyes closed, I lean my head back, my gasp of pleasure becoming an odd squeak as his fingers slide along my thighs.

"I want to hear you tonight," he says against my breast.

When his hand finds my warmth, burrowing under my panties, my gasp is perfectly audible. And so is my moan when he thrusts a finger inside me. My back arches as a reflex, pushing my breasts into his mouth.

Greedily, he suckles me, his fingers busy between my legs. Sensations wash over me, heady and intense. His hands are everywhere, wanting all of me, and I let him. I open myself to him, surrender to his control.

"These need to come off," he says huskily, pulling at my panties.

I've never taken underwear off so quickly, tossing it over my shoulder to land somewhere on the bed. He settles me back on his lap, pulling me against him so I can grind against his hardness.

I haven't seen it, haven't touched it, but I want it more than anything right now.

Wyatt's mouth searches for mine again, his hand cupping between my legs. "I'm going to make you come now," he whispers.

Maybe I want something more than what's in his lap first. I whimper against his mouth, a wordless signal that I want that too.

I want all of him.

I don't realize I'm moving against him, my hips thrusting frantically as his fingers slide in and out.

In...and...out...

Stopping the rhythmic plunder only to brush against my nub, sending waves of pleasure through me.

There are noises in the room; the sounds of his fingers in my wetness, my laboured breathing, and soft sounds somewhere between a gasp and a cry. They don't even sound like me.

Wyatt can hear me. I can hear myself making noises I've never made before.

My noises get louder my whimpers turning to throaty moans, to cries that fill the cabin as his fingers work me faster and faster.

His lips are on my neck, biting and sucking, pressed against my shoulder. I clutch him, pressing against him. Moving against him.

"More," I gasp, begging for the release that's coming. "Please."

He moves those biting, sucking lips to my breast, his nips painful but pushing me over. And when he rubs my nub urgently—

"Come now," he urges.

So close, and I arch into it, stretched as tight as a bowstring, reaching, closer and closer, until it hits, crashing over me like a wave. I cry out, my hips wild as Wyatt's fingers continue to dance.

"Fuck me," I say, even before my heart settles.

"Now?" Wyatt asks with disbelief. "Because I can—"

"Now."

"I can't say no, even if I wanted to." With a strong arm, he lifts me off his lap and I land on the bed. "You like that?"

I can't catch my breath but I giggle. Another giggle escapes when Wyatt laughs.

Then my giggle cuts off as Wyatt strips off his cargo pants, taking his boxer briefs with him, leaving him hard and thick and gloriously naked.

I drink him in, not remembering the last time I felt so loose and carefree. It's like the orgasm opened something inside me that I'd kept locked up for too long.

"How do you want it?" Wyatt demands as he rips open the foil wrapper.

"Anyway?" I can't tear my eyes away from his cock, watching as he smoothes the condom on like he's done this a thousand times.

How do I know? Maybe he has. The thought makes me feel just a little bit safer as well as inexplicitly dirty.

I like feeling this way. Dirty.

"You have to say it," Wyatt says, his hand fisting on the base of his cock. It's a thing of beauty, even wrapped tightly. I'm hit with the urge to take it in my mouth. I want to touch it, to taste it...

But I want him to fuck me more.

"From behind." The voice doesn't sound like mine. Breathy and gaspy, like I can't get enough air. "I want you to fuck me from behind."

The words are definitely not mine.

But Wyatt smiles, with a devilish light in his eyes. "I can do that." Grasping my legs, he flips me over and I give a gasp of laughter as he pulls me to the edge of the bed. Taking my hips, he forces me to my knees, pushing my shoulders onto the mattress when I try to rise up.

"This is nice," he says, smoothing a hand over my cheek.

Before I can brace myself for that thick cock to be inside me, it's something else between my legs. I give a strangled cry as his tongue plunges inside me. Then he drags it the length of me, again and again, and again.

"Oh, my god," I groan, my face buried into the duvet. His tongue laps politely at my clit, before he surrounds it with his mouth and sucks rudely. "Oh, please."

I'm not sure exactly what I'm begging for, but begging seems like a good thing to do. He repeats the move—in and out, up and down, around and around, until my head is spinning and my words are an incoherent mass of moans.

One last suck of my clit, and then he's gone.

"I'll come back to that," Wyatt promises. My groan of disappointment quickly becomes a moan of pleasure as he thrusts into me. Tight and painful for only a moment, and then he starts to move.

Fast and hard; not anything that I'm used to. But my hips are right there with him, and surprisingly, my moans transform into words, and I'm back to begging. Begging for harder, faster, *more*. Fuck me more.

I even say the f-word without being asked.

"You like that?" Wyatt shifts so that somehow he's even deeper inside me, fucking me soundly, solidly, without pause.

And then he slaps me, his hand cracking against my ass with enough force to make me gasp. "You like that?" he asks cautiously.

I find that I do. "Yes," I pant, pushing myself back at him.

"Good." He slaps me again, and then reaches between my legs, his fingers finding my nub—my clit. The centre of my world.

Wyatt seems to know exactly what I want like I've given him detailed instructions, but I've never said a word. He just knows.

It's like Wyatt just knows I want to be fucked hard and fast, his legs slamming into the backs of mine. He knows I want the feel of his hand on my ass cheek, a sharp smart, only to be replaced by his fingers on my clit. He knows when I'm close and he slows everything until I find myself begging for more.

Begging, pleading, crying out, my entire body awash with sensations until I can't control my cries, and push my face into the duvet as I scream, my body convulsing as the orgasm hits. So intense, going on and on until Wyatt groans above me and with a final thrust that pitches me forward, comes as well.

Basil

"I'M NOT EXACTLY SURE how to go about this," I admit as the door shuts behind me, leaving me and Clare alone in my cabin.

Our cabin—mine and Jasmine's, who, I have no doubt, is now busy fucking Wyatt. I don't even want to think about what the kids are up to right now. Things have gone X-rated way too fast.

It's like every one of my thoughts is a dirty one. Looking at Clare in her pretty sundress makes me want to rip it off her and throw her down on the bed.

"Do you not want to?" Clare asks, giving me a look like I've seen her give Billy a hundred times before. Not a good look, not the *I want to do nasty things to you* look that I've seen her give Billy after a night of too much wine.

I want her to look at me like that.

"I'd be an idiot if I didn't want to," I tell her, giving her an easy smile while trying to get my mind off Jasmine fucking Wyatt.

"And you're no idiot, Basil."

"I like to think I'm not." Even though Jas thinks I am at times. I don't want to think about my wife, and I definitely don't want to talk about her. "I'm not sure how to start," I admit.

"How about like this?" Clare reaches down and takes the hem of her dress and pulls it up and over her head. She's not wearing a bra, and her breasts will be small enough to fit perfectly in my hand.

"Wow." My gaze travels from her chest to the tiny thong she wears—I would never have suspected Clare was the thong type. She definitely has the ass for it, plus the long legs that seem to go on forever. "You've got a great body. I mean, I knew that, but seeing it up close and personal—wow."

"Thank you. I think."

"It was definitely a compliment."

"If you want one back, you better take your clothes off."

I don't have to be asked twice. I should have known Clare wouldn't go for the seduction scene; matter-of-fact, let's get on with it. Quickly, I pull off my polo shirt and my shorts, folding them neatly on the chair before I slip off my boxers.

I wish I was hard. It's about halfway there, but still, my cock hangs limply between my legs instead of jutting up, large and in charge.

Claire notices. "Hmm." Using her fingers, she shimmies her thong down those long legs and steps out of them.

That helps.

"Why don't you lay on the bed?" she suggests.

That also piques my interest and Mr. Bas takes a few swings, preparing to hit the home run. I position myself on the bed, head propped up on the pillows and grin at Claire.

She grabs my feet and tugs, stronger than I thought, and my head hits the mattress. "When's the last time you went down on Jas?" she asks conversationally as she hops onto the bed.

"What?" She's not getting into a position to give me a blow job, at least any position that I know of.

"I hope you're not out of practice." And with that, she swings her legs over my shoulders, and just like that, her pussy is inches from my face.

Oh, wow.

This is new. This may be a bit out of my comfort zone because it has been a while since Jas and I partook in oral sex.

Or at least oral sex for her.

But I'm game with Claire. And it's hot, knowing that she's taking charge of her pleasure. Gripping Claire's hips, I lower her a bit so my tongue can hit the right spot.

And I know it's the right spot because she gasps and a shiver runs through her.

Closing my eyes, I begin to explore Claire with my mouth.

I start slowly, with teasing touches but that doesn't last long before Claire is pressing down on my mouth. Keeping it slow, dragging my tongue the length of her, teasing kisses on her inner thighs, all before plunging inside her.

She seems to like that.

She also likes it when I find her clit, focusing my all attention on it with frantic flicks, using my tongue like I tease Jas with my cock or my finger to get her going.

From Claire's response, she's going to go all the way, especially when I take her clit in my mouth and suck, the sound of the suction blocking out her gasp. But I hear her moan, her cries that seem to go on and on. Energized, and really turned on by now, I shift her hips, pulling her back and forth above me.

She leans forward just enough to take my now, fully hard cock in her hand.

Why don't I do this more with Jas? This is fun. This is hot, the way I'm completely surrounded by Claire's pleasure, her scent and taste. I feel her jerk above me, her hips moving with a mind of their own.

She leans all the way over and takes my cock in her mouth.

Oh...wow.

This is good, this is great. This is distracting.

All I want to do is lay there and receive because it feels so good. Claire does something with her tongue around the tip when it's in her mouth, then slides her lips down the length of me, with just the right about of suck. And then—

I groan, the pursuit of pleasuring Claire completely forgotten.

And then she takes her mouth away. "Don't stop."

Giving myself a shake, I return to the task at hand.

Angling her enough, I get my hand between her legs and thrust my fingers inside her as I play with her clit.

Oh, she likes that.

She likes it so much that I keep doing it, licking and sucking and fingering and trying to keep my focus both on what's making her happy and the amazing things she's doing to my cock.

I should put a stop to this; part of me wants to flip her over and go balls deep into this pussy that tastes so sweet. But the other part of me wants to keep on doing what I'm doing.

And then the opportunity passes because I'm pretty sure Claire is coming.

Having a woman come when her mouth is on your cock is like nothing I've ever experienced before.

I really need to do this with Jas.

I clamp a hand on Claire's ass to try and keep her still because her entire body is trembling with little hip thrusts against my mouth. I keep my fingers going, and suck on her clit, lapping it with my tongue.

Sucking one last time, I feel her fall apart above me. Her moans become sharp cries—and she keeps my cock in her mouth the entire time.

That puts me over the edge and with a jerk of my own hips, I come with a low groan.

Chapter Nine

Jasmine

"What do we do now?" I primly tuck the sheet around me as Wyatt rolls onto his side, lying with his arm tucked under his head. The sheet is draped over his hips, leaving his chest bare.

Somehow he got me into the bed after he fucked me. I'm not sure how—things were a little hazy after I screamed.

He made me scream.

My ass is a little warm from his hand. I wonder if he left a mark. The thought of a red handprint on my bum, something I'd have to explain away, makes me dizzy.

Or maybe it's the sight of Wyatt lying beside me that makes my head spin. I can stare at his chest all day. In fact, I'm tempted to run my finger down his muscles, but I can't. That was...a lot for me.

"We wait for a few minutes and then we go again," Wyatt answers my question with a grin. Already I recognize his smiles—the sexy confident one, the one where his eyes are half-closed and it looks like he's about to eat me alive, the smug I-did-something-right one.

I like the grin. "Again?"

"You say that like it's a bad thing."

"No! It's not, it's just...I've never done this before."

"Which you've told me several times."

"I wanted to make sure you knew what you were getting into."

He narrows his eyes at me. "You make it sound like you're something I paid for. I told you; I wanted you the moment I saw you."

"When you heard me laugh."

"Exactly." He trails a sleepy finger down my arm.

Now it's my turn to frown. "But it was my choice. *You* were my choice."

"And I'm very glad I was. But it was planned. I told Carson I wanted you—she made it happen."

"How?" I stare at him in awe.

"Did Carson make any comments about me?"

"Well...I guess. It was kind of the way she smiled when she mentioned you."

"To intrigue you."

"And the way you kept looking at me. Was that part of the plan?"

Wyatt leans over and kisses me, his lips gentle against mine. How can a man who may have left a bruise on my ass have such soft lips? "I kept staring at you because I couldn't stop," he confesses in a low voice.

"I couldn't stop looking at you, either."

"I know," he says, in a perfect imitation of Han Solo. I laugh, and he smiles.

There's another smile for me to keep in my memory bank; the one where he's happy. I think that one might be my favourite.

"How long have you been doing this?" I ask to get my mind off Wyatt's smile. I'm having an even harder time not touching him, clutching the sheet with hands that want to wander.

He obviously doesn't have an issue with post-pillow talk that involves wandering fingers. They skate up my arm, with goosebumps erupting in their wake.

"About ten years."

"And so is this something you do fairly regularly? Meet other couples?" I ask carefully.

"Or was I completely swept away by your beauty and charm and told Carson that I had to have you?" Wyatt teased.

"Well, no, I'm sure you didn't..." I trail off, feeling my cheeks warm.

"Actually, this was the first time in a while that I picked first," he says giving me a sideways glance that sends tingles to the furthest reaches of my body.

"Really?"

"Is that your favourite word?"

"No. I don't know."

"Or do you just have difficulty believing people when they say nice things about you?" Because that is the absolute truth, I can only shrug in response. "What's your husband like? What's his name—Bane? Do you still like him?"

"Bas," I correct, feeling a guilty thrill that Wyatt was too into me to learn his name. "Basil. And yes, I love him."

"But do you *like* him?" Wyatt persists. "That's the problem with marriages—you still love each other, but there's not a lot of like. You get bored. Life gets in the way of having fun together."

"It definitely gets in the way of a lot of things." I try to think of the last time Basil and I had fun together, alone, without anyone else. Sometimes we'll get a babysitter and go out, but there's constant talk about the kids and our schedules.

I don't remember the last time we lay in bed and *talked*. Or laughed together.

It makes me sad that I can't think of anything.

"Carson and I were both married before." Wyatt flips onto his back beside me, still touching me with his hand. "I still loved my wife, but I was bored with her. And I didn't like her much because she wouldn't make time for me. It wasn't just the sex, although that suffered *a lot*."

I shake my head at the thought of a woman not making time for sex with Wyatt.

"I can't blame her, but part of me does," Wyatt continues, staring at the circle of light from the bedside lamp. "I had an affair."

"With Carson?"

Wyatt nods. "She was already divorced; her husband had cheated as well, but she always says her marriage was over long before she found out. It was just a one-time thing for me with her, because after it happened, things got a lot better with my wife. I was excited to be with her again, started making more of an effort. It might have been guilt," he adds, mirroring my own thoughts. "But things were good. Until she found out."

"And that wouldn't have been good."

"No, not good," Wyatt chuckles. "Long story short, Carson and I got together after that, but both of us decided that monogamy isn't all that it's cut out to be. We started looking around for other like-minded people, as she calls them."

"And you found us here."

"And we found you. And here we are." He leans over and brushes my temple with his lips.

"Here we are," I echo.

"Somewhere you never expected to be."

I shake my head. "Never. I always expected Bas and I to be together forever."

"And you might well be." Wyatt turns to face me again. "Stop looking at this as cheating because it's consensual, between all six of us. Go back to your husband and be excited about what you learned from me."

"What did I learn from you?"

Another kiss on my temple, then Wyatt trails it down to my mouth. "You learned how to say a dirty word," he says with a sly smile. "And you told me what you wanted. Bet that was the first time for that."

I smile shyly. "It was."

"It won't be the last."

Basil

"WELL, THAT WAS FUN." Claire grins at me.

Both of us are still naked, Claire lying flat on her back on Jasmine's side of the bed. She's still a bit breathless from her climax.

I'm stunned by mine. It's like Claire cracked me over the head with a baseball bat and I'm collecting my senses. That might well have been the best blow job of my life and I can never tell anyone about it, or even admit it to myself.

"It was," I manage.

Claire raises her eyebrow. "That's all you can say?"

"Give me a minute and I'll rain the compliments on you," I promise.

"I'd rather do something else in a minute," she says in a husky voice. My alarm must have shown on my face because Claire laughs. "Don't worry. Billy can never go two rounds so I don't expect you to as well."

"It's not that," I stammer, my face flushing. "Give me a couple of minutes for that."

"It's okay," she says.

"It's not," I argue. "Not if you want to..." I trail off and give my head a shake. "This is awkward, isn't it?"

"It doesn't have to be." She rolls over, curling into my side and I automatically slide my arm around her. "We're friends, so we can keep this purely friendly."

"Your mouth did not feel purely friendly a few minutes ago," I tell her in a low voice.

"Yeah, well." She chuckles. "I didn't feel purely friendly."

I reach out with my other hand, dancing fingers along her arm, the curve of her hip. Claire has a beautiful figure—not that Jasmine doesn't, but Claire is more lean and lanky. Sharp edges, where Jasmine is soft curves. I push at her hair, fallen over her cheek back behind her ear.

"So you thought I was cute?"

She chuckles again. Even her laugh is so different from Jasmine's, wry and rueful, instead of Jas's playful giggle.

I have to stop thinking about my wife because soon, I'll get my senses together and start wondering about what she's doing with Wyatt when I've been lying here naked with Claire.

I'll focus on naked Claire a little longer. That should help.

"I told you what I thought of you. You can tell me what you thought of me," Claire suggests.

"I never thought I'd be doing this," I admit. "I might have thought it would be a good idea, a really great idea, but I never thought I'd get the opportunity."

"I wonder what would have happened if we'd known this place was for swingers that first summer when we met? Do you think something would have happened?"

I think back years ago, the summer when we met Claire and Billy. We were younger, with more excitement about our marriage. More energy.

We had been with Matt and Shawna. Because of Jasmine and Matt's long friendship, we had been friends with them for years, but we'd gotten closer after we both married.

Despite this, I'd always felt a tinge of resentment toward Matt. Jealousy, that he had a part of Jasmine that I never could win away from him.

"I don't know what would have happened that summer," I confess. "Matt and Shawna were with us when we met you."

"And I doubt Shawna would have gone for it. She doesn't seem the type."

"And you do?" I cock my eyebrow at her. "Or Jas?"

"Maybe there's no type." Claire rests her head on my chest, her hand over my heart. "Do you think Matt would have wanted to? With Jasmine?"

It takes me a long minute to answer a question that I've spent years wondering about. "I don't know," I finally say. "He's never said a word about her to me. Not like that."

"Has Jasmine?"

"Maybe I should ask you. You're her best friend."

"I think Matt takes precedence," she admits ruefully. "They're like family."

"You are, too," I tell her staunchly. "Both you and Billy."

"I hope that doesn't change." Her voice is wistful and I feel her sigh more than hear it.

"We won't let it," I repeat Jasmine's earlier words, wondering if I really believe them.

Claire is quiet and it isn't until I hear her deep, even breaths that I realize she's fallen asleep. I tighten my arms around her and enjoy having her in my arms.

CHAPTER TEN

Jasmine

T HE NEXT MORNING, BASIL wakes me when he leaves for his run like he always does. But instead of crawling out of bed to be ready for the kids, I roll over, luxuriating in the empty space, the empty cabin. The only sound is the creak of the floorboards outside as Bas stretches on the porch and the sweet sound of the birds. There are no kids sleeping, or squabbling. They're still at the big house, and won't be back until after a pancake breakfast at eight.

I have over an hour to myself. The staff at Aurora really deserves a good tip this year.

The day is already warm and I kick the blanket off my legs. My nightshirt is tangled around my waist, leaving my ass bare, covered only by my modest cotton panties that will never be the same after last night.

I run a tentative hand over my ass cheek. I'm not sure *I'll* ever be the same. Stretching, I take inventory of my body, of the minor aches that come from a night of lovemaking.

These are different from waking up after being with Basil because it wasn't Bas last night. It was Wyatt.

I hug the pillow into my stomach, a smile spreading across my face. Who would have imagined last night could have happened, and that I was the one who had given the go-ahead? I don't even begin to wonder what it was like between Basil and Claire—I can't stop thinking of Wyatt.

Of the way his hands roved roughly over my body, taking what he wanted. Of the feel of his cock inside me, in a private space that had been reserved for Basil for so long. At the way he kissed me. A giggle erupts at that thought. For such a big, rough man to be so gentle with his mouth...

I'll never forget him.

The creak of the porch rouses me from my Wyatt reverie. Is Basil back already? He must have forgotten something. I close my eyes, pretending to sleep as I hear the door open. I know we need to talk about last night, and we will, probably in more detail than I'd like, but not now. Now I want a few more minutes of thinking about Wyatt.

I sense Basil in the room but keep my eyes closed. He stands in the doorway, probably checking his watch, adding a heart rate monitor or something. I should open my eyes, say hello, open myself to that conversation, but I don't. I want these few last minutes to myself.

A step forward, and then another as he comes to the bed, and I screw my eyes tight. I can't with Basil—not now, not yet. How can I be with Basil when my mind is still full of Wyatt?

Basil touches my ass, runs a gentle thumb against the spot where Wyatt spanked me. It's still tender.

"Hope that doesn't leave a bruise," he says in a low voice.

Looking over my shoulder, my eyes flash open with amazement to find Wyatt standing beside my bed with a dimpled smile on his face. "What are you doing here?" I breathe.

"Finishing what we started last night." His fingers quickly find the cleft between my legs, where thoughts of him have already gotten me excited, rubbing me through my panties.

"But Basil," I begin, his touch tearing the words from my throat. Pushing aside the fabric, Wyatt zeroes in on my clit with demanding fingers.

"Has gone for a run. I saw him leave. I even talked to him, asked about his route, and how long he'd be. So I know we've got a bit of time to finish things unless you'd rather go back to sleep."

"No!" The word burst out of me with excitement. I had been thinking about his touch and how he was right here, his hands on me. Then my face falls. "But I haven't washed or brushed my teeth..."

"You smell like me," Wyatt says roughly, his hands on my legs rolling me onto my back. With a yank and a wiggle, my panties are off, flying across the room. "And I'm not kissing your mouth this morning."

"Oh," I say as he lays down at the end of the bed, his head even with my—

He props my knees up and spreads my legs, leaving me wide open for him. My breath comes in quick gasps as his fingers caress my inner thighs.

"Did you have fun last night?"

I'm so engrossed in what his fingers are doing that it takes a moment for me to realize he'd spoken. "Yes," I say in a rush.

"Were you thinking about me when I came in?"

I lower my eyes. "Yes."

"I was hard when I woke up," Wyatt admits and my gaze flies to his face. "I wanted to be back inside you."

"Okay." I can't stop the smile breaking over my face, feeling like I've been offered a grand prize of some contest I don't remember entering.

"I'm going to do this first."

My eyes widen as his mouth finds me, as gentle as when he first kissed my lips. But still, I lie stiff on the bed, listening for Basil to return. What if he came back and found Wyatt like this? What would he say? What would he do?

What if he joined in?

Wyatt takes his time, his tongue exploring my cleft, his lips dropping nibbled kisses on my sensitive skin, his finger sliding in and out of me slow enough to feel like his touch part of a dream.

A very nice dream, one that I can't remember having for a while.

And then the nice dream gets a little more exciting as Wyatt gets a little more demanding. I feel myself relax, respond to his touch. The quiet of the cabin is filled with my breathing, the sound of wetness, of—

"Oh, god!"

My hips arch as Wyatt does it again.

I've read about women being *devoured* but I've never had it happen to me. Wyatt feasts, he savours, he satisfies with every touch of his finger, with every plunder of his tongue. The tiny bedroom is now filled with moans and gasps, and I'm so focused on my pleasure that I don't realize I'm the one making those sounds.

And then it gets even better as Wyatt brings me closer to the edge.

"More," I gasp. "Please..."

He gives me more. His tongue...his mouth...I only had a taste of what it was capable of last night and now I can't help but beg for more. *Moremoremore...*

"I'm coming..." I moan. "Please...Oh, god, *now!*" I crash around him, practically sobbing with relief. Shudders of sensation are still racing through my body when Wyatt lifts his head to smile at me.

And then he's inside me, thrusting hard and deep, taking what he wants from me.

His hands curl around my hips, pulling me close, going deeper, and my eyes flutter shut.

"Open your eyes," he instructs.

I do what he asks because right now, I'd do anything he asks. I hold his gaze, watching as flickers of enjoyment cross his near-expressionless face. I fight to keep my eyes on him as my body reaches for another release.

I stop thinking about Basil, of the rhythmic creaking of the bed as he thrusts even harder. Faster. His hips take me closer, his cock—

Oh, my god, his cock.

The second wave hits almost without warning. There's no time to warn, no time to plead for more as I explode, clutching Wyatt to me. My arms and legs wind around his body, begging for more as I come again.

A second thrust...a third...Wyatt closes his eyes as his body tenses above me, a low groan his only sound as he empties into me.

It takes a long moment before I can let him go.

Basil

I DON'T KNOW WHAT happened with Jasmine and Wyatt last night, but Jas is in the best mood this morning. She dances to silent music as we head up to the Big House for a late breakfast, her smile widening as she sees Wyatt and Carson at a table with Billy and Claire.

I'd be upset if I wasn't so happy to see Claire.

Last night was a bit of a revelation. I got to see another side of Claire—definitely the naked side—and I liked it.

I liked the naked side too.

She gives me a sideways glance as I sit on the bench seat beside her.

"When do the kiddies need to be picked up?" Carson asks as we settle at the table with plates of eggs and bacon from the buffet.

"After breakfast," Jasmine says, punctuating her words with a soft sigh that makes everyone laugh.

"You should try an adults-only vacation," Carson suggests. "It would be a game-changer."

"I've no doubt." I smile at Carson, thinking how attractive she is with the mane of blonde hair swinging down her back.

"I think last night can be called a game-changer too." Claire's words are what everyone is thinking, and I brush my leg against hers under the table.

"So everyone had a good time?" Carson asks with an innocent smile.

"Oh, yeah," Billy cries and I'm happy that Claire laughs along with the rest of us. Billy has always lacked a filter, but it never bothered me until I saw the new side of Claire.

Not just the naked side. The part of her that let herself be vulnerable. The side that snuggled against me and fell asleep, forgoing a second round.

I think I would have liked a second round.

"Do the kiddies have their camp today, even after the sleepover?" Carson asks. I've noticed she does most of the talking between her and Wyatt, the big man seeming content to sit quietly and eat a second plateful of eggs and sausages.

Somehow Jasmine got to sit beside him too. I resist the urge to check under the table to see if they're touching body parts.

Not that it should matter since they obviously did more than touch body parts last night. Not that I know for sure.

No questions asked. This was Carson's instructions and we'd all promised to abide by the rules.

"They do, after lunch," Jasmine replies. "I think this morning will be pretty quiet, let them recover."

"Meet on the beach after lunch?" Wyatt asks, surprising everyone, but making Jasmine beam with pleasure.

If she smiles that much over breakfast with him, what did she look like last night? I wonder darkly.

No questions, I remind myself. It's better not to know. Now if I can only stop my mind from going places I don't want it to go.

CHAPTER ELEVEN

Jasmine

I LIKE CARSON.

Even though I had sex with her husband, I like her. I wasn't sure if I would. And I'm happy that I can still talk to Claire like we always did, despite the fact I know exactly what she did with Basil.

Actually, I don't know exactly and I think I'd like to keep it like that. I don't want Basil to know about Wyatt either.

It's better no one knows anything. No questions asked, so no one needs to lie.

I don't want to lie, but Basil doesn't need the details.

It's only a little awkward during the afternoon as the six of us lay soaking up the sun on the beach. I have my book—historically, I've taken this week to really catch up on my reading—and as soon as I pull it out, Carson asks what I'm reading. Turns out we have similar tastes in authors.

Claire naps, because she always takes this week to catch up on her sleep. As she flips over on her back and Billy adjusts the umbrella shading her, I wonder if she's extra tired because of Basil.

What did they do together? Did he like it better than when he's with me?

"The first time isn't easy," Carson says in a low voice. I turn to see her watching me.

"It's...I don't know," I admit. "I don't know how to do this."

"I think you'll be fine. You need good communication and trust, and from what I've seen, all of you have that. Married couples as well as friends. You seem close to her."

I glance over at Claire again. "She's my best friend. Even though we don't live next door to each other, she's always there for me. And me for her."

"I'm jealous. I don't have a girlfriend like that. I have Wyatt, but it's not the same."

"No, it's not. I have Matt, but it's not the same."

"Tell me about him," Carson invites.

"Matt?" I shift on my chair. Wyatt has gone off to fill the cooler with beer, with Billy and Basil trailing after him for lack of something to do. The day is hot and hazy, making any physical activity other than swimming uncomfortable. "I've known him all my life."

"Are you in love with him?"

I blink at the bluntness of her question. "Why does everyone assume that? When I met Basil, he couldn't get his head around how Matt and I were such close friends."

"Because he's jealous. He's never had a close female friend, right?" She gestures with her chin to the sleeping Claire. "They may be friends, but it's not the same."

"No, it's not." I chuckle softly. "I'm not sure if Basil would know what to do with a female friend. There are times when he doesn't understand me and I'm his wife."

"Not all of them do. It goes both ways though—Wyatt is on very good terms with his ex-wife, but I can't understand the friendship. They've said too many hurtful things for me to ever forgive her."

I scan the lawn for the boys but they must be holed up in the cabins still. "What was she like?"

"That's Wyatt's story to tell."

"I'm sorry," I say, feeling reprimanded.

"Don't be. With this lifestyle, you need to have respect for each other. I'm sure Wyatt wouldn't mind if you asked about his marriage, but he needs to be the one to tell it."

"That makes sense." I can't help but wonder about Wyatt. He's a complete mystery to me, and I don't do well with mysteries. I need facts.

Do I need to know everything about Wyatt? Chances are, after this week, I'll never see him again. The thought hollows my stomach painfully.

"Don't fall for him," Carson says quietly.

I choke back a laugh. "Can you read my mind?" I ask with amazement.

"No, but your face is very expressive. It's obvious to me, because I know my husband. He's very...Wyatt."

"He is very Wyatt," I agree.

"And I've seen the effect he's had on other women."

That hits me like a bucket of cold water. Wyatt has been with other women. Not that Wyatt has a wife—I'm bothered more by the thought of him with faceless women, each more beautiful than me, all more experienced. What did they do for him? What did he do to them?

"Stop," Carson says firmly. "It's all over your face."

I stare into the lake, the glare from the afternoon sun on the water making me squint even through my sunglasses. "How?" I ask finally. "How do you do it?"

"It takes a bit of work," she admits. "But the first rule is, don't let your mind wander to places you don't want to know about."

"I think that's a good rule."

"Can I give you a piece of advice?"

"Sure." I turn to face her and my book falls into the sand.

Carson picks it up, dusts the sand off the cover and hands it back. "I don't know if you plan to continue this, or if this will be a one-time thing, but tread carefully if you involve your friend Matt," she says, speaking so softly I have to strain to hear her.

"Why?"

"From what I've gathered, whatever your friendship is, it's a different dynamic from the four of you. This might not have happened if he was here."

"It wouldn't have if Shawna was here," I agree, thinking how Shawna would have never even considered it.

But maybe if they had considered it, maybe if we'd done this with them, it might have saved their marriage.

"I don't know you," Carson admits. "But I can read people."

"You clearly can read me."

She glances over to a still-sleeping Claire. "I think feelings would be more involved if you included this Matt," she says. "More chances of someone getting hurt."

"Who would get hurt?"

She shrugs delicately. "No one? Everyone? Just be careful. This lifestyle can be addicting, but you have to choose carefully. Not everyone can handle it."

I go back to my book after that.

Basil

BILLY AND I PICK up the kids from camp and bring them back to the beach for a swim. Jasmine and Claire stay on the beach with Carson, all of them with stainless steel glasses filled with wine that Wyatt produced.

He joins us in the water.

I can't stop staring at his tanned, muscular back, with the tattoo of his son's name inked on his shoulder. He looks rough and tough—Jasmine should be afraid of him rather than watching him with hungry eyes, but I watch nervously as he tosses the more hesitant Dominic into the water, and realize he's not. There's a gentle side to Thor, especially with kids.

Is he gentle with Jasmine too?

Claire and I promised each other not to think of what had happened with our spouses and while I liked making the bond with her, it's really difficult to keep up. How does Jasmine do it? I wonder as I watch her laughing with Claire. She has no idea what happened between us last night and she looks like she doesn't care.

She's always been good at compartmentalizing. Even when she comes home after a bad day at school, she is able to set it aside to give the kids her full attention.

Jasmine is a great mother.

My gaze tracks to Claire beside her, her long legs crossed demurely, her one-piece Speedo making her look like she's on a swim team. She's a good mother too, although her maternal abilities were the last thing I was thinking about last night.

Claire laughs and swings her legs around to stand. The sight of her standing on the beach, hand raised to brush the hair off her face hits me like a punch to the gut.

I want to fuck her.

I need to fuck her.

Last night was great foreplay, but I need the real thing tonight.

"I'm heading in for a sex—a *sec*," I call to Billy, shaking my head at my slip. Billy doesn't hear me and waves me in as I splash through the waves. The wind has picked up, breaking the humidity and creating rolling waves on the lake that the kids love. Wyatt easily organized them into an impromptu game of volleyball with Lilly's bright pink ball.

It's more like a simple throwing-and-catching game than any real sport, based on the age of the kids. Wyatt keeps trying and there is a lot of laughter.

"He's great with the kids," I say to Carson as I join them, sinking onto the end of Claire's lounge chair with a spray of water. I'm conscious of her closeness; back on the chair with a refill of wine.

"He is." Carson shades her eyes and watches her husband. "It's my fault we don't have kids. I keep saying it's because of the lifestyle, but we could make it work. I just don't think I have enough maternal anything to be a mother," she confesses.

"It's not easy," Jasmine says.

"And it's not for everyone," Claire adds. "And that's okay."

"So you think you can be a swinger and have kids?" I demand.

Claire chuckles. "Way to be blunt about it, Bas."

Jasmine looks at me, her dark eyes filled with an expression I can't bring myself to read. Longing, but regret; hope and fear.

We have to have a long talk when this week is over.

I smile at her. "You going to go play with the kids? We should feed them soon."

"I was thinking about it," Jasmine admits. "I'm pretty hot sitting here."

Yes, you are, I mouth and she smiles.

"I'm going in." She stands up. Even though I was with Claire last night and have all these new feelings going on—mostly lust—I still love my wife. She's still the sexy woman I know and love. "Wish me luck."

"I adore her," Carson says as Jasmine picks her way across the sand.

"Jas is great." Claire's tone is firm, effectively shutting down any conversation about my wife.

"All of you are." Carson's smile widens as she turns to us. "Now, let's talk about the three of us."

"There's the three of us?" I ask, trying not to sound nervous.

"Not yet, but there could be." She lowers her sunglasses and gives me the same look she did the first day. "There could very well be."

CHAPTER TWELVE

Jasmine

BILLY AND CARSON DISAPPEARED soon after we got to the bonfire.

Carson and Wyatt ate dinner with us and the kids, and watching Wyatt with my children turned me on so much that I could barely stand to sit beside him. I could only give the kids half my attention, the rest focused on how close Wyatt was to me, and how desperately I wanted to touch him. And how long I had to wait before I got him alone.

So much for this being a one-time thing.

After dinner, we split up—for me and Basil to put the kids to bed, and for Carson and Wyatt to do whatever couples without kids do. A slow patter of anticipation begins as I watch Wyatt glance back at me with a smile as he walks off with Carson.

"Are we doing this again tonight?" Claire asks in a quiet voice. When I looked over, I see her watching me watch Wyatt. I shrug, unable to formulate an answer let alone the correct one.

What am I supposed to say?

But Claire takes my silence as approval. "We can do the same," she says.

Meaning she wants to have sex with my husband again.

And what do you say to that?

Back in the cabin, the kids are exhausted from their sleepover last night and more than a little grouchy, now that the distraction of Wyatt and Carson is gone. Basil steps up to get them into bed, and they fall asleep in record time, even before the storytime is over.

Basil finds me as I'm tidying up the tiny kitchen. Coming behind me, he slips his arms around me. "We don't have to do this again," he warns.

"I know." Like Claire, I don't know what to say to him. How do I tell him I've been in a state of heightened arousal since Wyatt left this morning? I haven't even told Basil that Wyatt came by, and I don't think he would suspect that he might of.

For the first time, I wonder how easy it would be to cheat on Basil. Would he be like Matt—completely clueless if I was having an affair?

"What do you think?" I finally manage after he moves away. I only turn to face him when I hear his chuckle.

"In for a penny, in for a pound, as my mum always says," he says, sounding more British than usual.

"Please don't mention your mum," I beg.

On the beach, Carson waits with Claire and Billy, the three of them sitting in a row of chairs facing the fire.

My stomach plummets as soon I notice Wyatt isn't with them.

"Wyatt will be here soon," Carson says off-handedly, more interested in Billy than any thought of my hookup with her husband.

Nothing else is said about Wyatt, especially after Billy and Carson quickly disappear. I sit quietly, my disappointment becoming worse the more Basil and Claire laugh together.

I'm not sure if Basil is trying to distract Claire from Billy's disappearance, or their reminiscing about last night, but the two of them seem to be the best of friends, helped along by the second bottle of wine.

I can't let it bother me since this was my idea in the first place, but it's difficult to watch them together, feeling more alone as the night wore on. When they decide to take a quick dip in the lake, I take it as my signal to leave.

My feet are heavy as I push them through the sand, only to pick up more weight as I reach the grass leading back to the cabins.

"Where are you going?"

The voice halts me, and I turn to find Wyatt striding across the grass toward me, his blue eyes searching my face with sweet concern.

Something inside me stands up and cheers.

"Back to the cabin," I say, which seems like the stupidest thing ever.

"Feeling left out?" Wyatt gives me a wry grin. "Didn't Carson tell you I'd be over as soon as I could?"

"She did, but then she left with Billy, and you never came and Basil and Claire..." I trail off, not wanting to verbalize the pity party I'd been having.

"He seems to be into the idea now." Wyatt grabs my hand before I can respond. "Let's go for a walk and let them have their time together."

"Where are we walking to?" I can't help the smile spreading across my face and the new lightness to my step. We pass the first row of cabins and the trees close over our heads, with only the full moon breaking through the leaves.

"I like the woods at night," he admits as I clutch his arm with my other hand, trying to stay close.

"It's...quiet." I jump closer as branches snap. "Or it would be if there wasn't a monster animal about to eat us."

"Don't be scared," he says with a quick glance. "I won't let anything eat you...anything that isn't me."

My breath leaves my chest in a flurry of excitement. "Are we going somewhere in particular," I say, trying to sound casual and failing miserably.

"There's a spot close by..." He glances down at me again. "This okay? Me spiriting you into the dark woods late at night?"

"It's fine, but I can't go far." I show him the baby monitor I shoved in the pocket of my shorts.

"It's close. I found this little spot once, right around—" We step between two trees into a clearing. A huge oak tree stands in the middle as if the size of it had chased away any other tree. Leaves cover the ground in a thick blanket.

"This would be perfect for a picnic."

"That's what I thought." Letting go of my hand, Wyatt darts to the tree in the clearing, and grabs the plastic bag at the root. "It might not be your average picnic. I didn't bring any snacks."

"I could be your snack," I say in a quiet voice.

"Ah." Wyatt pulls me close with a sly grin, twirling me so that my back is pressed against the trunk of the tree. "You're learning."

"You're a good teacher."

He smirks. "So I've been told."

I slap gently at his shoulder, remembering the feel of his hand on my ass last night. My breath catches with anticipation. "So modest."

"As long as you enjoy yourself, that's all that matters to me." He brings his hand to my mouth, running his thumb over my lips.

I kiss his thumb, my body already responding to him. It had only been that morning that he came to me but it seems like forever.

"Did you like it?" Wyatt asks in a hoarse voice. His hand winds around my back, over the curve of my ass. I lean closer, spreading my legs so I straddle his thigh pushed between them.

"Yes."

"Do you want it again?" A soft moan escapes as I feel his hardness between my legs. The image of him taking me from behind swims before my eyes and I clutch his shoulders to keep my balance.

"*Yes.*" He's smiling as he kisses me with demanding lips and tongue, gathering me close until he lifts me off my feet.

It's a complete mystery how I wind my legs around his waist, but he shifts, holding my ass in his hands as his mouth devours mine. I've finally climbed him like a tree, which is what I've wanted to do since I first saw him.

I press myself against Wyatt, already desperate to feel more of him.

"I need to taste you again," he whispers urgently against my mouth.

He must sense my wordless approval, or because I unwrap my legs and he sets me gently on my feet.

The night was warm by the fire, so I wore only a simple sundress, the one I pull on over my bathing suit. The ruched top is tight enough to forgo a bra, and when Wyatt pulls the dress up and over my head, his eyes widen at the sight of my bare breasts, nipples already pebbling from the chill air. As his mouth finds one, and then the other, sucking deeply, his fingers push under my panties.

I lean against the rough bark of the tree, letting him have me how he wants.

His fingers rub and caress before thrusting inside.

His tongue follows, as he kneels before me in the carpet of leaves, his hands on my hips as he opens me with his mouth.

The only sound in the clearing is the roughness of my breath, loud in my ears, and the soft groan as Wyatt picks up one of my legs and drapes it over his shoulder. I groan again, louder, as his hand joins his mouth; fingers thrusting inside me with a frantic rhythm, licking and sucking. I've never felt so wanted, or wanton as Wyatt makes me come under that tree.

It happens so fast that it surprises both of us; all of a sudden my moans become cries and I grip the back of his head, urging him on until my body tightens before the release.

"Oh, god," I gasp, fighting to keep my balance. All I want is to sink into his arms, but Wyatt is not finished yet. Only pausing enough to catch my breath, he finds me again, teasing me with his lips until my gasps once again become moans.

I've never come twice, not one right after the other, but if anyone can make me, I'm sure Wyatt can. I lean against the tree, my head lagging onto my shoulder. My eyes are almost closed when I see the flash of colour between the trees.

They flash open. Nothing.

I relax again, falling into the sensations, at whatever Wyatt is doing between my legs, and he's doing a lot. Already a second climax is building and I push my hips forward, greedy for more, murmuring wordless cries.

As I'm reaching for it—so close—I see another flash of colour.

It's a shirt, bright in the darkness. A figure stands on the edge of the clearing. "Wyatt," I hiss. "Oh—please...there's someone here. Watching."

"Do you want me to stop?"

"No, please...no!" The last word becomes a loud cry as I tumble into another orgasm, this one urgent and intense and demanding, taking all of me and leaving me wanting still more.

"Please fuck me now," I beg as Wyatt gets to his feet. I reach for his shorts but he gets there first, pulling down the waistband so his cock, thick and ready juts out. A drop glistens on the tip, gone in an instant as he slides a condom on. Then he lifts me up, pushing inside me without a pause as my legs wrap around him again.

His mouth finds mine and I taste myself. Desire builds and I meet his tongue with my own.

The bark is rough against my back as he fucks me, his hips working a rhythm that I don't understand, but feels so good. Winding my arms around his shoulders, I bury my face in his neck, my heavy panting meeting his thrusts.

The snapping of a twig lifts my head and when I look up, I see Billy standing there.

He's staring at us. With his cock in his hand.

Basil

THE WATER IS COOL at night but does nothing for my need for Claire, other than hiding my hardness. I haven't been able to stop thinking of her all day.

We slide into the water at the far end of the beach, the furthest away from the light of the fire. Claire wears a different bathing suit; this one a simple black two-piece, but it shows off her lean body, especially the curve of her ass where I grabbed her last night.

How did I get here? From being pissed about the whole idea to wanting to bend Claire over right in the water. I'm uncomfortably hard at the thought of it.

I haven't even fucked her yet, but if I don't soon, there's going to be a problem.

Claire splashes me lightly as she sinks below the water, hiding her body from view. "It's nice."

"We should skinny-dip," I suggest as I bend my legs to sink into the water up to my chest.

I think Claire considers it for a moment, which surprises me. She's full of surprises this week. "Too many people."

"They can't see us. I can barely see you." I splash her and she turns her face with a laugh. "Besides, if this place is really the swinger resort that they say it is, then everyone on that beach will be doing the same thing. We'll just be doing it a little quicker."

"What are we doing, Basil?" Her tone is serious, and she bites her bottom lip. The sight makes my cock twitch with need.

"Whatever you want," I say automatically. "We're just having a swim." She nods her head, and suddenly sinks under the water. "Claire?"

Resurfacing after a moment, she pushed her wet hair out of her face. "I wanted to get my hair wet," she explains. "And also take off these."

The bottom of her bathing suit is in her hand, and as I watch, open-mouthed, she lets them float on the water before undoing the strap at the back of her top.

"I'm going to have to stay under because I'm pretty white." She glances down with a mischievous grin. "At least my boobs are."

"I'm okay with white boobs," I say.

"Don't tell Jas that," Claire warns.

"I have no idea what to tell her about any of this," I confess as I reach for Claire through the water, my hand sliding around her waist feeling the coolness of her skin.

"I think it's better if we don't," Claire says. "Just like Carson says. I have no desire to find out what she did with Billy. I think it would mess me up."

"What do you want, Claire?" My hand slides onto her breast. She's smaller and firmer than Jasmine, but no less desirable. I roll her nipple between my fingers.

"For you to touch me."

"I can do that." I pull her closer, my other hand sliding over the curve of her bare ass. "Do you want me to kiss you here? In front of everybody?"

She shakes her head. "Everything but. I don't want them to see."

"It's kind of sexy, hiding it in plain sight." My fingers find the cleft between her legs. The water has cooled her heat, but she pushes herself against my hand as I slide a finger inside her.

"It is." Her eyelids droop, heavy with desire and her breath comes faster as I thrust inside her, then pull out to find her clit.

It was sensitive last night when I used my tongue. And when I sucked it...I pinch her clit gently with my fingers and Claire gasps. I watch her face. She's not usually overly expressive, but now, her expression reacts with every touch of my finger.

As she bites her lip again, I realize how much I want to kiss her. Kiss her until she can't see straight, smothering all of the soft gasps.

But I don't. I only stand and watch her face as she climaxes with a wordless cry, her body shuddering in the water.

Even before she opens her eyes, she's reaching for me. "You don't have..." I manage as she reaches for my cock, rock hard and extremely sensitive from watching her.

From knowing I just made her come in the water, in full sight of everyone on the beach. It's like I want to pat myself on the back for that little move.

"I know," Claire says, her whisper husky as it floats across the water. Her hand slips under my shorts and I stiffen as she grasps me. "I want."

"Okay." It's really the only thing I can say as her hand moves up and down. My eyes flutter closed, a sigh that is part relief, part gratitude escapes. "O-*kay*."

Jasmine has never touched me the way Claire does, like she has a right to me. She pushes my trunks around my hips, letting my cock loose in the water.

But it's not loose, because Claire keeps a grip on it, one that I don't want to break. She moves closer, and I feel her breasts brush against my arm. "I want you inside me," she whispers, the feel of her breath a tickle against my neck. "I want you to fuck me."

"Uh huh," I manage, barely able to form the words.

"I want you to fuck me so hard…" Her hand tightens, her stroking grasp coming faster. "But not yet. I'm going to make you come first, just like you made me come. I liked that, you know."

My only response is a strangled gasp.

"I like your fingers and I *really* like your mouth, but now, Basil, I want *this*." Her hand moves faster, mimicking my own hand when I need to get off. Fast and tight, the water surrounding us gives the moment a surreal quality.

"I want you to fuck me, Basil," Claire repeats. "I want it…now."

With a strangled cry, I come into Lockport Lake.

CHAPTER THIRTEEN

Jasmine

"**B**ILLY!"

Wyatt pulls back enough to glance at my face. "Wyatt," he growls.

"No, Billy," I gasp. I point to where Billy stands under the tree. He's moved close enough for me to see the expression on his face—a mix of guilt and desire. "Here."

Wyatt glances over his shoulder, his thrusts never faltering. "He wants to fuck you too."

"No—Billy," I gasp, torn between embarrassment at him seeing me like this, and pleasure from Wyatt's cock relentless inside me.

"You can have her next," Wyatt calls over his shoulder. "Wait your turn."

The words are an invitation and Billy steps closer.

And then something strange happens—I want him to watch me. The hungry look on his face excites me even more. And as Wyatt fucks me, pulling my legs apart to go deeper, I stare at Billy. And when Wyatt comes with a growl, biting my neck as he pushes ever closer, I watch Billy's hand moving on his cock.

Wyatt has barely pulled out, setting me on my feet lightly when Billy is there. Without a word, without an invitation or explanation, he roughly grabs my hips and pulls me towards him. His cock is hard and he guides it inside me, pushing my legs apart with his knee.

I gasp with the first thrust. Not that I'm not ready and wanting, but because Billy isn't what I expected. Thicker than Wyatt, longer than anyone, Billy stretches me as he fucks me roughly, searing my delicate skin with every thrust.

I lean over, closing my eyes, feeling the sensations building once again.

"Slap her ass," Wyatt instructs in a gruff voice. "She likes that."

I gasp again as Billy does what he says.

I do like that.

"Where's Carson?" Wyatt asks.

"With Bas," Billy says between thrusts. My eyes fly open with shock. Basil had been with Claire, but now Carson too—

"Get your mind out of there," Wyatt says.

"What?" I gasp.

"Look what you're doing right there, so don't say anything about Basil. Who would have thought," he adds, moving beside me. The condom is gone, his cock thickening again as he strokes it. I watch with fascination as he reaches between my legs with eager fingers, finding my clit with easy strokes. "That my little mouse is such a little monster."

"She's not a mouse," Billy argues, his thrusts practically lifting me off my feet with the force of them. "But I knew she'd be amazing."

"That she is." Wyatt sees me watching his cock and moves his hand. "You want more of this."

I lean forward and take him in my mouth, my hands gripping his hips for balance as Billy picks me up. My moans are muffled and garbled by Wyatt's cock, and I have no sense of finesse as I take him deep, but I had to taste him.

Two of them at once...both wanting me. It's a heady experience.

Billy grunts with every thrust, louder as he gets closer to his release, mixed with Wyatt's breathing, like a strange grateful panting. I wonder who is going to come first, then as Wyatt's fingers continue against my clit, I realize it's going to be me.

I climax with a harsh cry, Wyatt's cock still in my mouth, and too soon, Wyatt erupts as well. And with a final thrust and a shout that might be heard at the beach, Billy comes inside me.

It takes a while before my legs are steady enough to walk back to the cabins.

Basil

CARSON MEETS US AT the edge of the water. "Can I interrupt?" she asks with a smile. "Or, rather, join in?"

"Here?" Claire asks nervously.

"No. But I have a free cabin. Wyatt and Jasmine went for a walk."

"A walk? Where?"

"Into the woods. But does it matter? She's safe with him."

"I know, but—"

"And Billy?" Claire interrupts.

"Back to your cabin, I assume. So how about a nightcap in mine?"

Which is the ultimate euphemism for sex, I decide as we collect our clothes and follow Carson, dripping onto the already damp grass. "If you could spare a couple of towels?" I suggest.

"I can spare many things for you, Basil."

Carson takes Claire's hand as they walk in front of me. I enjoy the view but I also take the opportunity to get my breathing in check. This will be my first threeway and I don't want to mess it up.

When we get back to Carson's cabin, I take another moment to dry off outside, giving myself a reassuring pep talk. I've never had any complaints, but I've never had two women at once.

By the time the door closes behind me, soft noises from the bedroom draw me in. Carson and Claire have already begun.

As I watch, Carson slowly tugs off Claire's bikini bottoms with a questioning glance. Claire's top is already on the floor and once she steps out of the bottoms, Carson wraps a towel around her.

"I can dry you if you like," she says huskily.

Claire nods and Carson takes the towel and crouches on the floor at her feet. Beginning with her legs, Carson pats Claire dry, moving slowly and carefully, leaving no part of her untouched.

I hover by the doorway with a full view of Claire. Her eyes are half-closed and she bites her lower lips with either nerves or excitement.

I hope it's excitement because I'm already excited. I just don't have a clue about what to do.

Carson pauses when she gets to the area between Claire's legs. "Have you ever been with a woman?" She dries her legs, nudging her thighs apart.

"Once," Claire admits.

"Did you enjoy it?"

"Yes."

I swallow audibly. "I had no idea," I mutter. Both women look over at me and I suspect they might have forgotten about me.

"Have you ever been with two women, Basil?" Carson asks. She stands, gently touching Claire's taut stomach with the towel.

I'm in awe of Claire's body. I've always known she was in good shape, but last night I should have taken the time to really admire her. I do now. Long lean muscles from yoga, still firm high breasts. They're nothing like Jasmine's pillowy goodness, but each one would fit nicely in my hand, the tight nipple pushing against my palm.

"No," I say shortly, watching, as Carson does exactly what I had been thinking about—cups one of Claire's breasts in her hand.

I can't pull my gaze away as Carson rolls Claire's nipple between her fingers before running her hand up to Claire's shoulder and tucking it behind her neck. "Would you like to join us?" she asks.

"I...I can watch for a bit," I admit. I'm not sure if I can physically step across the room to them. I hold the towel loosely in front of me; my cock is rock hard, straining against my wet trunks.

"Whenever you like," she says lightly, and then she kisses Claire.

I watch them for long minutes; deep kisses with flashes of tongue that make my balls tighten with desire. Claire keeps her hands chaste, touching only Carson's cheek and her shoulder, but Carson has wandering hands. She massages Claire's breasts, strokes her back, her ass, her thighs.

I don't know where to look, and I can't turn away.

I hear Claire's gasp as Carson touches her between her legs.

That's when things start to get blurry.

Carson and Claire take things to the bed, with Carson asking me again if I'd like to join in. I do want to, but right now, watching two women together is fascinating.

It's also an amazing turn-on.

The way they touch, the way they kiss is unlike I've ever seen. I've seen my share of porn, but live and in-person is different, and way more exciting. Long legs, soft skin, fingers...lips... The way Claire moans makes my dick throb and I want nothing more to get in there with them. When Claire comes with a long-drawn moan, I feel like I'm about to come in my shorts and fight not to grab my own cock and take myself out of my misery.

I won't be any good if I give in now.

I'm actually learning more by watching.

Claire likes it rough, both giving and receiving. The way she thrusts her fingers inside Carson, pushing her legs apart, biting her nipple until Carson cries out. When Carson moves between Claire's legs, licking and sucking, Claire grabs her by the hair, greedily demanding more as she jerks her hips to Carson's rhythm.

Carson is content to work Claire with fingers and mouth until she climaxes a second time.

"My turn," Carson says, lifting her head. Still with her hands on Claire, Carson moves up the bed to straddle Claire's shoulders.

"Holy shit," I breathe as Carson lowers her pussy to Claire's waiting mouth. That was me last night, underneath Claire but it looks so much better when they do it. Carson reaches behind her with a tanned arm for Claire's pussy and Claire bucks her hips.

I can't stop staring at the smooth lines of Carson's back, the way her breasts thrust sky-high as she arches her back.

Maybe it's time for me to get in there.

Before I can make a move, Carson swings a long leg around and falls to the bed beside Claire. Without waiting to be told, Claire positions herself between her legs, crouching with her ass jutting up like the prettiest full moon, and continues.

Both of them look like they're enjoying themselves, and then there's me who is having fun just watching. I like I need to do more than just watch.

Apparently, Claire thinks so too. "Basil," she says over her shoulder. "Fuck me."

I don't need to be asked twice.

I drop my shorts and suit up with one of the condoms Carson left on the bed in no time flat. Once I'm on the bed behind Claire, uncertainty hits me. I hate to disturb them— "How do you want—?" I stammer.

"Just fuck me," Claire instructs, her voice low in contrast to Carson's loud cries.

So I fuck her. At the first thrust, as I sink into her warm goodness, my eyes close and I smile.

Chapter Fourteen

Jasmine

T HERE'S A LIGHT ON in the bedroom when I get back to the cabin.

I open the door quietly, listening for any sound that would indicate the kids are awake, or that there might be something going on in the bedroom.

Both rooms are silent, save for Sebastian's soft snores. I glance into the kids' room, deciding not to wake him to roll him onto his side. The last thing I want to deal with now is a wide-awake child and having to explain where I've been for the last hour.

"Why, my little darlings, your mommy was having sex in the woods with Wyatt and Billy."

Billy.

My legs are still trembling.

I glance into the bedroom to find Basil lying in bed, reading. A mixture of relief that he's come home to me as well as guilt that I just had sex with one of his best friends hits me, making me pause before I go in.

But Basil looks up. "You okay?"

Am I okay? My ass is still sore from where Billy slapped it and between my legs is tender from his size. But I'm satisfied...satiated...and smiling.

Please don't want to have sex with me right now, I silently plead as I enter. "Fine. You?"

"Good."

What does that mean? Was it good for him?

Of course it was.

It was easier the first time when Basil had been asleep when I returned and I didn't have to talk to him until the morning.

I can't help but wish Wyatt will be able to wake me up in the morning again but know it's impossible.

"I'm going to go wash up," I say quietly, hoping the light will be out and Basil asleep by the time I get back.

The book is away but the light is still on. Neither of us says a word as I crawl into bed beside him, feeling chilled from being in the night air. I cuddle under the blankets, wanting to be held, but afraid to move closer to Basil.

He turns out the light and I lie there, my eyes adjusting to the darkness, the sound of Basil's breathing beside me.

"Did you have fun?" he finally asks.

"I did." There's no point pretending I didn't; Basil knows me well enough to be able to tell that I had a good time, from the flush on my cheeks to my mussed hair.

I wish I didn't feel so guilty about it.

"I think I'd like to do it again sometime," Basil says awkwardly after a long pause.

Can he tell in the dark that I'm smiling? That his words magically make all the guilt go away? "Okay."

Then I move over to cuddle against him. Maybe I'll tell him sometime.

Basil

I'M SURPRISED AT HOW quickly the rest of the week goes by. Soon it's early Saturday morning and our bags and cooler are packed and waiting to be carried to the car. The kids race around the lawn with Claire's girls as we say goodbye.

"Now, I'm going to friend you all on Facebook as soon as I get home," Carson says as she hugs Claire. Her kiss on the cheek misses its aim and hits the corner of Claire's mouth.

"And I've got your addresses for Christmas cards." Claire winks at Jasmine, some inside joke that I don't understand. I'm surprised Jasmine noticed; she only has eyes for Wyatt this morning.

"If you're ever in the area, our door is always open," Wyatt says to her, pulling her into his arms.

"Same with us," I say when it's obvious Jasmine isn't going to respond.

"We're thinking of going to Mexico this winter. Why don't we all meet there?" Claire gives me a wink.

I think about the way she sounds when she comes and know that is something I'll be thinking about for a long time to come. "Sounds great."

I'm still thinking about it when we pull out of Aurora half an hour later. At least I have a week in Mexico to look forward to.

One Week

CHAPTER ONE

Claire

THE CURTAINS IN THE room are so thick that not even a sliver of the hot Mexican sun breaks through. I have no idea about the weather outside the hotel room until I open them an inch.

Not that I need to. Billy and I have been here for two days and it's been perfect since we got here.

Unfortunately, Billy hasn't had time to enjoy the weather, or the resort, or even me for that matter. Our vacation is piggybacking on his work conference, but today is the last day, and I'll be glad to have my husband back.

There's a groan from the bed, which means Billy is awake before he needs to be. I've never met any man who enjoys sleep the way Billy does. He can fall asleep anytime, anywhere—

Yes, he once fell asleep when we were having sex.

He always teases me that it was because I took too long to come, and I always shoot back that if he had done anything to help me out, it might have happened a lot sooner.

Our sex life is consistent at best. He won't agree, but I think we need some excitement added to it like a Vitamin B shot to the butt.

Whenever I think about my sex life—which actually is quite a lot—I can't help but think about this past summer. The week at Aurora Resort with our friends Basil and Jasmine definitely gave us a shot in the butt.

Turns out friends can easily slide into becoming swingers. Of course, we had help. Meeting Carson and Wyatt was a game-changer, as well as finding out that Aurora Resort, where we'd spent our summer vacation for the past six years, is a resort for swingers.

Billy rolls over. The sheet falls off him, giving me a glimpse of his back which is still the same pasty white as when we got here. "It's so early," he rasped.

"Your alarm will go off in ten minutes," I say, yanking open the curtains. Bright, beautiful sunlight floods the room, accentuating the heap of clothes that Billy stepped out of before crashing into bed last night.

Billy gasps and hides his head in the pillow. "Bright!"

"Only because you drank too much."

He flops onto his back, red-rimmed eyes blinking warily at the brightness in the room. "Giles wanted shots and apparently the tequila is not watered down here."

"Good to know."

We've been to three different resorts in the Mayan Rivera, and I've come to the conclusion that all the bars water down the alcohol in Mexico. I've never drunk so much as I do here; starting early, finishing late and I'm still able to be bright-eyed, and bushy-tailed in the morning.

"And then he wanted Scotch—who drinks *Scotch* in Mexico?" Billy sits up in bed to reach for the bottle of water on the nightstand beside him. "I don't even think the guy behind the bar knew what it was. At least he didn't know what the good stuff was."

"I take it you didn't have the good stuff?" I perch on the edge of the bed.

"Ah—no. Whatever it was tasted like piss, if I've ever drank piss. It was more like—" His eyes rest on me and like the pop of a beer, he focuses fully. "Hey, you're naked."

"Good of you to notice," I say sarcastically. "It usually happens before I get into the shower."

"You're going to have a shower *now*?"

I laugh at the hopeful tone in his voice. "You are not having hungover sex with me!"

"Does that mean I can have it with someone else?" My laughter fades at Billy's question. Before Aurora, that might have been a playful question between spouses. Now—everything's changed.

"We haven't really talked about that, have we?" Billy adds with a wary smile.

"Not really. I thought you didn't want to."

"You're the one who didn't want to go into details."

Billy's right. I didn't want to tell him what it had been like with Basil, or when Carson had joined us. And I didn't want to know anything about *Billy* being with Carson. That's uncharted territory.

Maybe there's a swinger course I should take to make things easier. Because hey—I think I might be a swinger now.

We might be swingers now.

"I thought we were waiting for Jasmine and Bas to get here?" I ask, easily bypassing the details comment. We invited our friends, Basil and Jasmine to join us in Mexico. We met years ago at Aurora, and because we live an hour and a half away, we don't normally see them very often.

But after this summer, I thought it would be nice to get together again.

But we also invited Matt and his new girlfriend, who knows nothing about the summer. Matt and his wife, Shawna, started going to the resort with Basil and Jasmine and then met us there. Because of the recent split, Matt didn't make it to Aurora this year, and now it seems he's more than moved on from Shawna.

"I think we should figure it out ourselves first, in case we need to direct the conversation." Billy grins at me. "I am an advisor, after all."

"A financial advisor, which is a little different than thinking you can advise our friends whether they want to have sex with us again," I say.

I'm not entirely sure if Billy did have sex with Jasmine.

Basil and I—yes. Basil and I and Carson—again, yes.

But Jas had been with sexy fireman Wyatt, and Billy had his world rocked by Carson. While I'm content with my own sexual prowess, I assume Billy was rocked by Carson, since I know I was. That had been a bit of a revelation.

It wasn't the first time I'd been with a woman, but the previous one had been a drunken fumble at a party and couldn't begin to compare with Carson's silky caresses.

I shouldn't even call it being with a woman since it had been about as sexy as masturbating.

I guess that can be good at times though.

While I'm not the type of woman who needs to express every emotion to her husband, Billy and I have always been able to talk to each other. But it's been five months since Aurora, and we haven't had a proper conversation about it.

"What happens at Aurora, stays at Aurora," Billy had said that first night and since I had been hit with an overwhelming wave of guilt for what I did with Basil, I was happy to agree.

Now looking back, I think we should have talked about it. Obviously, Billy has had a change of heart as well.

Billy reaches out and traces my tan line, dipping his finger between my breasts to follow the line of my bikini. "You've gotten some sun," he says, his eyes fixated on how my nipples harden under his touch.

"I have. You will too, whenever you get to see the sun."

Billy smiles. "Today. One o'clock and I'm a free man."

"And I get my husband back."

"Has it really been so bad?" Billy asks. His hand is warm as he cups my breast. "'Cuz I could try to make it up to you?"

I swat his hand away. "You know you're no good to me when you're hungover."

"It's hard to concentrate when my head hurts." Billy laughs as he rubs his temples.

I flip the blankets off him, pleased to see his cock jutting out of his boxers. "Have I shown you how proud I am that you made the cut-off to the conference this year?"

"Showed? Ah..." He trails off when I slide my fingers along his heavy cock. "You're the best wife, ever."

"You better believe it."

Billy

I HAVE THE BEST wife.

After my morning wake-up, I head to the last morning of the conference with a smile on my face and a spring in my step. Not only does she give an awesome blowjob, but she's also been pretty understanding about how busy I've been with the conference. The last two days have been packed with workshops and meetings, not to mention golf games and sailing trips that significant others weren't invited to. There are a few other wives along, but they already knew each other and didn't feel obligated to invite Claire along on their shopping excursions. There's also someone's husband, but Claire said he was sleazy and wanted nothing to do with him.

She's been alone since we've been here, and I know she's used to it, but it's hard thinking about your lonely wife wandering around a beautiful resort wearing only a bikini. Claire's a beautiful woman, and while I trust her completely, I'd like to be the one hanging out with her. But she never complains and I even got a blowjob this morning.

That's some wife.

Our room is a five-minute walk to the lobby, which leads to the conference rooms. This morning is the wrap-up to what we've done and I'll be free by lunch. I'm happy to be done with it. It's my first year attending; I almost made the cut last year, but losing a big client at the end of the year put a dent in my commission. This conference is work, but it's also a reward, as shown by the golf and sailing and parties at night.

Last night was a doozy.

I'm tempted to stop at the lobby bar for a shot of something to put in my orange juice but Claire delayed me just enough to make that impossible.

It's not the end of the world if I'm a couple of minutes late. I'm sure I won't be the only one.

My cell signals an incoming text and for a second I think it's the conference head reminding me to be on time. But as I pull it out of the pocket of my cargo shorts—wearing shorts to work is another perk of this trip—I recognize Basil's number.

We're on the plane!

Great! Meet for a beer at the pool when you get in!

When are you finished?

1 pm.

I add a happy face emoji.

C u soon. Hi to Claire.

Even though Bas and I have always ended our text threads by throwing a wave or a greeting to the wives, it feels different since the summer.

Since Basil had sex with Claire.

I honestly don't know the details of what happened between them because Claire and I agreed to keep quiet about that. While I like that she doesn't know about what happened in the woods with Jasmine and Wyatt, it's slowly driving me crazy not knowing what Claire and Bas got up to.

I imagine things—things that should be only seen on Pornhub.

And while I know Claire isn't into the dirty stuff with me, and I'm pretty sure Bas and Jas have a sex life relatively free of depravity, I have no idea what Claire and Bas did together. Or if anything happened that second night.

I took off with Carson early, and by the time I got back to the beach after checking on the kids, everyone was gone. A helpful couple pointed out that Jasmine and Wyatt had walked off into the woods, and I'm still not sure what led me to follow them.

Jasmine and I have always had a good relationship—playful, slightly flirtatious—but nothing that would suggest that I should follow her into the woods and *watch* while she has sex with Wyatt.

And then, after getting caught with my dick literally in my hand, to join in.

It was a messed up night.

Or not. Jasmine was...completely unexpected.

And that's why I haven't been able to stop thinking about her. Even this morning, when Claire had me in her mouth, doing all the cool things she was doing with her tongue it was Jasmine I was thinking about.

And I can't stop wondering if it will happen again when they get here.

With Jasmine, not Claire giving me a blowjob. At least I hope Claire will be up for doing that again. It would be easy to make a cozy foursome with Basil and Jasmine for this trip, but Matt's joining us with his new girlfriend.

No one has told Matt anything about what happened this summer.

It would be one thing if he was still with Shawna; then the answer would be a big, fat *no*. But Claire and I haven't met the new girlfriend, and Bas has only said that she's nice, so I have no idea what to expect.

It's not easy asking your best friend if your other best friend's new girlfriend is fuckable. Or swinger-worthy.

Is that what we are now? Swingers? I don't mind the label, but I'd like to know if we're going to have a repeat performance. I'm semi-hard every time I think of Jas, so I'd kind of like to know if I should shut that down.

Or not.

I hop up the sweeping staircase into the lobby, wishing like I have every morning, that I'm there only to book some excursion for me and Claire and, rather than showing up for a day's work. At least it's only a half-day.

My mind happily swims with the thoughts of this afternoon, free from the confines of rooms filled with numbers and strategies and smelling of coffee and body odour, rather than salt and sunscreen. In the lobby, there's the usual chaos of suitcases piled as new guests check in with excited kids running around.

I miss the girls. It's nice to be with Claire, but I still miss them.

Kids are forgotten as I do a double-take as a blonde wearing the smallest bikini I've ever seen passes me on the way to the bar.

Maybe I do have time to grab one for the road—or at least the trip down the hall to the conference room.

"Billy!"

I turn to see Matt, part of the group lined up at the concierge counter, waving his arms. "Buddy!" Swerving to avoid running headlong into an older couple wearing matching shirts and hats, I head over to the line and give him a brotherly hug. "I thought you weren't getting here until tomorrow?"

"Emmy got the day off after all and we got an earlier flight," Matt says. "Here." He gestures to a woman standing beside him in line. "This is Emmy."

I turn to her with an easy smile, hand outstretched but as soon as I see her face, I fall back into the past like I'm tumbling down the stairs of the lobby.

"Emily?"

Emily Hartnell—it's the same sweep of blonde hair, same sweet smile. At seventeen, I'd been madly in love with her, ready to slay any dragon or duel to the death for her; at eighteen, I'd been ready to go down on one knee for her until her father packed up the family and moved across the country.

I didn't even get to take her to prom. Instead, our first time had been a scramble in the back seat of my brother's car the night before she left.

"Billy?" Her smile grows wider, eyes amazed as she clutches my hand.

"Emily!" I'm ready to pull her into my arms when Matt's voice steps into our moment.

"Hey, Bill, how do you know my girlfriend?"

CHAPTER TWO

Claire

AFTER LEAVING MY HUSBAND with a smile on his face, I head out into the bright sunshine. Wearing the brand new bikini that I'm still a little self-conscious about under a gauzy cover-up, I have my Ray-Ban aviators, my sunscreen and my book in my bag, and I'm ready to spend a morning relaxing by the pool.

I miss the girls.

I wouldn't be honest if I didn't admit that walking alone anywhere gives me a pang. Used to feeling one or more little hands in mine, there's an emptiness that I can't shake. I feel like I'm missing something.

But to be honest, it is nice to move around without a delegation of toys and snacks and the usual last-minute arguments about what to bring and what should stay home. Billy and I are lucky enough to have both sets of parents living nearby who love to spend time with the girls. We're in Mexico for nine days and my parents are taking them for the first four days, before moving them to Billy's parents' place until we're home. They'll feed, clothe and take them to school, and probably be exhausted by the time our flight sets down.

But it's nice. Everyone enjoys this time apart and together, and the girls will be ecstatic to see us knowing our suitcases will be full of things for them.

After grabbing a coffee and a smoothie for breakfast, I stake out my claim near the pool. There are a surprising number of chaise lounges already filled for the early hour and a smiling, very buff staff member leads an enthusiastic group in AquaFit.

This is my vacation—no exercise for me.

I can't do anything about waking up early. My body is hotwired to get up by six. The girls wake up at seven and I need a little time for myself.

As I pull out my book, I smile happily. This is a nice time for me.

But an hour and a half later, I've had all the me-time I need for the day.

As a stay-at-home mom to Rachel and Rosie, my day is my own from eight-forty am to three-twenty pm. Other than that, my life revolves around the girls—making sure that they are happy, driving them to dance class and other activities, keeping our life moving smoothly. It's not a bad deal, but after the girls both started school, I found I needed to keep busy. I started back at the gym and created a group for other stay-at-home moms. It's a cross between a book group, therapy session, and a way to basically keep us sane.

Stowing my book in my bag, the cover-up comes off and I hit the pool. The clear blue water is refreshing and empty save for a few kids now that the exercise class is over. I have a nice paddle, but then get distracted by the swim-up bar.

Since we're on vacation in Mexico, it's always a good time for a daiquiri.

The bartender grins as I take a seat. He's blond and tanned with a cheerful smile that reminds me of Billy—a perfect distraction. "And how are you this morning?" he asks with an accent I can't begin to place. Whatever it is, it's pleasing to the ears.

"Better now," I say as I slide onto one of the stools partially submerged in the water.

"Ah. And what was the problem earlier." He leans his elbows on the bar and looks over with an admiring smile.

He's cute. I had a good opening line, but that's all I've got. It's been too long since I've flirted with anyone and I'm sorely out of practice. "I didn't have a drink," I say with disappointment.

"Well, I'm the best person to deal with that." He narrows his eyes. "You look like a Pina colada girl."

Girl. He called me a girl—not a woman, or a ma'am or a mother, but a girl. Gratitude, something akin to love, warms my heart. "Daiquiri actually," I say faintly.

"I've got a mango-passion fruit one that you'll love."

"Sounds perfect."

As he makes my drink, I catch sight of his name tag. *Benoit.*

What does it say for my status as a swinger if I can't even flirt with a bartender?

I've never considered the label—for months, I've thought of that week at Aurora as a one-time thing. It wasn't until we arrived in Mexico, waiting for our friends to arrive that I even considered it happening again.

That doesn't mean I haven't thought of Basil. Or Carson.

The evening I spent with them has been on the highlight reel when I can't sleep and my hand drifts under the blanket. Or the times when I need a little push to come before Billy finishes.

Basil was a surprise. Knowing he and Jasmine had been together since university, I suspected neither had much experience outside their relationship, but he did well, holding his own with me.

Not that I have film reels of experience, but there have been some. Joel—my first, when I was seventeen. He left me a month later with a broken heart and a taste for sex. Robby, John and Mike followed, leaving me with a bit of a reputation in school; completely unwarranted of course, because regardless of how many partners I had, slut-shaming is wrong.

My appetite didn't wane after graduation but luckily, I had more tolerant and admiring friends. In university, I started to figure out what I was doing and being more vocal about what I wanted. That was when I started to experiment more.

I can safely say there's not a lot I haven't tried, so the swinger lifestyle is like picking up where I left off. But I've been completely faithful to Billy. Not even tempted once.

Our marriage is a good one, and we're happy together. But since the summer, things are coming back to me, including how strong my libido is.

Marriage and kids and scheduled Saturday night tends to put a damper on things.

Carson made me remember that a little variety can be a good thing.

Benoit slides a daiquiri across to me, complete with a lime on the rim. "Thanks," I say, and bend my head to suck at the straw.

Much like I sucked Billy's cock earlier. I smile around the straw.

"You look deep in thought," a voice beside me says. Still, with the straw in my mouth, I look over to find a woman with white hair piled on her head who has taken the seat beside me. "Happy thoughts," she adds and gestures to Benoit. "I'll have one of those, please."

"Of course, Miz Morena." Benoit gives her a wink.

The cold of the daiquiri gives me a brain freeze as I swallow. "You must be a regular."

"I have been known for my morning constitutional," she says with a smile. "It's nice to find I'm not alone in my morning happy hour."

I raise my glass. "It's five o'clock somewhere in the world."

We sit in silence as Benoit readies her drink, the splashes from the pool seeming far away. As he sets it in front of her with an easy smile, she lifts her glass to me.

"To Mexico mornings," she says.

"And to mango daiquiris," I add.

"I'm Morena."

"Ms. Morena," I correct. "Is that what you'd like me to call you?"

"I don't think so," Morena muses with a cat-like smile. "But I would like you to call me."

I fight to keep my expression neutral. It was a simple statement, an overture of friendship so why does Morena's low voice send a tingle through me. "I'm Claire," I say instead.

I can't guess her age; from the whiteness of her hair, I'd say over fifty, but her skin is relatively unlined save around the corners of her eyes. She's a beautiful woman.

"I saw you reading earlier," Morena says, seemingly unaware of my appraisal. Or maybe she's used to it. "But since I was engrossed in my own book, I didn't want to interrupt us both."

"What were you reading?"

That smile again. "I'm not sure it would interest you."

I shrug, suddenly unnerved. "I like a variety of genres."

"Variety is always good, even in reading. What were you reading?" She nods when I tell her. "Book club?"

"It got me back into reading after my girls were born, so I can't complain."

"I love book clubs, but I wish some of the offerings were more...titillating." Morena rolls her tongue around the word like it's candy.

"Like a dirty book club? I'd go for that."

"Exactly. Maybe you would be interested," Morena muses and raises her glass to me.

Somehow it feels like I've just won the lottery.

Billy

"I 'VE MISSED YOU SO much, Billy."

The lobby magically empties and it's only Emily and I. She's wearing the same tiny bikini the blonde was wearing, only on Emily, it looks so much better, leaving nothing to the imagination.

Or maybe it's because I don't need an imagination—I remember exactly every inch of her. Her small, perfect breasts with brownish-pink nipples pebbled when I ran my thumb over them. There was a birthmark on her hip that I kissed and a mole on her collarbone that I nibbled. She liked it when I breathed onto her neck, the spot right under her ear.

I remember the softness of her thigh, how her ass curved into my hand. Her hand was so small, her fingers barely reached around when she held my cock.

She gave me my first handjob.

"I missed you, too," I stammer, my shock giving the scene a dreamy quality.

"I thought of you every time I made love." Emily runs her hand over my chest, down my stomach towards my raging hard-on. "No one was as good as you."

"He is really good, isn't he?"

Somehow Jasmine is there, standing in the now-empty lobby with a nearly naked Emily. And Jasmine's nearly naked too—wearing the same bathing suit she had on that night. Slowly, ever so slowly, she turns her back to me and bends over, her ass a luscious, perfectly ripe peach. "Miss me too?" Jasmine asks over her shoulder.

"Is this your wife?" Emily asks in a breathy voice, her hand wandering in the region of my crotch but thankfully never touching my cock. I won't last long if she does.

"No, she's—" How do I describe Jasmine? She's my friend, who I got to have sex with? Someone I hope to have sex with again, especially if she keeps showing me her ass like that. I reach a trembling hand to touch Jasmine, my finger trailing along the elastic of her bikini bottom to between her legs.

"I'm his wife."

And then Claire is there, wearing the same two-piece she had on when she left the room this morning. She wipes a hand over her mouth like she always does after I come in her mouth.

What the—

"I like your wife," Emily said in the same breathy little girl voice that I've never heard her use. "Would you like to watch us together? I can make her come right here—"

"Billy!"

I jump back in my chair, hands jerking up. "What? No, it's okay—" I glance around wildly.

There's no lobby, no Emily, or a bent-over Jasmine. Thank god there's no Claire because I have no idea how to explain this to her. There's only a darkened conference room with twenty people around the table, watching the PowerPoint presentation and listening to some VP drone on about year-end.

"You okay, bro?" Walt, who has been my partner in crime these past few days, elbows me. "You were out of it. Just staring, with this stunned expression on your face."

"Yeah. No." I wipe a shaking hand across my face. "Just out of it. Tequila," I finish apologetically.

"I get it. You need hair of the dog," Walt guffaws. "Let's hit the bar during the break. Last day," he reminds me.

"Yeah. That sounds good."

I need more than a bar. I need to get laid. And then I need to see Emily again to make sure she's real.

CHAPTER THREE

Claire

I SPEND THE REST of the morning drinking with my new friend.

"You own a resort for *swingers*?" Three daiquiris have affected my whispering skills and the word skitters across the bar loud enough for the balding loudmouth three stools down to catch it. He gives us an appraising stare, which along with the admiring glance we got when he sat down, the leer when he approached us, and his scowl when Morena told him in no uncertain terms to leave us alone, give him bonus points for most annoying creep of the day.

Morena stands up. "Let's go find a couple of chairs."

"I don't know if we can take our drinks in the pool—" My warning is cut off as she picks up her half-drank daiquiri and wades into the pool.

"Later, Benoit." Morena blows him a kiss.

"Always a pleasure, Miz Morena, and the lovely Claire." He winks as I follow Morena, keeping close to the edge of the pool except when we have to go deeper to avoid kids.

"Isn't this place adults only?" She asks as an energetic little boy learning to swim kicks water at us.

"I thought so."

"Let's go to the beach," Morena suggests after we reach my chaise lounge, still with my bag stowed underneath. "It'll be quieter, so we can talk."

"Talking sounds good." I grab my bag and follow her.

I won't deny that I'm already completely in thrall to this woman. Everything about Morena is interesting and exciting and now she owns a whole resort for *swingers*?

"So, what exactly do you mean, the resort is for swingers?" I ask as we step onto the white sand of the beach. Neat rows of beach chairs fill the space, all, except for two, empty and waiting.

"Drop your bag." Morena points to a nearby chair. "I need to go into the water. I prefer the ocean to a pool." She finishes her drink and puts the glass on the sand, soon to be found by a member of the staff paid so little to serve us so well.

"Me too." I set my glass beside Morena's and hurry to catch her leggy stride as she heads to the water.

I've spent so many years at Aurora that I learned to love the cool wildness of the lake. But this little patch of the ocean is nothing like Lockport Lake. I step into the clean, blue water and feel the salt prick my newly shaved legs. My toes look like wriggly worms and I realize I forgot to paint my toenails before we left.

"This is nice." We walk until the water reaches mid-thigh, and then Morena sinks down, sitting on the sand.

The gentle waves crest around her shoulders as she glances up at me, suddenly serious. "You do know what a swinger is, don't you, Claire?" Morena asks with a questioning smile.

"Of course. I am one." It's a bold statement and as soon as I say it, I want to take it back. I sit down beside her, fighting to find the right words. "I mean, once. We did it once. Well, twice. Two nights. We go to a resort in the summer and last year...We had no idea what kind of place it was," I admit, my tongue loosened, thanks to the three daiquiris. "Then we met this couple..."

"What was it called?" When I tell her, she smiles wistfully. "I remember Aurora. I've spent time there as well. It was way before your time, though."

What if I'd met Morena at Aurora? This summer...or years ago? The thought sends tingles through me. Morena at the lake. Morena with Carson—

I don't like that idea.

"So you're a swinger," I say, hoping I sound cool and casual, not like an awe-struck little girl. Because I am. I'm not exactly sure where Billy and I stand in the swinger lifestyle, or if we stand there at all, but I'm so intrigued by Morena.

"Was. Am," she says with a vague wave.

So what is it? Past or present? "You and your husband—?"

"Oh, I don't do husbands." Morena is quick to interrupt. "At least not my own. I like other people's husbands, though."

"Other people's..." Billy?

"Jed and I—I think we're better off not making it official. I like how things are and I seem to mess up marriages. My own, not other people's," she adds with a smile.

"So tell me what it's like being a swinger?" I ask eagerly.

Morena waves her arms through the cool water, her fingers spread and ghostly white. "What do you want to know? And why?"

And so, sitting on the soft white sand with the odd fish coming close enough to poke at my toes, I tell Morena about this summer.

"It sounds like a good first attempt," she says after I finish. "No lasting consequences."

"We haven't spoken about it since then," I confess. 'I have no idea if they want to try it again."

"Well, you definitely need to be able to communicate," Morena says. "And be honest and respect each other. You can't ever push too hard, either. This isn't a lifestyle for everyone."

"No, I can see that." I wonder, not for the first time, how Jasmine has adjusted to knowing I slept with her husband. "What else do you need?"

"Trust between partners. An adventurous side." She winks. "And of course, a healthy libido."

"I've got that," I say wryly. "And I've been known to take a few risks, especially when I was younger. But now..." How do I tell her that finally, at thirty-six, I feel comfortable in my body, with my wants and desires? I know what I need now, more than ever before. "I'm happy in my marriage, but I want more," I say slowly.

Morena nods. "It's the age. It's a good age."

"Things are good with me and Billy, but I think maybe they could get better. More exciting. More...new."

"Things get stale in a marriage. I should know, I went through three of them." She laughs wryly. "What do you want? New positions, new...people?"

"I was with a woman this summer," I say slowly. "I think I'd like to try that again." I've never admitted that to anyone, not even myself, but there was something about Carson's touch—softer but still urgent, firm, but different than a man's—that was intriguing. Intoxicating.

Even thinking about it makes things tingle down below.

"With Carson, I didn't...participate much. I mean I did, but I wasn't sure what I was doing. I'd like to—"

"Try again?" Morena interrupts.

"Learn."

The waves lapped at my chest and my nipples responded to the water. Or maybe they responded to the touch of Morena's hand on my leg.

"I like the sound of that," Morena says. "Maybe I can help you."

Billy

WE BREAK AT TEN-THIRTY and I'm the first one out the door, rushing back to the lobby on the off chance that Matt and Emily are still waiting in line.

Of course, they aren't, because the *Palacio Valiente* has great service and knows better than to keep guests waiting an hour and a half to check in.

After I check to make sure neither of them may be hiding in one of the sitting nooks around the concierge counter, I head to the lobby bar with a heavy heart.

"*Cerveza, por favor*," I say to the bartender. They frown on drinking during the workshops, but there's no way I'm waiting until lunch. My head feels like it's floating into space and a beer will tether me nicely. When a beer slides across the polished surface to land in front of me, I slump against the bar and drain half the bottle.

How did Matt end up with Emily Hartnell?

Earlier, when Matt had asked how I knew his girlfriend, there hadn't been time to go into details. I could only stand, blocking someone's attempt to get to the counter, staring at the love of my young life.

Of course, Claire is the love of my life, but back then, for a lot of years, Emily was everything to me.

"Long story," I had said in response to Matt's question.

Emily looked as shocked as I did. Maybe it was my imagination, but she looked almost as thrilled as I was to find her here. "I'll let you tell it," I said to Emily, drinking in the soft curves of her face. "I have to run. But I'll be finished after lunch and we can catch up then." My words had been directed to Matt but my gaze was still on Emily. "Claire's around, check the pools."

"We'll find her," Matt said. "Get to your conference and we'll catch you later."

As I hurried away, I heard Matt ask. "How do you know Billy?"

I wondered what she told him.

I'm still wondering, as I stand by the bar, staring at the exact spot where I saw her. It took me years to get over Emily; moving through countless women, in and out of bad relationships. It wasn't until I met Claire that I managed to vanquish Emily from my thoughts, like a magician's final trick.

Emily had been everything to me. As I grew up, and probably away from the guy she had loved, she remained the big unanswered question in my life.

What if her family hadn't moved away? What if she listened to me, instead of her mother, and tried to make things work long-distance? What if I tried to keep in touch, rather than burying my head in the sand and missing her?

I'd been eighteen and stupid, so of course, I never did anything right. But there's always been the wonder and the regret whenever I thought of Emily over the years.

It died away when I met Claire because I know we're meant to be together, but seeing Emily brings back all of that regret.

I press the cold bottle against my forehead and close my eyes. She's with Matt now. What am I supposed to do about that?

"Hey, bro, you okay over there?"

My eyes fly open as I turn to face the guy beside me wearing a wildly patterned bathing suit. "What?"

"You look freaked out." His shaggy blond hair is pushed off his face by a pair of sunglasses and his expression is one of concern. "There's no reason to be freaked out in this place." He waves a hand around the lobby. "Beer. Babes. The sun. It's paradise."

"Yeah," I say in a shaky voice. Things are good. There's no reason I should be freaking out to see a face from my past, even if it is Emily. "I just got a bit of a shock."

"Bad?" My new friend leans against the bar.

"I don't know. I just found out that my old girlfriend is now with one of my best friends. Here. In the resort," I say. I give him a bewildered expression. "I don't know what to think."

"Are you here with someone?" he asks.

"My wife."

"Well, then you get to catch up with your old girl, but not really catch up, if you know what I mean, because you're with the wife. Unless she'd be okay with something like that." He raises an eyebrow. "You think?"

I close my eyes again. Matt and Emily. What if...? "I have no idea," I admit.

"You'd be surprised how many women are okay with it," he surprises me by saying. "I'm Jed, by the way. Want to grab another beer and tell me about your troubles? I'm a good listener."

I take his offered hand. "Billy. Listen, another beer is really tempting, but right now I've got to get back to this conference. Today's the last day and I can't wait to be free of it."

"Are you staying for the rest of the week or taking off?"

I grin with relief. "Got the whole week ahead of me. Maybe I'll see you around and we'll get that drink."

"Sounds cool, man. Better get back to work and I'll catch you later."

As I head back to the room, I'm thankful for Jed's interruption because now I think I can get through the rest of the morning without another embarrassing daydream about Emily.

Chapter Four

Claire

I GLANCE OVER AT Morena staring into the distance. Her hand rests on my upper thigh, as gentle as a question you don't know if you want to answer.

I can ignore it.

Instead, I brush her fingers with my own.

Her mouth creases into a smile. "Since you're so curious, I wonder if you'd like a lesson."

Touching my leg and seductive smiles are one thing. What Morena is suggesting is—

What is she suggesting?

I answer with a question. "Here? Now?" I cringe at the sound of my voice, so high-pitched and nervous.

"Only if you're comfortable," she soothes.

"I'm...comfortable..."

At my stumbled words, Morena moves from beside me and spoons me from behind, her long legs resting against mine in the water, her fingers brushing a bit of sand off my shoulders. My heart is racing like I've just run one of Basil's marathons.

Why did Basil pop into my mind?

I try to slow my breathing, my mind flitting to different scenarios, all involving me making an idiot of myself. And someone seeing us, but that's a distant second.

"Ready?" Morena asks in a teasing voice, her breath brushing my ear. Her full breasts press against my back.

"Not really." I hear the nerves in my voice. "But okay."

She drops a kiss onto my shoulder and stretches out her arms so her hands rest on mine resting on my thighs. "When I'm with a woman, I like to be touched," she begins quietly. "Constantly. Everywhere."

I nod. My throat dries as she trails her fingers up my arms, leaving goosebumps that could be from the water, or from her.

I think it's from her.

"Most men want to get down to it as quickly as they can like it's some kind of race. I like to take my time, so it's enjoyable for both." She brushes her palms over my breasts and I give an involuntary jerk. "Do you like your breasts played with?"

"Some."

Morena cups them, her thumbs finding my nipples already hard to the touch. "Most men are fascinated with a woman's breasts, but do they ever ask what you want them to do? They go straight to the nipples, and do whatever they want with them." Morena slips her hands inside the top of my bathing suit and plucks at my nipples. "Bring back memories?" she asks in a teasing voice.

"A little."

"Men are such babies," she says fondly. "The quickest way to bring a man to his knees is to present him with a pair of breasts. You have a very nice pair, by the way."

"Small," I manage. I'm dizzy from listening to her low voice and the sensation of her fingers. Anticipation has taken over my nerves, and my body sits ramrod straight with Morena curved around me.

"But sensitive?" She carefully rolls my nipples with her fingers. Billy does the same thing, but with Morena, it's more deliberate.

It feels like there's a cord between my nipple and between my legs, so everything Morena touches above the waist affects down below.

I nod and Morena kisses my shoulder again. I want to turn my head and press my lips against hers, but I have a feeling that's another part of the lesson.

"Not all women like breast play, so you have to pick up their clues. Men leave their focus there because it's an area they understand, but I prefer the more mysterious regions." Morena's soft chuckle grazes my ear like a caress as she runs her hands over my breasts onto my stomach like she's smoothing fabric.

For the first time, I don't have the urge to pull in my stomach as it's touched.

"Don't think that I have anything against men." Morena dances her fingers along my side, onto my thighs. I spread my legs wider as an invitation. "I love men. I love a good penis, especially if the man knows how to work it. I've had a great deal of pleasure from men over the years."

Her fingers drop to my inner thighs and I draw in a shaky breath. "But I've given a great deal of pleasure to women over the years."

Here we go.

Morena dips her hands between my legs and pushes them wider apart. "I like to take my time," she says, one of her hands now at the waistband of my bikini bottoms. "You might be ready and waiting for a quick fix, but there's so much fun to be had down here." Her other hand brushes against my pussy, still covered and a soft whimper escapes. "Maybe you do want the quick fix?"

"No..."

I feel her smile as she kisses my neck, her tongue pressing into the area under my ear. "You taste salty," she breathes. "I wonder if you'd taste salty all over."

I don't answer because I can't seem to breathe properly.

"I'd like to find out, but later. Now, let's just see what my fingers can do. Never go right for the little nub," she instructs in a no-nonsense voice. "It makes it so much better if there's teasing first. Not too much, don't worry," she teases. "But this is all so sensitive, isn't it?" Her fingers stroke my inner thighs, trailing patterns that bring them close to the apex, before skittering away.

I thought being in the water would make my skin less sensitive, but being out in the open only heightens it. We face away from the shore so no one can see what Morena is doing, but they can wonder.

My head lolls to the side as an invitation for her to kiss my neck as her fingers slip into my bottoms. "This is all good, isn't it?" she asks she strokes me, carefully avoiding the touch that I'm almost begging for.

"Yes." My voice is ragged, my breath catching as she moves closer to the bundle of nerve endings between my legs.

"You want a quick fix now, don't you?" She finds my clit with a confident finger, and I fall back against her with my eyes closed.

"Just so you know, if I had you on a bed, or a floor, or even a table, I'd lay you out like a feast and really take my time." She thrusts a finger inside me and I gasp aloud, spreading my legs with a tilt of my hips. "But you want it now."

"Please," I whisper.

"So polite. I like that." She croons into my ear but I lose focus of what she says as her fingers rub and tease and thrust. My hips jerk as I meet each thrust of her fingers, the heel of her hand hard against my clit, but when she stops, when her focus is my clit, I'm still, except for a trembling that begins as my climax approaches.

It's like the speedboat in the distance. Faster and faster, closer and closer.

My moans are louder than the sound of the waves.

Thrusting again, her fingers have a knobbiness rubbing inside me that a smooth penis lacks, faster and faster with a corkscrewing motion.

Faster and faster, until she touches my clit with a firm touch and I come with a cry that scares the fish away.

Billy

I BREATHE A HUGE sigh of relief as I walk out of the conference room for the last time. Some of the other guys talk about grabbing a beer but all I want is to find Claire.

And then find Emily and Matt.

I head straight to the dining room with the buffet-style food stations to meet Claire. I'm on my second beer and first plate of food when she finally gets there.

"I have to tell you something," Claire says, excitement brimming in her eyes as she sets her bag on the chair. She's wearing her cover-up but my gaze heads straight for her chest, with the wet patches that tell me she must have just gotten out of the pool.

"I have to tell you something too." I take a deep breath. "I know Matt's girlfriend."

"I met a woman," Claire blurts at the same time.

"Wait. What?"

"A woman. She's a *swinger*," she hisses, taking the seat opposite me and leaning across the table.

"Here?" I glance around the restaurant. "Is this place for swingers too? My work conference is at a swingers resort?" I laugh with disbelief. "I think I missed the memo on that one."

"I don't know. I didn't ask her."

"What did you ask?" I ask, wondering how this will change things. If it will change anything—it's hard to say since Claire and I haven't decided on what kind of vacation this will be. The kind where I go back to the room with her at night or someone else does.

Claire shifts her gaze, the way she does when she's guilty of something. "We...talked..."

"About?"

She pauses, biting her lip.

"Claire? What happened?"

"Billy!" I look up to see Matt coming towards us with a tray of food, Emily smiling nervously at his side. "I knew we'd find you around the food. Claire!" Matt drops his tray on the table. "How are you?"

Claire jumps to her feet and hugs him. "You're early! It's so good to see you."

"Matt's already here," I say weakly. "I was just about to tell you."

"We got an earlier flight," Matt explains, pulling away, his shirt damp in spots from Claire's exuberant hug. "Meet Emmy."

"Hi!" Whatever was bothering Claire a moment earlier, is shrugged off in the excitement of meeting Matt's new girlfriend. "So glad you guys could come. On the trip," she adds hastily.

"Thanks for inviting us," Emily says, her gaze flitting toward me with a nervous smile.

"Apparently Em knows Billy," Matt says, like it's the best thing in the world. He takes the seat next to me, leaving Claire to move her bag for Emily to sit down.

I'm on the edge of my seat to find out what she told him, and how different is it from how I would have explained. I know Emily loved me as much as I loved her, so maybe she called me her first love. The one that got away. The boy who broke her heart.

"Really?" Claire turns to me, but it's Matt who answers.

"I guess they went to high school together," Matt says in his usual cheerful voice and my heart sinks.

I turn to Claire, who looks expectantly at me. "*Emily*," I mouth. Because I don't keep secrets from my wife, Claire knows all about my past, at least as much as I felt comfortable telling her. She's got the gist of how it had been with me and Emily.

Matt, it seems, knows absolutely nothing.

I can't explain how this makes me feel.

Claire's eyes widen so much that I'm afraid they might pop out of her head. "*Really?*"

"Really," Emily—or Emmy, as Matt calls her—agrees. "Small world, isn't it?"

I down my beer. I don't know how much of this I can take.

"Wow." Claire stares at me, blinking quickly, obviously at a loss for words.

I don't know what to say either. About anything. "Yeah. Did you eat?"

Claire shakes her head, held back in her usual ponytail. "I was so excited to...uh, meet you guys, that I completely bypassed the food." She pushes her chair from the table. "Be right back."

"Hang, on, I'll come with you." Matt drains his beer as quickly as I did moments earlier. What's leading this guy to drink? "I need another one of these. I'll get one for you, Bill."

"Hey, thanks." I turn my head to watch Claire and Matt walk off before I round on Emily. "What did you tell him?" I hiss.

She throws up her hands. "What am I supposed to tell him? We went to high school together, and that's what I told him."

"We did more than just go to school together."

"Yes, but I haven't told him that. I've been only dating him for six weeks, Billy. We haven't gone that far back."

"You haven't told him about me?"

"Have you told your wife? She seems nice, by the way."

"Yes, because she's my *wife*."

"Well, Matt *isn't* my wife. Or my husband. We're still in the getting-to-know-you phase."

"You came to Mexico with him during the get-to-know-you phase? Wow, things have really changed since we dated," I mutter.

"We were seventeen," she reminds me.

"I wanted to marry you!"

"We were seventeen," she repeats, her voice gentle. "You really think we'd still be together?"

"We might!"

"And you'd miss out on your lovely wife. And kids? Do you have kids?"

"Two," I admit, feeling guilty that I even had the remote thought about a life without them. "Rachel and Rosie."

"I have fifteen-year-old twins. Boys."

"You have what?" I rear back in shock. "But that can't—you're not—"

"I was twenty-one when I got pregnant."

"But that's only a couple of years after you moved!" Was I over Emily when I was twenty-one? I fucked anything that moved at that age, so maybe not.

"You can see why I haven't gotten as far back as my teen years," Emily says wryly. "There was a lot going on in my twenties."

"Yeah." I stare at her, drinking in her face, the smile I remember so well. "I want to know everything."

"I can't tell you everything." She glances up, tracking Matt's location. "I don't know what to tell him about you."

"Tell him the truth. It's not like Matt will mind. There's no point keeping secrets."

"He's coming," Emily says without moving her lips. "Would you really want to know that you had sex with the same woman as your best friend?"

I'm going to figure out what that's like as soon as Basil and Jasmine get here.

CHAPTER FIVE

Claire

HOW DID AN OLD girlfriend of Billy's get to be here in Mexico with Matt?

And not just any old girlfriend—*the* girlfriend. The only other serious relationship he had before me. And the one that messed him up for years.

She's not what I expected.

I've had a hate for the spectre of Emily Hartnell since Billy first told me about her. Who could blame me? The guy I'm crazy about says all this wonderful stuff about another woman. He didn't go so far as to say Emily was the love of his life or the one that got away, but he said everything but.

The night he told me about her was the first time I gave him a blow-job. Bet your precious Emily can't do that!

She's not as pretty as I expected. She's still really pretty, but not model-beautiful.

Maybe a bit beautiful.

I tune in to Matt saying something just as he veers off toward the bar area. I head to the closest food station, which happens to be quesadillas.

At least the arrival of Matt will take my mind off what just happened with Morena. I can't believe I was just in the water with her...fingering me. Finger fucking me. Fucking? I don't know what to call it. It's more than simply fooling around, plus it was in the *ocean* and anyone could have walked up and seen us.

I didn't care.

I have to figure out how to get more of her.

"So," Matt says as we meet back at the table. "I didn't hear much about Aurora from Jas. How was it this year? I hated to miss it," he continues as I fight the urge not to look at Billy. "But with everything that happened..." He gives Emmy a rueful glance.

It's been five months since Aurora and while I know Billy and Matt have kept in touch via texts, it's obvious that no one has broken the pact to tell him what happened.

I'm still not sure what Jasmine's reasoning behind it was, but I made a point not to say anything. What could I say anyway? *"Aurora was great this year. Because you and Shawna weren't there, we met a new couple and tried out swinging. No, not swinging on a swing-set, the kind where you have sex with another couple. Basil and I hooked up twice, the second time with another woman..."*

"Yeah, I can see how it would have been tough," Billy says when it's obvious I'm still stuck in my head. "How are you doing anyway?" he asks, full of sympathy.

"Good," Matt says, as hearty as ever. "First bit was tough, but then Emmy and I—"

"How did you two meet anyway?" I interrupt. He's been split up with Shawna for *five* months and already he's brought a girlfriend to the group vacation?

I had no idea Matt could move so fast.

Emmy smiles, but I notice that it doesn't quite meet her eyes. "We've known each other for a while," she admits.

"When Shawna left, Emmy was a big help. We've been friends for years—"

"Friends," I echo. "And Shawna was the one who left."

"Just friends," Matt says with a chuckle. "Nothing happened until a few weeks after Shawna left. I know you two were close."

Actually, I have my issues with Shawna, but I'm not about to bring those up. My problem now is the expression on my husband's face when he looks at Emmy. I know he still sees her as the perfect ex-girlfriend, and if that's not the case, I want him to know *right now*.

This is our vacation and I'm not having him mooning over her.

"I was," I say instead. "But we're Team Matt for this, so..." I don't mean to sound threatening but I have a feeling it kind of comes out that way. I glance at Emmy who studies me like I have the answers to an important test.

"Thanks, Claire. It's good to have your support." Matt grins, looking like the same Matt I've known for years.

But I'm not the same Claire.

"What was that all about?" Billy hisses. After lunch, we move to the closest pool, which happens to be the same one where I met Morena.

As soon as Matt takes Emmy off for a splash in the pool, Billy turns to me. "You don't have to be so hostile to Emily."

"Her name is Emmy," I correct. "And that wasn't hostile."

"I'd hate to see when you are. Look, Claire, I had no idea she'd be here."

"How would you? Did he tell you who he was bringing?" When he shakes his head, I sigh. "I don't like being blindsided like that."

"You think I do? She doesn't mean anything."

I laugh, low and humourless. "Ah, yes, but she did. Anyway, I don't want to talk about Emmy, or Emily, or whatever her name is right now."

"Emmy, I guess. And sure. I don't want to talk about her either." Which is a lie, but I'm not about to call him on it. Especially, when I see a certain someone waving to me from across the pool.

"That's her," I hiss with excitement.

"Who her?" Billy asks.

"Her—Morena. The woman I told you about before we were rudely interrupted by your past."

"My past—the swinger?" Emmy is forgotten as Billy peers across the pool where Morena has settled into a chair. "That's her, with the white hair?"

"Morena. We...talked..."

Billy's head whips around so fast that I'm afraid of him getting whiplash. "Talked?"

"We went for a swim," I concede. It sounds innocent, but Billy knows me too well to be taken in.

"A naked swim?" he demands, looking interested despite his annoyance

"No, clothes stayed on. But she...and I...*she made me come*," I hiss. "With her fingers. In the water."

Billy rears back. "Seriously, Claire? When I was working? That's not fair."

"You're upset that it happened when you were working?" I laugh with disbelief. "Not the fact that I...and her..."

He looks at me closely, seeing the excited gleam in my eyes, the way I can't hide the smile. "No. I don't think I'm upset about that."

"What does that mean?" I ask slowly.

"It means that I don't think we have to have that conversation. Just have to talk to Jas and Basil."

Talk to them about being swingers. About swapping. Sharing.

Having sex with other people; other people being our friends.

He's okay with it. Deep down, I suspected he would be, but there was always the chance that Billy would have been upset to hear about me and Morena.

"So, what happened?" Billy glances over at Morena lounging in the sun, her low-cut one-piece leaving nothing to the imagination. Her body is firm and sexy...

Very sexy.

"She reminds me of Carson," I muse. "Older, confident."

"And that's what you like," Billy says, still staring. "Maybe I like that too."

Billy

I NEVER WOULD HAVE thought that my wife telling me about how she hooked up with a woman would be a good distraction, but it definitely takes my mind off Emmy for the half an hour she's in the pool with Matt.

It turns me on. Twice I have to adjust my swim trunks as Claire tells me about her ocean fun this morning. Even though this is a new side of my wife, I have no trouble picturing Claire with another woman, especially when I can clearly see the other woman in question across the pool, and appreciate the way she fills out a bathing suit.

For a few minutes, I'm *Emily, who?*

Emmy. Even in my head, she needs to be Emmy. It's clear my Emily is gone.

"So, you really want to do this again?" I ask Claire, her cheeks flushed from more than the heat.

Right there in the water, where anyone could have seen. What's gotten into my wife?

Right now, I'd like to get into her.

But clearly, we have things to discuss before I can drag her off to have my way with her.

"It might be a little late since I've already done something." She looks at me with the same expression she gets when she buys a new, expensive pair of workout pants—she knows she's in the wrong because she spent too much money, but she knows I love seeing her in the pants.

Guilt, mixed with a knowing expression, because my wife does know me very well.

"Yeah, you have."

"Are you mad?"

I sigh, shading my eyes with my hand so I can take another glance at this other woman. "How can I be mad when you've given me this huge hard-on?"

To my delight, Claire looks right at my crouch. "Sorry about that," she says with a giggle.

"You will be if you're not about to do something about it later," I say, only half-joking.

"Two blow jobs in one day?"

"I didn't say it was only going to be me. I can take you in the water just as well as anyone else can. We could slide into the water right here; I'd push you up against one of those jets and spread your legs...have my way with you right there."

"Where anyone can see?" Claire asks in a voice that is suddenly husky with want.

"You didn't have a problem with it earlier."

"I didn't." Claire stares at the brilliant blue water of the pool. Matt and Emmy have moved on to the swim-up bar. She's quiet for so long, I think she's moved on to some other thought in her mind, and do my best to think clean thoughts so I can get rid of the raging hard-on.

"Okay. Let's go."

"Go?"

"In the water."

My jaw drops. "Really? I never—"

But I never get to finish because a shout cuts the air, and I look up to see Basil and Jasmine walking toward us.

Damn it.

"Hey!" Claire jumps up but I have to swing my legs to the side and adjust before I follow her.

And suddenly Matt and Emmy are there. It's obvious Bas and Jasmine have already met Emmy. The sight of Emmy kissing Jasmine on her cheek doesn't help the hardness factor.

Jasmine looks...good.

It's been months since I've seen her, but even the gauzy dress and bright smile can't erase my favourite image of her—bent over in the woods with beautiful breasts drooping like ripe melons as Wyatt thrusts into her from behind.

The look on her face is one I'll never forget.

"Hi, Billy." Jasmine is wearing a shy, almost embarrassed expression so I know she's thinking of the same thing.

She's thinking of the way Wyatt invited me to join them; how I thrust into her, slowly at first, feeling her tightness grip me.

The feel of my hand on her ass.

"Hey." I lean down to kiss her, easily finding her mouth instead of the cheek she offered. And then I can't resist taking her in my arms.

I know the moment she feels my hard-on press against her because there's a quick intake of breath and then she presses herself tightly against me.

I've *got* to stop thinking about sex. I don't know how I'm supposed to get through the afternoon.

CHAPTER SIX

Claire

I'M NOT SURPRISED WHEN Billy makes an excuse to head back to our room.

I don't even remember what he said to the others, just that I'm chatting to Jasmine and all of a sudden, Billy is calling me.

"I'm going back to the room for a sec. Do you want me to grab your book, or come with me?"

There is nothing in his voice that suggests otherwise, but we've been married for almost ten years and *I know.*

"I'll walk back with you," I say just as casually.

He takes my hand as we walk away. Not a word about Basil or Jasmine or Emmy—or nothing that gives any indication of what is about to come.

The resort is set up with rooms scattered throughout, buildings leading to common spaces. Our room is a short walk, and my eyes blink as he holds the door for me to the building, trying to adjust to the sudden change from the brightness.

We head up the stairs, still not speaking, my heart hammering with anticipation.

Billy swipes the door with the key card and steps back to let me enter. The room is cool and dark, with the beds already neatly made by the hotel staff.

Maybe we can mess up the bed a little before—

Billy grabs me before the door is even closed, pushing me up against it. Untying the knot on my sarong, he throws it to the floor before yanking down my bikini pants.

"Wow, what—" Then he drops to his knees before me. His hands are between my legs before I can finish the thought.

And then his mouth.

"Oh."

There's no preamble, no gentle foreplay. Billy goes right for the gold.

Pushing my legs apart roughly, he dives in with his fingers. With only a quick lap of his tongue, his mouth surrounds my clit and sucks, sending sensations racing down my legs and forcing a choked gasp from my lungs.

"Oh...god..."

Did he know that I've been looking at Morena sitting across the pool all afternoon, wondering what it would be like to have her mouth where Billy's is?

How can he know that I've been so turned on all since Morena; like a mousetrap, trembling, ready to snap?

It's not going to take me long to snap.

With a throaty growl, Billy pulls one of my legs up and over his shoulder. I grab the door handle for balance, the cool of the metal door against my overheated back. His tongue replaces his fingers, his hand cupping my ass to move me in response to his thrusts.

Then he's back to my nub of nerves, his tongue sending shivers through my legs. I push his head deeper...harder...more...

"Don't stop."

But to my ever-lasting disappointment, he does. "Did she fuck you like this?"

"What? No," I gasp. I try and push his head back. "Please...don't..." Billy pushes my leg down and stands up. "What are you doing? You can't just—"

And then his cock is in his hand, thrusting it into my slick wetness. There's the moment of pain from his size, like a screech of tires on wet asphalt, and then it's all good.

So good.

"—Leave me like this," I finish.

"I'm not leaving. I'm going to fuck you." He punctuates his words with forceful thrusts sending my hips against the door. "Did she use her mouth on you?"

"Morena? No...fingers..." Oh, his cock. As much as I love the feel of Billy's mouth between my legs, his cock is something else. Thick and long and so hard...

He pulls out, rubbing the tip along my clit. "She played with you. Like this?"

"Fingers," I whimper as the over-sensitive nerves react.

"Not with a cock, because she doesn't have a cock. You like this, don't you?" He slowly, ever so slowly, enters me. So slowly that I'm about to scream.

"God, yes! Don't tease."

"You've been teasing me ever since you told me about this Morena. Only telling me enough to imagine...do you know what I've been thinking?"

"Tell me," I pant.

"I want to watch you with her...see what she does with her fingers...and her mouth." He slants his mouth over mine, suffocating my gasp as he lifts me, my feet dangling as he thrusts. Hard...deep...his tongue sweeps through my mouth and I taste myself.

I can't bring my legs up around his hips, only hang, propped against the door like a rag doll as he fucks me slowly, too slowly. I want him to take me like an animal, fast and feral like he can't get enough.

"Can I watch?" Billy asks in a husky voice, his mouth inches from mine.

"I want you to fuck me," I plead. "I want to come...make me come..."

"Use your fingers like she did," he says. He sets me down, my legs trembling enough to make standing difficult. I wrap one arm around his neck, and dip between us with the other, feeling the base of his cock as he thrusts, searching for...

My eyes flutter closed as my fingers find my clit and I rub. Hard. Fast. Like he knows how desperate I am, how close to release, Billy picks up speed, slamming me against the door with the force of his thrusts. His mouth over mine again muffles my gasps, my moans, the long-drawn-out cry as I climax with a thrust of my hips.

I wrench my mouth away from Billy. "Oh, fuck!"

A thrust, and then another, and Billy comes, his face buried against my hair.

I can tell he's smiling.

Billy

"WHAT WAS THAT?" CLAIRE gasps as she pulls up her bikini.

I tuck myself back into my shorts. "Are you complaining?"

"Well, no, but..." She looks at me with a concerned expression. "Are you mad? About me and...Morena?"

"Do I seem mad?"

Claire reaches for her sarong and wraps it around her hips, leaving her stomach bare. Her breasts, small and perfect, press against her top. "Billy, talk to me."

"We couldn't talk at the pool with the others. That's why I brought you here."

"No, you brought me back because you wanted to fuck me." She smirks. "That much is obvious." She reties her ponytail, looking as composed as when I pulled her back to the hotel room.

"That is true." I pull a bathing suit out of the drawer as Claire sits down on the edge of the bed.

"What do you think?" Her tone is hesitant, uneasy. This whole thing makes me uneasy. On one hand, is as sexy as hell thinking about my wife with another woman, but on the other, this is *my wife*, and I don't want to lose her.

"You want to do this again." It's not a question. Basil and I talked about what it had been like when he and Jasmine had the initial conversation at Aurora, how it was so hard to agree to have sex with others, without seeming like you really wanted to have sex with them.

I have a picture in my head of Bas and Jasmine dithering. *"Do you want to do this?" "No, do you want to do this?"*

There's no point in beating around the bush with Claire. I know what she wants.

"You want to do this again with Jasmine and Basil and this Morena woman and whoever she's with?" I ask slowly, holding my breath as I wait for her response.

The cock of her eyebrow is almost imperceptible at the mention of Jasmine, but I notice. I never told her about what happened in the woods with Jas and Wyatt. About how I watched, and then joined in.

Maybe I should tell her. Maybe I should—

"Yes." I look up at the decisive tone in her voice. My wife is not one to beat around the bush. "I mean, it hasn't done much to hurt our relationship," she adds with a grin, gesturing to the door.

"Do you like being with women more?" I ask. "You and Carson...and now Morena..." The thought has been in the back of my mind since Aurora. I know Claire wants me, wants my cock because she's told me in no uncertain terms. But I want to make sure she still wants me *more*, wants me more than anyone else.

And that includes Basil, too. I know the basics, but neither one of us went into details about what happened in the summer. I don't know if that's better or worse. I have an imagination, and it's not easy to guess what they did. How Claire sounded, what she looked like when she was with Basil.

"No. But I do like it," Claire admits. "I'm not going to lie to you."

"Carson said we need to be open and honest about our feelings." I quickly tie the string on my bathing suit and sit down beside my wife. I pick up her hand—the hand she used to make herself come as I fucked her.

Knowing she was getting herself off was hot. I can't deny that. I've watched her touch herself a few times over the years, and make a mental note to do more of it.

Would I really want to watch her with another woman?

A flash of the woman lounging across the pool; her head with the long, white hair, bent between Claire's legs.

Yeah, I could watch that.

"So we'll talk to Basil and Jasmine?" Claire asks, as direct as ever. "And Morena?"

I nod. And then, trying to make it sound like I couldn't care less, I ask, "What about Matt and Emmy?"

CHAPTER SEVEN

Claire

IT WAS A QUICK conversation, as quick as the fuck against the door, but at least I know Billy and I are on the same page.

We're going to try swinging here in Mexico.

Try swingers...be swingers...I'm not sure of what to call it. Playing, swapping, sharing. I don't care what it's called, because I'm still tingling from Billy. His mouth between my legs, devouring me. Fucking me against the door. Sex is always good between us, but it hasn't been that hot for a while, and if that was the result of me telling him about Morena, what's going to happen when I tell him more?

When we return to the pool, Basil greets me with a smile.

I don't think I'll tell Billy about Basil. Not everything.

Someone has piled my things on a chaise lounge beside Emmy, and as I arrange my towel, Billy drops onto the edge of Matt's chair, on the other end of the line of chairs. Jasmine lies next to

Emmy, with Basil beside her, and then Matt. So much for any sweet, post-sex chatting with my husband.

With a tight smile in Emmy's direction, I watch out of the corner of my eye as Billy laughs at something Matt says. The two men look at bit alike, both with their blond hair and open, easy expressions. While Billy has always been more of the laid-back, surfer dude type, Matt is the epitome of the boy next door—sweet, polite, earnest.

Neither of them is anything like Basil, with his dark good looks and his compact body with—

His body. I want to pull down my sunglasses and stare, but instead, I use them as a mask to seriously check him out. I've seen Basil in a bathing suit too many times to count. A few months ago, I saw him naked. But that was five months ago. I've never seen Basil so fit and firm and...

"Damn," I say, unable to help myself. "Jas, what has Basil been doing?" I don't need to raise my voice for Jasmine to look over.

"I know, right?" She smiles in appreciation. "I thought he was in good shape before, but now—we're taking the kids to Disney after Christmas and he wants to do the marathon when we're there. But not just the regular one; it's a full marathon one day, and then a half the next day, or vice versa. I have no idea, but it's *a lot*, and all he does is run. But now he looks like that." She smiles again.

"Impressive," Emmy says. She hunches her shoulders with embarrassment. "I had no idea he looked like that under the teacher's clothes."

"Those khakis do nothing to show off his ass." Jasmine laughs.

"Are you talking about my ass again?" Basil asks. "It's all she talks about," he adds ruefully to Billy and Matt.

Matt shrugs. "It's just an ass."

"Maybe it'd be different if you had an ass like that," Emmy mutters under her breath, giving me a grin.

I don't like that she's Billy's long-lost love, but I like her for that comment.

And she grows on me more and more as the afternoon wears on and Billy shows no sign of budging from his perch on Matt's chair. It doesn't take long before I realize he's there so he can talk to Jasmine.

In fact, it seems like everyone is talking to Jasmine—Matt, Basil, and even Emmy. Everyone except me, and I'm supposed to be her best friend.

I'm not a jealous person, but it's hard not to be annoyed when you get ignored.

Matt flags down a white-clad waiter, who brings *cervezas* for the boys, and Pina Coladas for the ladies.

I can't stand coconut but I take a polite sip. "Nope, not drinking that," I say, putting the drink in the shade of my chair.

"I don't love them either," Emmy says with a grimace. "At least not the ones here."

"I had a good daiquiri at the bar earlier," I tell her.

"Let's go grab one," she suggests.

Luckily, she can't see the surprised look on my face. "Uh—sure." I glance at Jasmine, who is sucking her straw with all of the intensity that I gave to Billy this morning. "Jas, you can have mine. We're going to grab a couple of daiquiris," I say.

"Be back soon," Emmy says. She stands and pulls off her gauzy cover-up.

Of course, she's got bigger breasts than I do.

Pale and full, her creamy breasts rise over the edge of her bikini top like overflowing ice cream cones. Emmy is curvy with hips and thighs and even the hint of a belly, but it works for her. I never expected her to be so sexy.

By the expression on Billy's face, neither did he. Things must have changed since she was seventeen.

While I'm not as sexy as Emmy, there's no denying the attraction of my own body. Yoga, spinning, running—it all adds up to a pretty package, tight and firm. Tearing my sarong off, I run my fingers under the edges of my bikini bottoms as I head to the stairs of the pool, knowing all eyes will be on my ass.

Like Basil, I have a very nice ass.

The water is cool and crisp against my skin, and I want nothing more than to dive in and swim a few laps. But there are too many people dotted through the water, so I'm forced to wade across to the bar, Emmy by my side.

She tells me about her boys—twins—as we cross the pool.

"Fifteen," I groan as we reach the pool bar. "I can't imagine that. Rachel is eight and that seems old enough for me." I quickly do the math. "You must have been a kid when they were born."

"Feels like it." She grimaces. "Were you good friends with Shawna?" she asks, the question coming out of left field.

"Did you know Shawna?" I counter.

"A bit. Obviously, not as much as Matt."

"Well, same for me. Shawna was...Shawna. I'm sorry for Matt that his marriage broke up but no one is crying over Shawna being out of the picture."

She smiles, her first real smile, I decide. "Good to know."

She stops as we notice that nearly all the stools are filled at the bar. "Looks like we're not the only ones with this idea."

A man—a very good-looking man with shaggy, dirty blond hair—glances over his shoulder. His face lights up with a cheerful grin. "Take mine," he offers. The only available stool is beside him. "As long as you don't mind me squeezing in beside you."

It could have been an offensive, smarmy comment, but when said in such a friendly tone, it's not. "Thanks," I say as he slides off, standing quite close to me as I sit down. "Very gentleman-like of you."

"I try. And I'll try harder. Benoit," he calls, waving a hand at the same bartender that had been there earlier. "Duo mango daiquiris, *por favor*."

Emmy laughs, just as charmed as I am. "Good guess."

"Not really." He leans close enough for his shoulder to brush mine and I smell sunscreen and man. "My girlfriend mentioned she had a drink with you earlier and how much you liked it." He draws away as my jaw drops. "I'm Jed. I was hoping I'd get a chance to meet you."

Billy

E MILY IS NOT THE girl I remembered.

Emmy. She's Emmy now.

She'd not a girl any longer, either. Clearly, she's all woman. I fight not to stare as she and Claire walk off together.

Emily and Claire—my past and my present. And I can't say a word about how weird that is because Matt doesn't know. He has no idea that my first time was with his girlfriend.

Come to mention it, Basil has no idea that my first time, my first threesome, was with his wife.

I have to look away to hide my smile. What kind of vacation is this going to be?

I turn back when Jasmine mentions Emmy's name. "I'm really glad Emmy could come." She glances at me with a smile. "She's really nice."

"I know. We went to high school together." I try for casual, even though there's nothing casual about how nice I think Emmy's ass is. "Happy for you, bro." I clink my bottle against Matt's.

"Thanks," he says, his eyes on Emmy easing into the water. "Guess I forgot Claire doesn't do coconut."

"No worries," Jasmine says, reaching over to snag Emmy's drink. "More for me."

When she leans over, I can't help but notice the curve of her hip, the dark skin of her leg seeming to go on forever. But her legs have nothing on her breasts. The V-neck of her bathing suit is just enough to show the crevasse of cleavage, enough to make me take a healthy swig of my beer.

Claire wants a repeat of Aurora. Does that mean me and Jasmine again? My eyes travel along her body, thankfully hidden by my sunglasses. I wouldn't mind that.

My cock throbs as if it remembers what it was like.

I wouldn't mind that at all.

Basil asks me about my conference, and I wrench my mind away from the pleasures of his wife to answer. But after he moves on to ask Matt something, I'm right back there, surreptitiously watching Jasmine.

And then I catch her watching me.

Not just watching me—I catch Jasmine staring at my crotch. My cock gives more than a throb at that. Her gaze moves up my body, and she bites her lip when she sees me watching.

Oh, it's on.

But Jasmine...or Emmy? Fighting the urge to adjust, I turn away from Jasmine's lip biting and glance across the pool. Emmy is my past and I—

There's a man talking to them at the bar. There's something familiar about him, the way he leans over, brushing Claire's shoulder as he says something to Emmy.

Both women laugh.

"Are they picking up?" Jasmine asks, following my gaze.

"Looks like it."

"How do you feel about that?" Her tone is pointed like there's an underlying meaning to her words.

Maybe I'm just imagining things, but it's better to be safe than sorry. I lean forward over Basil's legs. He continues to chat with Matt and doesn't notice. *I missed you*, I mouth.

Jasmine drops her chin with a wide smile.

I'm glad I got that in, because a moment later, Matt brings Jasmine into the conversation and I don't get more than a word in edgewise. But I know I'm the reason for her smile.

I stand up and pull a nearby lounger close. Pulling off my shirt, I wonder if I should ask Jasmine to put sunscreen on me as I lie down.

Probably not a good idea. Even after me and Claire's little up against the door, I'm still half-hard at the thought of Jasmine. At the possibility of a second round.

And a third round...

I'd be rock hard in a minute if she laid her hands on me. I settle back, arms over my head and let the nearby conversation wash over me. There'll be time enough to talk to them, I decide. A nice little nap would be a great idea right now.

With a last glance at the bar across the pool, my half-closed eyes fly open.

A woman has joined Claire and Emmy. I'd recognize that tumble of white hair piled on the top of her head anywhere.

Morena.

CHAPTER EIGHT

Claire

TOO MUCH SUN AND a steady stream of afternoon drinking lead to a dinner with lots of wine, which makes it an early night for all of us. But that also means an early morning the next day.

At least for me. Stopping for a coffee and a smoothie, I meet Jasmine by the pool. It's early enough to get our pick of chairs, and we find a nice spot with the shade of a tree blocking the heat of the morning sun.

I haven't seen her in months, and while texting and Facebook posts can tell a lot about a person's life, it's not the same as face-to-face contact. We chat about the kids as we settle in.

"I kind of feel like I should try the aquafit," I admit, watching the well-built instructor lead the women in a not-too-vigorous routine at the other end of the pool.

"A vacation is to relax," Jasmine says, sipping her own coffee. "You know they're only doing it because he's hot. I've done Zumba with you. That's no workout for you."

"You might be right." I glance over with a grin. "About how hot he is."

"It's a nice distraction. Birds singing...half-naked cute guy in the pool..."

"It's a nice life."

"Speaking of cute, I saw that guy at the bar with you yesterday." She nods her head slowly. "Nice."

I nod my head in agreement. "He was." Taking a deep breath, I wonder if this is the best way to bring this up. Before he fell into a drunken sleep last night, Billy told me to talk to Jasmine about "doing the thing with them again."

His words, not mine.

"Funny you should mention him," I say.

"Is this going to be about what happened at Aurora?" Jasmine asks bluntly.

"Am I that obvious?"

"I'm sure it's been on your mind as much as mine. Or maybe not," she backpedals quickly.

I chuckle. "Just a bit. You know, my new friend Jed? Cute guy at the bar you mentioned? Well, he and his wife Morena are swingers."

Jasmine pulls down her sunglasses, her brown eyes wide and disbelieving. "Is this a swinger resort too?"

I burst out laughing. "Billy said the same thing when I told him."

"So Billy is...into the idea?" Jasmine fails miserably at casual. So much that I want to ask her what I've long suspected—that something happened with her and Billy. That last night, when Carson was with me and Basil, no one asked where Billy was. I like thinking that he was alone, asleep in our cabin, but the doubt has always been in the pit of my stomach.

Jasmine's reaction only reinforces my doubt.

Or maybe not. Maybe she just wants her chance with my man.

"He's in," I confirm, pushing away my questions. I'll ask Billy. I don't want things to be awkward with Jas, because if I ask her about Billy, what's to stop her from asking about Basil? "What about Bas?"

"Oh, he's all for it," she says ruefully. "Surprising, since he was almost the holdout in the summer. You did a good job of converting him."

"It wasn't—I didn't..." I stumble over my words. "I never..."

It's only when Jasmine gives a big belly laugh that I realize my cheeks are warm to the touch.

"It's okay," she reassures me. "As long as things are good with me and you then it doesn't matter."

"Good with me," I say. "How are you and Basil?"

"Never better," she says with surprise. "Who would have thought sex with other people would bring us closer together? And between us..." she trails off. "I'm not going to give details."

"Good, though?"

"The best!" I join in her laughter, thinking of the improvements with Billy and I. More impulsive, more enthusiastic, just *more*. Sex with other people does improve your sex life.

"What about Matt?" I ask after the laughter fades. "Emmy met Jed and Morena, but we never said...I don't think she knows..."

"I never said a thing to Matt!" Her vehemence surprises me.

"It okay if you did," I assure her. "If you want them to join in—"

"No," she snaps, like the slamming of a door. "Absolutely not."

Billy

THE NEXT MORNING I meet Basil after his run. There used to be a time when I went with him, but I know there's no hope in hell of that these days, not in the shape he's in. He can run circles around me, and then go sprint through a couple of marathons, all before breakfast.

He's a machine.

I wonder if that makes him better in bed.

I've never been one to be curious about what other men do in bed. In fact, I do my best not to think about it. There had been a guy in high school who scored with any girl he wanted. The rest of us—virgins, the lot of us—had been in awe of his success. There had been a lot of talk of exactly what he did to make him so popular because he wasn't all that good-looking. But I never found out.

It's different when it's your wife and the other man who had sex with her is your best friend.

This is the first time I've seen Basil since the summer, so I suppose it's only natural that when I look at him, I see him with Claire. And then the unspoken questions begin—did he make her come?

I know that's a yes because Claire is always insistent on getting her piece of the pie.

Did he make her come more than once? Did he come more than once?

Did they do things I don't do? There's not much I wouldn't do, so I can't see that happening, but still, it's a question.

I can't stop the images of them, but luckily, it hasn't done anything to our friendship. Just something to be curious about and to make sure I don't drink too much and suddenly start demanding answers.

Basil is in dire need of a shower when he meets me at the smoothie shop. Claire found it a few days ago, and while I like my big breakfasts, these are great for a snack, or when I want to suck something through a straw that isn't alcoholic.

"How's it going?" Basil asks, still panting.

"Good with me, but are you going to be all right? How far did you run?"

"Only seventeen." He smiles at the girl at the smoothie shack and asks for some complicated protein-based smoothie that will probably taste like grass. Training for the marathon has obviously affected Bas' eating habits. It's a good thing he hasn't given up drinking.

"Only…" I roll my eyes. I walked Claire to the pool to meet Jasmine earlier and that had been enough exercise enough for me. "Good thing we had an early night."

"Yeah. I didn't expect that. Matt totally bailed."

"He did." A twinge of frustration remains at the image of Matt, with his arm around Emmy—my Emily.

She's no longer my Emily, and it's time I accept that.

Basil nudges me with his elbow. "Guess that's what happens when you get a new girlfriend." I don't answer. I can't answer, because I'm too busy still accepting she's only a part of my distant past. "What's wrong? You don't like her?" Basil asks.

"I think she's great," I say honestly.

"Did I hear something about you going to school with her?"

"High school. Long time ago." My reply is crisp and curt and to the point.

"I'm sure she's changed since then." Basil accepts his smoothie. "Both of you."

He thinks she was a bitch, I realize with a twinge of guilt. Emily is nothing but sweet and kind to everyone, but until she tells Matt, my true opinion of her will stay locked up. "What is that?" I ask instead, looking at Basil's smoothie with disgust. The colour looks more mud-like than green, and I can't imagine it tasting very good.

"It's good for you. Kale and lemongrass, with beets and carrots and pineapple." Basil ignores my grimace as he takes a long suck of his straw. "Jas really likes her too. Emmy. It's a big change from Shawna, but I think she's good for Matt. He's more—"

"She was my high school girlfriend."

So much for keeping it under lock and key. I don't mean to say it, definitely don't mean to blurt it out like that, but I can't help it. The secret has been churning up my insides more than the mud smoothie is going to seriously move Basil's.

"What?"

"I spent more than a year madly in love with her," I say morosely. "She was my first, my everything. Back then—obviously Claire is everything now. But she hasn't told Matt so she doesn't want me to say anything—"

"Emmy? You and Emmy?"

"I called her Emily then."

"Seriously? You had sex with her?"

"That's what you're getting out of this conversation?"

"No, but—" Basil looks he wants to say something else, and I can only imagine it's something about Aurora. How that if I've had sex with Emmy, then I've had sex with all the women here?

Only he doesn't know about me and Jasmine. Or maybe he does. I don't know if he knows.

I've had about enough of the secrets flying around.

"Small world," Basil finishes.

"Tell me about it."

"Are you going to say something to Matt?"

"I'd rather she did, to avoid any unpleasantness between him and me. Not that it's unpleasant, or a big deal. I'd just like it out in the open, you know?"

"Yeah." Then after a pause. "Claire knows?"

I finish my drink and toss it into a nearby garbage can. "Yeah. I told her about Emily years ago, so it wouldn't have taken much for her to put two and two together. Not that there's anything to hide." I throw up my hands. "Just tell him! Matt's my friend and I don't want to keep things from him."

"Yeah." The way he says that makes me sure that he doesn't know about me and Jasmine, so now I feel like a shit about that.

"Look, bro," I begin then stop myself. What if me saying something about it gets Jasmine into trouble with Basil? Again, not that there should be secrets, but I don't want things to be awkward.

Having sex with your friends is more difficult than expected.

"Yeah?" Basil turns to me, trusting light in his eyes.

I don't know what to say about Jasmine, about Matt, so I grab something completely different. "You want to have sex with Claire again?"

Chapter Nine

Claire

"So why doesn't Jasmine want to include Matt?" Billy asks later than evening when we're back in our room getting dressed for dinner.

I wondered how long it would take him to ask.

"I don't know." Billy stands behind me and I glance at his reflection in the mirror. He looks good in the loose shirt and khakis with his hair damp from his shower.

He smells good too.

"You must know. The two of you were all cozy when we came up this morning."

"We have lots of things to talk about other than you husbands," I say archly. Billy narrows his eyes, and I relent. "She's always been...weird about him. I know they've been friends forever, but sometimes I wonder if maybe there was more. Maybe there were feelings on one side, or both, that they never acted on.

"Wouldn't this be a good opportunity to do that?"

"Maybe it would rock the boat. Besides, if you've gone your whole life wondering what it would be like with someone, wouldn't it be kind of a letdown when it actually happened?" I can tell I've got him from his expression; shifting eyes and his jaw clenches. It's the same expression when I catch him doing something wrong.

This time he hasn't done anything he should feel guilty about, but I know he wants to. Billy wants Matt involved because then he'd get a chance with Emmy.

And I'm not sure how I feel about that.

"I don't know about that," he says, still not looking at me in the eye.

Should I call him out, ask if he wants to have sex with his old girlfriend?

I don't see the point. Billy is a man, and Emmy is an attractive woman. They have a past together. Why wouldn't he want to have sex with her?

That may be the case, but I've never come right out and asked Jasmine what the deal is with her and Matt. They are friends; I've lost track of the stories, and the *remember when* moments they've shared over the years. But no one—at least not me—knows exactly how friendly they are, or have been.

"I don't want to push Jasmine on this," I say, pulling my hair back into a ponytail. Billy likes me better with my hair down but I don't like how the heat makes it stick to the back of my neck.

"Why? She owes you for letting her have sex with your husband again," Billy jokes.

It takes a moment for his words to register. "Again?" I turn to look at him.

"Yeah." Billy smiles, still thinking it's funny. What's funny is the expression on his face when he realizes what he's said. "Oh."

"I didn't realize you had sex with her the *first* time."

"Oh, well, it wasn't really sex..."

"Did your penis come in contact with her vagina?"

"Well...kind of."

"When was this?" My voice turns colder than the air conditioning in the room, and Billy knows he's lost. Slowly, he tells me about following Jasmine and Wyatt into the woods that night at Aurora and Wyatt inviting him to join in.

I only nod, turning back to the mirror. Here's the difficult part—I shouldn't get upset with Billy for having sex with Jasmine, because that would make me a hypocrite. I'm two and hopefully more with Basil.

"You didn't tell me," I accuse in a low voice, trying to keep my hand steady while I put on mascara.

"Carson said don't ask questions. You didn't ask so I thought that meant you didn't want to know."

I frown at his logic. "She also said it's important to be honest about this."

"I didn't think you'd want to know," Billy repeats.

"I didn't need details but I would have liked to be told that the act took place. Does Basil know?"

"I have no idea." Billy shrugs. "I haven't seen Jasmine in months, same as you. I can ask her."

"I would have liked to know this before I spent the day with her," I fret. "I talked to her about the very same thing this morning."

"Would anything have changed?" Billy steps behind me and puts his arms around me. "Look, babe, I'm sorry I didn't tell you, but I honestly didn't know how. It's bad enough I know you were with Basil and Carson, but I don't want to know details." He drops his head to nuzzle my neck. "Except for Carson. I wouldn't mind details about that."

I pull away. "If you honestly think you're going to sex your way out of this, you've got another thing coming. I hope you luck out with someone else tonight because it's not going to be me."

My annoyance with Billy lasts the rest of the night. We meet Basil, Jasmine, Matt and Emmy for a nice dinner. I thaw towards Billy enough that no one knows anything is amiss, but I can feel the distance between us. Technically he didn't lie to me, although it feels like he did.

I keep staring at Jasmine.

She's been my friend—one of my best friends—for years but I look at her in a new light tonight. It doesn't help that she's lit up like a candle. Smiling, laughing, her eyes shining with happiness. I know things are good with her and Basil, so I have to wonder how much of this inner glow has been brought about by seeing my husband again.

Or Matt.

Jasmine and Matt sit across from each other at the table; girls on one side, boys on the other, just like we do at Aurora. Did. Past tense, because Matt and Shawna weren't there this year. Or Matt and Emmy.

The more time I spend with her, the more I understand the attraction. Not only is Emmy good-looking; the halter-style dress she's wearing is sexy in an unobtrusive way, but her personality is the complete opposite of Shawna.

Where Shawna was opinionated and strong-willed, Emmy is easy-going and sweet. Shawna was the leader of the group, needing control of every last detail and the force of her personality was such that everyone went along with it, like a stick being washed downstream by a strong current. When they were together, Matt tended to fade into the background, only yanked to the forefront by Jasmine.

With Emmy, Matt talks more, laughs louder, and looks like he's enjoying himself. Gone is the pinched expression I've noticed in the past, the carefully chosen words, and the pained look in his eye whenever Shawna pulled a Shawna move. This Matt is the full-colour version.

I like him much better than the black-and-white copy.

And as much as I didn't want to, I like Emmy too.

I'm pulled back into the conversation by Matt's loud bark of laughter as Jasmine tells some story about the kids. Jas and Matt may have a past, but these days the kid connection is just as strong.

Like yesterday at the pool, Jasmine has the attention of all the males at the table, something else that wouldn't have happened had Shawna been here. On my other side, Emmy picks up her nearly empty wine glass.

"The two of them are like this all the time," I say out of the corner of my mouth.

She nods. "I've noticed." I can't tell from her tone if this annoys her. It's got to be difficult for her to come on this trip, joining the rest of us for the first time. She may know Jasmine and Basil, but vacation Jasmine is a little different than everyday Jas.

And vacation Basil...

As if he knows my thoughts have strayed once more to him, Basil looks up to find me watching him. He sits directly across from me and as he shifts his gaze, I feel a nudge against my foot.

Looking away, I hide my smile. How can I be upset at the thought of Jasmine and Billy, when the thought of me and Basil makes me smile like a schoolgirl in the midst of her first crush?

Billy

AFTER DINNER, I'M READY to head to one of the resort bars when Matt announces he's off to bed.

"What do you mean, you're off to bed? You went to bed early last night. We're on vacation, for god's sake!" I exclaim.

Matt takes Emmy's hand and pulls it up to drop a kiss on it, a move that would make any woman swoon.

I don't like it.

"I've spent all dinner neglecting my brand new girlfriend," Matt says with all the cockiness of someone who has a brand new girlfriend. "I'm about to go make up for it."

Emmy smiles but doesn't meet my eyes as the two of them say their goodnights.

"Want to take a walk on the beach?" Matt asks Emmy as they walk away. I can't hear her response but they veer off toward the sand.

"Did that just happen?" I ask in a strangled voice. "Did *Matt* just announce he's going off to have sex?"

"I think so." Jasmine looks as deflated as I feel.

"That wouldn't have happened if Shawna was here."

"Well, no, because he would have been having sex with Shawna," Basil says drily. "I can't see Shawna being into having Emmy join them."

There's a pause before the four of us bursts out laughing.

"Are you going to bed?" Claire asks, glancing between Basil and Jasmine. I'm glad to see that things seem to be fine with her and Jasmine. It's not her fault that I never told Claire.

I still don't know why I haven't told her.

Basil shakes his head before Jasmine can answer. "Hell, no. Vacation, remember. Let's go find another drink."

We head to the main lobby, a fair walk away. Of course, the conversation turns to Matt and Emmy.

"They seem happy," Claire says, walking ahead of me and Bas.

I watch my wife's hips sway under her dress, thinking of the quickie yesterday afternoon. I haven't made love to her today. A few years ago, during our first trip without the kids, I made a vow to have sex with her at least once a day. This trip is our second without them, and so far I've kept up my end of the bargain.

Maybe I should specify *having sex* rather than sex with my wife. Because I can't stop looking at Jasmine's ass either.

"They are," Jasmine says, the tone in her voice begging to be challenged.

"Are you trying to convince yourself as well as us?" Claire asks, picking up on the same thing I did.

"No, of course not. Emmy is great and makes Matt very happy. Shawna is in the past, and I'm glad for him."

"I kind of miss her telling us what to do," Basil muses.

Claire glances over her shoulder. "Do you *like* being told what to do?"

It's one of those flirtatious comments that we've all made countless times over the years. We're adults, all in fully committed relationships and very comfortable with each other. We flirt. We make inappropriate comments. Innuendos fly across, even better when naïve Jasmine misses them.

This is the first time since Aurora that the four of us have been alone, and as the realization hits, we fall silent.

I have no idea if Claire meant it as a joking innuendo or if Basil really likes it when she tells him what to do.

Maybe being a swinger with your friends isn't the best idea.

Luckily, the awkwardness is saved by the brightly lit lobby looming ahead. As we enter, close to the bar, there's already a healthy crowd gathered, watching the bartender do one of those cocktail shaker flipping tricks.

When Claire gasps, I think it's because the guy almost lost the shaker. I turn in time to see that her cheeks are pink and she's giving a little wave.

A tall woman, with white hair, wearing a red dress, waves back.

"That's Morena," Claire says to me.

I do the classic double-take. "*That's* Morena?"

She frowns. "I pointed her out to you yesterday."

"Yeah, but that was across the pool...maybe the sun was in my eyes." I drink in the sight of the older woman—red dress nicely hugging curves in what is still a trim figure. Her smile is wide, there's interest in her dark eyes, but it's the hair that gets me. She's wearing it tucked onto the top of her head in a bun, and all I can think about is what she would look like with the tumble of silver-white hair falling to her shoulders.

Naked shoulders.

I smile widely. "Why don't you introduce us?"

CHAPTER TEN

Claire

"Hey, Lobby guy!" Jed exclaims as Morena draws him forward.

I look at Billy with confusion. He has a similar expression on his face until something clicks.

"Hey," he says. "Lobby guy. I bumped into Jed during a break during the conference yesterday," he adds.

"You looked like you could use a couple of these." Jed raises his bottle.

"Right now." Billy grins at him. "I'll go get us a round. You grab a table."

"Who's that?" Jasmine whispers, eyebrows raised with interest. With all the introductions, drink orders and finding a table, it was a bit before I had a moment to answer Jasmine's question.

"Jed...and Morena...Bar guy." Jasmine continues to look at me like she knows there's more than my simple explanation. "They're...swingers," I admit. "I told you about them."

"How exactly do you know that?" she demands. My face must give her an answer. "Claire! Without us?" Jasmine hunches her shoulders with embarrassment when she realizes how loud her voice carries.

"It was just me," I hiss, throwing Morena a sideways glance across the table where she's busy laughing at Billy's jokes. She catches it and smiles, seeming to know that Jasmine and I are discussing.

"With...Morena?" Jasmine follows my gaze. "Really?" I shrug. "So, how was it?"

Mentally I count how many drinks Jasmine has had tonight and calculate it's enough for her to ask that question. "Good," I confess. "We went down to the beach for a little swim." My smile might be a bit too gleeful, but I can't help it.

"Wow," Jasmine marvels, sneaking a glance at Morena. "I've never been with a woman and now, you've been with two."

"Three actually." I try not to sound too smug. "But the first was a long time ago and now that I've—" I hunch my shoulders with another grin. "I shouldn't even include it."

"Look at you." Jasmine brushes her shoulder against my arm. "Serious swinger now, are you?"

"As serious as you are." I lean. "If we...if *they*...want to..." I trail off as both Jasmine and I turn to glance at Jed.

He grins at us.

"Hell, yeah," Jasmine says under her breath.

Jed takes a shine to Jasmine. Which is fine, because I'm still not ready to process how she and Billy ended up together that night in Aurora.

I don't know if I want details, just *how*.

So if Jasmine ends up with Jed, then that leaves Morena for Billy, and Basil for me.

Me and Basil again.

As the empty glasses add up, I watch Basil across the table. While Jed and Morena sit at opposite ends of the table, it's clear to everyone that they are together. The way Jed looks at her for approval or agreement, how Morena's eyes light up when she catches him looking at her, and the quick touches of a hand whenever space allows.

On the other end of the spectrum, Billy barely glances at me.

I don't take it personally. Billy is loud, fun-loving and loves attention, especially when he's drinking. And he's definitely drinking tonight. His blue eyes have a glittery quality that suggests he's about to fall asleep or keep drinking all night long.

I hope he doesn't fall asleep on Morena.

Since Billy is preoccupied with Morena, and Jasmine is practically falling over herself with Jed, I have plenty of time with Basil. And after I finally move around the table to sit next to him, it's clear he's come to the same conclusions that I have about the rest of the night.

"Are you okay with that?" Basil jerks his chin towards Jed laughing with a pink-cheeked Jasmine.

"I should be asking you." I stir the ice in my vodka and tonic, the tiny clinking sounds lost in the noise of the bar.

"I am," he assures me. "I didn't know if you wanted to...you know. Him."

"Is this your way of telling me you want to have sex with your wife tonight?"

"No, but...I mean..." He narrows his eyes at me. "Don't try and confuse me."

"What am I confusing you about?" I widen my eyes, batting my lashes for good measure.

"I thought we—"

"We, as in you and me?"

"Yeah. I thought we—"

"Okay."

"Okay? Just like that?"

I lower my voice and lean close enough for me to smell his spicy cologne. At Aurora, Basil smelled good, but never this good. "Is that what you want?" I whisper. "Do you want me, Basil?"

"I've wanted you every day since the summer," Basil says in a strangled voice. "Every damn day."

Warm explodes inside me. It's good for the ego to know someone wants you, but it really feels good knowing Basil feels the same way I do.

Billy

WE SHARE A FEW drinks at the bar, a lot of laughs, and then things get serious fast when Morena asks if I would like to walk her back to her room.

A glance around the table shows the others perched on the edge of their seats, like birds waiting to take flight.

Claire gives me a quick nod, and I know things are fine with us.

"Sure." I try for cool and suave but my voice cracks like an adolescent's. Claire smirks as I stand up. "Do you...ah, do you have the key?" I ask. At the shake of her head, I pass her the keycard, wishing we'd thought to bring both.

Of course, I didn't know this was going to happen. At least not happen this fast. I just met Morena, and *whoa bam*, I'm toddling off to fuck her.

At least I think that is what's going to happen.

With an awkward wave, I follow her out of the bar and she takes my hand like I'm a child. "It's going to be okay," she says in a soothing voice.

"I know."

"You look a bit shell-shocked. Should I have waited? Did you want to make the first move?" She glances up at me, her eyes dark, a smile hinting at her lips.

"This is good." Thankfully, my voice no longer cracks.

"I think so too. I think it will be very good."

We don't say anything else until we come to her building. Their room is on the main floor, looking out to the garden, which I don't see because the curtains have been pulled tight. The room is neat but looks lived in. I notice the book on the table, along with a pair of glasses. Shoes line along the wall; flip flops and sandals and a pair of running shoes that must be Jed's.

I'm in another man's room.

I swallow with difficulty.

"Are you all right, Billy?" Morena asks gently. I can only nod. "We don't have to do anything, you know. Although, I think you want to. I can always tell when a man wants me."

She steps close enough so that I can smell the faint tinge of her perfume. Her chin reaches my shoulder, so it's not much of a reach for her to slide her hand around the back of my neck, pulling me down to her. "Show me how much you want me," she whispers before her lips find mine.

It's a quick kiss, but it does the trick. My nerves vanish at her touch, and I lean into her, demanding more.

"That's a good boy." Morena runs a hand through my hair as she pulls away. "I knew it would be you as soon as Jed told me he met you. I was interested even then."

"You were interested in me?" I ask stupidly. I feel drunk, like there's a toxin on her lips that confuses me.

I think it's just her.

Morena smiles. "Well, you and your wife, but we don't have to talk about her right now, do we? Unless you want to."

"I...don't know..."

"Did she tell you about it? How I made her come sitting in the ocean? That was a first for me." Slowly, she runs her hand down my chest, all the way to my cock, which gives a solid twitch in response. "Goodness." Her smile widens as she slides her hand down my length. "This might be a first as well."

"Ok," I say, my head spinning. I'm drunk. I drank my fair share tonight but I'm drunker on Morena than anything I had at the bar.

With a squeeze that has my half-mast cock racing to full, she steps away. You can do whatever you with me," Morena says as she works a hidden zipper under her arm. "Except for hurting me. I don't do well with pain, other than the odd spanking."

"Spanking," I repeat, mesmerized at how she pulls her dress up and over her head in a swift movement. That dress looked complicated and Morena pulls it off like it was nothing.

"Have you ever spanked a woman?"

I can feel the smack of my hand against Jasmine's ass, how she jerked at the touch. I nod.

"Did you enjoy it?"

"I'm not sure," I say honestly. I could barely look Jasmine in the eye the next morning, and now every time I speak to her, I want to start off with an apology. I'm not sure if it's for me.

"Don't feel obligated," Morena reassures me. "What would you like?"

"I don't know." I'm overwhelmed by her offer; carte blanche to do anything I want with this beautiful, sexy woman. I should have all the dirty thoughts of my generation running through my mind, but I can't.

All of a sudden, the only woman I think about is Emily and I know I'm about to screw this up so badly.

"You could pretend," Morena says softly, turning away from me to undo her bra.

I look at her bare back, smooth and silky, her hair held up by an unseen clip. And then she releases it and a cascade tumbles down, almost silvery blonde in the low light.

I take a step forward and grab a fistful of Morena's hair. "How could you forget me?" I demand in a low voice, my arm sliding around her waist to pull her back against me.

"I didn't."

"You did. You were everything to me, and you walked away from what could have been. You forgot about me. Aren't there enough memories for you to tell him what we shared?"

"Remind me," Morena begs in a voice that's not her own. I only hear Emily's voice.

I kiss her neck, sucking against the soft skin, tonguing my way along her jawline. When I turn her to face me, she makes a noise that might be a protest but I ignore it, feasting my lips against hers.

It's been a long time since I've kissed like this.

Slow, long kisses, my tongue sweeping into her open mouth. Morena winds her arms around my shoulder, cradling my head and her hips nudge against mine as I deepen the kiss.

Suddenly I'm back to being seventeen when a make-out session was the most I could hope for, taking pleasure with my mouth and trying to give as much as I could with my hands.

I pull Morena closer, running my palms down her back, cool from the air conditioning. Her scent surrounds me, her skin so smooth under my hands. When she pushes her hips against me again, I reach for her ass, firm and tight under the briefest of lace panties.

I feel like I'm seventeen, but I know I'm with Morena because this is so much better than being a simple horny teenager. I'm a horny man, with an experienced woman in my arms, who can give as much as I can.

Still holding her, I back up to the edge of the bed and fall onto it. Morena fits between my legs, my neck barely straining to keep kissing her.

I don't want to stop kissing her.

But as my hands find her breasts, full and ripe with cherry-like nipples teasing me, I want those too. Kissing my way down her neck, her chest, I lick at each one before setting my lips around the bud.

Morena sighs.

Her breasts are works of art. I'm used to Claire's smaller size, and even Jasmine's fullness can't compare to Morena's. I want to live between her breasts. Die here...

Consumed with my feast, I don't notice that Morena has straddled one of my legs until I feel her rub herself against it.

She needs more.

Lifting my head, the room is a blur as I sit back on the bed. Morena straddles my lap. As my lips find hers again, she starts to grind against my cock, still trapped inside my pants.

I groan into her mouth, the friction making my head spin more than any spirit.

My hands tight on her ass, I help her thrust against me, faster and harder, kissing me with an urgent mouth. I let her take her pleasure, not wanting to stop her, praying I can hold out until she stiffens with a low moan.

As soon as she relaxes against me, I stand up, holding her ass in my hands, and throw her on the bed. Before I join her, I yank off her panties, the scrap of lace flying over my shoulder. My hand between her legs, my mouth back on her breasts, she comes again with a louder cry.

And then I'm inside her, thrusting urgently, as her feet scramble to find the edge of the bed. Again and again, thinking only of myself. Driving hard inside her, hearing her cries, her hands reaching for me, urging me on until I come with a low growl.

When I open my eyes, Morena is smiling. "You just made sure I'll never forget you," she promises.

CHAPTER ELEVEN

Claire

B ASIL AND I ARE the last to leave, not wanting to walk back to my room with Jed and Jasmine.

She looks like a deer caught in the headlights as Jed leads her away from the table.

"You still okay with this?" I ask as Basil finishes the last of his drink with a quick swallow.

"Hell, yeah."

We don't say anything else until we're back in my room. The only sign of my nerves is how I fumble with the key card.

This is Basil. I should be more excited than nervous.

I am excited.

When the door shuts behind him, Basil grabs me around the waist. For a moment, I think he's about to tug me back against the door.

"Oh no," I mutter, wriggling out of his arms. I lead him over to the bed instead, as far away as yesterday's afternoon delight as possible.

I don't need Carson's advice to know that for me, I need to keep Basil and Billy completely separate.

Which means doing things I don't normally do.

At the end of the bed, I tug at Basil's polo shirt. A quick pull and he's bare-chested before me.

"Wow," I murmur. Trailing my hands through the soft curls covering his chest, down along his impossibly tight abs—"You've got one of those V things," I marvel, running my hands along the tight muscles of his lower abdomen before popping the button on his pants.

"You like?"

"I like." I cup his cock through his pants, already hard, before I pull pants and underwear off in one swoop, leaving Basil standing in a puddle of fabric.

"Don't waste any time, do you?"

My answer is to push him onto the bed. Basil props himself on his elbows and looks at me with a bemused smile. His dark eyes are heavy from the drinks tonight, but there's also lust and desire. The sight encourages me, readies me.

That, and the sight of his cock resting against his leg, hard and waiting for me.

Taking the condom out of my purse, I toss it onto his stomach and pull off my panties. Basil struggles with the foil wrapper, so I straddle his legs to help and take it from him.

"I've had a lot to drink tonight," Basil tells me, watching as I roll the condom on his cock like I do it every day.

"Oh, I know." I wrap my hand around his cock and squeeze. Basil can't compare with Billy in the cock department, but there's more than just size. There are positions and moves...I slide my hand along it, rubbing myself against him.

"Jas always says I last too long when I'm drinking."

Holding him upright, I slowly lower myself onto Basil's cock. "I don't think there's a too long in sex."

"Jas says—" His words cut off when I begin to rock my hips.

"I'm not Jasmine."

"No." The word comes out in a huff as I raise and lower myself. "You're Claire. I like being with Claire."

"I like being with Basil."

"Can I ask a question first?" At my nod, he tugs at the skirt of my dress. "Can you take this off? I want to see you ride me."

And I do ride him.

Once I pull my dress off, Basil's hands are everywhere—circling my waist, guiding my hips, pulling me back down onto him when I raise up enough so only the tip is inside me. He spends long moments on my breasts, caressing, kissing, and not for one minute do I think he wants them to be bigger.

My breasts are tiny but never before have my nipples been so sensitive as I lean over Basil so he can reach with his mouth.

All this is while I'm riding him. Setting my own pace, taking him as deep and as hard as I want. Bracing my hands flat against his strong chest, I let my hips take over, finding the rhythm that's right for me. Billy has jokingly called me demanding before, but never has it been like this. I use Basil for my own pleasure and I think he likes it.

The sounds from Basil are definitely no complaints.

"Jesus, Claire," Basil groans as I adjust my hip movement. "Thank God I drank all that tequila because I can go all night like this. I don't want to come for a long time."

I squeeze my muscles and he groans again. "Oh, I'll make sure you come when I'm ready."

"Not before you." Reaching down, he easily finds my clit. Even the quick rub sends me arching, a gasp escaping from my open mouth. "Not so much the machine now, are you?" He smirks, his fingers knowing what to do to bring me closer to the edge.

As he rubs, I struggle to keep my rhythm, distracted by the new sensations. There's nothing like coming from straight fucking, but there's also nothing like having your clit rubbed just the right way.

"I want to hear you," Basil says. Something has shifted; it's like I've lost control. I'm no longer taking, using. "Tell me what you want."

"I want to *fuck* you," I gasp, pressing against his hand. "But I don't want that to stop."

"I'm not stopping anything. I'm just getting started." Suddenly Basil thrusts up and his cock finds that magical, mystical spot inside me. He does it again, and I cry out.

"There she goes," he murmurs with a smile. It takes four more thrusts and frantic fingers for me to fall apart above him.

My legs are still trembling as he manhandles me, flipping me onto my stomach. "Now, I'm going to fuck you," he says, pulling up my hips to slam into me.

I lean my head on the mattress, my whole body jerking from the force of Basil's thrusts.

"I want to hear you come again," Basil instructs. He goes deep, as deep as he can, and hard enough that the sound of his legs slapping against mine fills the room.

This time I reach between my legs. "Just like that," I moan, finding my clit with my fingers. It's sensitive to the touch, but still ready for more.

This time, Basil is the one who takes, and I let him. He fucks me fast and hard, his fingers kneading my ass, taking what he wants.

But he's not alone. My fingers, trained for years in the art of self-pleasure, helps me reach for the release. This...this mindless fucking is good...so good, but I need more.

I give myself what I need, and just as Basil's thrusts become even more frantic, I tense, feeling the climax like the weight of a freight train bearing down on me.

"Don't stop," I beg. "Please...no...yes...oh...*yes!*" My back arches as I come hard for the second time, feeling like my body is collapsing into itself as Basil keeps thrusting.

And then he suddenly pulls out, like I've asked him to stop. "What...? Wait, no."

Instead, he eases me onto my back and slides into me again.

My body, my mind is muddled from the force of the orgasm and it takes a moment to realize his thrusts are slower, deliberate; completely different.

"What is this?" I stare up at him, my arms instinctively stroking his muscular back, gripping his ass, so tight from the running.

A lock of hair drops into his eyes, and he sweeps it away without breaking his rhythm. "You fucked me, I fucked you...I want different now," he says, his breathing laboured and hoarse.

"I like…different." It's like he's a different man. No longer urgent and frantic, Basil is still forceful, but there's a gentleness to him now. He's giving, rather than taking.

He's giving himself.

"Me too." I reach up and claim his mouth in a kiss—our first kiss. It had been something I hadn't wanted to do, to bring such intimacy into the situation, but somehow it seems right.

Basil groans as my mouth finds his, my tongue sweeping into his mouth, as eagerly as I gave myself to him. His hands pull me closer, his thrusts deepening. The kiss swallows our gasps, our cries of pleasure as Basil suddenly stiffens above me.

I run my hands down his back as he comes inside of me.

Billy

THE NEXT MORNING, I see that Claire is still asleep, lying naked beside me with only a sheet thrown across her ass. I take my time waking up, enjoying the sight of the smooth skin of her back, feeling my cock shift and shiver as he slowly wakes up as well.

She was asleep when I got back to the room last night, alone in the bed with no sign of Basil.

I'm not sure what I think about Basil being here with her last night, so I push it from my mind. I find that's the best way to deal with it. My wife had sex last night, and not with me.

This morning is another story, however.

I can't help but wonder. Last night was the third time she'd been with Basil. That's...I wish I could say that's more sex she'd had before our marriage, but it's not. But that's a lot.

I smooth my hand down her back, noticing the smoothness of her skin, the different tan lines from her bathing suits. Why haven't I ever noticed how nice her back is? Like most men, I've always been more concerned with the front.

Morena's front is very nice, as is Jasmine's.

I am not thinking about Jasmine this morning. Or Morena. I have a naked wife in bed with me and that's who I'm going to focus on.

Claire shifts under my touch and rolls over, still asleep. My hand ends up on her stomach, just above her belly button.

Also, a nice place to be.

Her eyes flutter open and she focuses on me, giving me a sleepy smile. "Good morning," I say.

"Hey."

"Are you still mad at me?"

Claire blinks and opens her eyes wide like she's forcing herself to wake up. "I was mad at you?"

"Well, you weren't that happy with yesterday."

She smiles as her eyes drift closed. "Ah. You and Jasmine doing the nasty."

"It wasn't all that nasty."

"Do I need to know that?"

Leaning over, I drop a gentle kiss on her belly, before blowing a loud raspberry. Claire shrieks and rolls away. I pull her back.

"Seriously," I say, resting my head on her stomach. "How much should we share about this?"

Claire runs her fingers through my hair. "How much do you want to know?"

"I'm not sure. That's the problem, isn't it? If I say I want to know everything, what happens if I can't handle it?"

"I think you can handle it."

"I think *you* can. After all, you've already been with Morena."

"Yes, I have." There's a tone of proud smugness in her voice. I kiss her belly again, nipping with my teeth. "I was surprised you were with her. I thought you'd want Jasmine to yourself."

I had thought about Jasmine last night—long and hard. But the problem with doing this with a small group is that one decision affects everyone. "I wasn't getting in the middle of her and her man. Jed seemed pretty set on her. Not that he wasn't impressed with you," I quickly add.

Claire chuckles. "I'm not jealous of Jasmine."

"I'm not suggesting you are."

"Jealousy has no part in this," she says, suddenly serious. "It's not going to work if we let jealousy take over. So whatever you're thinking about me and Basil, just get over it. Or ask. Don't sit and stew about it."

I raise my head and gaze at her in disbelief. "How did you know?"

"How long have we been married?"

Another kiss, my tongue dipping into her belly button to hear her laugh. "Not long enough."

"So, what's bothering you?" she asks.

How do I say it? How do I put my thoughts into words—about my wife and my best friend? "Three times," I say finally.

"Three times," she agrees.

"And it's...good?"

"I'm not sure how you want me to answer that." Her fingers return to playing with my hair, digging deep to massage my scalp. I close my eyes, enjoying the sensation. "Basil is very different than you in many ways. I'm not saying one is better because I'm not comparing. You're different, and that's all you need to know."

"You mean, that's all you're going to tell me. What if I need to know more? What if it...turns me on?" I drop my voice suggestively but Claire's only reaction is to laugh.

"You don't need me to tell you things to get turned on. At least, I hope not." I glance up at her wistful tone. "I hope I still turn you on."

"Always," I promise, sliding up to kiss my wife. "That will never, ever change." As I pull away, she grabs the back of my head, and I kiss her again, feeling her mouth open under mine.

My cock jolts into full wakefulness.

"We never kiss anymore," Claire says after we pull away.

I think of Morena in my arms last night, how I enjoyed the simple kissing part. "I'll kiss you anytime you want."

"Maybe that's something we can do after we brush our teeth," she says with a smile.

"We can do other things without brushing our teeth." And then I slide into her, spreading her legs with my knee, sinking into my wife.

CHAPTER TWELVE

Claire

THERE HAD BEEN A discussion last night about going snorkelling with Jed and Morena. It sounded fun, but I chalked it up to drunken talk, making a mental note to look into it later in the week.

But I'm surprised when we join Basil and Jasmine for a late breakfast, to find Jed and Morena there already, and Jed having already booked an excursion for us.

"We leave at eleven," Jed says with a cheerful grin. "Who's in?"

"Me," I say automatically, feeling loose from Billy's love-making. A dip in the ocean would be the perfect thing.

Jasmine looks chagrined. "I'm not great with boats," she admits. "I think I'll pass, spend some time with my book in the sun."

"I'll stay on land as well," Morena says. "If you'd like the company."

"Of course," Jasmine says. Was that interest in her eyes? She seemed intrigued about me and Morena last night. I wonder if that's something she'd like to try.

Out of all of us, Jasmine has surprised me the most. I can't believe how open and eager she's become. It's like a part of her decided to wake up and join the party.

"What about Matt and Emmy?" Billy asks, pulling my attention away from Jasmine. "We're here with another couple as well."

"They go to bed a lot," Basil complains with mock seriousness. "Miss all the fun."

"Well, maybe we can help them make up for what they missed," Morena says lightly, but there's no doubt in what she's referring to.

"I don't think they'd be interested," Jasmine says flatly.

Matt and Emmy are interested in the snorkelling trip, however, and happily join us onboard the boat later.

"It's so beautiful," Emmy says, standing beside me on the deck. She shades her eyes to gaze out onto the crystal blue water of the Caribbean.

"Is this your first time in Mexico?" I ask.

"I'm a single mom with twin boys," Emmy says with a smile. "I've only ever been to DisneyWorld. We're due to go back next year. One of the boys is a Star Wars freak."

The more time I spend with Emmy, the more I like her. She's different than Shawna in so many ways. And once I get her on her own, away from the boys, cocooned in their boisterous tangle of maleness, the awkwardness Billy brings out in her vanishes.

I don't mind spending the afternoon with Billy, Basil, and Jed; throughout the years at Aurora, it's always been me who does things with them; Jasmine and Shawna preferring the less strenuous activities, like reading and lounging. Emmy seems more like me. Already, we've talked about trying the free scuba diving lessons in the pool and taking the kayaks out.

Unlike me, she's obviously trying to keep her distance from Billy. As we suit up for snorkelling, Emmy sticks tight to Matt, almost like she's nervous about the water, which I know for a fact she's not. Billy barely says two words to her, which is very unlike him.

I'm not sure how Matt doesn't see that there's something going on between the two of them.

"Emmy," I begin in a low voice, my hands gripping the railing as the boat sets anchor. "Billy told me about...well, about you. Before."

She looks at me with a frightened expression. "I haven't said anything to Matt," she whispers.

"I won't say anything," I assure her. "But...why not? You and Billy were kids. I don't know what it was like for you, but Billy—whatever." I stop myself from saying too much. I'm sure Billy doesn't want me to spill his innermost thoughts that he confessed to me one drunken night, especially if they're vastly different than the feelings Emmy had for him.

"I don't want him to get upset," Emmy says.

"Who? Matt or Billy? Because both of them are two of the most laid-back, easy-going guys around. I can't see anyone getting upset about a teenage fling."

"It wasn't a fling." Emmy stares out to the water. "I don't know what it was like for Billy, but he was...he was everything to me."

To hear her say it like that is like a sharp thrust into my heart. Billy is my everything and to hear another woman say it...it hurts. Plain and simple.

But I push it aside. "Ok...but why didn't you tell Matt when you got here? It's just making it more awkward the longer you wait. Billy doesn't know what to say to you and he's been friends with Matt for a long time."

"I don't know," Emmy says, lifting her shoulders. "Well, I do, but I can't..." She trails off, leaving me staring at her, waiting for her to finish. "My ex-husband was horrible," she finally says in a flat voice. "He never trusted me, always got upset when he thought I was lying. It took me years to get away from him, years to get over what he did to me."

"And you think Matt is going to react like him." I take a deep breath, sympathy running through me. "Let me tell you one thing. I've known Matt for a long time too, and he's nothing like that. Nothing at all. He might get upset that you didn't tell him right away, but it'll be nothing like what you experienced."

"How do you know that?" she whispers.

"I just do. Trust me."

We spend an amazing hour snorkelling; cutting through the clear water to see turtles, which are surprisingly fast, and fish that dodge and weave through the coral. It's so peaceful under the water and I'm able to clear my mind from everything that's going on.

I don't think about sex once; at least not until we've been called back to the boat.

Billy and Basil are a little ahead of me, leaving me and Jed together on our way back. Suddenly, Jed grabs my hand, pointing to my right where a huge turtle has just pushed himself off of the bottom, leaving a cloud of sand behind him.

"So cool," I say, the words garbled with my mouthpiece. But Jed seems to understand, giving me a smile and a thumbs up. And then he looks at our hands, still clasped together.

And then he looks at me—or rather my body—as I drift lazily beside him, held up by the life jacket. It's just a moment, and it's difficult to see his expression, but there's no denying the jolt of electricity that zips through me. I like to think I know what he's thinking because I'm thinking it too.

Maybe it's time to take a break from Basil.

Jed holds my hand all the way back to the boat, swimming along beside me, often looking over with a smile.

At least it looks like he's smiling.

I like to think he's looking at my ass as I haul myself up the rope ladder.

Matt and Emmy are cuddled up by the railing as we head back to the resort. I stand with the boys, basking in their interest.

"This has been great," Basil says with a happy sigh. "But I hope Jasmine's had a good day."

Jed gives a low laugh. "It's been a good day if Morena's had anything to do with it."

Billy

I CAN'T HELP IT—MY mind slides all the way to dirty thoughts at the mention of Jasmine and Morena. Of them in the water like Claire said, or lounging by the pool, the sun warming their skin, or maybe in Morena's room, the air cooled by the air conditioner...

"I think Jasmine was going to spend the afternoon reading," Basil says.

Claire and Jed look at each other and laugh.

"What?" Basil asks.

"Nothing," Claire says with a grin. "I'm sure she'll have a great time."

I tune out Basil's continual *what*s and Claire's laughter and lean against the railing. The sun is warm on my back and easily makes me forget about the three days I spent in the conference room.

Finally, this is my vacation. Lots of sun, sex; a goodly amount of *cervezas*, and drinking them with friends.

Speaking of which, Jed arrives with his hands full of bottles and hands them out. "I talked to the captain," he says, clinking his bottle against mine. "Made a little arrangement with him."

"Perfect end to a good day," Basil says. "Did you see that huge turtle?" He and Claire talk about the sea life they saw, while Jed leans on the railing with me.

"So Morena and Jasmine?" I ask, trying for casual.

Jed shrugs. "I wouldn't put it past her. Morena is...something else."

"Yeah," I agree. "You been married long?"

"Oh, she won't marry me," Jed says cheerfully. "I've lost track of how many times I've asked her. I love her like crazy. It's really the only problem we have."

"So her...and you...with others...that's not a problem?"

Jed shakes his head. "Nope. Morena's been...*with others*..." He grins. "For longer than I've been alive. Maybe not that long."

"How old *is* she?"

"I'm not asking and she's not telling."

"Fair enough. She's cool."

"She's amazing," Jed corrects. "You guys have got to come to her place in Nova Scotia."

"That's the resort for swingers?"

"She's got a pretty good set-up there. People come from all over to visit, and enjoy the perks."

"And you're okay with it?"

"Sure. I mean, it's nothing new for me. The girl I was with before I met Morena was big on polyamory."

"Really? This is a big thing?"

"For a lot of people, but not for everyone. It can be tough, but me and Morena can handle it. She told me that you guys, that this is a new thing for you?"

"Pretty new," Billy admits.

"It's fun. Never a dull moment."

"I can see that."

"You and Claire..." Jed swallows a mouthful of his beer. "You ever think of bringing someone else in?"

"Well, we kind of brought other people into things..." I'm not sure what Jed is getting at.

"I mean a threeway."

At least I don't have to wait long for him to explain.

"Ah...not really. Hadn't really given it much thought."

"Maybe you should."

"Ah...do you mean with Morena?"

"No. I meant with me."

The boat pitches over a wave, knocking me off balance. Or maybe it was because of what Jed said. "Oh."

"Think about it. Talk it over with Claire. It'll be fun."

"Claire...I don't know about that."

"You don't think she'd go for it?"

"No, it's not her. It's...I don't know if I could...you know, watch her with someone else. It's okay knowing her and Basil, but, you know, I don't want to *see* it. At least not with another guy. A woman..." I give a rueful shrug.

"I get you," Jed says easily. There's a pause as we finish our beers. "What about Jasmine?"

CHAPTER THIRTEEN

Claire

WHEN THE BOAT RETURNS to the resort, we find Jasmine at the pool where we left her, with no sign of Morena. Jed waves goodbye and says something about seeing us after dinner.

"Have a good day?" I ask, dropping to the lounge chair beside Jasmine.

"Jas, you should have come!" Matt towers over Jasmine, his shadow leaving her in the shade. "Turtles and fish and Emmy says she saw a stingray but I think it was a shadow."

"It was a stingray," Emmy says firmly.

"It was also a big boat, which I've never done well with," Jasmine says. "You remember that time we went out on Vic Solley's dad's boat and I threw up over the edge? I wasn't looking forward to a repeat performance."

Matt gives a wave. "That's different. It doesn't matter what you did in high school."

Claire shot a glance at Emmy. That was the perfect opportunity to tell Matt. *Hey, guess what I did in high school?*

"Matt, I think I'm going back to the room to change," Emmy says instead.

"I'll walk back with you," Billy says quickly.

"Good idea," Matt says, clapping him on the shoulder. "Let's stop at that bar for more of those blue drinks we had the other day."

Matt really has no idea what's going on.

"You coming, Claire?" I hear the tightness in Billy's voice. I know he's been trying to talk to Emmy. Hopefully, our talk on the boat will help her come clean to Matt.

Not that there's anything to come clean about. Like Matt said, it doesn't matter what you did in high school.

"In a sec," I say. "I want to ask Jas about all the cute guys she saw today without you guys trying to butt in."

"Then I'll go change too." Basil leans over to drop a kiss on Jasmine's head. "I think I smell of turtles."

"What do turtles smell like?" I ask and Basil sticks his arm under my nose. "You're a bit salty but no worse than usual."

"Are you saying I smell?" Basil slaps a hand on his chest, pretending to be offended.

"No worse than usual."

That's when he threatens to throw me in the pool.

I'm still laughing as the four of them head back to the rooms. "You seem like you had fun," Jasmine says.

I ignore the vulnerable tone. "Yeah, it was great. But I spent more time with Emmy than anyone else, which I will tell you about in a minute. But first." I lean closer. "What happened with you and Morena?"

Jasmine pulls back with surprise. "What makes you think something happened?"

"Oh, just something Jed said. So?" I raise an eyebrow and watch Jasmine start to squirm. "You did say you wondered what it would be like with a woman."

"Oh, my God, Claire!" Jasmine gives a whispered shout and swings her legs around on the lounge chair. "It was—"

"I know, right." If we were men, we would be high-fiving right now, but because it's Jasmine, I give her knee a squeeze instead. "Did she rock your world?"

"She rocked something, that's for sure." She gives me an embarrassed smile.

"I want all the details," I say, then think better of it. "Actually, no. I have an imagination and you, know, *I've been there first.*" I say this last part in a gleeful whisper.

"Yeah, yeah," she says with a smug smile. "But I've had Jed."

I start to laugh then, a snort of disbelief than leads to a big belly laugh. It's contagious because soon Jasmine has joined in and I don't think either of us really knows what we're laughing at.

"What are we doing?" I wipe the tears from my eyes.

"We're laughing about something."

"I know but, this—" I gesture to her, the chairs around us. "Did you ever imagine we'd be sitting here talking about other people like this? About *having sex* with them?"

"No." Jasmine instantly sobers. "Never. Never ever, ever...never. I'm still not sure—"

"You're not backing out, are you?"

A quick shake of her head sends her ponytail flying. "No."

"Me neither."

"Did...was there talk on the boat? What'd I miss?"

"I'm not sure. Billy and Jed were talking on the way back, but nothing much was said because of Matt and Emmy." I look at her closely. "Do you want to say something to them?"

"No." Her reply is as quick and firm as her previous refusal.

"Why? Emmy seems really cool." It's on the tip of my tongue to tell her about Emmy and Billy, but I stop myself just in time. It's not my secret to tell.

Jasmine stares at the blue water of the pool, at an older man cutting through the water with smooth strokes. "I don't know," she says finally. "But I can't see it happening. I don't want him to see that side of me." She stands up and begins collecting her book and sunscreen, throwing them into her bag. "I'm going back to the room to get changed."

"Ok." It's all I can say. Jasmine has changed from this, and I think it's for the better. I'm not sure if it's the added attention from Billy and Jed, or the fact that Shawna isn't here, but she's got a new confidence. She's come out of her shell.

I don't want to tell her that Matt is sure to notice this new side of her.

Billy

It's Matt who invites Jed and Morena to dinner with us. We have reservations at the Japanese steakhouse, and when Claire and I got to the restaurant, we found them waiting for us to be seated. Jed is beside Jasmine, sitting with an arm around the back of her chair. Her cheeks are pink from laughing, her smile wide and bright.

It makes me kiss her, hello, and then I have to kiss Morena, which isn't a hardship at all. She smells of fruit and flowers, wearing a different red dress.

Morena looks good in red. Here in Mexico, most women wear flowered dresses, bright colours, and a lot of white. Morena stands out in red.

I think she'd stand out in any colour.

"How was your little boat trip?" she asks, her hand lingering on my arm. I think of the other places that hand touched last night.

"There was nothing little about it. It was a very big boat," I say.

"I'm sure it was. Very big." Her dark eyes are full of laughter.

"Very big," I add firmly.

Beside us, Basil shakes his head. "I don't think you're talking about the boat, but I don't want to know."

Morena gives me an approving smile and my ego, among other things, swells. "We're waiting for the lovely Emmy and Matt, and then they'll seat us."

"Matt's not lovely?" I ask.

"Well...I wouldn't know." Morena has the sexiest smile, and the ability to turn everything into an innuendo. "And I've heard that they won't be joining us for our after-party tonight."

"They're not?" Disappointment hits me. During the afternoon on the boat, it was on the tip of my tongue to mention our new arrangement, but something stopped me. I thought it would be better coming from someone else, Jasmine maybe. Or Jed could have said something, like he asked me to have a threesome with Jasmine.

I still can't believe he came right out and said that. The fact that it shocked me makes me feel I still have a long way to go to get comfortable with this lifestyle.

But all afternoon I'd been full of anticipation, sure that tonight Matt and Emmy would join us and things might happen. I don't know what might happen, but something would.

It's the reason I didn't give Jed an answer. It's like I'm saving myself for Emmy.

"They're not," Basil confirms. "Jasmine doesn't think Matt would go for it. She doesn't want to put a wedge in the friendship. She thinks it would be awkward."

"And what do you think?" I can't help but ask.

"I think it would be fine, but she knows him best," he says, like the dutiful husband he is. "And we really don't know Emmy."

I do. Or, I did. Honestly, I don't know what Emmy's reaction would be. I don't know her anymore, and all I want to do is talk to her. Find out what this Emmy is like to find out what I missed out on.

Claire finishes flirting with Jed and moves to Morena. They kiss hello as well, and every man in the restaurant lobby stares.

No, I didn't miss out on anything. Claire is everything and she makes me very happy. Firmly, very firmly, I push away the tinge of regret.

I shove it away.

"Well, if they don't know, I'm not going to be the one to let the cat out of the bag," Morena says. "I'll behave myself."

Basil looks at her standing arm and arm with Claire and I can see the naked desire in his gaze, probably because I have the same look in my eyes. "Don't behave too much," he says in a low voice.

"I'll save it for later." She winks.

"Hey, sorry we're late," Matt calls out and Claire steps away from Morena.

We're shown to our table, and there's an awkward shuffle to see who will sit beside who at the horseshoe-shaped table.

Matt and Emmy end up on one end, Jed and Jasmine on the other. Morena and Basil flank Claire, who doesn't seem disappointed in the seating arrangements.

Or the fact that it seems to make a clear divide in the arrangement for tonight. For the after-party, as Morena called it.

If Matt and Emmy won't be joining us...I catch Emmy's eye and force a smile. Another night where I won't have a chance to talk to her.

And then I feel the nudge of a knee against my leg and look down to see Jasmine nestled beside me.

I don't think there'll be much talking tonight.

CHAPTER FOURTEEN

Claire

I T'S THE BEST NIGHT we've had so far.

The steakhouse is amazing, with the chef slicing and dicing right in front of us. He's so adorable with his white cap hiding dark curly hair that I spend as much time watching his dark eyes as his incredible knife prowess. I know I'm not the only one who notices since Morena is also full of smiles for him.

Morena touches me a lot.

Not that I'm complaining; every stroke of her finger or touch of her hand, as simple and friendly as it can be construed, has the effect of sticking my hand closer to the fire.

It makes me hot. Super sensitive.

It turns me on.

After dinner, when we're thanking Miguel, the sexy chef for the food and the entertainment, Morena turns to me. "We'll keep this going for a bit longer?"

Her hand drops to my leg, and in a quick move, runs a finger under the hem of my dress.

And then Basil's hand is on my other leg. "Okay."

Is he asking or telling? "Okay."

Like Basil, I don't know exactly what I'm agreeing to, but the dull throb between my legs isn't going to give me a chance to turn anything down.

"Let's go dance!" Matt cries as we file out of the restaurant and I hide my grimace. Right now I want nothing more than to have my own little dance party with just Basil and Morena.

But we go to one of the discos and order another round of drinks.

There's a different atmosphere tonight. Maybe it's the addition of Morena and Jed; maybe it's how we all know how this night is going to turn out. But Matt has to be an idiot not to realize there's something more going on, and he's not a part of it.

Jed pulls me onto the dance floor, and there's more bumping and grinding than outright dancing. Then Jasmine has a turn, leaving us staring at her sexy moves.

"What's going on with Jas?" Matt demands, his expression one of shocked admiration at her moves. Jed is right there with her.

"She likes to dance," Basil says with a shrug of his shoulders. "And Jed's a lot better than I am."

"I don't know about that," I whisper in his ear.

"Look at her," Matt exclaims. "She practically making out with him."

"What happens in Mexico, stays in Mexico," I say.

"Well, let's go join them," Morena announces. Giving Emmy no time to protest, she grabs her hand, motioning for Billy to follow.

"I need a drink," Matt mutters, sliding out of the booth to head to the bar, leaving Basil and I alone for the first time that night.

"Maybe he doesn't know what's going on," I say with a laugh. "But how can he not?"

"I have no idea," Basil agrees. "But maybe Jas is right; maybe he wouldn't go for it."

"He might think it's too close to cheating. He got burned with that with Shawna."

"I never thought of that," Basil muses. "That must be why Jasmine doesn't want to tell him."

"Maybe. But it's a bit of a pain to hide it."

He turns his shoulder to his wife on the dance floor, now joined by the others. "What are you hiding?"

"Well, we are alone in a dark corner, all by ourselves."

"That's usually what alone means." Basil moves closer, his fingers caressing my arm on the table. "Would you like me to put my hand up your skirt like Morena did at dinner?"

"I'd like you to put something else up my skirt," I tease and Basil laughs.

"It looks like it's going to be me and you again tonight," Basil says, his laughter fading.

"And Morena. I think she has every intention of joining us."

"Are you all right with that?"

"I am." I hold his gaze, trying to let Basil see how the thought of being with both of them is exciting to me.

"I mean, are you all right with me again? Wouldn't you rather Jed...?"

"Would you?"

"He's not really my type."

It's a pathetic attempt at a joke. "Be serious, Bas. We have to be honest here. If you would rather be with just Morena for the night—" The thought of them together, of Basil with anyone other than me, bothers me more than I want to admit.

"She scares me," he admits with a rueful smile. "Sexy as hell, but me with her?"

"I don't scare you?"

"You terrify me." Basil puts his hand over mine. "But I can't seem to get enough of you."

"Well, then, it's good that I can't seem to get enough of you. I'd rather you tonight than Jed."

Or Billy. The thought is too disloyal to dwell on and I push it away.

"Are you sure?"

His uncertainty warms me. "Basil." Glancing over his shoulder, I see Matt has been swallowed up by the crowd at the bar. And the dance floor is so packed that I can only see the back of Billy's head.

Basil and I are to all extents, alone.

I touch his face, my hand cupping his cheek and the day-old stubble that appeared this morning. I like him with a bit of a beard.

I like him.

"I want more of you," I whisper, leaning closer so that my lips are a breath away from his. "I want all of you."

Basil kisses me, taking my mouth with a surge of hunger that takes my breath away. A noise escapes me, part moan, part whimper as his hand skates up my thigh, landing right where the heat between my legs seems to be pulsing.

My hands are on him, reaching, searching, wanting, and the only thought in my head is Basil.

I want him. Now.

But slowly, I'm aware of someone tapping my arm. Pulling away, the realization that Basil and I are making out in the corner of a bar where anyone can see hits me like a bucket of cold water.

"Oh, God," I gasp, jumping away from Basil, who looks as stunned as I am.

"No, just me." Morena towers over me, her hand on my arm and a knowing smile on her face. "But I suggest you two shelve it for a bit in case you want your friends to notice."

"Matt." Wildly, I look around to see him still at the bar. Only a moment had passed, but it seems so much longer.

It seems like Basil was kissing me for hours.

I want him to kiss me for hours.

"No one noticed," Morena assures me. "But seeing you here like that—goodness. It makes me very excited about later. Are we in agreement that the three of us...?" Her gaze studies me and then Basil.

"Yes," he says in a strangled voice.

"Great. Why don't you come and dance with me?"

I can't think of anything but Basil's mouth on mine as I follow Morena onto the dance floor.

Billy

I SEE CLAIRE KISSING Basil.

The sight of it jolts me enough that I stop dancing which prompts Morena to look over to see what had caught my attention. With a wink, she disappears back to the table.

I'm not sure what she said, but when Basil and Claire join us, they stand at either side of the cramped circle we've created. I catch Claire's eye and smile, trying to let her know that everything is okay because from the expression on her face, she's a little shaken.

From kissing Basil?

Matt finally returns, his hands full of drinks. "We lost our table," he says ruefully as he hands me a glass.

"I'm not sure how much longer I want to stay," Emmy says loudly. "It's really crowded in here."

"Drink up and we'll go then," he says, handing her a glass. But Emmy shakes her head and hands it to Jasmine, who takes a mouthful.

Matt brushes his shoulder with mine. "She's drinking a lot," he says, his eyes on Jasmine.

"She's having fun."

"I'm not used to seeing her like this," he admits.

I'm looking forward to seeing a side of her later—the naked side. But of course I can't say that to Matt. Maybe Jasmine is right. Maybe he wouldn't be able to handle it.

"She's having a great time," I say firmly, not wanting Matt to ruin our mood. "Stop acting like a jealous husband."

"I'm not her husband."

"You're not her boyfriend either, and that's what you're acting like."

Matt shrugs, with a frown on his face. I glance at Emmy, to see her watching us. Suddenly she moves over to my other side.

"Did you tell him?" she hisses.

"Of course not. But I wish you would. I don't like lying to my friend."

A man—stumbling drunk, from the looks of it—suddenly slams into Emmy from behind, almost knocking her off her feet. I grab her just before she falls, tucking my arm firmly around her waist.

"Hey, watch out!" Matt cries, turning to the man with anger so quickly it surprises me. "You almost knocked over my girlfriend."

"Sso verra' sorry," the man sings over his shoulder and resumes his wild dancing.

"No, you need to apologize," Matt demands, his face contorted with rage.

"He did apologize, bro." I clap a hand on his shoulder. "It's cool. Emily's all good."

"It's not enough," he insists, turning back to the man.

I've never seen Matt like this before. Usually, he's so laid back but now he seems almost ready to throw himself into a fight.

"Stop it, Matt." Emmy stands before him, her face drawn. With anger, I wonder.

Then I see the look in her eyes. No, fear.

Is she afraid of Matt?

"I'm defending you," Matt says. "Don't get mad at me for the guy being a jerk."

"I don't need you to defend me," Emmy cries. Then without a word, she pushes out of the circle. Throwing a backward glance at Matt, I'm right behind her.

"What was that about?" I ask as I catch up with her by the door.

"I need some air." She shoulders open the door, taking deep gulps.

I catch her by the arm and lead her to the corner of the building, away from the busy doorway. "Emily, what happened?"

"He was so upset," she whispers.

"At the guy who knocked you over, not you," I assure her. "I've never seen him like that."

"Can you see why I can't tell him?" she pleads.

"But I've never seen him react like that before. Have you? What's going on between the two of you?"

Emmy draws a shaky breath. "He's never been like that," she says. "He's always so sweet and even-tempered. It just threw me."

"Guys sometimes feel the need to defend their girlfriend's honour. Do you remember that party we went to when Tim Cole spilled his beer all over you?"

Another shaky breath, and then the hint of a smile. "I thought you were going to hit him."

"I almost did. So I get Matt's reaction. But...I don't get yours."

Emmy takes a step away from me and leans against a planter filled with flowers. Away from the club, I can hear the low hum of bees still busy gathering.

"My ex-husband," she admits. "He got mad a lot."

"Did he hit you?"

"I got out," she says, which isn't a denial. "I got the boys away from him before he could hurt them."

"Did he hurt you?"

"I don't like fighting," she admits in a low voice. "Or raised voices. Or conflict in general."

"Does Matt know all this?"

"I've told him things weren't good with my ex. Not everything. Not..." she trails off, glancing down at her hands.

"Which is why you're not going to say anything else to me." I run a hand through my hair. "Matt's a good guy, Emmy. You need to open to him if you want this to work. Shawna wasn't a treat either. I think the two of you can really help each other."

"I've been on my own for a long time." Her face sets in a stubborn scowl. "I don't need help."

"Everyone needs help. And you should always be honest with him."

I want to say more but Matt rushes out the door of the club. "Emmy!" he cries. "What happened? What did I do?"

Emmy looks at me. "I don't like fighting," she says, letting him draw her into a hug. "I don't like to see you angry. It...scares me."

"I scared you?" He takes her arms gently. "That's the last thing I want to do."

"I know. It's just..." She looks at me now and suddenly I feel as unneeded as a third shoe.

"You guys need some time alone." Backing away is tough, but I do it. "I'll leave you be, go back inside."

"The others are coming," Matt says, still staring at Emmy with concern. "Let's go for a walk," he adds. "We can talk. You can tell me what I did."

"It's not what you did," she protests. "It's just..."

"Let's go sit on the beach," Matt suggests, taking her hand. He nods his chin at me. "See you tomorrow."

"Goodnight." Emmy lets herself be led away without a backwards glance at me.

I stand watching them disappear into the darkness until the door opens and Jasmine tumbles out with Jed.

"Did they go to bed?" Jasmine asks, still pink-cheeked at happy. "I thought they'd never go!"

CHAPTER FIFTEEN

Claire

"LET'S TAKE A WALK along the beach," Morena suggests. I don't answer, too busy watching Billy walk off with Jed and Jasmine. It seemed only natural to split up after Matt and Emmy left, and I hope Jasmine can distract Billy. He seems upset as Emmy and Matt walk off.

I may like Emmy, but I don't like what she's doing to Billy or Matt.

"Sure," Basil says, taking my hand.

I glance down at our clasped hands. We've never held hands before. Last night was the first time we kissed. It almost seems like Basil and I are doing things backwards.

And then Morena takes my other hand. "Let's go."

The three of us hold hands until we reach the white sand of the beach, looking like drunken teenagers. If anyone saw us, would they think we're off for a rendezvous? And interlude?

To have sex?

I slip off my sandals, the sand cool between my toes. Basil takes them from me. "Go play," he says with a smile. "You're always the first to dip your toes in the lake at Aurora."

He's right. The half-moon reflects on the still water, the only movement the low waves breaking over the sand. For a moment it's no different than Lockwood Lake at Aurora, but then I remember we're in Mexico, which is very different than Eastern Ontario.

I'm a very different from the person I was there.

Morena follows as I skip toward the water. "Would you rather be alone with Basil tonight?" she asks in a low voice.

A glance back shows me Basil walking by the row of chaise lounges, hopefully out of earshot. "Why?"

"I've gotten a vibe from the two of you tonight. You seem very...together."

"We're not. We're married to other people."

"I didn't mean that," Morena says quickly. "Just that you two have a connection. It's obvious."

"He's the only other man I've been with," I blurt out. "I mean, not ever. Just since we've started this. Jasmine has..." I trail off, not wanting to give words to my flash of jealousy. Truly, I'm not jealous. Basil and I...Morena's right. There's something between us.

But right now I'm sure that's a good thing.

Morena takes my hand again, her thumb stroking the back of my hand. "I understand completely. But you know, some of my most exciting interludes are the ones where I have a connection with the person, rather than a random stranger. When I know them so well that it feels safe and so easy." She squeezes my hand. "But the sex is still really good."

I smile to myself, thinking of how good it was with Basil last night. The way he held me at the end, the way he kissed me. The way it felt like we were making love, rather than having sex.

I've heard books talk about the difference, but I've never realized it before now.

"Let's head over to one of those cabanas," Morena says with a note of girlish excitement in her voice.

"Are we allowed to?"

"I don't think so." Morena laughs. "That's why it'll be fun."

Feeling more carefree than ever, I let Morena tug me towards the small tent at the far end of the beach, smiling as Basil races us there. Inside, a bed takes up most of the space.

"That's it?" I scoff. "I thought there'd be more in here, like a fridge or a fireplace."

"Just the bed." Morena lays down, the skirt of her red dress sliding up to reveal a pair of tanned and toned legs. "For afternoon naps and midnight rendezvous." She smiles mischievously at us.

"Are you speaking from experience?" Basil immediately lies down beside her, reaching out a hand to brush a strand of hair off of Morena's face. She responds by pressing her lips against his.

It's a chaste kiss, over before I know it, but the sharp pain, like a punch in the stomach that I get from the sight, lingers.

What was that? Basil is married and not to me.

I stand at the end of the bed, watching as if hypnotized as Basil trails his fingers down Morena's bare shoulder, along the strap of her dress until his hand cups her breast.

"Have you ever been with two women?" Morena asks, allowing Basil to push the strap off her shoulder, freeing her full, rosy-tipped breast.

"Once," Basil says, tearing his attention off Morena to look at me.

"Ah. I'm disappointed I'm not the first."

"I was more of a spectator," Basil admits.

"So you like to watch?"

"I like...lots of things." Basil glances at me again. I can't read his expression—I'm not sure if he wants me to leave or to join them. With Carson, it was true that Basil was more of an observer than a participant, but does this mean he's ready to join in?

Am I?

"Why don't you join us?" Morena raises her arm to offer me her hand, which allows me to clearly see Basil's hand, now inside her dress. "Claire?" It's like she senses my hesitation.

But why am I hesitating? This is what I want. Morena excites me, and Basil...I'm not sure what Basil does, but it's definitely something.

Basil reaches out his hand. "Coming?"

If he hadn't taken his hand out of Morena's dress, I'm not sure I would have moved. "Not yet," I joke, kneeling at the end of the bed. "But hopefully soon."

Morena gives me a cat-like smile. "Oh, I think I can help with that." She shifts on the bed, allowing me to lie between them.

Basil bends to kiss me, his lips firm against mine. That's the problem right there—once I start kissing him, I don't want to stop. The crash of the waves and the hiss of the wind against the sides of the tent fade away as I lean into Basil's kiss.

He cups my face as his tongue sweeps into my mouth and suddenly I don't care that it's the same hand that cupped Morena's breast. I only want Basil to go on touching me.

But it's not Basil sliding fingers up my thigh, under my dress, nor is it Basil who pulls down my panties with eager hands. As he kisses me—becoming more urgent—it's Morena who pushes up my dress and crouches between my legs. It's Morena who tastes me with her tongue, her fingers demanding their share of me against my inner thigh.

Her fingers explore my wetness, her tongue skimming my slick folds and I moan against Basil's mouth.

He breaks off. "Whoa," he says as he watches Morena, her head buried between my legs, tasting and teasing. "That's so hot."

"You," I whisper, reaching for his lips. His mouth against mine, his hands on my breasts, dipping into the V-neck of my dress are quick and urgent while Morena takes her time with me. But just as quickly, my fingers begin the search for the zipper on Basil's pants at the same time I push Morena's head deeper, in a wordless plea for more.

She gives me more. Hot, wet—her mouth takes and takes, devouring me like she's woken up starving for a midnight snack.

Basil's mouth falls to my neck, kissing and biting his way to my breasts as my gasps become moans, my hips meeting the thrust of Morena's fingers. I cry out as the sensations wash over me like the tide over the sand, but she doesn't stop, only takes more.

And more.

Three times, I come; each more intense than the last, my cries reaching for the stars as I become no more than a writhing, moaning mess of arms and legs.

When Morena finally lifts her head, it takes a moment for me to realize Basil is behind her, thrusting, his hands on her hips. The added vibration that pushed me over the edge was Morena's moans as she came.

"Enough," Morena commands in a husky voice. "Finish with Claire."

"I can..." Basil begins to protest he pulls out.

Morena kneels on the bed, looking at me with an affectionate smile as I fight to catch my breath. "Together," she adds. "I've taken what I wanted, and now I'll leave the two of you alone."

"Wait," I say as she slips off the bed, straightening her dress as she stands in the sand.

"I'm sure we'll see each other tomorrow," she says. And then she's gone.

Basil watches her leave, jutting cock still hard and pants around his ankles. And then he's on me.

My arms wind around his shoulders as he slides inside me. "You're so hot when you come," he mutters, his lips against my neck.

"I thought there'd be more," I say with confusion.

"I'll give you more." He grins down at me.

As Basil thrusts with a rolling movement of his hips, I sigh with satisfaction. Morena was...my body still sings from her touch. But Basil...

I cry out as he goes deeper, his hands on my ass as he gives me more.

This is what I want.

Billy

"I THINK WE NEED to make some rules," Jed says. He still holds Jasmine's hand and swings it gently between them as we walk back to Jed's room.

"This is my vacation," she says with a giggle. "I don't want any rules."

Jed glances at me. "I think Billy might."

He's right. As eager as I am to get hold of Jasmine again, I'm at a loss when it comes to another guy joining us. It was one thing with Wyatt; I joined in at the last minute and he let me take the lead with Jasmine.

Sort of.

I got to fuck her, he got the blow job and there was no touching between us. I don't even think I looked him in the eye.

I think it might be different with Jed.

"What do you suggest?" I ask as we stop before his door. For a moment before he opens the door, I have a fear that Claire didn't go to our room, that I'm going to walk in some threeway scene with her and Morena and the lucky bastard Basil, and never be able to unsee it.

I know I'm lucky too. Jasmine is incredible and any new experience has the potential to be a good one.

But when Jed unlocks the door and ushers Jasmine inside, I'm happy to see an empty hotel room; the air cool and the bed perfectly made just like it was last night when I was there with Morena.

Jed sweeps Jasmine off her feet and tosses her onto the bed. The sound of her nervous giggle hardens my cock. "Have you ever been with two men?" he asks as he flops on the bed beside her.

Jasmine nods, her eyes shining with excitement. I hope its excitement and not from alcohol. "Once."

"And what happened that one time?" Jed motions me onto the bed and I sit awkwardly on the end.

"Billy fucked me and I had Wyatt in my mouth," Jasmine says with a gleeful smile at me.

"I don't think I've ever heard you say that word before," I marvel.

"I fuck, you fuck, you're both going to fuck me," she sings.

"And I don't think I've ever seen you drink this much."

Jasmine giggles again. "I'm actually not that drunk. I'm just really nervous...and surprisingly excited about this whole..." She trails off and waves her arm around the room. "Thing."

"I'm not surprised," Jed says. "Are you horny, baby?" His Austin Powers' impersonation is dead on and Jasmine and I laugh.

She hunches her shoulders. "I am," she whispers.

Jed rubs his hands. "So let's begin. There's a couple of ways this can go with the three of us and I want to make sure nothing goes where you don't want it to."

"You sound like you've done this before."

Jed nods. "Couple of times." But the way he says it makes me think it's more than that.

"I think I'm okay with that," Jasmine says slowly.

"Really?" My shock is evident and Jasmine shrugs in response.

"What about you?" Jed turns to me, and my balls tighten at the thought. "Any place you don't want to go?"

I don't think twice. "I like you fine, bro, but I don't think I can go there."

"Fair enough."

"Will you kiss?" I turn to see Jasmine with a question in her gaze. "I've never seen two men, and I don't even know if I want to, but I've heard two men kissing is really hot. And I'd like to see it," she finishes with a bold lift of her chin.

"Up to you," Jed says.

"If the lady wants to see..." It's just a kiss, I think as Jed shuffles across the bed on his knees. But as Jed reaches for me—giving me no chance to prepare—I'm quick to realize it's not just a kiss.

I had no idea what to expect from a guy kissing me, but it's not this.

Jed's lips are as soft as a woman's without the slickness of lip-gloss. And then way he holds the back of my head is firm, but not dominating. When he sweeps his tongue into my mouth...well, things happen. They shift and surge, and for the briefest of moments, I wonder if I spoke too soon.

Jed pulls away and both of us glance at Jasmine for approval.

She claps her hands with a big smile. "That was nice!"

"Nice wasn't exactly what I was going for." Jed frowns. "Did I rock your world?"

"World is definitely rocked," I say, trying for casual so as to not let on how much the kiss did get to me.

I think I'll keep that to myself.

"Well, if the lady is satisfied, then I've done what I've come to do." Jed moves to climb off the bed.

"Hey!" Jasmine protests. "I don't think so."

"Did I forget something?" Jed asks with a mischievous grin. He leaps onto Jasmine and she laughs. "Let's get you naked."

This is a whole new side of Jasmine, and I have to admit, it's a huge turn-on.

Sex has always been good with Claire but rarely is it fun. Even before the kids, we had been so caught up in our need for each other that we never took the time to make it fun.

Jasmine laughs and giggles. It's obvious from the shyness in her tone that she's out of her comfort zone with Jed, but she's into it with her hesitant replies to his questions. And when Jed finally has her naked and spread on the bed, taking the position between her legs, this is another new side to her.

"You good that I start her," Jed asks, his mouth inches from Jasmine's neatly clipped pussy.

"Go crazy." I wave my consent. "I'm good to watch."

"Not forever," Jasmine protests. "I want—" Her head tips to the side as Jed lowers his mouth. "That."

I've never seen another man go down on a woman, other than Wyatt and Jasmine, but it was dark that night and I imagined more than I saw. This time, I have a bird's eye view.

From Jasmine's responses, Jed seems to be very good at this.

He takes time with his tongue, slowly lapping the length of her, dipping inside, before he begins to tease her clit.

It doesn't take her long to come after he starts to suck it.

One moment she's lying still, eyes closed, and the next she grabs the back of Jed's head with both hands, pushing her hips up with a mew-like cry that makes my cock hard as a rock.

Jed only lifts his head as Jasmine sinks back into the pillows with a satisfied giggle. "Don't worry, I'm not done yet."

"How?" Jasmine murmurs. "I'm never that quick."

"I've been told I'm pretty good at this." With a grin, Jed begins to kiss her inner thighs and Jasmine sighs.

I take a moment to study how his fingers and tongue never stop touching her but avoid the sensitive area until she moans. Even I can tell the sound is tipped with frustration, and he bends his head to her once again.

But this time, he pulls one of her legs up, resting his head against the other as he thrusts his fingers inside her.

Jasmine cries out, and I start. I'd better start doing something or this is going to be over before it begins.

As I bend to her breasts, nipples peaked and irresistible, Jasmine's hips jerk as Jed finds something she likes. I'd begun to suspect there was more to meet the eye with Jasmine, with her hockey mom attitude and teacher sensibilities giving off a strong maternal vibe, but I had no idea there was such an uninhibited sexy beast inside her mom jeans. It's a total turn-on.

I watch Jed out of the corner of my eye, making a note of what Jasmine likes and responds to with the sharp cry or moan that fills the room. I remember Basil making a bad joke years ago about how quiet she was. That is not the case anymore.

Her hips take on a desperate rhythm as her cries become louder and I keep my mouth and hands on her breasts to help. But then Jasmine's hands fumble at the waistband of my shorts.

My eyes drift close as she eagerly takes me in her mouth. But kneeling gives me a better view of what Jed is doing and if he's as good as he says he is, I want to take notes. I watch as he slides a finger gently into her ass just as she comes for a second time.

After that, things get hazy.

Jed lies on the bed, with Jasmine astride him. After letting her take the lead and both of us enjoying the sight of her unfettered breasts as she rides him, Jed pulls her onto his chest, leaving her ass for me.

This is a first for me.

I nudge my cock against her ass. Slowly and carefully as to not hurt her, stopping often, I press inside until my head is inside of her.

I hear Jasmine's intake of breath, and then I slide all the way in. "Ok?" I whisper. She nods again, and I start to move within her, loving the tightness around my cock.

I slowly, carefully, gently thrust, my mind blanking because nothing has ever felt so good. So tight...

This is one thing I've never done before.

"You okay?" I hear Jed ask, and Jasmine nods, her dark hair falling in a puddle across Jed's chest. I move gently and she moans, either because she likes it or as an encouragement to keep going. I take it as both and thrust a little harder at the same time as Jed plunges up and Jasmine cries out.

"Oh my god," I mutter, griping her hips with shaking fingers to stop me from going too fast. I want this to last.

But it's evident it's not going to last as the tight grip pulls me to the edge. I thrust hard—once, twice and come inside her.

And then I lay back and watch as Jed brings Jasmine to her third climax.

CHAPTER SIXTEEN

Claire

"ARE YOU OKAY?" BASIL asks as we walk back along the beach.

"I'm fine." I'm more than fine, I want to say. I'm relaxed and happy and very, very satisfied.

I'm also a little confused.

"Do you think we'll do this again?" Basil asks, sounding as confused as I feel.

"Do you think we could? I mean, do you think it's a good idea?"

"I don't know." He reaches for my hand and links our fingers. "I've always liked you, Claire, but lately...especially these last few days..."

"I know." I don't wait for him to finish, because I'm thinking the same thing. "It's changed something."

"I think it's good for us. I mean, I like thinking about you like this. But I'm not sure if it's good for the rest of us."

"We need to be able to compartmentalize," I say firmly. "Not let emotions get involved."

"Maybe we should ask the experts," Basil suggests. "See what they think. Because Claire..." He stops and tugs me towards him, and I let him. We stand in the sand, arms around each other. "I don't want to stop doing this. Or feeling this way when I'm with you."

"I love Billy." I rest my head on his chest, feeling the thump of his heart.

"And I love Jasmine. But I like being with you."

"I like being with you, too."

"If we can do both..."

"Why shouldn't we?" I finish, giving him a tight squeeze. "But don't fall in love with me."

"Don't fall in love with me," he counters, his hands sliding down my back to grab my ass. "I'm very irresistible."

"You're okay." I squeal as he pinches my bum. "A bit gropey."

"I'm making the most of it," Basil says, his hand now finding my breast. "I'm going to have to keep my hands to myself tomorrow."

"Yes, you are." I hug him tightly, not wanting to let go. A heavy weight of tiredness rests on my shoulders, but I don't want this night to end. I sigh, kissing Basil's neck.

A cry cuts through the air.

Basil stiffens. "That wasn't you."

"I think you'd hear me," I say with a grin. I lean away from him, and glance over my shoulder to where the cry came from.

"There's a couple on one of the chairs," the sharp-sighted Basil says quietly.

"Should we move? Give them some privacy." If I squint, I can see two figures darker than the night sky. I can tell from the hair that a woman is straddling someone on the chair.

I can't make out anything, but I can picture it in my mind.

"I'm kind of enjoying watching them," Basil admits.

"How much are you enjoying them?" Basil pushes his hips against me and I feel his hardness. "I thought that was because of me!" I cry, pushing him away with a playful slap.

Basil laughs and reaches for me as I lunge across the sand, running away from the couple in the chair. It doesn't take long until Basil catches me, sending me tumbling into the sand.

He rolls me over, his weight heavy on top of me. But I don't push him away; I shift so he lies between my legs and I wrap my arms around him.

It's a moment. A very nice moment, one that I'd be happy to continue. But a second cry cuts the air, and I take that as a sign. "We should leave them alone."

"I'm not about to go over and offer to join in."

"I thought you want to watch."

"I'd rather watch you come again."

My breath leaves me in a huff as my entire body tightens at his words. A good tightness. It would be so easy to let Basil in—I could have him right there in the sand.

I want him right there in the sand. I want him to watch me come again.

But as I lift my head to kiss Basil, he rolls off me. "I guess this isn't the best spot for this," he says ruefully.

"There's always tomorrow night," I say, hiding my disappointment.

A third cry, louder this time, follows us as we leave the beach.

Billy

"**W**ELL, THAT WAS A nice surprise," I say with a sideways glance as I walk Jasmine back to her room. It feels good to hold her hand; it's strange that I didn't even kiss her.

Neither did Jed, come to think of it.

When it was over, Jasmine seemed flustered and embarrassed, but Jed quickly pulled her into a hug that seemed to relax her. He asked if she'd like to stay, and when she shook her head, I offered to walk her back to her room.

And here we are, after our second time together.

I'm sure it had more of an impact on Jasmine, but I definitely enjoyed myself.

"I aim to please," she says.

"Jed seems cool."

"Ah—yeah." A long pause. "Are we supposed to talk about this? How does this work?"

"I have no idea."

"Maybe we shouldn't."

"Whatever you want, Jas. I'll do anything you want."

"Especially now?" She smiles archly and I raise her hand to my lips.

"Definitely now." Giving a happy hum, we turn down the hall towards her room. Mine is on the lower floor, but I'm nothing if not a gentleman. "I want to know something, though."

"For you? Anything," she teases.

"Why didn't you want to include Matt and Emily? Emmy," I correct.

Her smile fades. "I don't know. It seems...strange...to think of sharing this with him."

"Have you ever thought of him like that? Other than just your friend?"

Jasmine gives me a sad smile. "I've been in love with Matt from the moment I met him, to the moment I met Basil. Maybe the day after I met Basil."

"Does he know?" When she shakes her head, I press on. "Why didn't you ever tell him? Maybe he was in love with you, too?"

She gives a quick shake of her head. "The way he ran after every girl but me? I seriously doubt it. There was one night I was planning on telling him," she adds, speaking slowly as if she doesn't know if she should continue.

"What happened?"

"It was the night he met Shawna. Obviously, she got there first." I squeeze her hand. "Poor Jas."

"It's okay," she says gamely. "It all worked out for the best. I'm happy with Basil, and he's no longer happy with Shawna." She gives me an impish grin.

"You don't hold many grudges, do you?"

"Not really, no," she admits. "But sometimes, when he's being a pain, I can't help but think should've-would've-could've and it makes me feel better."

I nudge her with my shoulder. "I know what else would make you feel better." She giggles, and I don't think I'll ever be able to hear that sound without thinking about this night.

"I'm sorry, though," she says.

"Sorry for what? You haven't done anything wrong."

"Basil told me you and Emmy have a…a history. He didn't go into details. I'm sorry if you wanted to reconnect—actually, no I'm not sorry if that's what you wanted, because I love Claire."

"I love her too and it wasn't like that. Emmy meant a lot to me once, but things change."

"They do."

"You've changed," I say with another brush of my shoulder against her. "I had no idea you had that in you."

"Stop it!" She ducks to avoid me, and I grab her around the waist, laughing as she giggles in mock protest.

I hold her in my arms and press a kiss against her forehead. "You know, I've done all this *nasty* stuff—" I drop my voice to a husk and she giggles again, "—with you, and I haven't even kissed you."

Jasmine raises her chin. "What's stopping you? Only tonight, though," she adds and I don't waste any time.

I kiss her like she's a woman I've been intimate with, and not just a friend. I kiss her like I want to, like I want to do more with her. Standing in the hall, long after midnight in faraway Mexico, I kiss her until I'm tempted to push my way into her room and do more than kiss her. And she kisses me back.

I kiss her until a voice rings out down the hall. "What the hell?"

Jasmine freezes in my arms.

"What do you think you're doing?"

My heart sinks as I turn around to find Matt swaying slightly from too many drinks, keycard in his hand. Emmy stands wide-eyed beside him.

"Crap," Jasmine whispers.

One Night

CHAPTER ONE

Emmy

THE LIGHTS PULSE AND the music vibrates through me. For such a tiny disco in the resort, the place is packed, the tables around the dance floor stacked with laughing partygoers, each with at least one colourful cocktail in their hand.

I've had several colourful cocktails, which has definitely improved my dancing abilities.

Due to the fact I was raising babies in my twenties, most of it by myself, I missed out on the bar-and-club going years where twentysomethings normally would spend weekends drinking too much and dancing all night, so I'm a little out of practice.

But thanks to the availability of delicious drinks in this place, plus how comfortable I am with my new friends, I'm doing some serious dancing. For me, anyway.

My skirt swirls around my legs as Jed twirls me one last time. Strands of hair stick the back of my neck but I resist the urge to tie it back as I move on to Claire, doing a little innocent bumping-and-grinding to the delight of the men. I laugh with her, sing along to the music, having a wonderful time—

And then Billy spoils it.

Billy leans in to talk to Matt on the dance floor. Neither is smiling, which says a lot for both of them. Matt's forehead has a furrow, which only happens when he's upset about something. They could be talking about anything—about the dancers, about how Basil seems to be unable to tear his gaze away from Claire tonight, to how sexy Morena is in that dress. But of course, I jump to the conclusion that Billy is telling Matt that he had sex with me.

I can almost hear the words.

Best night of my life.

I gave it to her good.

It was like there was a wild animal in the back seat of the car!

It was one time. It happened.

Emily, who?

I have no idea of the words Billy might use to describe our one night tonight together because I haven't talked to him about it. One year, eighteen years ago, and I haven't spoken to him since.

Until I turned around in the lobby of the resort and saw him walking towards me. For a moment, I was ecstatic—the years fell away and here was Billy, my Billy, walking to me. He found me. He didn't forget me. He—

And then Matt called out to him, and my mind quickly clicked things into place as my heart fell into my shoes.

Matt knows Billy.

Matt is friends with Billy.

This trip to Mexico with Matt's friends includes Billy and his wife.

And no one knows about my past with Billy, the love I've kept hidden in my heart for all those years.

When Matt turns away from Billy with a frown on his face, I abandon Claire mid-song and dart around the dancers to Billy's side. "Did you tell him?" I hiss.

It's the third night of our trip to Mexico, and the worry that this will get out seems like it's burning a hole in my stomach.

Keeping the secret has ruined any happiness of seeing Billy again.

"Of course not," Billy says, leaning close to me so I can hear him over the 80s music playing loud enough to vibrate the cheap wood floor of the disco. "But I wish you would. I don't like lying to my friend."

I don't know why I haven't told Matt yet. It's nothing—a blip from my past. But even a blip would have upset Ed, and the memory of my ex-husband's anger is a memory I can't seem to shake. I'm not afraid of what Matt would say if he knew about me and Billy, but I am afraid of how he'll react.

Suddenly, I'm slammed from behind, like I'm on the ice during one of my son's hockey games and got caught with my head down. I stumble forward into the circle of dancers, tripping over my feet. As I feel myself falling forward, Billy grabs me by the waist and yanks me upright.

"Hey, watch out!" Matt cries. The anger in his voice came from nowhere and sets me to stone. "You almost knocked over my girlfriend."

"Sso verra' sorry," the man sings over his shoulder and resumes his wild dancing.

"No, you need to apologize," Matt demands, taking a step towards him, his face contorted with rage.

"He did apologize, bro." Billy claps a hand on his shoulder. "It's cool. Emily's all good." He keeps his arm tight around me. I can't catch my breath.

"It's not enough," Matt insists, turning back to the man, looking like he's about to throw a punch.

I have to stop this. Dragging a deep breath, I push away from Billy, feeling all eyes on me. "Stop it, Matt."

I've stood up to Ed threatening me with a knife, so I can stand up to Matt in a bar fight. Another breath. Another.

Breathe.

"I'm defending you," Matt cries, his arms raised like he's defending himself from an attack. "Don't get mad at me for the guy being a jerk."

"I don't need you to defend me." Ordering myself to breathe isn't working and I feel the room closing on. Pushing my way out of the circle, I rush to the door.

Billy catches me by the door. "What was that about?"

It's Billy who followed me, not Matt. That little detail helps.

"I need some air," I gasp, shouldering open the door. The night air is hot and sultry, like a tango dancer. Staggering out, I take giant gulps of air.

Billy catches me by the arm and leads her to the corner of the building, away from the busy doorway. "Emily, what happened?"

"He was so upset," I whisper, still fighting to force air into my lungs. I haven't had a panic attack in years, and it's been just as long since I woke up screaming from a nightmare where Ed was once again after the boys.

And now, after an innocent bump from a drunk, I'm a mess again, like no time has passed.

"At the guy who knocked you over, not you." Billy has a confused expression on his usually cheerful face. "I've never seen him like that."

"Can you see why I can't tell him?"

Billy gapes, slow to see the connection between the two. "I've never seen him react like that before. Have you? What's going on between the two of you?"

My lungs finally seem to be working and I draw in a shaky breath. "He's never been like that," I admit. "He's always so sweet and even-tempered. It just threw me."

Out in the warm air, with Billy's solid presence beside me, I realize how much I've overacted. What am I supposed to say to the others? How can explain this? My head pounds a response, a combination of my fear and embarrassment, as well as the numerous cocktails I've had tonight.

"Guys sometimes feel the need to defend their girlfriend's honour," Billy says, as I rub my temple. "Do you remember that party we went to when Tim Cole spilled his beer all over you?"

Another shaky breath, and then I manage a smile. "I thought you were going to hit him."

"I almost did," Billy smiles with relief to see me regaining my composure. "So I get Matt's reaction. But...I don't get yours."

Realizing how close Billy is standing to me, I take takes a step away and lean against a planter full of colourful blooms. "My ex-husband," I admit, unable to come up with a suitable excuse. There is no excuse. "He got mad a lot."

Billy's jaw tightens. "Did he hit you?"

"I got out. I got the boys away from him before he could hurt them."

"Did he hurt you?" His eyes were dark and stormy and despite myself, I feel another twinge of fear.

Breathe, breathe.

"I don't like fighting," I manage, my voice low. "Or raised voices. Or conflict in general."

"Does Matt know all this?"

"I've told him things weren't good with my ex. Not everything. Not..." I stare at my hands, unable to look him in the eye.

"Which is why you don't need to say anything else to me." Billy runs a hand through his hair. "Matt's a good guy, Emmy. You need to open to him if you want this to work. Shawna wasn't a treat either. I think the two of you can really help each other."

"I've been on my own for a long time." I'm so tired of everyone thinking they know what's best for me. No one knows what I went through, what it was like for me. What I feel, what I need help with. "I don't need help."

"Everyone needs help. And you should always be honest with him."

I look at Billy and I don't see any remains of the boy I used to love with all my heart. I had to throw out the notebooks with *E + B 4 evr* inscribed in colourful ink, but I remember what it looked like. I remember how it felt to write Emily loves Billy in my best cursive.

But he doesn't look anything like my Billy.

Tall and broad, with flopping blond hair and a laughing expression that suggests he doesn't have many cares in the world. My Billy was tall and thin, with wide shoulders he had yet to grow into, and he cared about me.

Maybe too much?

Matt rushes out the door of the club. "Emmy!" he cries. "What happened? What did I do?"

For once I'm not happy to see him. "I don't like fighting," I say, reluctantly letting him pull me into his arms. "I don't like to see you angry. It...scares me." My words are aimed at his shoulder and for a moment I don't think he heard me.

"I scared you?" He takes her arms gently. "That's the last thing I want to do."

"I know. It's just..." I glance over at Billy, wanting him to stay, but knowing he can't. He has a wife, and I'm here with Matt.

Matt is...I like Matt. It was a big step for me to go away with him, leaving the boys, taking that next step to trusting someone.

I'm not sure what was the most difficult.

Do I love him? Not yet. But I care about him, and I can see that love might be on the horizon, like waking up early to see the sunrise.

"You guys need some time alone." Billy backs away as if realizing he's overstepped. He hasn't and I hate that he thinks it. "I'll leave you be, go back inside."

"The others are coming," Matt says, still staring at me with concern. "Let's go for a walk," he adds. "We can talk. You can tell me what I did."

"It's not what you did," I protest. "It's just—"

"Let's go sit on the beach," Matt suggests like I haven't spoken. He takes my hand, firm in his grip and nods to Billy. "See you tomorrow."

"Goodnight." I smile weakly at Billy and let myself be led away without a backwards glance.

Matt

"I'M SORRY," I SAY as we walk away from Billy.

"You didn't do anything wrong," Emmy says, her tone telling a very different story.

I'm not used to this. When I was married to Shawna, she liked to tell me, in no uncertain terms, exactly what I did wrong, how I did it, and what I'm going to do about it. Shawna was a difficult woman to live with.

Sometimes I feel like a new man being away from her.

"It kind of feels like I did," I admit as we reach the beach at the edge of the resort. The cool sand lies flat and undisturbed, already raked for the night. I feel a twinge of guilt as I step off the path, but I see other footprints. They should rake in the morning because we're not the only ones walking on the beach at night.

If Shawna was here, she'd have a revised schedule for beach raking ready to bring to the manager's attention.

But Shawna is not here. I'm here with Emmy.

But if she's so great, why am I struggling to focus on her? It's the first time I've been with Billy and Claire since last summer at

Aurora, and being with them and Basil and Jasmine brings back a lot of flashbacks of Shawna. Either I'm trying to push my ex out of my thoughts, or I'm hit with all these thoughts about Jasmine.

I haven't been able to stop thinking of Jasmine since we got here.

We've been friends since we were kids; platonic, easy, relaxed. I can tell her anything, and she's been a huge support after Shawna left me.

She was the one who pointed out how hard on the ego it must be when your wife leaves you, even when you weren't sure you wanted her in the first place.

"You need a boost," Jasmine had said. "Do something you're good at, or you have fun with. Something that will make you happy and make you feel good about yourself."

So I asked Emmy out for dinner. I don't think it was exactly what Jasmine had in mind, but it worked for me.

"It's not you, it's me," Emmy says, pulling me away from thoughts of anyone else. She slips off her sandals, holding them in her hand.

"That sounds like the beginning of a breakup speech." My stomach flips nervously. We've only been dating a few weeks, but I've known Emmy for over a year, and I like her. I don't want a breakup speech here; now. In Mexico.

"I'm not breaking up with you, Matt." Her smile reassures me more than her words. Emmy has a great smile—full and bright and always so cheerful. It's what attracted me to her in the first place.

It's what made our friendship so easy, seeing her smile every time I was in the arena with the kids. And then it got so that I wanted to see her smile more than just a few times a week.

"I'm trying to explain why I got freaked out," she adds.

"You said you didn't like fighting. I get that, but I wasn't about to start a bar fight."

"It seemed like you were on the verge of it," she points out. "My ex-husband would get angry." Emmy bows her head like she's speaking to her shoes. I can tell it's not easy for her to talk about it. Not only does she hardly ever mention her ex, but she's also speaking in such a hesitant voice, I feel like whispering in response.

"How angry?"

"Very. He...he hit me. When he got angry."

Two emotions—one, I want to pull her into my arms and vow to protect her from the world. Two—I want to find Emmy's ex and kick the shit out of him.

Instead, I do nothing, just wait for her to continue.

"He pushed me into a closet once...I had bruises that I needed to cover up. I wore a lot of long sleeves," Emmy continues. "But I got out. The boys came and things didn't stop...I left for them."

"You should have left for you," I can't help but say.

"I might have," she admits. "But they were the most important."

"I hate that you had to go through that."

"Me too," she says with a hint of a smile. "I have a lot of regrets, thoughts of *what if*. I'm over the worst of it."

"Are you?"

"I don't like fighting," she concedes. "Loud voices. Threats of violence. That's why I won't let the boys play hockey at a higher level—I can't stand the thought of body checking."

"I get that."

"So that's what upset me," she finishes with a shaky sigh.

"Thanks for telling me." Emmy and I have never had a problem talking, but usually, it's about the kids or Shawna. I think this might be the first time she's truly opened up to me.

The thought makes me a little sad. I'm dating this woman—I've brought her on vacation with me, but how much do I really know her? I knew she was divorced and it wasn't easy for her, but I had no idea her ex abused her.

What else am I missing? Have I been so caught up in my own problems that I haven't let Emmy talk about hers?

We walk down to the shoreline. The thin, white-capped waves lap at the damp sand and Emmy pushes her big toe into the sand. "I had such a good day," she frets. "I loved the snorkelling, and dinner was so fun." She pauses. "I like your friends."

"They're great." An image of Jasmine across the table at dinner, practically tucked up under Jed's arm hits me. "At least Bill and Claire. I don't know much about this Jed and Morena."

"I think they're lovely."

"Lovely," I echo. "He flirts a lot."

"It's a vacation." Emmy gives me a sideways glance. "Flirting is allowed."

"Are you giving me permission to flirt with another woman?"

"You don't need my permission for anything, Matt." She smiles ruefully. "I'm not one of those women who need to police every action of their—their man." For a moment, I wonder if she slipped, about to say *husband*.

Like I slipped when I was checking in and called her my wife. I'm still not sure if Emmy caught that.

"I hate that the day ended like this," she adds.

I take her hand and swing it back and forth. "It doesn't have to end this way. We're good now. You've explained, I understand. I've apologized...all friends again. Well, more than friends."

"More than a little," she agrees, looking up with a smile.

"The night is—maybe not young, but we are on vacation. Still lots to do."

"What did you have in mind?" I'm encouraged by the flirtatious tone in her voice. I've quickly realized that Emmy has difficulty showing affection in public, or to initiate things in the bedroom, so it means a lot when she does.

"I have many things in mind." I swing her around to face me, so that a wave splashes over her feet, making her squeal. "But the first one starts with a question."

CHAPTER TWO

Emmy

A QUESTION.

I freeze at Matt's words. Literally, freeze; my legs lock, my fingers curve in a bad impression of a claw, and the breath is forced from my lungs in a huff.

No No No No...

"How are you about late-night swims?" Matt asks.

It takes a moment to recover and when I do, everything sags like an old pair of pantyhose. "Swim."

"You like to swim?"

"Of course!" My voice is too loud, too excited for a simple question about swimming. I rein it in, take a deep breath to stop my heart pounding with great thumps and smile.

It's more like a grimace than a smile because Matt looks at me funny.

I thought he was going to propose!

Two of my girlfriends and my mother predicted this trip was going to be Matt's way of asking me to marry him. I said no, that we weren't there yet, that he wasn't ready.

I didn't say anything about me not being there yet; so far away from being ready that it's laughable. There's no way I'm ready to marry *anyone*, not even a great guy like Matt.

The great guy that is suggesting we go for a late-night swim instead of dropping down on one knee in the sand to suggest we spend the rest of our lives together. Perfect.

"We used to go in some nights at Aurora," Matt is saying, and I tune in with a guilty shiver. "Claire was always the first to jump in, especially after she'd been drinking."

I like Claire. I think she's a good fit with Billy, much better than I would have been.

I need to tell Matt that I knew Billy. It's a bad lie to have hanging between us, and not fair to Billy. And now that Claire knows...

"So do we go in wearing our clothes?" I ask, wrenching myself back from the thoughts of Billy. Old Billy, new Billy; my Billy, Claire's Billy.

"Or not," Matt asks, the delight from my suggestion evident in his voice. "Looks pretty empty."

I cast a long glance up and down the beach. The only sound is the hiss of the waves and the odd call of a bird. The lights of the resort shine brightly only a few feet away from the sand and I see people walking, but no one heads in our direction.

For the moment, we're alone on the beach.

It would have been a great time to propose if we were ready to take that step. Which we're not.

Which we might not ever be.

"Okay," I say finally. "I'll just take my dress off and leave it here?"

"Hang on." My knight-in-shining armour drops my hand and runs to pull one of the chaise lounges out of its neat line over to us. "I don't want your dress to get sandy."

"You go first," I whisper, sudden excitement making me shiver more than the thought of the cool water. I'm not impulsive. I don't do things like go for midnight swims anywhere, regardless if there's a sign that says the beach is closed at eleven pm.

There is such a sign; I saw it earlier today.

Matt wastes no time in chucking off his polo shirt and cargo shorts. I catch my breath as he stands in his boxer briefs with an embarrassed grin.

There's nothing at all for him to be embarrassed about.

Before Matt, I had a long stretch where men weren't allowed in my life. I had enough to deal with—the aftermath of leaving Ed, relocating, the boys, and a love life wasn't a priority.

Neither was sex.

When the mood arose, which wasn't often, I did quite well on my own.

Now that I'm with Matt, it amazes me how I lasted so long without sex. I still can't tell him what I want or when I want it, but I make sure he knows that I'm as eager and excited as he is.

I reach out and brush my fingers against his bare chest, my thumb rubbing against his nipple, which hardens under my touch. He has the perfect amount of hair on his chest—enough to run my fingers through but not enough to itch when I lay my head on his chest.

"Your turn," he says, his eyes on my legs.

The look in his eyes helps wipe away my earlier stab of fear of his anger. This is Matt—nice guy. Good guy. Trustworthy guy. Look at how quickly he apologized for scaring me.

The look in his eyes also brings about a throb of desire between my legs. Reaching down, I pull my dress over my head. It's held up with thin straps and tight across the bodice, with a built-in bra. My breasts react to the sudden freedom by my nipples hardening into tight pebbles.

As I toss my dress onto the chair, my nipples catch Matt's attention right away.

"A little chilly, isn't it?" he says with a smile.

"A little." Despite our intimacy, I instinctively cover my breasts with my hands, but he holds out his hand.

"Race you?"

"It takes me forever to get into the water," I complain. I take his hand and let him tug me into the waves.

The water is warm and clear. Moonlight carves a path through the small whitecaps pulsing toward the beach and we follow the path. The lights and noise of the resort are far enough back that it feels like we're alone.

Matt leads me deeper, laughing at my squeals as the waves lap at my bare skin until the water is around my waist. Then he stands behind me and wraps his arms around me.

"It's beautiful out here," I say wistfully, staring at the moonlight on the water.

"I'm really glad you came with me. I know it was a last minute, but I thought it would work out. I hoped it would."

"It's been great so far," I assure him.

"Do you miss the boys?"

"Every minute." I push down the lump in my throat when I think about them. "But I think it's good for me to get away. I've never been away without them."

"What about your honeymoon?"

I shake my head, being careful that my hair doesn't blow in Matt's face. "No honeymoon. I was already pregnant by then. Ed always promised to take me after the babies but that never happened."

"I didn't know anything about your marriage, how bad it was." I hear the sympathy in his voice, but like always, it hardens me. I don't like being pitied. I was stupid enough to marry an abuser and luckily got out before any lasting damage.

Considering my overreaction in the bar, I should correct that to say *too much* lasting damage.

"I don't talk about it much. I don't like to think about it," I say coolly.

"I get that," Matt says easily. "But having bent your ear so much about my marriage, it's not exactly fair that you didn't have time to tell me about yours."

"Like I said, I prefer to leave the past in the past. Besides, I'm a good listener."

His arms tighten around me. "You're a very good listener. I don't know how I would have gotten through these last months without you."

"I think you would have been fine. You have your friends—at least Basil and Jasmine are close by."

I've known Jasmine for a while. Our town is small enough, that when kids play hockey or any other sport, it feels like everyone knows each other. While my boys are older, they've played at the arena their whole lives. Adam still plays hockey, but Josh switched over to baseball but works at the rink; in the concession and helps coach the younger teams. I've seen Jasmine and Basil there for years, but have always thought Jasmine was some clone of Shawna. It's nice to see that I was wrong about her.

What I can't put my finger on is Matt's relationship with Jasmine. One of the first things he told me was how he grew up with Jasmine, that their friendship has lasted over thirty years. It's an envious relationship for anyone, but especially a man and a woman, who, from all I can pick up on, have kept things platonic their whole lives.

Having never had a male friend, I wonder how that's possible, especially considering how pretty Jasmine is, with her dark eyes and lush figure.

I've never asked Matt about her, but I'm ashamed to admit that since we've been in Mexico with them, I've watched every interaction between Jasmine and Matt with the intensity of a jealous wife.

Not that I'm jealous; I just think there's more to their friendship that either of them is admitting to, maybe even to themselves.

"Jas has always been there for me," Matt says, his matter-of-fact tone etched with the possessiveness of a long-time friend.

"And Basil?"

"Sure. This has been great, all of us together, especially since I wasn't able to go to Aurora this summer. But it's funny; now that Shawna's gone, I'm enjoying spending more time with Bill. She never really liked him," Matt confesses. "I'm not about to tell him that."

"How can anyone dislike Billy?" I demand, more heatedly than I should. "He's so nice and laid back."

"I think that's what annoyed her," he says. "She thought every-one should be intense, like her."

"You're not intense."

"And look at what happened." I feel the vibration of his chuckle more than hear it, and tighten my hands on top of his. Matt's become more self-deprecating about his divorce. I can tell he's accepted that Shawna's gone, but I'm not sure if he's dealt with it.

I should know since there are things in my past that I still haven't dealt with either.

"I'm glad you're here with me." Matt folds his arms across my chest and hugs me. "Asking you out for dinner without the kids that time was the best thing I ever did."

"If you'd waited a little longer, I might have asked you." I'm only half-serious because I've never asked a man out in my life. And how do you ask out a man whose wife recently left him? How would you know when he's ready?

I still find myself wondering if Matt is even ready now.

"It's been a while since I've had a woman chase me," he says. I can tell he's smiling at the thought, so I step out of his arms.

"I'll give you a head start and chase you back to the beach," I tell him. "I'm cold."

Matt

Emmy is as good as her word and chases me through the waves back to the beach. I let her catch me once and laugh as she tries to take me down with a half-assed tackle.

I like her laugh. I remember one day bringing my boys to practice and found her outside the locker room laughing hysterically with a group of fathers.

Shawna never laughed like that.

I also liked the way the men looked at her—like she was some sort of Wonder Woman reincarnate.

Now that I know her better, I think Emmy is even better than Wonder Woman. Raising twin boys on her own, and now that I know about her ex...she's amazing.

When we get back to the beach, I kiss her before she can put on her dress, drawing her close like I'm trying to warm her.

I just want to feel those nipples against my chest. I've wanted to touch them since she pulled off her dress.

Beautiful breasts. Beautiful body. The breasts aren't as full and ripe as Jasmine's but there's nothing I would change about Emmy.

Maybe if she was a little more into sex.

The kissing is nice; she responds quickly, her arms around my neck, her mouth open and eager. I like kissing her. It's an almost-forgotten art since Shawna wasn't into it.

Or maybe she just wasn't into me.

Emmy clearly likes to kiss, and we spent numerous nights making out on my couch, jumping apart at any sound from the kids upstairs. But once we started sleeping together, I cut out the make-out sessions since I was eager for more and time was always limited.

There's no time limit here. No kids ready to pop up at the worst possible moment.

My hands skim the sides of her breasts before returning to cup them. It's a nice weight in my hands and I caress, massage...my thumbs strafing those tight nipples.

I want them in my mouth.

Breaking the kiss, I lead her to the chaise lounge and sit down before settling Emmy on my lap. And then I go to work on those nipples, teasing the hard buds with lips and tongue.

For one brief flash, I imagine Jasmine sitting astride me.

Emmy gasps when my teeth graze her nipple, and I lessen the intensity, trying to calm my need. But it's hard when she's slowly pushing herself against my cock, trapped and hard as a rock under my wet boxer briefs.

Does she even realize she's moving against me? I feel the heat of her pussy through the thin material. She's almost grinding against me.

She wants it now.

Reaching down, I fumble with the waistband until I can pull out my cock. Emmy reaches for it, eagerly stroking with both hands.

"Put it in," I whisper. Emmy looks at me with expressionless eyes, and I wonder if I should wait, rein in my urge. But she pushes her panties aside and adjusts so that she can sink down onto me, ever so slowly, like she's trying to tease me.

I don't want to be teased.

My eyes close at the feel of my cock trapped inside of her, the warm wetness caressing me. I grasp her hips and move her, up and down, back and forth until Emmy finds her own rhythm.

Her rhythm is a fast one, drawing herself up until only the tip is inside her, before slamming down astride me. Her breasts swing with the force, her nipples still tight and tempting.

It's good—too good. I'm going to come in no time if she keeps this up.

This time I fumble with her underwear, searching for her clit. Shawna used to touch herself when we had sex, needing to make herself come before I got off. Because she did it herself, I'm out of practice bringing a woman to orgasm.

But I'm not opposed to trying...again and again.

Emmy's soft cry lets me know that I've hit the right spot, and her hip movements slow as I circle her clit with my finger.

"Faster," she says breathlessly.

I add a finger and quicken my pace. I may be inexperienced with women, but I'm willing and eager. I remember how much fun it is to make a woman come.

Emmy is close. I can tell from her movements, her rhythm more urgent. She grips the arms of the chair and bucks frantically, her gasps becoming groans as I rub her clit faster.

I've never seen her like this. It's such a turn-on watching her; her mouth open, eyes closed. Her breasts are so tantalizing, swinging as she rides me that I fix my mouth on one.

She cries out as I suck hard.

Cries out again, her body tensing above me.

"Are you coming?" I whisper, thrusting up inside her, desperate for my own release. Again, I thrust up and her cries become louder.

"More," she breathes. "Don't stop! Don't—" I spear her one last time with my cock and she cries out, body arching above me as she comes.

Thank God. Grabbing her hips, I move her against me, burying my groan against her shoulder as I come inside of her.

CHAPTER THREE

Emmy

WE WALK BACK TO the room holding hands.

Matt can't stop smiling. He's very happy with himself. The first time we made love was awkward. I was out of practice—Matt only being the fourth man I'd been with. Billy, my first; Ed, my husband for three long years; and then a drunken pickup after my divorce, an experience that came about more from a hidden rebellious streak than any real desire. I don't even remember his name. Tom, or Todd. Maybe Tony.

The first time with Matt, I'd been nervous, and he was accustomed to how it had been with his wife. It made the experience uncomfortable, for both of us, and made me doubt that I wanted to go down this road with him.

But I gave him a second try, and I'm happy that each time has improved. We're slowly finding our groove, discovering what turns each other on.

Matt's turned on by just about anything.

For me, the sex is good but controlled; it's like Matt is trying too hard to please me. I'm sure that's because of Shawna—she was a ball-buster if ever I saw one. But when I lie awake beside him, or even in my bed, I wonder if we're missing something.

In the books I read, there's always so much passion between the lovers. I know life isn't a romance novel, but I'd like a little more passion with Matt. I'm attracted to him...I want him...but is this all there is?

I don't say any of this to him, because it would only hurt him and that's the last thing I want to do. Matt's a good guy.

I shouldn't want any more.

"I wonder if the others are still there," Matt muses as we walk by the disco on the way back to the room, music still pounding into the night.

"I'm not going back in there," I say with a laugh. My dress has wet marks across my chest and goosebumps dot my arms.

"C'mon, one more drink?" He tugs me towards the building practically vibrating from a Billy Idol song.

"No." This time I'm firm. And too cold to think about anything other than crawling under a blanket.

"They're probably gone," Matt says as we continue past. "Jasmine likes early bedtimes. She's probably tucked into bed by now."

That's an odd statement. Why is he thinking about being Jasmine tucked up in bed when he's headed there with me?

Of course, now that he mentions Jasmine, it opens the floodgates for me to think about Billy. I picture him curled around Claire, his long arms cuddling her close.

He was always a good hugger. So long and lean. When I knew him, he was all arms and legs. Lanky and gangly with a haircut that encouraged him to spend more time and product on it than I did for my hair.

Now, with the shoulders and the floppy surfer hair, he is almost unrecognizable from the boy I knew.

I keep telling myself that whenever I see his smile—the same smile that used to send butterflies fluttering in my stomach.

But I don't mention Jasmine or Billy. After a busy day and a late night, I'm tired. There's no need for further discussion tonight.

Matt opens the door to the building where our room is. There are units like this spread over the resort; three-storied buildings with a wide hallway open at the ends. Somehow our room is on the same floor as Jasmine and Basil, with Claire and Billy downstairs on the main floor.

Our room looks out onto a garden vista, with palm trees, colourful flowers and lizards that sun themselves on the rocks. It's everything I imagined Mexico would be like. It's been a good trip so far, I think to myself as Matt follows me up the stairs, his hands warm on my hips.

Just the simple touch makes me wonder about a repeat performance. Would he want to make love again tonight? Because...I'd be okay with that.

I think about how to suggest it, without really seeming too eager as we start down the hall. The hallway is dim without sunlight pouring in, but lit enough for me to see the couple halfway down the hall.

We're going to have to pass them to get to our room, and from the looks of things, they don't want to be interrupted.

Matt

A COUPLE BLOCKS THE hall, almost outside Jasmine and Basil's room. Arms entwined, looking like they have a need for a room, or things might be starting to happen right there in the hall.

I squeeze Emmy's hand and glance down. We were kissing like that not too long ago. Will she want—?

That's when I notice Emmy has stopped walking, staring at the couple.

That's when I realize who it is.

"What the hell?" I demand, my voice slow and unbelieving.

At the sound of my voice, Jasmine stiffens in Billy's arms. Jasmine and Billy.

Jasmine and Billy.

"What do you think you're doing?" I don't recognize my voice. The disappointment sounds like my father, the hurt makes me think of the times when Shawna pulled something, but the anger—the anger is mine.

Jasmine and *Billy*?

"I—" Jasmine detangles herself from Billy's arms, but he *won't let her go*, keeping a possessive hand around her waist.

I want to snap off his hand at the wrist so he can't touch her anymore.

"Matt," she says breathlessly, eyes darting around the hallway, lips still moist from Billy's kiss. The sight of them makes me want to throw up and punch something at the same time. "What are you doing here?"

"I'm going to bed and it kind of looks like you're doing the same. With *him*." Two strides get me before them, and I stab a finger into Billy's chest. "What the hell, Bill?"

"We can explain," Billy says. But he's looking at Emmy instead of me, with an apologetic expression on his face.

"Did you know about this?" I round on Emmy. "That they're screwing each other?"

"No," Emmy gasps.

"Are you sure? Because you don't look all that surprised."

She does look guilty. I know that expression all too well. "Matt, no," Emmy pleads. "I don't know anything."

Her words fall on deaf ears because the roaring of anger is so loud I can't see straight. "You're lying. That's why you wanted to come with me, because you knew Billy's here, and you want a piece of him too?"

"Did you tell him?" Billy demands of Emmy, confusion written all over his face.

"Tell me what?" When I see the horror on Emmy's face, the tiny seed of doubt I'd felt that first day seeing Emmy's reaction to seeing Billy morphs into a huge tree of jealousy. "High school—there's

more to this than going to school together. What else is there?"
The glance between them speaks volumes.

"Matt....it's nothing. I wanted to tell you—" Emmy begins.

"Tell me *what*?"

"We went out," Emmy admits in a low voice.

"Like, dated?" I stare at her with astonishment. "Why didn't
you tell me? Don't you think that's something I should know?"

"No. I don't," Emmy says stiffly. "But I *was* planning on telling
you because Billy is your friend."

"And you *fucked* my friend," I growl, like the easy-going fun of
the last hour never existed.

Emmy gasps as if I've slapped her.

Billy steps up like he's about to stand between us. "It was a
long time ago, man. And I was in love with her." The buzz of
Billy's words increases the size of the tree of jealousy so that it
towers threateningly over my head. "I wanted to marry her, but
they moved."

He fucked Emmy. He fucked Jasmine—my *Jasmine*. Rage boils
under the surface of my skin and I turn to Emmy with cold eyes.
"You had sex with him."

"Matt—"

"Listen, bro," Billy says as he grabs my arm.

I shake him off. "You had sex with my girlfriend. This is why you
came isn't it?" I turn to Emmy, not caring about the pained expression on her face. "So you could get another chance. But you're out
of luck 'cuz you found out he's moved on with Jasmine."

I turn to Jasmine with disgust. Jasmine, my oldest friend. Now,
a liar and a cheat and no friend of mine.

"I can't believe I brought you here," I say to Emmy, disgust underlying my words. "You're nothing but a liar. You all are."

"Matt, stop it. You don't know what you're talking about," Jasmine cries.

"Really? You're fucking Billy, right outside the room where your husband is sleeping. I think I know what I'm talking about because that's what I'm seeing. *Cheater*." The word seeps out like its toxic. "Is that who you've become, or have you always been like that? Who are you?"

I can't stand the sight of her. Of them. Emmy and Billy...Jasmine and Billy. Everybody betrays me. The bile rises in my stomach and I turn and stomp down the hallway.

No one follows me.

Chapter Four

Emmy

"What just happened here?" Billy takes a step towards me, which I neatly sidestep. "Emmy, it's not what you think."

I raise my hands as I skirt past him, not wanting to share the same space. How could he? "None of my business."

"It is," he insists.

"No, it's really not. I came here on vacation, against my better judgment, just looking to get to know Matt a bit better, and I find this. This..." I search for the words. "You're cheating on your wife!"

"No, he's not," Jasmine says angrily. "Damn him. I've got to explain things." She hastens down the hall, the *flip flop* of her sandals becoming faint as I'm left alone with Billy.

"You don't have to explain anything to me," I say in a quiet voice as I try to get past him. "It's none of my business what you do, or with who."

"We're swingers."

I pause, blinking with surprise. "Well, that makes it all better," I say sarcastically.

"Emily." Billy grabs my arm, and I stiffen, willing my face to go blank.

Never let him see you scared. "Let go of me."

He drops his hand and takes a step back from me. "I want to explain," he says in a low voice, the urgency in it stopping me.

"I don't want you to. But what do you mean—swingers? Is that a thing?"

"It's...swingers. Couples that...swing." Billy's expression is a contradiction in emotions—guilt and shame, but pride. Happiness. "We share. Wife-swap."

I step back. I did not expect that. But maybe it's an excuse, although I have no idea why Billy would lie to me. "Are you serious?"

"No...yes. It just started. It's all-new, and I'm not sure how to explain it."

"You're going to have sex with Jasmine." I study his face, see the mussed hair, the shirt that he forgot to button properly. My stomach drops with the realization. "No, you *had* sex with her."

"Emmy..."

"Where is Claire?" I demand, anger coating my words, although I don't know why I would be mad. What Billy does is none of my business. I keep telling myself that. "With Basil?"

"And Morena." Billy shifts, staring at his feet.

"Morena? And Jed?" I ask incredulously. "They're involved with this too?"

My first thought is that I've somehow walked into some perverted porno; an adults-only resort that caters to swingers. I know nothing about the lifestyle; my only experience was watching a movie years ago and being confused at why all the parents went to a party and dropped their keys in a big bowl by the door.

I'm still confused. If you're married and having sex with someone else, that's classified as cheating. Infidelity. Adultery. A betrayal of your wedding vows.

Billy nods. "It happened in the summer. Once. At Aurora. And then here, we wondered...and then we met Jed and Morena and that's what they do."

"They're *swingers*." Billy nods again. "And you wanted to be one of the cool kids?" For a moment, I slip into my Mom's voice, faced with my boys and their juvenile explanations.

"No." Billy gives me a half-smile, and memories of a younger Billy flood my mind. "It's not like that. We've been married for years and sometimes—"

"Excuse me for not understanding what it's like to be married," I snap.

"Emmy, I'm trying to explain here, not piss you off."

I cross my arms across my chest. "Explain then."

"We were all looking for some excitement. It's as simple as that."

As simple as that. Couples switching partners, looking for more excitement. Maybe it is that simple. Even though my marriage had been rotten from the beginning, there had been moments where I'd wondered and wished for someone else, for something *more*.

The same sensation I had with Matt. Wanting more passion. I thought it had been me—that I wanted that because there had been something wrong with my marriage, with me. But now, the realization hits that maybe I'm not alone in this. Marriages can grow stale, like Matt and Shawna's. But instead of looking for clandestine moments of excitement, with lies and excuses to justify and cover up, Billy and the others are looking elsewhere...and have permission to do it.

It makes sense. It might not be what I would have done in my marriage, but I see the merits. But Billy...Billy with someone else. Billy is a swinger, and he's been with someone else.

When I was right in front of him.

The awareness of *that* makes me catch my breath, suddenly feeling as flattened as if a giant rock had rolled over me. My shoulders sag; the events of the day and night suddenly leave me exhausted.

"Why not me?" I whisper.

"What?" Billy demands. "Why not you what?"

Tears prick at my eyes. "You didn't think I was exciting enough?"

"Emmy..." The regret in his voice stiffens my spine and I blink away the wetness in my eyes.

"Don't. You've been running after me since I got here, and now, suddenly, I'm not good enough? You forgot all about me, because of Jasmine?"

Jasmine. They all want Jasmine, and she's gone running after Matt. To confront, to console...I don't understand what is between them, but Matt's reaction to finding Jasmine and Billy together wasn't how someone who is just a friend reacts.

And I just let her go after him. What's going on between them?

Billy shakes his head like he's clearing water from his ears. "What are you talking about?"

My anger and hurt rears up and threatens to swallow me. "Why didn't you ask me?" I demand, my voice rising. "If you're a swinger, and get to have sex with whoever you want, why didn't you ask me? We could have been together one last time."

Billy stares at me, wide-eyed and slack-jawed. If I wasn't so angry, I might laugh at the sight. "Is that what you want?"

"I don't know," I snap. "And now I'll never know."

My shoulder brushed against him in my hurry to get to my room. To get inside before all these emotions rush out even more and leave me blubbering on the floor.

Or worse.

"Emmy," Billy calls after me.

I look at him one last time—tall and broad and so confused. I want to go to him, rush into his arms so badly that I slam the door harder than I mean to and the whole room shakes.

Matt

I'M OUTSIDE BEFORE I realize it. The air is warm, sticky and I turn in a circle, wondering where to go. The beach is out, but it's a short walk to the lobby and the bar is always open. I take a step on the path, stop. My head is swimming.

Emmy and Billy.

They've all lied to me, just like Shawna. Cheaters, the lot of them. Everyone lies. Everyone cheats.

"Matt!" Jasmine bursts out of the door. All I can see is the image of her in Billy's arms. Kissing him, her hands in his hair, moaning her response. Wanting him.

It's a shock how much it hurts.

"No." I push away, heading up the path to the lobby. "I don't want to talk to you."

"Yes, you are going to talk to me." Jasmine grabs my arm and swings me around to face her. She's breathing hard from the run, her eyes determined. "I'm going to explain."

"That you're fucking Billy?" The words spit out, popping like bacon fat.

"No! I mean, yes, but we all are."

I take a step back. "You're *all* fucking Billy?"

"No." Jasmine takes a deep breath and for a moment it looks like she's about to laugh. "Things happened at Aurora this summer. We met another couple, and decided to try it."

"Try what? Cheating on your husband?"

"Swinging," she says. "I guess that's what you call it. Wife-swapping. Sharing."

"Sharing Billy?"

"No." She closes her eyes for a moment. "Not just Billy. We all...this summer, I was with Wyatt, and then Billy. Here, it's been Jed...and Billy..."

I take a step back from her. "You've had sex with other men while you've been married," I say in a flat voice. Who is this person? "Other than Basil."

"Yes. And Basil has been with Claire." There's no hint of remorse in her voice. That's when I know she's serious.

Jasmine with someone else...I know she's only ever been with Basil. And for years, I've seen her with Basil, accepted her with Basil, become friends with him so I can stay in Jasmine's life.

I need Jasmine in my life, and the only way I can accept thinking of her with Basil is to see her happy with him. Thinking of her with Billy...with Jed...with whoever feels like someone poured a bottle of tequila down my throat.

It burns.

"Why didn't you tell me?" Despite the burning inside, my voice is cold, enough that Jasmine drops my arm but still raises her chin defiantly.

"I didn't know what you'd say."

"You didn't know what I'd say," I echo, unbelievingly. "I've known you my whole life. There's nothing you don't know about me."

"You've been through a lot with Shawna and I wasn't sure—"

"You didn't want me involved," I interrupt, my voice flat. Jasmine didn't want me. Even though it's been evident for years; she's happy with Basil and probably never thinks of me, the realization hits me like a kick to the crotch. And like a kick, it almost brings me to my knees.

"I didn't know how it would work," Jasmine has a desperate quality in her voice like she's trying to talk her way out of it. I remember the tone from conversations with Shawna, after accusing her of having an affair, listening to her try and turn it onto me.

"I know how sex works," I say coldly. "You put the cock in the—"

"I didn't know how it would work out with us," she bursts out. "I don't want to ruin things with you and I can't deal with the thought of you being with Claire or Morena. Or anyone else because I would want you for myself."

Her words roar through me, setting the burning on fire again. "You want me?" I manage to choke out.

Mutely, Jasmine nods, her eyes huge in the dim light.

I can't speak, can't think. I can only do.

A step forward brings me to her and I wrap my hand around the back of her neck and pull her to me. The roaring in my head tells me this is wrong, but I don't listen.

I kiss Jasmine.

CHAPTER FIVE

Emmy

I LEAN AGAINST THE door, my body tingling like I've stuck my finger in a light socket.

Billy.

Since I first saw him in the lobby, I haven't been able to get him out of my mind. There was so much left unfinished with us.

I'd loved him from the first moment I saw him walking down the halls of high school, but Billy was the Golden Boy and never noticed me. It took two years before he smiled at me. And then he spoke to me. And then it happened so fast—one minute I had watched longingly as he grinned at what seemed like every other girl in town, and then he was mine.

All mine, until the day my parents told me we were moving. And then all the light Billy brought to my life began to fade.

We were together once—a terrified sixteen-year-old and the king of the school who liked to pretend he had experience, but the reality was that he knew no more than I did about love.

Twenty years later, my memories of that night are still as vivid as ever.

He never even considered another night with me.

It's not until I hear the soft scuffle outside the door that I push myself away from the door. A quick peek out of the peephole shows an empty hall. Billy's gone back to his room, back to his wife. Or maybe back to Jasmine.

I have no idea what the situation is. Where would he go?

Swingers? What does that mean?

Quickly and quietly, like I'm trying not to wake Matt, I get ready for bed. But there's no way I can wake Matt since I don't even know where he is. He left, with Jasmine quick to run after him. Whatever he might say to the contrary, I know there's something more than friendship between them.

I stare at my reflection in the washroom, the pained look in my eyes as clear as the still-white skin around them, that's been hidden from the sun by my sunglasses. What am I doing here? I've been dating Matt for *weeks*; what has he pulled me into?

How could he not know his friends were swingers? Maybe he lied—maybe he's in on it too? Or maybe Matt and Jasmine had something together, and how she's passed him over for Billy.

That can't be right. Matt was just as surprised to see them together as I was. Shocked, upset. If I didn't know better, I'd say seeing Jasmine with Billy might have broken Matt's heart.

I have no clue about the relationship between Jasmine and Matt, but it doesn't excuse the things he said to me. He called me a liar. A cheat.

A ball of anger grows in my belly, like I'm smoothing out a snowball, ready to make my last pitch. I've been called worse, but I'm none of those things.

Matt thinks I came because of Billy, that I'm using him.

Matt is in love with Jasmine.

I don't know what is worse.

What am I doing here? I want nothing more than my own home, my own bed, as far away from this mess as possible. I avoid even looking at the bed I've shared with Matt for the last few nights, and pull back the covers on the second double bed. I am not sharing a bed with him tonight.

I wish I could take back the sex we'd had on the beach.

Huddling under the cool sheets, I begin to untangle my thoughts like I'm brushing out my hair after the day on the boat. Was that only today that we went snorkelling? It seems like forever ago.

It was so much fun. I liked Jed...I like Basil and Claire and Jasmine. And I couldn't help developing a tiny crush on Morena, even as she intimidated me with her mature beauty. What does Billy mean, they're swingers?

To me, swingers came from the seventies; married couples wearing bad clothes, too much makeup and toupees throwing keys in a bowl to pick out a new partner for the night. How can Morena be a part of that?

How can Billy?

How can Billy, and not want me a part of it? A wave of humiliation washes over me as I close my eyes tight. What exactly did I say to Billy? How could I even suggest he include me in whatever games he plays?

I hear the soft beep as Matt unlocks the door. Lying as still as I can, I pretend to be asleep.

I don't want to talk to him tonight. It doesn't matter that I had been in his arms only an hour ago, watching the moonlight on the water—I need some space from Matt.

He kicks off his shoes and leaves them by the door. I hear him bump into the table, his quiet curse. I keep my eyes shut, willing him to move on, get into the other bed and go to sleep.

Instead, he stands at the end of my bed.

I can sense him; smell the combination of salt and sand and sweat, as well as the sweet scent of the alcohol. How drunk is he?

This is *Matt*. He won't hurt me. But the old fear tries to slip in the cracks.

"I'm sorry," he whispers.

Sorry for what? What's happening? What is he going to do to me?

Instead of answering, he pats the end of the bed and heads into the bathroom. I lie awake for a long time until Matt's quiet snores somehow lull me to sleep.

Matt

W HEN I WAKE UP in the morning, Emmy is gone.

For a moment I lay in the darkness, the hum of the air conditioner breaking through the quiet and think about what it would be like if Emmy hadn't come on the trip with me.

If she hadn't been pulled into the drama of my friends. If I didn't have to feel the double guilt of kissing Jasmine.

I never meant to kiss her. One moment I was angry—furious, hurt, embarrassed—directing all of these emotions onto Jasmine, and then her words cut through everything.

I can't deal with the thought of you being with Claire or Morena. I want you for myself.

My cock came to life with a hungry roar as I stared at Jasmine in the dim light, like I was seeing her for the first time. Her lips, the full breasts that I've spent my life dreaming about, the body I've watched become a woman...

Not only did I kiss her, I grabbed her and pushed her against the light pole, my mouth demanding, my hands scrambling against the thin fabric of her dress.

But Jasmine didn't push me away or tell me to stop. She didn't slap me or knee me in the balls like any woman should have done when faced with that behaviour.

She moaned into my mouth.

Her hands dove into my hair, hauling me against her, her body warm and welcoming as she pressed against me. The sound of her quiet moan filled my ears. For a moment I thought...I wanted...

Until one of the golf carts that the resort staff drove blew past, the driver giving an appreciative toot on the horn.

I backed away from Jasmine, stumbling over the uneven ground and stared at her like I'd been kissing a snake.

"Look what you made me do," I spat.

"I didn't make you do anything!"

"This!" I waved my hand between us. "I don't do this."

Jasmine made a point of smoothing her dress where my hands had pulled it up onto her thighs. "Feels like you do it. Don't blame me," she snapped, her dark eyes as cold as the night sky. "You wanted it as much as I did."

"You wanted..." My anger faded, leaving only confusion.

Jasmine drew a shaky breath, then another. "Clearly, we have things to discuss. But

not tonight. Go to bed, Matt. We'll talk tomorrow."

And now it's the next morning and I'm as confused as I was last night.

Jasmine has been a part of my life since kindergarten. I remember the day; standing outside the locked door of the bathroom, hopping from foot to foot with my hand on my cock, desperately trying to hold in my pee. But just as the door had opened, I couldn't wait any longer and the wetness had spread across the front of my pants.

It had been Jasmine in the bathroom. Instead of laughing at my misfortune like any other five-year-old, she had been apologetic, rushing to get the teacher while I disappeared into the bathroom, my cheeks as hot as the urine that stained my pants.

Someway, somehow, no one ever found out about my mishap. I know I had Jasmine to thank for that.

She's been my best friend ever since; the two of us dealing with my parent's divorce, my numerous broken hearts, the end of my hockey career.

When I look back, it seems like Jasmine had always been there for me, but I'm not sure what I ever did for her. She supported and encouraged and how did I repay her? By groping her like a horny teenager in the middle of the night.

It wasn't the first time I'd kissed her—that had been back when we were fifteen and nervous about a party we'd been invited to. Jasmine had confessed she'd never kissed a boy. Arrogant, full of what I thought was plenty of experience—I'd kissed two girls, plus grazed a boob—I had offered to kiss her.

It had been a kiss, and not a particularly good one and neither of us had felt the pull for a repeat performance. Jasmine had always been there, growing more beautiful by the year, but she had been firmly in the friend category. I loved her like a sister and treated her as such, until the day I watched her walk down the aisle to marry Basil.

I'd never seen a woman so beautiful, not even my own wife. I'd stood at the front of the church and watched Jasmine in her white dress promise to love Basil and my heart had shattered. Regret tinged the pain—why wasn't Jasmine marrying *me*?

I've been in love with her ever since. To be honest, I've probably always been in love with her but seeing her like that brought it to the forefront. But my love for Jasmine had been manageable; something I could easily control and hide from others, including a very suspicious Shawna. It wasn't until I saw her kissing Billy that it rushed through me again like a tidal wave, blotting out everything in its path.

Including Emmy.

What have I done? What did I say to her? My words are a blur; I can't even remember the details of our time together on the beach. We made love, and then I kissed Jasmine. What kind of man am I?

My only thoughts are to find Jasmine until I see the empty bed. And then I realize I need to look for Emmy too.

It's too early for Jasmine to be awake, and I can't find Emmy anywhere. I check the beach, the pool, the breakfast places, but no sign of her. It's not until I try the lobby, half afraid that she got a ride back to the airport, that I have any luck.

"Ah, yes, Miz Emmy," the smiling girl behind the counter says. "I booked her a trip into Playa del Carmen this morning." She cranes her neck to look out the front doors. "You just missed her."

"She went into town?" I ask, hearing the words but not understanding them. "Without me?"

"Since you're here with me, it looks like yes, she went without you."

"Is there an airport there?" Her bags were still in the room, but I'm worried. I might not exactly want her to be here, but I don't want her to leave.

I need to sort out my head with Jasmine before I can deal with Emmy, but I don't want her to go like this.

"No, sir, no airport. Lots of boats though, and shopping. She went shopping, to buy you a present maybe?"

"I doubt that." I push away from the counter without thanking her. I hear my name float across the lobby.

It's the last people I want to see—Morena and Jed. Neither of them looks put out by my scowl though and greets me with big smiles.

"Hey, how's it going?" Jed slaps me on the back. "What gets you up so early?"

"Looking for Emmy. Apparently, she hopped in a van going to Playa del Carmen."

"Oh, no," Morena cries. "That was probably the one we should have been in. I told you we didn't have time—" She cuts herself off with a mock frown at Jed.

"We can book the next one," he says and Morena hurries off without another word. "A buddy is in Cancun and Playa is about halfway between us. We're meeting him there for the day."

"Did you have sex with Jasmine last night?" I hiss, not listening to his explanation.

"Whoa." Jed rears back like I punched him. "What's going on?"

"Did you have sex with her?"

"Well, yeah, but she was cool with it." Jed puts up his hands like he's about to fend me off and I think it's an overreaction until I realize my hands are balled into fists. "Everybody's happy," he adds. "Didn't mean to step on any toes."

"You didn't step on anything."

"To me, it looks like I stole your girl and you're ready to lay a beating on me." Jed tries to laugh. "What's going on?"

"Nothing." I turn away from him just as Morena returns.

"The next van leaves in a half an hour so I got us on that," she says before her eyes fall on Jed's defensive position. "What'd I miss?" she demands, her voice turning to ice.

"Matt was asking about our after-party last night."

"Well, it's about time you found out," Morena says with a disgusted shake of her head. "They should have told you all along. I don't like secrets, even when they don't concern me. Come on." She takes my hand. "We've got a half-hour to wait. Come have a morning drink with us."

Chapter Six

Emmy

WITH EVERY MILE THAT takes me away from the resort, I feel more and more unsure of what I'm doing.

I left a message for Matt, but I didn't wake him before I left. And even though I've been on my own for six years, during those years with Ed, he did his best to instill the number one rule in me—don't do anything without his say-so. Ed is long gone, but that morning I realize that I still defer to Matt for most things.

I thought I was fixed but apparently, I still have a long way to go. Ed really did a number on me.

I stare at the jungle that lines the highway. What's in there? And how are the windows of the van so clean? No sticky fingerprints or the remains of hearts traced over fogged glass mar my view.

I wish it was as easy to remove the remnants of Ed from marring my life.

This isn't the time to dwell on my ex-husband when there are issues with my current boyfriend. Again and again, the events of last night roll through my mind like one of those Harry Potter movie marathons that the boys love to watch.

Not long later, we arrive in Playa del Carmen, a bustling little town in the middle of the Yucatan peninsula, halfway between Tulum and Cancun. I did my homework for the trip, learning as much as the geography and history of the area, so places and names aren't entirely foreign to me.

Still, it's a new feeling as I step out of the van—I'm all alone in a strange place. Even though English-speaking tourists already crowd the streets, I'm a stranger in a strange land. And I'm by myself.

I miss my boys. I've only ever travelled with them; spending more time concerned with their enjoyment and well-being than my own. Even on the flight down, I'd been preoccupied with sending their exam schedule to my parents, who were looking after them.

Today, I have only myself to look after.

I clutch my bag close as the van deposits the last of the group on the street corner and roars away. He'll return to take me back to the resort, to Matt, but until then I'm on my own.

Falling into a group headed to the marketplace, I trail behind and try to take in everything at once. Mid-morning and the streets are already busy with voices mingling above background music; sexy music that my hips want to sway to.

My hesitant smile becomes wider.

And then I'm almost knocked off my feet as a tall blond man pushes past me at a run. I spin around, stumbling into the older couple behind me.

"Watch it," the man shouts. The hair on the back of my neck prickles, not wanting a repeat of last night. He takes my elbow to make sure I have my balance, but I pull away.

"Watch where you're going," I call after the man.

"Is this the group from the resorts?"

When I glance over my shoulder, the blond man is staring after us. I don't know if it's his expression of concern that prompts me to answer, or the movie star good looks. He literally takes my breath away.

"They just dropped us off," I say, my steps slow and heavy as they take me away from him. Brad Pitt with a mix of Ryan Gosling and Tom Hardy—he looks like a compilation of romantic heroes all morphed into one.

"No one else? I'm supposed to meet friends here."

I shake my head and with a last look, reluctantly turn back to the group, which has gotten ahead of me.

"Hey!" This time I stop and turn with a scowl. "Sorry about the shove," he calls. "My bad—very bad of me. I should be spanked." And then he grins, a completely infectious, irreverent smile which somehow makes him even better looking.

It must be the dimples. I can't see his eyes behind his sunglasses but I bet they're blue. And twinkling.

"You should be," I say with a grin of my own. Then with a twirl of my skirt, I turn and hurry after the group.

I can tell he's watching me walk away.

As I start to wander down the busy street of the market-place, with no destination in mind, I have to admit, being alone feels...nice.

Freeing.

My smile widens as I begin to explore.

Matt

I DON'T ARGUE AS Morena leads me to the bar in the corner of the lobby and, with a smile for the bartender, she orders three mimosas.

"I'm not drinking that girly drink," Jed complains.

"Shush, and stop trying to look like the big man. It's barely ten am, so there's no way you should be having a beer," Morena tells him. Jed gives me a grin and a wink behind her back.

I wonder about their relationship. The age difference is...considerable, although no one would bat an eye about it had the roles been reversed. Jed seems quite content with Morena telling him what to do.

I wonder what things are like in the bedroom.

Swingers. I don't even know what that means, exactly.

"So you heard about our little party last night." Morena pulls her glass towards her and takes a delicate sip. She's a beautiful woman, with dark eyes and all that hair.

"I did." I pick up my glass and drain half of it while Jed laughs. "That good of a morning, bro?"

"Emmy's gone." The concern hits me; pushing aside the hurt that she left without a word, I can't help but worry about her. We're in Mexico, a foreign country with police armed with assault weapons and a jungle pushing against the boundaries of the resort. What if something happened to her? What if she's hurt or—

"Why don't you tell us what happened?" Morena interrupts just as my worry is about to morph into full-fledged fear. "And stop worrying. She's a big girl. She can handle herself."

"What if she can't?"

Morena studies me, her dark eyes full of sympathy like she can read my mind. "She can. You had a fight and she's gone off to get some time to herself. She'll be fine, back by the end of the day with a smile on her pretty face."

"How can you be so sure?" I demand, my hand gripping the stem of my glass hard enough to break it.

Jed snorts. "Because she's Morena. She knows all. Relax, dude, and tell us what happened."

Because the only other option is to worry myself sick, I tell them about last night. Leaving out my time with Emmy on the beach, I tell them about walking back to the room and seeing Billy and Jasmine in their full-on embrace in the hall.

"They left you to have their own make-out session?" Morena raises her eyebrows at Jed with a teasing smile. "Are you losing your touch, hon?"

"I didn't think I was."

I look from Jed to Morena, and back again. "So you're saying, you and Billy and Jasmine...last night...?"

"I am." Jed grins without an ounce of smugness or conceit. "I hope they aren't upset by me admitting that."

"I think this lifestyle only works with openness and honesty." Morena sips at her drink. "It's not for everyone, but it isn't as terrible as some make out."

"What exactly is this lifestyle?" I ask carefully, trying not to admit my ignorance. I had a wife. I had sex with her. That was it. Did I want other women? An image of Jasmine flashes before my eye. Well, yeah, but that went against my marriage vows, so it wasn't an option for me.

Shawna obviously didn't have the same belief in our marriage.

I take a deep breath. "You say you're swingers, but what does that mean, exactly?"

"We don't believe monogamy is the only option in a relationship. I think that a person can love more than one person at a time. It's called polyamory," Morena explains with the patience of a woman used to justifying her life. "Open marriages can be beneficial."

"So the two of you just...whatever...with who you want?"

Jed turns to Morena with another grin. "That was my old life. Since I met her, she's kept me on the straight and narrow. There has to be a connection with the person. It's more fun that way."

"You're saying you have a connection with Jasmine? And...Billy...?" Billy and Jed? My mind swings with the image of my friend and Jed.

"I like to think so," Jed says honestly. "There's attraction, interest. I like them. I like it when I like people. I like you." I blink with surprise and Jed chuckles. "It's cool though, nothing has to change. I'm not about to jump you here and now."

Morena touches his hand. "Be serious."

"Oh, I am." It's the first time I've seen Jed without a smile on his face. "Sex is a very serious business for me. But it's also a lot of fun. People forget that."

I drop my eyes under his gaze. I've never considered sex to be fun. Sex is good—at least it had been with Shawna. With Emmy...it's good as well, but it's almost like something is missing. Maybe it's our inexperience. Maybe it's time we allowed more fun in the bedroom.

Maybe we can change things when she comes back.

CHAPTER SEVEN

Emmy

WANDERING AROUND A NEW place is a novelty and one I think I can get used to.

I disappear into the shops of the Playa del Carmen marketplace; poking into anything that catches my fancy, looking for knick-knacks and souvenirs for the boys. I buy a new sunhat for myself, one of the sarongs that Claire has, as well as cutesy lizards that I can put on my desk at home to remind me of the trip.

Do I want to be reminded of it?

Yes. Other than last night, it's been a great trip. And even last night was fun, just at the end...when Matt kind of blew up.

I wonder if he's realized he's in love with Jasmine yet.

The streets become crowded as the morning wears on, even though a fine mist has begun to fall. Even the rain in Mexico is nice, like a cooling shower. It's enough for my hair to be covered with a helmet of water droplets, but not enough to soak my yellow sundress.

But I still take the opportunity to duck into a restaurant when I come across one, even though it's a little early for lunch. The place is nearly empty and my stomach growls as a waitress shows me to a table. The scent of fried meat and onions reminds me I was in such a hurry to get away from the resort that I missed breakfast.

I study the restaurant as much as the menu. Barely finished boards cover the floor, with cheap-looking tables and chairs dotted around the space. Neon lights advertising a variety of American beers hang on the walls and for the first time, I wonder if eating here is a good idea.

My gaze lands on the only other customer seated at a nearby table piling guacamole on a nacho chip. "I think this place is better than it looks," he says with a grin. His blond hair is mused and damp from the rain but doesn't detract from the bright blue eyes and blinding white smile.

An image of dimples jiggles my memory like someone trying the bathroom door and I drop my eyes back to the menu, embarrassed to be caught staring.

"Good guacamole," he adds. When I lift my head again, he's still smiling. "I still need that spanking, you know."

My mouth falls open and he laughs. "I'm really sorry I ran into you earlier but isn't it fate that I bump into you again?"

An image of the man running into me on the sidewalk clicks into place. "You!" I exclaim. "The guy."

"That's all I am?" He slaps a hand on his chest in mock offence. "*The guy*?"

"The spanking guy?" His grin is infectious and I smile, even as I wonder what I'm doing. It's been a very long time since I've spoken to a strange man like this with a mix of flirtation and irreverence.

Make it never. I've never bantered with a man; if that's what we're doing. Spanking?

"Oh, now, *I'm* doing the spanking. I like the sound of that." He stands, grabbing the bowls of guacamole and chips and crosses to my table. "I think it would be easier on the waitress if we sit together," he explains, towering over me.

I slowly look up at him. Long, tan legs lead into khaki shorts printed with tiny trees. A loose-fitting yellow linen shirt speckled with raindrops can't disguise the width of his shoulders. My first impression would be an entitled, preppy rich boy, but his smile is too nice, too genuine. I raise my eyebrows as he sets the bowls on my table. "I like to share."

"Sharing is caring." Why would I say that? And what does he mean? Is everyone in the world but me having casual sex with strangers?

"Although you do look like you're pretty happy with your own company," he says with an apologetic smile.

"I was."

"But you look nice, and I was hoping you'd take pity on me." Without waiting for an invite, he pulls out a chair and sits down. "I'm going crazy being by myself!" He holds his hands up by his face and shakes them comically and I laugh despite myself.

"Why are you by yourself?" I ask.

"Does this mean I can stay?" he asks with a hopeful smile. The dimples appear and something flips inside my stomach. I've never seen a better-looking guy.

And he wants to sit with *me*?

That question decides for me, despite years of being told to avoid strange men. I gesture to the chair. With a wide smile, he extends a hand. "I'm Coulter."

"Emmy." His warm hand engulfs mine, shaking it briskly.

"Thanks for letting me crash your table," Coulter says, holding my hand for a moment too long. "I promise I'll behave and won't say anything to offend you."

"What's the fun of that?" I ask. I don't know where that came from, but I can be anyone with this man.

I can be Emmy, who hasn't even met Matt.

For a moment, I want to be.

Coulter blinks with surprise. "I obviously picked the right table. By the way, don't go for the spicy margaritas. I had one in this place in Cancun, and wow!" He pantomimes his head exploding and I laugh again.

"Good to know. You think the regular ones are okay?"

"Why would you want a regular? You're on vacation, go for something different." He leans across the table to look at my menu. "Go for that one."

"How can you even read it? You're looking at it upside down."

"Passion fruit margarita. I can read that just fine." He winks.

"You've got me intrigued by the spicy one. I can take a little heat." I wink back at him.

Coulter gives a big belly laugh. "I definitely found the right person to bother. Do I want to know why you're alone? Did you run away from your tour group?"

I shake my head. "Well…" I reconsider. "Sort of. I ran away from my resort."

"Perfectly acceptable. Was there a reason for this escape? Not enough nacho chips. Ah, speaking of which!" I look up to find a waitress with a tight red T-shirt and tired eyes smiling at Coulter, hands full of tortilla chips and salsa. "I moved tables," he confesses. "Hope that's okay."

By the way she's looking at him, I think anything Coulter does would be okay for her.

"We need a round of margaritas," he continues. "Spicy?" He raises his eyebrows at me, and I nod in agreement. "And since I'm a wimp, I'll go for the passion fruit 'rita. On the rocks, please. And my new friend needs some of your amazing guac because I'm eating the rest of this." He scoops up another chip heaped with guacamole.

When the waitress leaves with our order, Coulter leans across the table. "You have to have them on the rocks. They water it down with all the slushy stuff."

"I've only ever had the slushy ones."

"Well, then, here's to expanding your horizons."

By the time I finish my second margarita, I feel like I'm already half in love with him. It's not only his looks that appeal to me, but Coulter is nice. And sweet. And funny. And treats me like I'm the only woman in the world.

I know he's a stranger, probably putting on an act the same as I am. I'm sure by the end of our meal, he's come up with a slimy sales pitch or will suggest I go back to his hotel room with him, but right now I don't care. I feel more of a tingle from the way he smiles at me more from the tequila.

This is a new Emmy, sitting with a man she doesn't know, talking and laughing and *flirting*. I didn't think I remembered how to flirt but look at me now.

"You never told me why you're all alone," I ask as the waitress brings the third round of drinks as well as a plate of nachos for us to share.

"I think your escape would make a much more interesting story." I shrug, unwilling to bring Matt and the others into my little Coulter bubble. "Just tell me one thing," he says nervously. "Do you have a husband out there who's going to be upset that I'm monopolizing your time?"

"I think it's up to me whether you're monopolizing my time."

"So I'm not?" A hopeful smile.

"Well, yes, but I don't mind. Yet."

"Ah, well, if I'm too much for you, feel free to escape from me. But I should tell you, that I'm a master at monopolizing. I've stayed with so many people, and no one has ever asked me to leave. I don't think you'll be wanting to escape from me. Unless, of course, we get caught and have to both escape."

"I don't think that's necessary. I don't have a husband and I doubt my boyfriend will be coming after me."

"Why ever not?"

"I think he's in love with someone else."

Coulter leans back in his chair with a chip covered with melted cheese in his hand. "I have to hear about this."

"For some strange reason, I feel like I can tell you."

"Of course you can tell me. Anything. It's much easier to admit things to strangers. But it doesn't seem like we're strangers, does it?"

"It really doesn't."

"I think we've bonded. And don't give me that look, the one where you're thinking that the other shoe is going to drop, that I'm suddenly going to switch into my hard press to get you into this awesome timeshare program." He laughs at my expression of surprise. "You were thinking that, weren't you?"

"I was," I admit. "That, and the possibility of you spiking my drink and dragging me back to your hotel room to take advantage of me."

I'm half-serious about this last part and I think Coulter realizes it.

"Well, there's no need to worry about that. I've never spiked a drink or taken advantage of anyone." He meets my gaze and gives me a devilish grin. "I've never needed to. Plus, my hotel is back in Cancun, so that's a fair drag."

"That is a little far," I agree, relieved at his honesty. At least I think he's honest. Years of Ed's warnings of the danger of men try and push their way in, spoiling my happiness. I don't want anything to spoil today. I think I'm safe with Coulter.

Plus, I've been taking karate with my boys for years, and I know how to defend myself.

"Now that we're cleared that up," Coulter says through a mouthful of chips and cheese. "Tell me about why you left."

So I do. I tell him about Matt and I coming across Jasmine and Billy last night, and Matt's reaction. I tell him what Billy told me, that they're swingers, or at least trying things out.

"They met this couple before we got there, and I guess that's what they're into," I finish, taking a long pull from my drink.

"Don't tell me." Coulter chuckles softly. "Gorgeous older woman with white hair. And a good-time guy who is nearly as cute as I am?"

My stomach falls and I glance around, looking for the trap. "How did you know?"

"Morena and Jed," he says with another chuckle. "I should have known. Jed's one of my best friends. They're who I'm meeting here."

Matt

AFTER I SEE MORENA and Jed on the bus—we're so deep in conversation that they miss the next van going to Playa del Carmen and have to wait another hour—I go in search of my friends.

I find them still at breakfast, sitting at a table for six, clearly waiting for me and Emmy.

Jasmine is the first to notice me and her eyes widen with alarm until I smile reassuringly. She's my next conversation, mainly to apologize, but I'll want to do that in private.

"Morning," I call out as I approach. "I'm going to grab some grub and then I'll join you."

A few minutes later I'm back with a tray of breakfast burritos, a plate of bacon, and another mimosa.

"Where's Emmy?" Claire asks, but it's Billy that I direct my answer to.

"Seems like she's gone off for a jaunt," I say lightly. "I got a message that she went into Playa del Carmen early this morning."

"I would have gone with her..." Jasmine smiles foolishly. "But I guess she wanted to be alone."

"I guess. Things got—I'm sure you've all talked about it." I look from person to person. "Maybe it's time to fill me in on a few things."

"I thought we should tell you," Basil says under his breath.

"And I didn't," Jasmine admits, looking me straight in the eye. "I had my reasons, and I can see that I was wrong to keep it from you."

"I would have liked to know what was going on." I pause and take a bite of bacon. "So what is going on?"

They tell me about Aurora, about meeting Carson and Wyatt, each tripping over the other with the effort of getting the story out.

"Did you have any idea the place was for swingers?" Billy asks.

I give my head a shake. "None. Do you think Shawna would have stepped foot in the place if she'd known?"

"Definitely not," Claire says, so despairingly that it gets me wondering what she really thought of my ex.

"So what happened?" I ask slowly. "With these...swingers."

I'm surprised when Jasmine is the one who replies. "We hooked up with them," she says with a defiant tilt to her chin. "Me and Wyatt, Billy and Carson, and Claire and Basil."

I nod, with no idea how to respond to that. Asking how it seemed rude, but it's all I can think about. What was Claire like? Did Jasmine like being with another man? Where did this all happen?

I don't even want to get into the logistics of the kids being there or the fact that for years, we've been bringing our children into a swingers resort for a family vacation.

I just shake my head about that one.

"So what about your marriages?" I ask instead. "What has this...sharing...done? Better? Worse?"

Again, it's Jasmine who answers, like she's been elected spokesperson for the group. "Things are good," she says firmly. "We keep things honest and open and I think our relationship is better for it." She glances at Claire for confirmation.

"I agree," Claire says.

"I think it's improved certain things," Billy drawls. "But I'm not sure you want to hear about that."

"Not really, no." I give a half-hearted grin. "But I do want to hear about you and Emmy."

"What did she tell you?" Billy gives me a shifty glance.

"That's the thing. She didn't say anything after I got back to the room, and she was gone when I woke up."

"Well, you were a bit—" Billy begins, but Jasmine cuts him off.

"Mean. You were very mean to her," she says with a shake of her finger. "I like Emmy. I think she's good for you."

"I like her too, but I think we might have rushed things a little, coming down here so soon after starting dating."

"I wondered about that," Basil says in a smug voice.

"Yeah, well, she's a great girl and I like her. But maybe I've got too much baggage right now to be in a relationship."

"Or maybe she does," Claire offers. "She said something about a husband. Sounds like he was bad news."

"She hasn't even told me half of it," I admit. "Which I guess is why she didn't tell me about you and her."

Billy meets my gaze. "I loved her. I was seventeen and she was my first everything. I was crazy about her, and then her parents moved and I was stupid about it. Never saw her again until you guys were in the lobby." He shakes his head. "You have no idea the shock that gave me."

"Talk about a blast from the past."

"And I've been tiptoeing around her because you didn't know, and I didn't want to cause problems. Sorry I didn't tell you."

"I think she should have been the one to say something," I say ruefully.

"Open and honest," Jasmine reminds me.

"I agree with that. Thanks for finally telling me."

"So...now that you know... what do you think?" Basil asks.

"I don't really know," I say slowly. "The fact that the four of you did this...are doing this...that's fine. It's your life, and I'm not judging. I just really hope it doesn't come between you, because after going through one divorce, I'm in no mood to go through another one."

"But what about you?" Claire asks. "Do you want to play?"

I look from one to another, my gaze finally landing on Jasmine. For once it's hard for me to read her expression.

"I'm going to have to think about that," I admit. "I need to talk to Emmy first. I have a feeling we're not going to be together much longer, so I can't answer for her." I glance at Billy, who is staring at his plate of congealed eggs to hide his expression. I can read this one. It's hope. Hope that Emmy is interested enough to try this out.

"As for me..." I shrug and pick up my glass. "Ask me again after a few drinks."

CHAPTER EIGHT

Emmy

THINGS GET A LOT more personal after we get to the Morena and Jed connection.

"Are you a swinger too?" I ask. I sound too eager, too desperate for information.

Why do I want more information on something I'm never going to do?

"Just because I'm good friends with those who follow that lifestyle doesn't mean that I do too," Coulter says archly. Then he grins. "I'm a single guy, so I'm not sure I classify as a swinger. Do I agree with open marriages? Yes? Am I comfortable with polyamory? Yes. I've been in love with a woman and a man at the same time. Do I judge others' ideas of love and commitment? Absolutely not. To each their own." He finishes his margarita and looks around for the waitress. "I'm going to need another one of these if we're talking about this."

"Me too." I feel so inexperienced. Naïve. Love and romance for me have always been with one person at a time; sex, when it happens, has been the same. Dealing with more than one man at a time would be complicated, and possibly exhausting.

But two men at a time would possibly mean more sex. What's possible about it? There would definitely be more sexual gratification coming my way if I included another man—say, Coulter—into my life.

I watch him across the table, trying not to seem like I'm staring. Why would I think about sex with Coulter?

Why *wouldn't* I think about sex with Coulter? If those full lips said anything about me and him, I might have a serious problem finding the word *no*.

"Tell me what's going on with you," he invites after the waitress brings us another round and takes away the remains of the nachos. "What's this boyfriend like?"

Matt. His name rips through my Coulter-haze and brings with it a twinge of guilt. Not only did I run away from him, but I'm also enjoying myself too much for a woman with a boyfriend.

"We've only been together a few weeks," I say weakly.

"This is a perfectly platonic lunch you're having with a new friend," Coulter assures me. "In case you're getting the guilts. I will admit to having a hope of the possibility..." He wiggles his finger between us. "But I'm not about to act on it unless you give me the go-ahead. We can sit here and flirt like mad for the rest of the day, and you'll still be safe and sound with me."

"That's good to know." Really, it's not. His words send my stomach sinking to my toes. Even though I would never do anything to betray Matt, it might be nice if Coulter seems a little more torn up by the fact I have a boyfriend.

But how much of a boyfriend is Matt? In love with another woman, most likely already planning a rendezvous with her tonight...

Still...

"What's the matter?" Coulter asks. "Your face is like an open book. All these emotions keep whipping across it."

I cover my cheeks with my hands. "I have the worst poker face," I admit. "And my kids can always tell when I'm mad, or when I'm teasing them about something."

"Or when you're happy," Coulter adds, leaning forwards with his elbows on the table. "You're happy when you mention your kids. Not so much when you mention the boyfriend. Can he still be called a boyfriend? I feel like I'm back in high school."

That, of course, reminds me of Billy, but I push any thoughts of him far back in my mind. Now is not the time for Billy.

"I don't think we've been together long enough for me to call him a partner. Partner." I try out the word. "It makes me feel like I work in a law firm."

"Not me, because there's no way I'd ever work in a law firm." With a loud sucking noise from the straw, he drains his glass.

"I think he's in love with someone else," I say slowly. "I think he's been in love with her for a long time. I think I'm going to feel like a third wheel when I get back because she's on vacation with us."

"So maybe it was a good thing that you met Jed and Morena," Coulter says.

"Maybe." Billy pops into my mind again. "I'm not sure how long he's going to be my boyfriend."

"So I met you at the perfect time." Coulter raises his eyebrows suggestively, and I laugh, grateful for the change in the mood.

I don't want to get into Matt, and Matt and Jasmine, or even Billy right now. There'll be time enough for that when I get back to the resort. I glance at my watch, noticing I have at least another hour before the first van heads back to the resort. "I'm glad I met you."

Coulter rears back. "You make it sound like this is the end of it. Uh uh. Drink up sweetie, and let's go find some trouble to get into."

Obediently, I take a long sip. "I thought you were meeting Jed and Morena?" I ask, feeling the rush from the alcohol as well as knowing Coulter isn't leaving me.

"They'll find us."

Feeling ridiculously pleased that he's picking me over them, I finish my margarita while Coulter pays for lunch. Then, grabbing my hand, we head back onto the streets of Playa del Carmen.

Coulter pulls me from one store to another, and the margaritas we drank make everything more fun, more amusing, and definitely sillier. I do my best to convince him to buy a three-foot-wide sombrero; he thinks I need a thickly woven poncho with a map of Mexico emblazoned on the front of it.

The number of bags increases from store to store with Coulter playing gentleman and carrying mine.

"I need another drink," he says. "Especially since I doubt Morena and Jed are ever going to show up."

"I hope I didn't take their ride." I've had nervous thoughts about that since Coulter told me they were supposed to meet him.

But he waves away my concern. "I'm glad they're late because I never would have met you."

"Well, you might have met me if I'd bumped into them," I say realistically. "Seeing as I kind of know them."

Coulter narrows his eyes. "How kind of? We never got into that."

"There's nothing to get into. I spent the day snorkelling with Jed. I danced with him. Morena...I haven't gotten much of a chance to get to know her."

"She's great. I want a clone of her. It'd probably be the only way I'd settle down."

"Mr. Anti-Commitment, are you?"

"Mr. Anti a lot of things," he admits. "But why waste a perfectly good day on my issues? Especially when we could be—" He suddenly grabs my hand and pulls me across to an open door. "Tasting tequila."

The chalkboard A-frame outside the door invites us in with a crude drawing of a bottle with the requisite worm inside, along with the words, "Best tequila to taste."

"Well, if it's the best." I shrug and lead Coulter inside. "We'd better try it."

Twenty minutes later, we're back on the street, this time swaying dangerously because of what might have been the best tequila I've ever tasted. The bag carrying three bottles bangs painfully against my leg as Coulter jostles against me in the busy street. The rain had stopped while we were drinking our fill of the different types of tequila, and shoppers now mill about what had been a quiet patch of stores.

"What next?" Coulter asks eagerly.

"Shouldn't you try and find Jed and Morena?" I hear the reluctance in my voice. I don't remember the last time I've had such a good time, with or without alcohol. Being with Coulter is easy and fun; there's no need for serious conversations or decisions and I've managed to put Matt completely out of my head.

I know that will change when we find Jed and Morena. Even if they know nothing about the events of last night, they're part of it and the inevitable questions about why I'm here without Matt will bring everything to a head.

"No!" Coulter cries and my heart sings. I'm sure it's the liquor that is making him so inconsiderate to his friends, but I feel like being inconsiderate today. It's not a common feeling for me. "They'll take you away from me." He tucks his free hand behind my head and pulls me close in an awkward hug. His bags full of souvenirs bang against the back of my legs, but I don't pull away. "Jed will tell me to *behave*. I don't want to behave. I want it to be like this for as long as we can."

With my face pressed against his chest, I breathe in his scent and think that sounds like a good idea. I wrap an arm around his waist and lean closer, hearing the quick intake of breath.

This might not be the best idea, because now I don't want to let go.

We stand on the street, forcing shoppers to pass around us. I can't let go. Being with Coulter today has made me feel like a different person. Forget about my baggage and my issues, and the questions hovering around my relationship with Matt—today I'm just Emmy who is fun and funny and has the attention of a really good-looking man.

Who is now hugging me, like he doesn't want to let go.

I think he might have sniffed my hair, but even that makes me happy. Makes me...

The happiness and contentment I've found today seem to suddenly congregate between my legs. Hugging Coulter turns me on. That's never happened.

I stiffen in his arms, unsure of what to do. This seems wrong now...but right.

"I like you," he murmurs into my hair. "I'm sorry."

"Why are you sorry?" I whisper into his shirt.

I'm never going to see him again.

Suddenly Coulter gasps. "There they are!" Without giving me a chance to look down the street, he grabs my hand and pulls me into the nearest store.

Matt

AFTER BREAKFAST, BASIL AND Billy talk about booking another snorkelling excursion. After a long look at me, Claire stands up to join them, leaving me and Jasmine alone at the table.

I wait impatiently until Claire is out of earshot. "Did you tell Basil about last night?"

"What exactly should I tell him about last night?" Jasmine asks, nibbling on the end of a churro.

"That I—you know..." I stumble with the words, filled with a fervent wish that maybe Jasmine forgot about how I threw myself at her.

But she kind of threw herself back at me, so I hope she didn't forget that.

"That you kissed me?"

My heart sinks. "Well, yeah. I should apologize."

Jasmine gazes coolly at me. "You're sorry that you kissed me?"

Maybe that wasn't the best thing to say. I try again, more diplomatically. "I was upset and angry and maybe I shouldn't have done it."

"Maybe...shouldn't have...Did you want to?" Jasmine presses. "Did you want to kiss me?"

I look everywhere but Jasmine, hoping to find the right answer among the tables and trays of half-eaten food. I'm not sure there is one. "I...uh...I'm not sure what you want me to say?"

"What do you want to say?"

I've always thought that while Jasmine is a good teacher, I'd be scared to be in a classroom with her. I throw up my hands with frustration. "Stop messing with me! I'm going through a difficult time here."

Jasmine leans back in her chair and bites the churro in half. I watch in fearful fascination as she chews and swallows. "What exactly is so difficult about it? To me, you overacted over something that was none of your business."

"I thought you were cheating on Basil! Of course it's my business!"

She narrows her eyes. "Is that what got you so upset? Because I don't remember you mentioning Basil much."

I exhale in a hiss. "Look, Jas, what do you want? Seriously?"

"Are you in love with me?" she asks as if we're discussing the weather.

"Why is everyone so concerned with that?" I mutter. I glance up as a couple sits at the table next to us. "Why don't we talk about this somewhere else?"

"No, this is fine."

"Are you mad? You're mad. I said I shouldn't have—"

Jasmine leans forward. "Matt, I've been in love with you since sixth grade. I've never said anything because I was afraid of ruining our friendship."

At her words, I stop breathing. *Love...friendship...afraid...*It seems like Jasmine is talking to me from a great distance. I cough once, take a deep breath. "You've been what?"

"You heard me," Jasmine says impatiently. "There was once—the one time I got up enough courage to tell you how I felt, was the night you met Shawna. I knew there was no way I could compete with her. She was tall and blonde and gorgeous, confident and totally in charge of her life and I was little Jasmine, who'd been tagging after you like a lost dog. I gave up that night. There would never be a Matt and Jasmine. You'd never see me in that way—as a woman. I was firmly in the friend zone and I've lived with that. I've gotten over it for the most part and went on with my life. I met Basil and I'm happy with him." She took a deep breath and reached across the table for Basil's half-finished juice he'd left behind. "And then last night, because you see me with *Billy*, you get all pissy and finally, after years of me wondering and wishing, you kiss me." She stares at me with spots of colour on her cheeks and her eyes blazing. "So yes. I'm a little pissed off with you."

I process her words slowly; carefully going over each word and the result is a swirl of emotions. "You love me?"

"I'm not going through this again. It's embarrassing enough the first time."

"Jas." I reach out my hand and touch her fingers tapping on the table. She stares at it like it's a kind of rodent.

"I don't want your pity. I've been an idiot and the last thing I want is—"

"I've been in love with you since I saw you walk down the aisle," I blurt out. "You got married and it was like..." I can't put into words how I felt seeing Jasmine in her white dress, hand in hand with Basil, professing to love him and knowing I had as much of a chance as a snowball in hell with her. How could I ever think I'd make her happy when she was clearly over the moon to be marrying Basil?

Jasmine stares at me incredulously for a long moment, leaving me wondering if I should say something more before she throws up her hands. "What the hell am I supposed to do with that information?"

"I don't know." The noise of the restaurant swelled as a large group walked past us, talking and laughing like they don't have a care in the world. Like there was no possibility of their world being turned upside down like mine has been.

"I'm happy with Basil," Jasmine says in a small voice.

"I know," I'm quick to assure her. "And I'm glad. Really. I only want you to be happy, Jas. I've always wanted that. I'm sorry if I messed it up."

"I don't know what you did." She taps her fingers on the table like she does when she's thinking.

"Do you want me to go?" I ask in a low voice. "Give you some time?"

Jasmine heaves a sigh. "I don't think time is going to help."

"Maybe not, but I don't know what else to do." I sit quietly for a moment watching Jasmine. "It wasn't the first time we've kissed, you know."

Jasmine looks at me and I'm grateful that her eyes have warmed slightly. "We were fifteen and you kissed me out of pity," she says wryly. "I don't count that."

"It wasn't the best." I smile at the memory; at Jasmine and I standing a foot apart, of not knowing where to put my hands, and the feeling that kissing Jasmine should be more fun. Despite the awkwardness, I also remember my bewilderment that I was hard from kissing Jasmine, and quickly pulling away.

Jasmine shakes her head at the memory. "It was horrible. At least you've gotten better." Her last words are said under her breath like she doesn't want me to hear."

"What's that you say?" I smile widely. "Better, you say?"

"It was okay," she says grudgingly.

At least she smiles when I laugh. I reach out and take the hand now fidgeting with the cutlery. "Look, Jas, you're important to me. In fact, now you are the most important woman in my life. I don't want to ever spoil that, and it kills me to think I put our friendship in jeopardy because I was jealous."

"It's not spoiled," she concedes.

"It could have been," I press. "But thankfully, you're sweet enough to forgive me, and maybe this could be a blessing in disguise."

"What's that supposed to mean?"

"We know where we both stand. And since you're taking a dip in the swinger pool, maybe this'll be a good chance to see where we *really* stand. See how good we'd be together."

An uncomfortable silence falls and I look around wildly once again, realizing I over spoke and wishing I could reel my words back, like catching a fish. Maybe she doesn't want that. Maybe she doesn't want me. She said she got over me—

"I love Basil," Jasmine says finally.

"I know." My shoulders slump miserably. That's it. That's over. How am I supposed to get past this?

"You really want to try it? You and me?" Jasmine's tone is both skeptical and hopeful. It's the hopeful aspect that makes me smile.

"Yeah," I say, still holding her hand. "I do."

CHAPTER NINE

Emmy

"THEY'RE HERE!" COULTER GRASPS my hand and swings into the store next door, claustrophobic with racks and piles of colourful clothes. "We have to hide. We have to hide," he repeats to the wide-eyed salesgirl. She only nods and motions us to the back of the store.

Coulter has a tight grip on my hand as he drags me along behind him. "Coulter, wait! I thought you were meeting them."

"I'm having too much fun with you." He pulls me deeper past the racks and piles, into a curtained alcove in the back corner. As he bundles me inside and yanks the fabric closed, we hear voices.

"Is that them?" I shudder with the urge to giggle.

"I don't know." Coulter must have the same need to laugh because his eyes are dancing and he claps a hand over his mouth.

"What are we doing?" I whisper.

"I don't know!"

One moment I was hugging him on the street, and now I'm crammed in a tiny changing room with him. I do my best to slow my breathing as I realize how small it really is. With our myriad of plastic bags crowding around us like an audience, Coulter is barely a hand-width away from me.

He sucks in his breath when we hear more voices and I try to suppress the laughter. With blue eyes open wide and his hand clapped over his mouth, Coulter looks like a cartoon version of a Man Afraid. The store is narrow and deep and when a couple picks through the stacks of colourful tourist shirts nearby, my eyes widen too, because we can hear every word.

It's not Morena and Jed.

But we still huddle in the changing room, shaking with suppressed laughter.

Coulter gently sets down his bags at his feet, shuffling closer to me, and rests a hand on the wall behind me. His scent surrounds me, hot and spicy, like the margaritas I had for lunch.

I don't know where to look. He stands before me, blocking the curtain with his wide shoulders. My gaze is fixed on his yellow linen shirt and with a blink, I see that it's still damp from the rain. Hesitantly, I put my hand on his shoulder, smoothing the material with nervous fingers.

I don't look at him, just continue to run my hands over his shoulders, feeling the muscles tense under my touch. His chest is broad and for a moment I have the urge to rest my head against it like a pillow. Wrap my arms around his waist, and push myself against him...

I feel his heartbeat as my hands drift lower, pretending I'm checking to see how wet his shirt is, but really just taking the opportunity to touch him.

He lets me. When I reach the waistband of his short, Coulter sucks in his breath with an audible gasp but I only tap the belt loops as I slide both hands around his waist. I step closer as my hands curve over his ass.

I cup his ass—firm and fine through his khaki shorts—and lean my forehead against his chest.

What am I doing?

It's as if my hands have a mind of their own, with the sole purpose to explore Coulter's body. It's a heady experience, letting want take over from knowing the right thing to do. I know I should grab my things and push past into the store, calling after Morena and Jed and letting them take Coulter away from me. But I don't want to.

As my hands slip under his untucked shirt, his bare skin is warm, smooth. Soft. I need to move closer to allow my hands to run up his back, under his shirt, and when I lean my body against his, there's a hardness pressing against my belly.

I inhale a shaky breath as his hands rest on my waist. His touch is light, gentle, in no way threatening, like an invitation to keep up my exploration of his back.

He makes a noise when I scratch my nails along his shoulders, and I bring my hands down to his ass again, cupping firmly.

I want to pull him against me. I want to pull him inside me.

The thought has me swaying to keep my balance.

But I let my hands continue to wander around his waist again, to where the hardness of his cock strains the front of his shorts.

I touch it. Running my hand along his considerable length, I finally look up and meet Coulter's gaze. I smile, my eyes crinkling at the corners.

His mouth crushes me with his kiss.

Coulter bounds into action like a tiger tired of watching his prey. My hands are trapped between us as he yanks me against him, his mouth practically devouring me. Fingers tangle in my hair; I realize a second too late that his other hand is already up the skirt of my dress, hot against my bare leg.

If I'm going to stop him, I'd better do it now.

But I don't.

His hand burrows between my legs, cupping my heat for a moment before his fingers snake under the elastic of my panties.

Coulter is touching me...his fingers probing...there's a moment of terror.

What am I *doing*?

And then his finger is inside me, his thumb against my clit and I gasp against his mouth. Instead of pushing him away, of running away *get away*, I push against his hand.

I forget the world exists; the feel of his hand, his lips against mine, his tongue tangled with mine is all I want. All I need.

Coulter pulls away from me, leaning back just enough to look at me, his fingers busy...so busy...

My eyes flutter closed as I surrender to the pleasure building inside me. It's close...already so close.

"Open your eyes," Coulter says in a ragged whisper. "I want to see you come."

His arm tightens around my waist as my legs threaten to buckle. "I can't," I breathe.

"Oh, yes, you can." His fingers thrust inside me, and I look down, at his arm disappearing under my skirt.

His fingers are *inside* me...

And then they're rubbing my clit again and the sensations that have built so quickly reach the peak. "Don't stop," I beg with a groan. "Please..."

Coulter claps a hand over my mouth as I come, my legs shaking, cries muffled. My body still tingles as he steps away.

"I need to fuck you," he says in a hoarse voice.

I don't say anything as suddenly his cock is free from his shorts, suddenly he has a condom in his hand, and suddenly he spreads my legs and thrusts inside me.

It happens so fast.

Coulter picks me up and I fight to wind my legs around his waist. One makes it, the other dangles lifelessly as he slams me against the wall. Hangers jangle, a gauzy shirt falls onto my head as he fucks me.

He fucks me hard enough that I see the curtain dance over his shoulder. It's like he's going to pound me through the wall; how can the whole store not know what we're doing?

But I don't care because I want more. It's not enough. "More," I gasp. "Harder."

I want to go through the wall; I want the store to know I'm fucking in the changing room, fucking a man I barely know.

Coulter thrusts harder, slamming into me like his life depends on it.

Maybe it does.

It feels like it does.

I reach overhead, searching for something to hang onto, to brace myself. The hangers jab into my shoulder, but I don't feel any pain because the most intense sensation builds in my core and I have to let it out. I need to scream because it's so very, very good.

Coulter slams his mouth over mine as my scream threatens, again muffling my cries as I come again, so quickly and so intense that my entire body tenses like a live wire until I collapse bonelessly in Coulter's arms.

Another thrust, and another, and he comes inside me. This time I muffle his cry.

Matt

I'M IN OUR ROOM when Emmy gets back; inside because the fine mist had deepened into a flash downpour, forcing those still around the pool to rush to find cover in a dead run. I wasn't fast enough and I rub my hair with a towel, but rain in Mexico is much better than the snow that falls back at home.

Already the sky is lightening in the distance and I know the rain won't last long.

I lay down on the bed, contemplating a nap when Emmy lets herself into the room. "Emmy," I cry, jumping to my feet like I'd last seen her months ago. "You're back."

"Sorry I left without saying anything." Her hair is wet from the rain, her T-shirt hugging her breasts. She doesn't look me in the eyes.

Feeling foolish, I sit back down. "Don't worry about it. I'm glad you're back. I didn't know if you'd come back."

This gets me a glance. "Of course I'd come back."

"Well, I wasn't sure. I'm sorry about last night. I didn't handle that well." She nods, dropping her bags on the table. One clinks like there are bottles inside. "You did some shopping."

"I went to Playa del Carmen. But I guess you got the message."

"Thanks for leaving one. Did you see Morena and Jed? I saw them before they left this morning."

"I did see them." I can't read her expression and that worries me. It almost seems like she's guilty, but I could be transferring my own feelings onto her.

I lean forwards on the bed. "Emmy, can we talk?"

"I think we need to." She fluffs up her hair. "Let me get changed."

"I don't mind the wet look." She smiles wanly and sits on the edge of the bed to take off her sneakers. "Will you tell me about Billy?"

She tosses a shoe by the door. "Do you really need to know, considering how fast you jumped to conclusions about me? Liar...cheat..."

"I apologize for that. It was...I was in shock."

"We need to talk about that too." A second shoe flies after the first before she turns to face me. "Jasmine?"

"I asked first," I remind her.

Instead of answering, Emmy gets up and goes to her clutter of plastic bags on the table. "I had a nice buzz going all afternoon and that bus ride took it away. Let's have a drink." She pulls a bottle out of the bag and sets it on the table.

"Is that tequila?"

She nods and unscrews the top. "I went to a tasting. It's good. Grab a couple of glasses."

Bemused at this new side of Emmy, I do as I'm told. She pours a healthy shot into each of the little glasses and we sit down, each on our own bed facing each other. "What do you want to know?" she asks.

"Everything?"

With a nod, she scoots back into the middle of the bed and crosses her legs yoga style. "I fell in love with Billy the first time I saw him, on my first day of high school," she begins. "Of course he didn't notice me for two whole years. Then we were together for over a year until my parents moved across the country."

"He was your first?" I ask.

"I guess that's the important part of all this," she says with a sarcastic curve of her mouth. "But yes, Billy took my virginity. Only once, because I guess that's all it takes. It was the night before I moved. Since we didn't make it to the prom, because that's the stereotypical time to do it. When did you lose your virginity?"

Her question catches me off-guard. "I—uh, I was seventeen. But why does that matter?"

"I don't know. Why does it?" she asks pointedly. "Do you really need to know how Billy was my first boyfriend, my first love, for a long time, the only guy to give me an orgasm—" I must have blanched because Emmy laughs. "Don't worry, you've made me come. Things seem to be working better down there these days. But do you want to know all that?"

I raise my hands. "I don't. You're right, it doesn't. I just want to know why you never told me you knew him."

"I didn't know how you'd react."

"Because of your ex-husband?" She nods and I press my lips together, not wanting to mention that she might have just as many issues as I do when it comes to exes. "Are you still in love with him?"

Because that would make this day just plain perfect.

"I haven't seen Billy since I moved," Emmy says. "I haven't thought about him in years. I have a lot of fond memories of him, but no, I'm no longer in love with him." She knocks back the rest of her tequila in one mouthful. "Now it's your turn. What's up with you and Jasmine?"

"I don't know."

"Shouldn't you figure that out?"

"I'm trying to. I kissed her last night," I admit. I finish my shot and get up to refill our glasses.

"Was that what the apology was for when you came into the room?"

I glance at her with surprise as I hand her the glass, the amber liquid sloshing up the side. "You were awake?"

"For a while. Was it a good kiss?"

"How can you ask that?" I lower myself back on the back. Was it a good kiss? Jasmine said it was *better* but was that the same as *good*? Did Jasmine feel like the Earth had shifted off its orbit as my mouth crashed against hers? Did she feel the urge to crawl inside me, to plot over every other emotion with her touch? "It was okay."

"How would you prefer me to ask it? Look, Matt, we're friends. Before the dating, having sex stuff, we were friends." She smiles and I'm reminded how much I like this woman. Before the sex stuff started, like she said, Emmy was a good friend. "I don't know what's going to happen with us, but I have a feeling we're not going to make it," she continues and I blink with surprise at her bluntness. "So let's stop pretending we're in the middle of this big love affair and just be friends for a minute. I think we both need a friend right now."

"Has that been what I've been doing?" I ask ruefully."Pretend ing we're in the middle of a big love affair?"

"Kind of. But it's okay. Both of us have got some serious bag-gage, and that's without Billy and Jasmine and your merry band of swinger friends."

"They can be your friends too."

"I like to think they are, but who knows what's going to happen. I doubt I'll see Morena and Jed again." She takes a deep breath and a big swallow of tequila. "Funny story—I met up with a friend of theirs in Playa."

"Really? They said they were going to meet someone."

"I saw them. They were late so I ended up having lunch with Coulter."

"Coulter—their friend? How did that happen? And do you normally have lunch with strange men?"

Emmy's eyes narrow at the self-righteous anger in my voice and once again, I wish I could take back my words. Emmy's right—we might be better off as friends, and considering what I dragged her into when I brought her down here, she has the right to do whatever she wants.

"If you're upset about me having lunch with him, then you're going to hate the fact that I had sex with him," she says.

I swallow the shot of tequila and pour myself another.

CHAPTER TEN

Emmy

I DIDN'T PLAN TO tell Matt about Coulter like that. It just happened; it irritated me how annoyed he seemed about sharing a simple meal, and I opened my mouth and the words popped out. It surprised me as much as Matt.

I see the look on his face—hurt, then a flash of anger. And finally resignation. He knows as well as I do that whatever we had, is over now, regardless of what happened with me and Coulter.

Coulter...

Everything still tingles. My skin feels alive, like a simple touch would send me into throes of ecstasy.

Maybe that's a bit much. But it's true that everything arouses me right now; Coulter's final hug almost had me dragging him between two cars for another go, the cologne of the driver of the van sent me daydreaming on the drive back, a fantasy that involved a flat tire and a tow-truck driver. Even Matt sitting with shoulders slumped on the bed has me wondering that if I climbed on his lap, would he feel better about things?

I've never felt so horny. I don't know if I have Coulter to thank for that, or it's just that my body decided to wake up. All of a sudden, it announces that, hello, I'm a woman and I have needs.

I like it.

When we came out of the store, my dress rumpled and wrinkled, my eyes glazed and with a silly smile on my face, Morena and Jed were standing outside, like they were waiting for us. Maybe they were. Maybe they saw us duck in; maybe they saw the way the building shook from the force of Coulter fucking me.

They didn't seem surprised at all to see us together.

But I didn't stay long enough to ask; with my face flaming, my body still screaming for more Coulter, I made my excuse and hurried back to where the van would pick me up.

Coulter followed me. "Emmy, wait."

"I have to get back," I throw over my shoulder.

"I will find you, you know. Just in case you think you can get away from me."

I stop so quickly, that Coulter runs into me. "You can't stop bumping into me, can you?" I say, fisting my hands in his shirt and pulling him closer.

"I can't help it."

"I need to get away from you now," I tell him, my voice fast and urgent. "But after...I don't know. But I will leave word with Morena about how you can find me." And then I kissed him, again and again, wondering why I was rushing to get away from him.

"So what's going on here?" I ask blithely, pretending like nothing I'd said mattered.

"I think you need to back up a minute." Matt stands and begins to pace in front of the beds. "You had sex with this guy. Don't you think I deserve some explanation?"

"You do." I fight the urge to rub my legs together. Twice! Coulter made me come twice and I'm still like a dog in heat, panting for more.

I swing the rest of the drink and climb across the bed for the bottle. Maybe it's the tequila. Maybe I'm just drunk.

Maybe I don't care what the cause it.

"I'm sorry."

I am sorry. I cheated on Matt. I never wanted to hurt him.

But I have a feeling I didn't hurt him. And I don't think he cares all that much about what I did with Coulter or anybody else.

To prove me right, Matt slowly nods his head. "I guess I can't blame you."

"You could..."

"I kissed Jasmine last night," he confesses stopping mid-pace and reaching for the bottle in my hand.

"That's a kiss. I did more than kiss." Why am I trying to one-up him?

"I would have done more. You with this guy—me with Jasmine—so what does this make us both?"

"Swingers?" The word pops from my mouth, as blithe and unconcerned as I've ever heard myself.

Matt stares at me for a moment, then laughs. "I guess so." He pours half a glass of tequila for himself before handing it back to me.

I swig straight from the bottle. "We don't have to be," I say quickly, feeling the burn of the alcohol, the haze of impending intoxication. Or maybe I'm just confused about what's going on. "We can just be two people who are messed up."

"I think I want to be a swinger." It takes a long moment for Matt to meet my gaze. "At least, I think I want to have sex with Jasmine."

"You think?" I ask, with a teasing smile twitching at the corners of my mouth.

"I do," he admits, sinking back onto the bed, glass clutched in his hand.

"I know." Flopping on the bed, I have to lean to the side to take another mouthful from the bottle. "Did she tell you what went on last night?"

Matt shrugged. "Jasmine had sex with two men. Jed and Billy."

"Really?" I prop myself up on my elbows, unable to conceal my interest. "What do you think that was like?"

"I have no idea. We didn't get into details," he mutters. "Would you want to do that?"

"Sure," I say automatically. "I mean, why not? I've got more lost time to make up for than you do."

"Would you ever want to be with two women?"

This is the last place I ever expected this conversation to go.

"I don't know." I think about Jasmine and Claire. Would I want to be intimate with them? Would I be comfortable caressing their bodies, touching them like Coulter touched me? And then an image of Morena in her cutoffs and T-shirt knotted to show an inch of stomach flashes through my mind. "Maybe?"

"I think that would be hot. To watch. Maybe join in."

"Every guy wants two women," I say scornfully. "That's the number one male fantasy."

"I guess." Matt shrugs with a lopsided grin. "What do you want? What's your fantasy?"

Coulter. "Rough," I say without thinking. "Hard and fast. I'd like to be overpowered. Not forced." I shudder. "I don't want that. But I want to be so turned on that I'd do anything for a man."

"Are you turned on now?" Matt asks in a low voice.

I glance over at his crotch. I can tell he's hard. I can tell from the sight of it pushing against his shorts, and I can tell from his voice.

Also, from the expression in his eyes. All three are enough to start a throbbing between my legs. I lick my lips. "Maybe."

Matt puts his glass on the floor between the beds and leans across the space to grab my ankle, then my knee. He pulls me across to the edge of the bed. "What did he do to you?" he asks, his voice thick with desire. "The guy you fucked."

"He fucked me." For some reason, it's important for me that Matt knows the difference. I might have made the first move on Coulter, but he was the one...

Twice.

"Same thing." His hands are hot on my legs, his grip tight.

"It's not. To me, if I fuck him, that means I'm on top. That I'm taking what I want from him. That's how it is with me."

"He took what he wanted from you instead." I can only nod as Matt's hands massage their way up my leg. "Did he make you come?"

I have to swallow before I can get the word out. "Twice."

"How?" Matt's voice is low and heavy, like a morning fog. I want to get lost in it.

"The first time was with his fingers—"

"Not his mouth."

"No."

"I think I'd like to use my mouth."

The air conditioning kicks on, making me jump. "Okay," I murmur.

"Do you like that? When a man uses his mouth?"

"I—I don't know." Instead of being embarrassed by my inexperience, I want Matt to change things. I want him to do a lot of things.

Right now.

His fingers dig into my calves, moving past my knees with quick efficiency and sending tingles through my body. "Has anyone ever used their mouth?"

"Once," I admit, dropping my eyes at the memory of the first man I'd had after I left Ed. "I didn't really like it. I don't think he was very good."

Matt gives a bark of laughter. "I don't know if I'm any good either," he confesses. "It's not something I did with Shawna. She didn't want to."

The thought of Matt...just the thought of it is turning me on. I stare at his mouth, wondering what it would be like, how it would feel. I thought Coulter was enough but now I realize he was just the warm-up.

"You can try with me," I whisper. "If you want."

Instead of answering, Matt grabs both of my ankles and yanks me to the edge of the bed, my skirt pulling up to leave my panties on display.

They're not on display for long as Matt pulls them off. "I want."

And then he kneels on the floor between the beds, stroking my inner thighs, massaging my muscles as he slowly works his way up, spreading my legs open. He stops briefly at the apex, his hand between my legs.

On my pussy.

Even thinking the word forces a shaky breath from me.

He palms my pussy before sliding a finger into my wetness. "He fucked you."

"You don't have to do this," I say weakly, already moving my hips with anticipation.

"I said I want to," he says, moving a finger slowly inside me. "I'm going to make you come better than he did."

I'm not sure that's possible but go for it, I think as he pushes my legs apart even farther, bending my knees and holding the backs of my thighs.

And then his tongue...

"Oh," I say in a small voice.

He starts with feather-light licks against my clit, then moves deeper into my cleft. Slow and languorously, Matt's tongue travels from my clit to my ass, stopping to explore everywhere in between. After the third time, I'm squirming with pleasure.

He spends countless minutes focused on just my clit, licking me with just the right amount of pressure so, all too soon, I cry out, begging him to make me come. But then he stops and begins to explore me with his fingers.

Matt's very good with his fingers and for a moment, I think he's finished with his mouth. I'm okay with that.

But there's still more to come. When he returns to my clit, he tries to suck it. It's awkward and it's clear this isn't what he's used to, but the sensation is exquisite, sending shivers through my legs and forcing me to grab the back of his head so he can take more of me into his mouth.

"You like that?" he murmurs into my pussy.

"Yes!"

"You like me sucking it?" He does it again, his mouth hot and demanding, and I shriek with pleasure. "I guess so."

When he starts licking my clit again, the pleasure is almost unbearable. The noises in the room startle me until I realize it's me. Me, who is so quiet that Matt once asked me if I came. Now I'm moaning, incomprehensible pleas for more, for him not to stop, to keep going, please, keep going.

I thrust against him, his fingers inside me – two maybe three – moving slowly but insistently. My orgasm builds, picking up speed like no climax I've ever felt before. Everything is pulled so tight that I feel like I'm about to snap.

"Oh, God, *please*," I beg, my hands on the back of his head pushing him deeper.

And then I come with a cry so loud I'm sure the next room can hear. It goes on and on and Matt keeps going, licking and sucking and finger fucking me like he doesn't have a care in the world. I writhe on the bed, coming again and again, unable to stop, not wanting to stop until Matt lifts up his head.

"How was that?"

"You need to fuck me now," I say, unable to catch my breath. Not even my vibrator can make me come like that.

Without warning, Matt rolls me over, pulling up my hips so that my ass is in the air, and then he's inside of me.

It's hard and fast; exactly what I want. His hands roughly grip my hips, thrusting deep. I moan, pushing my hips back against him.

"You like this too?" he demands. "Do you?"

"Yes." I don't need to say anything, because Matt can tell just how much I like it. "I like...so good...feels so good..."

"You like it hard."

"Yes!"

"Tell me how much."

"So...much..." His thrusts slam the bed forward and I fist the bedspread in my hands to keep my balance. "Harder," I beg. "Please! Don't stop—please, fuck me hard, so hard!"

"Fuck you so hard," Matt mutters, his words punctuated by deeper thrusts. I bury my face into the bed as my orgasm begins, begging for more until the moment it hits, sending my body arching up with a scream, and forcing Matt to come with an animal-like growl.

As he pulls out of me, I can only collapse onto the bed. "I think you should stop making love," I say in a breathless voice, turning my head so he can hear me. "And just fuck like that all the time."

Matt

NEITHER OF US IS in any shape to meet the others for dinner.

The next day, we wake up early and decide to spend the day together, just the two of us. Regardless of how good the sex was yesterday, I have a feeling we're not going to make it when we get back home. I spend the day enjoying Emmy and coming to grips with that.

By the time we return from exploring the ruins of Tulum, sunburnt and starving, I think I have.

I'm also excited about what's going to happen that night.

I bumped into Billy in the lobby before we left for the excursion. "What's going on tonight?" I asked, after giving him the PG-rated recap of my night with Emmy.

"Dinner, and..." He shrugs, like he's unconcerned, typical Bill. "Same as every night here."

"Is anything *happening*?" I ask again, with emphasis and a raised eyebrow. "Like, with you guys? Because I think we're interested." I finish with a casual shrug, mirroring Billy.

"Really? Emmy too." He can't hide the surprised expression, or how pleased he is at the thought.

"That's what *we* means. I don't think I'd do it without her."

"I'll tell the others. Nothing happened last night. Morena and Jed never made it back until late."

I don't tell him about Emmy meeting up with their friend. I don't want to know more about that, and I suspect Bill doesn't either.

I also don't mention my conversation with Billy to Emmy until we're back at the hotel dressing for dinner. "Are you sure about tonight?" My reflection hovers at the edge of the mirror as Emmy brushes her hair.

"Whatever you want," she says without meeting my eyes.

What I want is to put my arms around her and fuck her like I did yesterday, but there are too many things in the way.

Namely, Jasmine and the image of Emmy with another man. And then the image of her with Bill keeps slipping in.

I've spent the entire day trying not to think about sex and failing miserably.

"What do you want?" I ask instead.

Emmy puts down her brush. "We can go around and around on this, but it's pointless. You're intrigued enough to talk about it, so I know you want to try. And to be honest, so do I. I'm...inexperienced," she says with a rueful shrug. "And I'd like to change that to better understand what I want."

"You seemed to know what you wanted yesterday," I mutter.

"That's one day. I have a lot of years to make up for, years when other people told me what I wanted. It's time for me. I say we try."

"What about us?" I ask in a quiet voice. My feelings for Jasmine have been there for so long that they seem separate for what I feel about Emmy. And to be honest, I'm not exactly sure what I feel for Emmy. I like her; I think she's great. Do I think this will lead to something more, something deeper? I'm not sure. Do I think I should let it?

Again, I'm not sure about that. I have a feeling I might need to do some work on myself before I try to make a relationship work.

But I don't need to decide that now.

"I don't know," Emmy says. I'm glad we're on the same wavelength about that.

"You look great," I tell her, finally slipping my arms around her. "At least I want to make sure I tell you that."

She meets my gaze in the mirror and smiles sadly. I wonder if tonight will be as bittersweet for Emmy as it is for me.

CHAPTER ELEVEN

Emmy

MORENA IS THE FIRST one I see as we walk into to restaurant. The others are waiting, laughing at something Billy says. Morena is the only one facing the door.

"Emmy." Her smile is big and bright and she moves towards me with arms outstretched. "I missed you." She folds me into a hug and I return the pressure with surprise. "I heard you met Coulter," she whispers.

"I told Matt about him," I say in a low voice as I pull away.

"Ah." Morena's eyes flick to Matt and he reaches for my hand with a smile as he notices.

I still can't understand how he isn't more upset, but there's no point in questioning it.

The others greet us—the women with hugs and kisses, the men with slaps on the shoulders for Matt and kisses on the cheeks for me.

Billy keeps his hand on my waist a moment longer than necessary, letting me breathe in the scent of his cologne.

Jed isn't so polite. He leans in, kisses me firmly on the lips. "Coulter," he says with a shake of his head.

"He's a nice guy." I'm not sure what else I'm allowed to say about him. Does everyone know about it?

I glance at Morena, relieved when she gives me a quick shake of her head in response to my unasked question.

"He's a *great* guy." Jed squeezes my shoulder. "One of my best mates. I'm glad you bumped into him, glad he could amuse you for the day."

"Sounds like he definitely amused her," Matt says under his breath, giving me a wink.

That is not normal behaviour for a spurned man, but then again, none of this has been a normal vacation. I smile at him as the hostess leads us to the table.

As we sit down and go through the regular steps of ordering drinks, a glance at the others. Morena and Jed, as much as an outsider as I am, seem to fit in perfectly. I wonder if it's the after-parties, as Morena calls them. I guess it's easy to make friends with people if you're having sex with them.

Billy has taken the seat next to me like I know he would. Like I hoped he would. As several conversations swirl across the table, he leans close to me.

"Matt says you and him ...tonight...?" He says it like a question.

Has he been thinking about it too?

I've been thinking about Billy all day long. When I haven't been wondering what's going to happen with Matt, that is, or remembering how it felt when Coulter fucked me.

I think about that a lot.

I also think about yesterday with Matt as well, so I've been thinking about sex for the majority of the day. It's a first for me, and it makes me feel heavy, with a dull throb between my legs.

Matt mentioned something about how pink my cheeks were early and wondered if I had gotten sunburned. I couldn't tell him that I was just horny.

How do you tell your boyfriend that you're excited thinking about having sex with another man?

Although, the way he handled the Coulter confession, maybe he'd be fine with it.

"Matt and I what tonight?" I say to Billy with a teasing smile.

"That you...that we—"

"We?" Had things been arranged already? I know deep down that I want to be with Billy tonight, but I thought the whole arrangement gave everyone a choice.

I want to make my own choice.

"Maybe we," Billy concedes, shifting in his seat. "If you want."

I glance across the table at Claire and find Morena watching me with an affectionate smile. "What do you want?" I ask Billy, then change my mind. If I get a choice, it's about time that I let what I want be heard, loud and clear. "Because I want you."

"Me?" Billy asks like it's a surprise. Maybe it is a surprise for him to hear me say it.

It's kind of a surprise for me too.

"You," I say, leaning in so I can whisper in his ear. "I'd like you to fuck me tonight."

Matt

DINNER PASSES QUICKLY, WITH good food, lots of wine and laughs flashing by that we pushed the fast forward button. To me, it seems like everyone wants to get through with the pre-show and get on to the main event. Emmy's cheeks are pink and she keeps smiling playfully at Billy, who keeps staring at her like he can't believe his good fortune to have her beside him.

I know the feeling well.

But tonight, Emmy will be in good hands, leaving me free to focus on Jasmine, who can't stop smiling, her eyes twinkling with delight at everything, from the umbrella in her cocktail, to Morena's dress, and the warmth of the evening.

I'm glad I'm not the only one who is excited.

After dinner, the eight of us head to Jed and Morena's room, stopping first in mine to grab Emmy's partially drunk bottle of tequila. My idea, since it seemed to work like some kind of magical elixir for me yesterday.

I made Emmy scream—more than once. I don't know if that was the booze or just me, but I'm not changing a thing.

I pour shots all around as we stand around the hotel room, wondering what to do. More than once I think of asking Morena and Jed if they're used to everyone being together like this, but that seems rude.

Is this an orgy? Is that what we're going to do? I can't take my eyes off the king-sized bed.

One bed, one room and eight of us. How is this supposed to work?

It works by Morena giving Jed a long, lingering kiss, and then slowly taking off her dress.

Now I can't take my eyes off her.

For an older woman, Morena is sexy; she's sexy for any woman. And there's a confidence in her that most women lack. Naked, with only a brief pair of red lace underwear, she flicks Basil's chin, winks and saunters to the bed. She knows we're watching her, and with an exaggerated sway of her hips, it's clear that she likes it.

As she settles herself on the bed, tucking her arms behind her head, I'm not ashamed to admit I think twice about my choice of Jasmine.

Not that I've made my choice—this isn't one of those parties where you pick a person's keys. According to Jed, tonight we're going to see what happens.

What happens is that Basil steps forward. Whipping his shirt off, he leans over Morena and whispers something to her, something that makes Morena laugh. I watch, dry-mouthed as he kisses each of her breasts, licking the tight tips before settling between her legs.

Just like that. I don't know if I feel more awe or envy that Basil can do that, just like that. I know I also feel a bit uncomfortable as I watch. Another shot of tequila helps with that.

And another.

I've never watched someone else have sex. It's a lot different than watching porn.

First of all, I don't know where to look. It seems rude to move closer to see exactly what Basil is doing between Morena's long, slim legs, but she's clearly enjoying it.

That's the second thing I never expected. The sounds. Morena makes this noise in her throat that makes me hard.

"This is off to a good start," Jed says, reaching for Claire standing next to him. I don't know if it was planned or luck of the draw but Claire lets herself be tugged forward without a glance at Billy. "Feel free to stay or go."

"I think we'll go?" It's more of a question as Billy gives Emmy a long look. She doesn't even glance at me before she nods her head. "Have fun, babe," Billy says over his shoulder at his wife.

Claire is busy kissing Jed and doesn't respond.

I look over at Jasmine who is staring at Basil and Morena with rapt attention. "What do you want to do?" I ask in a low voice.

"He never does that with me," Jasmine says, the accusation evident in her voice as Basil slides a finger inside Morena, eliciting an appreciative moan from Morena. Sounds of wetness, of licking and sucking, fill the room, and I know Basil's using his tongue like I did with Emmy yesterday.

Jed has Claire positioned to straddle his shoulders and I watch, my mouth hanging open, as she lowers herself down to his waiting mouth.

"Or that," Jasmine whispers.

Morena has one hand on the back of Basil's head, urging him deeper, and reaches up with the other to cup Claire's breast. She rolls Claire's nipple between her fingers.

I have no idea how to respond to that; Jasmine's comments, not about Morena playing with Claire's nipple.

I have no idea if I'm supposed to be watching this.

Part of me can't seem to move. This is better than porn; this is live porn happening right in front of my eyes. This is my friends having sex in front of me.

This is Jasmine's husband in bed with another woman, making her moan and groan with his fingers and tongue.

The sight of it makes me hard as a rock and I wince at the tightness in my shorts.

"Are you okay with this?" I ask Jasmine in a low voice.

She drags her gaze from the bed, where Claire has just leaned forward to take Jed's jutting cock in her mouth, her cries of pleasure now muffled.

Morena isn't muffled by anything and it sounds as if she's about ready to come. My breath comes in heavy pants as I fight the urge to grab my cock and give it a quick few rubs to relieve this pressure.

But why would I do that, when Jasmine is right here.

"Jas?" I whisper urgently.

"This is turning me on," she says, wide-eyed and giggling. "I never watch porn so I didn't think...is this what it's like?"

"No," I admit. "This is way better." I reach out and take her hand, feeling like I'm fifteen and faced with the prospect of kissing my best friend. "What do you want to do?" She might want to stand here and watch; she might want to join in the foursome on the bed.

The foursome that suddenly switches position like a well-choreographed dance pack. Now Morena's head is buried between Claire's legs, her ass in the air and Basil sliding into her from behind. Jed's cock is still in Claire's mouth...

If I don't do something about *my* cock, my night is going to come to a short end.

She giggles and it sounds more nervous than excited. "That," she says with a wave of her hand. "All of that."

Sounds good to me. "Then let's get out of here."

CHAPTER TWELVE

Emmy

B ILLY LEADS ME BACK to his room, and awkward silence grows between us.

I have no idea how he's feeling after watching his wife get pulled to the bed by another man. Is he upset? Is he used to it?

There's so much about this that I don't understand.

Like how I can be almost unbearably excited by watching Basil and Morena.

I could have stood there all night, watching Basil with mouth and fingers pleasure her. Morena is sexy; the act was hot; a shirtless Basil is impressive, especially how he dove right in there.

My breathing comes in little pants as I follow Billy into his room and the heavy throb between my legs is impossible to ignore.

The door shuts behind me with a heavy click. The room is neat, without much visible evidence that Billy shares it with Claire.

I'm glad. I know we have her approval—blessing? Her okay?—but I don't want a reminder that Billy is married.

I don't want to think about Matt, either.

"You okay?" Billy turns to me with a questioning look in his eyes. I don't want him to question me or this or anything. For once I'm going to act on what I want, and forget about everyone else.

"I'm good," I say in a clear voice. I don't ask him the same, because that would be a reminder of everyone in the other room.

The other room where there were four people on the bed. Even now, they would have shed more clothes, shifted positions. Things would get more heated, louder…

"I don't—" Billy begins, but I take a step and put a finger on his lips to stop him.

"Do you want me?" I ask. He nods quickly, staring at me with wide eyes. "Then take me. Now."

He kisses me without another word.

He's not rough when he kisses me, but there's not much gentleness about it either.

I like that. I don't want to be gentle. I don't want to be soothed and coddled; I don't want to be made love to with soft touches—I want to be fucked.

His hands find my breasts; moulding, cupping, squeezing as he kisses me. It's like he's devouring me. Like he can't get enough.

Like we're eighteen, in the backseat of the car with one last night together.

I love the feel of his lips against mine, his tongue darting into my mouth. Pulling off his shirt, my hands are everywhere, touching every place I can reach, kissing him frantically like he's about to be stolen away from me.

Billy at eighteen was tall and lanky, with wide shoulders and a mop of blond hair that kept falling into his eyes. Billy, twenty years older, is tall and broad; he doesn't have the muscular fitness of Basil or even Matt, but everything is firm and still in place.

It's like I'm young again, but better. This time Billy isn't fumbling in the back seat, letting out muffled curses as his long legs tangle with mine, and headlights shine in the window. This time Billy knows exactly what he's doing.

His hands caress my back, my bare shoulders, my arms. He pushes my hair away from my neck and trails his lips along the sensitive skin, all the way down to the top of my dress. He shoves the shoulder straps out of the way so he can kiss my shoulder, hungry lips searching for more skin to devour.

"Take it off," Billy mutters.

With shaking arms, I pull at the zipper under my arm and Billy helps me pull the dress over my head. And then he looks at me.

I see the desire, the need. The want. I've never had a man look at me like that before. "You're different," he says, his finger tracing the edge of my bra and dipping between my breasts.

"So are you." I touch his stomach, running my hands over his chest.

"You're better," he says roughly.

"So are you."

He reaches for me again, unclipping my bra as he kisses me, his hands moving to my bare breasts. I run my hands over his torso, admiring the smooth skin, the sprinkling of chest hair, the firm arms. I kiss his shoulder as I yank on his belt buckle.

Billy keeps trying to kiss me as I undress him, pulling me close, stroking my breasts but I keep the distance as I wrestle to get his pants off. Once they're off, I take a moment to stroke the hardness straining his boxer briefs before I tug them off too.

He's naked before me and now it's my turn to admire. I want to touch everywhere, all of him, from the tanned arms and back to the whiteness of his bare ass. I take a turn around his body, my fingers the only contact with his body, darting out of his grasp as he reaches for me. And then I press myself against his back with a teasing smile, stroking his chest with both hands, to his stomach and then dipping lower.

The night we spent together was in darkness, and I never saw his body. I never fully appreciated his cock jutting out, thick and long and hard.

Moving around to the front of him, I touch the tip, my breath shaky. Billy inhales with a gasp as I stroke his cock with gentle fingers, then grasp it, running my hand up and down the length.

I want it in my mouth.

Dropping to my knees before Billy, I grasp the base with both hands, taking a moment to tease the tip, drawing my tongue along the length before I take it into my mouth.

Billy's groan enflames me, knowing I'm the cause.

I spend long minutes on the floor, his cock in my mouth, Billy's hands on the back of my head, guiding me, encouraging me. I bob up and down along the length, revelling in the taste and feel of it until finally, with an anguished groan, Billy pulls me to my feet.

"My turn," he says, and pulls me to the bed.

Sitting on the edge, I stand between his legs and his mouth finds my breast, his hand delving between my legs. My head tilts back with a sigh as he touches my wetness and his fingers slide inside me. With his mouth, he tugs on one nipple, and then the other, dragging his tongue into my cleavage and up the swell of my breast.

"How do you want it?" he asks. I feel of his breath on my sensitive skin and pull his head in for more.

"How do you want to give it to me?" I ask in return.

I feel the vibration of his chuckle against my nipple and it tingles all the way to the apex between my legs. "You sound like a dirty girl. It's not what I expected."

"I'm a very different girl."

"I know. I like it." His fingers move with lazy strokes like he's playing with me. I press my hips against his hand, wordlessly asking for more.

Playtime is over, Billy.

He gently bites down on my nipple as he thrusts his fingers in and out. My hips move with him, meeting everything thrust

"I want it hard," I tell him breathlessly. "Stop teasing me."

"You give orders now."

"When I know what I want."

"And what do you want, Emily?"

I close my eyes. Billy is still the only one who calls me Emily, and the sound of my full name on his hips brings back the memory of the girl I used to be.

The girl who would never ask for anything.

I'm a woman now. Reaching down, I grab his wrist, angling his hand so the fleshy ball of his thumb presses against my clit. And then I rub myself against it quickly until I come with a shallow orgasm. "I want you to fuck me."

"I can do that." I look down to see Billy looking at me with so much lust in his eyes, I almost come again.

Then he throws me down on the bed.

Matt

I'VE NEVER SEEN A woman take off her clothes so quickly. I'm in awe of Jasmine's speed in undressing…and also her breasts.

I've had fantasies about those breasts for many, many years, and finally seeing them in the flesh leaves me speechless.

"What's the matter?" Jasmine demands as she kicks her panties across the room. "You're staring at me."

"What do you expect?" I take a step so I'm close enough to touch, cupping her fullness in both hands. "I've been dreaming about these for years."

"They're just breasts," she says with a smile, dropping her gaze.

"Maybe for you." My thumbs strafe her nipples and I watch her for a sign that she's enjoying it.

Nothing. Her expression doesn't change.

"You don't like me doing this, do you?" I ask ruefully, my hands stopping the exploration.

"It's okay," Jasmine says slowly.

It's like I'm climbing Mount Everest and I'm told to stop a mile from the top. "I think you're breaking my heart," I say, only half-joking.

"Keep doing what you're doing."

"Nope." Reluctantly, I take my hands away. "I've been thinking about this for too long—this is what *you* want. I want everything." I give her a half-hearted push and Jasmine settles herself on the bed.

"All the fuss for these. Balls of fat."

My head pops out of my shirt in time to see Jasmine with her hands full of her own breasts, fingering her nipples. I stare for a moment before my eyes begin to glaze.

"They're so, so much more than that," I say in a hoarse voice and Jasmine laughs. But her laughter fades as she takes me in, standing shirtless beside the bed.

"Take the rest of it off." She bites her lip and my cock gives a jolt.

"Touch yourself again." I'm not sure where the request comes from, but seeing her fingering her nipples is a huge turn-on.

"You like that?" Her eyes brighten, and she touches her nipples again, rolling them between her thumb and fingers.

"I don't know but I think I do."

"What about this?" Jasmine runs a hand down her stomach. Spreading her legs, she touches herself, rubbing her clit with a quick finger.

"Oh, God." My voice chokes.

"Do you like it?" Jasmine runs her finger through her cleft, sliding it inside and I think I might explode.

"I do. Does it feel good?"

"It might feel better if you do it."

My pants are undone as I kneel on the bed. I remember her face as she watched Basil with Morena. "With my mouth?"

"Yes please," she whispers.

"So polite." I draw her knees farther apart. "You don't have to be polite with me." I cup her pussy, feeling her heat.

"I won't, so don't be polite with me." With a chuckle, I bend my head but Jasmine's hand on my shoulder stops me. "Matt?"

"Jasmine?"

"Are you nervous?"

I catch my breath at her expression—wistful and wary and eager. "No," I lie. "I only want it to be good for you."

"What about you? It has to be good for you."

"I know it's going to be good."

I start at her breasts, to give myself a little taste. Her skin is sweet, her nipples like cherry candies. I tell myself to move on, to give her what she wants when she gives a gasp and rests her little hand at the back of my head.

I can't help the swell of pride and with a smile, I move on, kissing my way down her body; under Jasmine's heavy breasts, running my tongue along my ribs, smoothing my hand down to her hip. I tongue her belly button, which makes her laugh.

And then I'm between her legs, nibbling at her inner thighs as I push her legs up. Her scent surrounds me as I hover, blowing the dark curls and Jasmine gives a whimper of frustration.

"I told you not to be polite," I tease, my tongue darting out to caress her nub with the briefest of flickers.

Jasmine responds by pushing my head down and I'm lost.

Slowly, carefully I explore her cleft, touching, tasting, teasing. Jasmine's moans turn into cries in the quiet room as my touches become more demanding. My tongue is everywhere, fingers quick to follow, probing inside her, replaced by thrusting fingers as I return to her clit.

I like the way she whimpers when I lick her, crying out as I surround her clit with my mouth.

I like the way her hips arch, her cries becoming breathless pleas. Her hands fist in my hair as she urges me on, to take more...all of her...

"Please...please...don't stop...oh, Matt..." she chants.

I thrust my fingers inside her as I tongue her relentlessly, wondering how much, wondering if she's close and then suddenly I can feel the build-up growing within her. She arches up with a loud cry, her spasms clutching my fingers as she comes, her hands kneading the back of my head.

I'm on her before she stops shaking, breathlessly kissing her so that she can taste herself.

"I'm going to fuck you now," I mutter against her lips, praying I can last long enough to get inside of her. My cock throbs with need, almost painful with the intensity. I need to slow it down, make it last for her.

But Jasmine doesn't want to slow it down.

"Please," she pants. "Please, please...now..."

I've never put on a condom so quickly. "Are you sure? I can wait..."

"Fuck me," she cries.

I enter with a thrust—too fast, too hard and Jasmine gasps with surprise. But once I'm inside, I can't stop.

"Jesus, Jasmine," I mutter as I bury my face into her neck, my hips moving full speed ahead as I thrust into her. "So good."

She meets every one of my thrusts, her hands on my ass, still begging for more.

I do everything in my power to stop, to slow down, but I know it's going to be too quick. "Touch yourself," I say hoarsely. "Make yourself come again because I can't last long."

The feel of her hand between our bodies almost makes me come, but I manage to hold off until she brings herself to a climax, and then I empty myself inside of her.

CHAPTER THIRTEEN

Emmy

BILLY IS BETTER THAN I remember; better than I ever could have imagined.

Maybe it's because it's been so long or maybe it's my newfound sexual awareness but I feel so *alive*. Wanton. Womanly.

He pulls me on top of him, spreading my legs and lowering me down to him. My eyes widen as I take in every inch of him.

"You fuck me," he says lazily.

As I ride him, picking my tempo, Billy easily thumbs me to a climax that leaves me hunched over his chest as I come with a harsh cry.

"That's two," he says proudly.

"It's not a race," I say weakly, still leaning on his chest.

"It is," he insists. "Every year I missed you."

"That's—no way!" I laugh. "I won't be able to walk."

"That's the plan," he says as he flips me over onto my back, somehow without pulling out.

But then he does pull out, replacing his heavy cock with a tongue.

I fist the covers on the bed as my eyes begin to roll back. His mouth is demanding, urgent, his fingers probing.

We didn't do this when we were eighteen. I sigh, my eyes fluttering shut as I think about what I've missed—not just Billy, but the years when I denied myself this pleasure.

Things are going to be a lot different when I get home.

This orgasm is slow, almost relaxing and feels as good as if I'm sinking into a bath.

"Three!" Billy cries as he rolls me over onto my stomach and pulls up my hips. I don't have a chance to respond as he thrusts inside me with a swiftness that makes me gasp. And relax time is over as Billy fucks me hard and fast. I feel every inch of him; wanting every inch of him. Letting him take me where he wants to.

I rest my head on the bed as he takes me. Hard and fast.

In and out...in and out.

His legs slam against mine, his hands gripping my hips. It's good...so good. So good that I'm breathless, unable to do more than gasp weakly under his onslaught.

"I don't want...to ever...stop...fucking you."

It's Billy who voices it but the thought is my own. I can do this forever.

When he reaches around my hip to rub my clit, I'm ready again, ready for Billy to push me over the edge. This time my cry is piercingly loud like I'm in pain and I thrust my hips back onto him, my body demanding more as I climax again.

"Four," Billy sings as he rolls me onto my back. I'm done; spent, and he must know it. When Billy slides inside me, he's gentle, almost tender and I marvel at the difference.

This is making love.

And it's over too quickly as Billy comes with a muffled curse, dropping a kiss on my forehead before he rolls off me.

As soon as he does, I feel the absence of his warmth and cuddle against him. His arms slide around me and I rest my head on his chest, feeling his heartbeat slow.

"I think I'm supposed to say something," Billy says after long minutes. "Or at least get you a blanket."

"I'm okay," I murmur. Even though the room is cool, the last thing I want to do is crawl under the covers on the bed. The bed that Billy will share with Claire tonight after I leave.

That little intimacy seems wrong.

"And I don't think you need to say anything," I add.

"I do," he insists. "That was incredible. Everything I ever dreamed about. And I used to dream about you a lot."

"So did I."

"Really?" Billy cranes his head to look at me and the hopeful expression on his face almost breaks me. Because as good as this was—it can't be.

"I never really got over you," I admit. "I guess I must have, but it took a while. I think it would have helped if I'd met a nice guy, rather than an ass like Ed—"

"I can't believe he hurt you," Billy interrupts.

"I don't want to talk about it," I say quickly. "He has no place here with us."

"Fair enough." A pause. "There's an us?"

"There used to be." I prop my head on my fist so I can see his face. Study every inch of it. "But now? No." I say it firmly, trying not to sound harsh, but I see Billy wince.

"You said you never got over me."

"You will always be important to me," I say. "My first love. You'll always have a place in my heart. But you made a life without me. A good life, with a good wife and kids...I can't be a part of it, Billy."

"But we could...this arrangement..." Again the hopeful expression, and I sigh.

"I can't do that to myself," I admit. "I don't want part of you. I mean, I do," I say with a teasing chuckle, glancing down his body. "*Obviously*. But I wouldn't be happy with only part, and I know I'd want more. And the last thing I would let myself do is come between you and Claire. I'm not that woman."

"But maybe..."

"How?" He knows I'm being reasonable, but still Billy screws up his face to try and come up with a solution for us to continue this.

I know he can't because there's no way. Being with him for only one night is going to be hard enough to move past. I can't do that to myself.

"What about you and Matt?" he asks finally.

"I think he's got some issues to resolve, and it might be better if he did that without me. He's a great guy. Maybe if the timing was different..."

"You don't want to be the rebound girl?"

"No." I shake my head before I lay it down on his chest. "Who was your rebound girl, after me?" I ask.

Billy pauses before answering. "I shouldn't answer this, should I?" he finally says. I glance at him in time to see the rueful smile. "Or I should say Claire?"

"Who?" I demand.

"Ami Cole," he admits.

"What? It had to be her?" If I had a mortal enemy in high school, it was Ami, with her breasts and body and popularity with both sexes. I wanted to be Ami, as much as I envied and disliked her. Rearing up, I slap at his chest, a little too hard to be completely joking. "How dare you?"

"It was only one night," Billy protests, moving away from my fists. "Maybe two...three..."

I launch myself at him, and for a minute we wrestle on the bed, laughing easily as I let him pin me.

Billy stares down at me. I can tell he's trying not to rest his weight on me. "Emmy?" he asks quietly.

"Don't say it," I whisper.

So he kisses me instead.

Matt

"THAT WAS NOT WHAT I expected." I lay on my side, looking at Jasmine, the chill of the air conditioning blowing on my ass.

The ass which might have evidence of finger marks. I'll need to look in a mirror to be sure.

"Was it better? The best?" Jasmine says jokingly. She crawled under the blankets after we finished, after she came with such a loud cry that I suspect those in the room next door will have heard her.

"You were..." I search for the right word. "A revelation," I announce.

Jasmine giggles at the description. "I do surprise myself at times."

"Are you...you and Basil." I pause, once again searching for the words. "Are you going to keep doing this? The swinger stuff?"

"I think so." Jasmine's voice is soft, tentative and sounds impossibly young.

"It's good between the two of you?" I'm not sure why I'm asking—out of concern? Hope? Guilt, because I don't want to be the one to come between my friends.

"It is. It was always good, but now, things are gotten better in certain areas."

"You're talking about sex, aren't you? You can say it."

Jasmine giggles again, and I can't help but reach out eager fingers and pinch the side of her breast. "I've known you my whole life and I've never once talked about my sex life."

"Well, now that I'm part of your sex life..." I trail off as I see her expression. "For the night, anyway."

"What about you?" she asks quietly. "Would you want to do this again?"

"With you?"

"Or anyone else."

"That's a stupid question."

"I'm serious. If Basil and I keep this up at home, would you and Emmy—"

"I don't think there's going to be a me and Emmy," I say heavily.

"Because of this?" Jasmine gasps.

"Because of me. Me the other night, me still messed up from Shawna. I think we're both going to come to the conclusion, if we haven't already, that I'm going to need some time on my own."

"I think that's a good idea," she agrees. "Not that I don't like Emmy—I think she's great. But it's been a long time since you were by yourself, and I think it'd be good for you."

"Me too. I'm glad I brought her because if not for all this, we might have limped along for a while before I figured things out."

"Limp?" Jasmine glances at my now flaccid cock resting against my leg.

"What do you expect? I'm not Superman."

"But you could be...right? With the right superpower?"

"I think you're more like kryptonite." I reach out and peel the covers off of her breasts and toy with her nipple.

"If Basil agrees," Jasmine begins hesitantly, "do you think you might want to, maybe *continue* this?"

"Now? Or back at home?" Hope surges through me, at the thought that this won't be the last time.

"Either? Both?" Jasmine has an eager expression on her face, along with what I already recognize as hunger, the sight of which sends a surge to my sleeping cock.

I pull off the blankets. "Maybe if you let me play with your boobs this time," I say with a grin, as Jasmine pulls me into her waiting breasts.

The End

Coming Soon...
Want more Emmy?
She's part of the next series!

OTHER BOOKS BY ANNA ELLIS

FANTASIES BOOK CLUB

Gemma

Emmy

Callie

Nia

Malcolm

One series

One Summer

One Week

One Night

Husbands and Wives series

Making Friends

The Husbands

The Wives

New Neighbours

Joe and Jacey

Husbands and Wives – The Collection

Interludes

Interludes II

Interludes III

Interludes – The Collection

Melissa

Paige

Office Plays series

Office Plays

Secrets and Lies

Love After Hours

Lost Weekends

Touch series

Touch

Touch – Iliya's Story

Touch – Del's Story

Caress

Caress – Iliya's Story

Caress – Del's Story

Embrace

Embrace – Iliya's Story

Embrace – Del's Story

Adults Only series

Shared Accommodations

Room Service

Late Check Out

No Vacancy

Short story collection

Peek-a-boo

About the Author

ANNA ELLIS LIKES TO writes about happily married couples having sex with other happily married couples. There's no werewolves or vampires, shapeshifters or tentacles involved - just good, old-fashioned sex. And maybe a little tying up. Or a spanking or two.

In the **Husbands and Wives** series, follow new neighbours Jacey and Dominic as they learn to navigate the slippery sidewalks of suburban swinger lifestyle. Being a good neighbour has never been so much fun!

Her new series, **One**, returns to the swinger lifestyle with three married couples looking to spice up their marriages.

Her **Office Plays** series takes you to the workplace to meet the most excitable group of office employees you would ever want to work with. They give coffee breaks a new meaning.

The series **Touch** is an unconventional love story about a woman who falls in love with a man...and his wife. All nine books are available now, *Touch*, *Caress,* and *Embrace.* Each has three separate points of view from Kenna, Iliya, and Del.

Adults Only follows Morena and Lorde, who run a B&B especially for swingers. The four book series includes characters from other series—Jacey and Dominic from **Husbands and Wives**, Callie, from **Office Plays**, and Iliya from **Touch**. While you don't need to read the other series first, it would improve your pleasure!

And her latest series, **Fantasies Book Club,** brings back a few favourites as a book club reads dirty stories that seem to mirror their own lives.

Anna also writes women's fiction/chick lit under the name Holly Kerr. If you're looking for something a little less steamy (but still hot!) check out her books.www.hollykerr.ca

Visit Anna at annaellis@wordpress.com or Facebook

Happy Reading!